BITTERSWEET
SUSAN STRASBERG

G. P. PUTNAM'S SONS   New York

Designed by Bernard Schleifer

Library of Congress Cataloging in Publication Data

Strasberg, Susan.
Bittersweet.
1. Strasberg. 2. Actors—United States
Biography. I. Title.
PN2287.S77A34   792'.028'0924 [B]   79–25832
ISBN 0-399-12447-0

Printed in the United States of America

ACKNOWLEDGMENTS

Many thanks to my friends and family, who encouraged me, held my hand, shared their memories, and tolerated my moods. Special gratitude also to Dr. Ellsorth Baker and the late Dr. Albert Duvall; my editor, Phyllis Grann; my agent, Morton Janklow; and Maggie Starr.

To Jennifer and to
Mother and Father

The bitter past, more welcome is the sweet.

William Shakespeare,
All's Well That Ends Well, V: iii

ENDINGS AND BEGINNINGS

Mother is dead. She died six weeks ago of cancer of everything. My brother, Johnny, is in County General Hospital in the intensive-care ward, a hundred stitches on his body and seven pints of someone else's blood running through his veins. He was on an LSD trip and went through a window. The doctors say he may live. My father is sleeping upstairs in the guest room. He arrived today, lines of grief etched on his face, looking defeated.

With my mother gone, I will never be anyone's baby again. I am the mother now. Across the room, in a lace-covered crib with tiny wooden angels dangling over her head, my own two-and-a-half-month-old baby, Jennifer, lies sleeping. Her breathing is irregular and shallow.

My husband, Christopher, is somewhere doing whatever men do when out at four in the morning. After four years together, we are still intimate strangers. The house is quiet now. The violence of our marriage has not yet penetrated to the nursery.

Jenny has a congenital birth defect. There are four holes in her heart, and it is hell not knowing if the drugs Christopher and I took in the past have caused her condition.

I am trapped in a welter of guilt, self-pity, fear, and doubt. I have fallen so far that perhaps it is too late to reverse the tide. How can I go forward in my life when I do not even know or understand what has brought me to this point. I dread returning to the beginning, remembering, but I know I must, in order to overcome the darkness I feel inside me now, because somewhere in the heart of my past lies the answer, the key which will unlock the door to my future. I must find the courage now to confront myself face to face, to begin to put all the fragments together again. And nothing in the past can be worse than this fear.

My mother once wrote me a postcard: "Darling, I made it, and so will you . . ." I had to try.

PART ONE

I WAS ONSTAGE shortly before I was born. My mother was playing a part in *Many Mansions* on Broadway. "But, Paula," the producer said to her, "the audience just can't accept a prostitute who's seven months pregnant." So *we* were fired.

I believe, as the Chinese do, that you are molded and influenced in the womb, so perhaps it was predestined that I become an actress. Floating around in my amniotic fluid, sound filtering through my mother's stomach, I heard the applause, felt the energy of the audience, and not realizing they weren't for me, stored away those sensations for future reference. Fifteen years later, I made my stage debut off-Broadway in the role of a young girl who was—what else?—an up-and-coming young prostitute. My prenatal indoctrination had served me well.

The only major event I've been unavoidably late for was my own life, and I've been rushing to catch up ever since. My arrival was scheduled for the twentieth of May but I waited in the wings until the twenty-first, and after forty hours of painful labor, finally made my entrance on May 22, 1938, at 12:00 P.M. Eastern Standard Time in Sydenham Hospital in New York City.

Mother wrote in my baby book, "At birth Susan was clear-

15

complected, eyes open and crying." All three conditions were to last for years.

My father did not come to see me immediately. He had been told that newborns were often red and wrinkled, especially after a long labor, and he was afraid that if I were ugly, he might be repulsed and unable to love me. When he finally worked up his courage and took a look, I was, he said, "beautiful."

I was not named for seven days. My father, immersed in studying sixteenth-century England, opted for Elizabeth; he felt that if I hated Elizabeth, I would have so many options: Betty, Beth, Liza, etc. Mama picked Susan from the Bible. So, finally, I became Susan Elizabeth Strasberg.

My birth announcement proclaimed: "A four-star hit! The *Golden Girl* in her long-awaited debut among *All the Living*" (titles of plays with which my parents had been involved). "A triumph of the Stanislavsky method" (the famous Russian acting teacher). Then followed reviews in the style of the leading critics of the day: "The labor movement's most impressive demonstration" —John Mason Brown. "No one but Lee Strasberg could have done this—I hope" —Walter Winchell. "Without scenery or costumes, the current Strasberg production simply must be seen at once" —John Anderson. "Couldn't have done better myself" —George J. Nathan.

According to Mama, I jumped feetfirst into everything and at two and one-half weeks I was "holding head erect and steady when held to shoulder, lifting chest from bed when lying prone." On May 5, 1939, just short of one year old, I took my first steps alone, and I didn't fall down hard again until I was twenty-four.

Multicolored dreams had brought my ancestors, the Sykes, the Sachs, the Strasbergs, the Millers, the Browns, and the Dinners, to the shores of America, the New World, the land of freedom. They came from Russia, Poland, England, and Austria. One had fought in the American Revolution.

My father's parents met one day when my grandfather, a

talmudic scholar, was driving to synagogue. He saw a beautiful young woman working in the fields. It was love at first sight. He drove directly to the matchmaker and said, "I want her." They were married immediately and began to have children. My grandfather left Austria and the family stone-quarry business when my father, the youngest son and last child, was born. In America he took a job as a presser and sent for his family one by one. My father was the last to arrive at Ellis Island. He was eight years old and had never seen his father.

The generation of children my father's parents produced was the distillation of the best of two thousand years of Jewish culture and discipline. One of their sons, Arthur, was a dentist; another, who died, had been a schoolteacher; but in their wildest dreams, none of his family could have imagined that my father would choose the theater. My grandmother moaned when informed of my father's aspirations, but eventually she became supportive of his efforts. After all, he was "the baby."

My mother's father was a tall, blue-eyed, good-looking, debonair Viennese. When I met him, he was retired, but he had owned a bar and grill in New York and rhapsodized at length about the virtues of Viennese pastry and cooking. Mama's mother was the "all-American" in the family, a daughter of the Revolution, of which she was very proud.

My mother was a lovely young actress, discovered by Eva Le Gallienne. She had been an honor student in high school and was filled with dreams of writing and the theater. Her parents were horrified by her acting ambitions, and only by running away to get married at the age of sixteen did she escape their parental wrath. She divorced this gentleman, from whom she was already separated, the same year that she entered the Group Theater and met my father. I remember her telling the story of how, upon learning of her impending remarriage, her ex-husband had come looking for her with a loaded pistol. "He was crazy," she said, "but my God, he was good-looking."

My father was one of the leading visionaries of the American theater, a co-creator of the Group Theater, which became famous for its searing social and moral indictments as well as the quality of its presentations during the 1930s.

All in all, it was a heritage to be proud of.

My first memory is of crawling around in diapers under a dining table, in and out of a lot of legs, and eating all the crumbs being dropped. Many of these were famous or soon-to-be-famous feet I was romping around. In those days our most frequent guests were Molly and Elia Kazan, Luise Rainer, Harold Clurman, John Garfield, Clifford Odets, Franchot Tone, Sidney Kingsley, Tallulah Bankhead. In later years people would ask me, "What was it like to be around all those celebrities? Weren't you intimidated?" I didn't know they were famous, and at that age I wasn't interested. The *star* in my life was Jonesy.

Martha Jones, my nurse, was an extraordinary woman, liberated ahead of her time, and one of the first Negro registered nurses. She was loving, tender, aggressive, and independent. Initially she came to care for me for two weeks, but she was with us on and off for six years. My mother recalled she would hear Jonesy singing to me, "I'm going to paint you black and then you'll be my baby." And because she gave me so much of her love, I was partly her child.

Other infants were lulled by "Twinkle, Twinkle"; my father sang me "Brahms Lullaby" and "Green Grow the Lilacs," from a play he had appeared in. At one month old, they were reading me Egar Allan Poe's tragic love poem "Annabel Lee."

My first memories of being attracted to the stage all involve Tallulah Bankhead. Even at the tender age of three, I knew enough to be deeply impressed by her flamboyance, her beauty, and her larger-than-life behavior.

On one occasion, Tallulah was visiting us along with "Uncles" Clifford Odets and Franchot Tone. They were discussing Russian ballet, the attributes of Nijinsky and Pavlova, and the tragedy of Nijinsky's madness. Inspired, I disappeared from the room and shortly afterward came tearing down the stairs wrapped in my mother's scarves and began to writhe and gyrate, improvising Nijinsky's death dance. Leaping and wheeling in the air, waving my scarves, I cried out, "I'm Jinsky, Jinsky!" I fell into a swoon at their feet, and they thought I had fainted until I opened one eye to see Tallulah's reaction.

Then there was Tallulah onstage. I saw her come down a white staircase in a red dress, and I knew I wanted to do that. Not act; I wanted to come down those stairs looking like that lady who came to the house and smelled good, talked like a man, and laughed a lot.

My mother had been friends with Tallulah for years and had worked as her jill-of-all-trades at Windows, Tallulah's country estate, before Mother had begun to act. Mama had gone backstage and offered to work for Miss Bankhead because she loved the theater and thought Tallulah was the most wonderful actress. Tallulah accepted her offer of service, and Mother went to stay with her for that summer. The relationship became a little bumpy when my father directed Tallulah in *Clash by Night*, but by the time I was growing up, things were back on an even keel. Tallulah asked mother to accompany her to Hollywood, where she was to film *Lifeboat*, her first movie, with Alfred Hitchcock directing. My mother's job was to be dialogue coach. When Mama went off to California, I felt she had abandoned me. I recall my father and me trying to cope for ourselves. He carried me as he ran around the kitchen cooking dinner and sang me to sleep at night holding me in his arms.

That is the last childhood memory I have of my father being overtly affectionate. He was caught in the seesawing philosophy about what was the correct behavior in raising a child. This was pre-Spock, post-Freud. One year you were absolutely forbidden to pick up your child when it cried; the next it was necessary to soothe the baby at the first sign of tears. Some well-meaning friend told my father that to touch a daughter often after the age of three had sexual overtones. In his vulnerability as a new father, my father accepted this and drew away from me. I was an outgoing child, and this sudden withdrawal of his energy made me contract, shrink

19

imperceptibly inside myself. When I climbed on Daddy's lap, he seemed uncomfortable; if I rushed to hug him, he tensed his muscles or became passive; and, as the time passed, I knew surely it must be that I was unlovable, not a good little girl.

Mother returned from Hollywood and regaled us with stories of her Hollywood stay. Tallulah wanted to make a conquest of the town and had behaved very grandly, expecting Mother to also. One evening Tallulah asked her to call the valet, which my mother did, pronouncing it as Americans do, "vallay." Tallulah screamed, "My Gawd, it's valit, not vallay. Don't you know anything?" The following night they went to dinner with Hitchcock. Mother, anxious to utilize her newly acquired knowledge, ordered "filit of sole." "Gawd," Tallulah roared again, "it's fillay of sole, you idiot." Tallulah could be overbearing. It was said about her, "A day away from Tallulah is like a month in the country."

Many of the actors and writers we knew were like that. Larger than life, flamboyant, temperamental—it was the style, it was almost expected. Franchot Tone came to the house one night drunk and bloody from a battle over some woman. It was difficult to equate this man with the tender, aesthetic, scholarly gentleman who had held me on his knee earlier that day. Clifford Odets would switch in mid-sentence from a poetic reverie to a towering rage. He was unable to stop himself from turning his anger onto the people he loved the most, his wife, his children. Although I was shocked, I was impressed by my parents' tolerance and kindness in the face of this erratic behavior. Subconsciously I deduced that this conduct was permissible only because of their extraordinary talent. Certainly I was not allowed such indulgence. I was too young to understand that the melodrama and thunder obscured an enormous amount of insecurity, immaturity, and fear.

We were very close to my father's family and they adored my mother. Before my parents were married, they lived together in Greenwich Village. My father had been widowed when his first wife, his childhood sweetheart, passed away. My mother was obviously a strong candidate for number two. My grandmother, accompanied by Cousin Ruthie, traveled down from the Bronx to meet my mother and check her out.

She opened the door dressed in a white silk shirt, pale blue jodhpurs, and riding boots, her blond hair bobbed fashionably short, her cobalt-blue eyes rimmed with mascara. One didn't see this in the Bronx. It was a successful visit, and on their way home, Ruthie asked, "So, Grandma, what do you think of her?"

"Well," said Grandma, choosing her words carefully, "thanks be to God, at least she's Jewish."

The main religious influence that I knew came from celebrating the Jewish holidays at Grandma and Grandpa Strasberg's. They would visit us in turn, but without Grandpa. We weren't kosher, and although he didn't judge us—"Better to eat a nonkosher chicken offered by a person with a good heart than to hurt that person by refusing his food. God understands"—he was unable to make that adjustment for us. I think he and my grandmother were more comfortable in their own territory than in our home with its bohemian flavor and strange, eccentric company. What would Grandpa have thought of Franchot Tone at a later Passover in our home, wearing his yarmulke tilted over one eye like a tam-o'-shanter?

I loved their home. Everything smelled older, worn but safe; the food aroma had baked itself into the furniture, and the lace curtains, which had seen sunlight in Galicia, smelled like chicken soup.

Grandmother was a strong woman, bearing traces of the beauty she had once been, but it was Zada, Grandpa, who made the deepest impression on me. He was in his early eighties, dressed in black, never without his yarmulke, the skullcap male Jews wear to cover their heads before God, and inevitably reading the Talmud, the Jewish Book of Law. It was an old book, pages yellowing around the edges, and I was terribly impressed that he could read it backwards. He was silent most of the time. This was partially his personality and partially because he spoke not a word of English. Coming to America in his sixties, and thinking he would die soon, he declined to learn the difficult new language. When he was seventy-five, his family begged him to study English. He said in Yiddish, "It's a little late, maybe if I were younger."

When he was in his eighties and grandchildren seemed imminent, his children said, "Papa, learn some English and you'll be able to talk to your grandchildren."

He shook his head no, saying, "How much longer can an old man like me live, anyway? It's not worth it." At ninety-seven he said, "If I'd known I was going to live this long, I would have learned English."

Grandpa and I communicated in our own way. He would lie down in the afternoons to take a nap, and I would stand beside his couch, stroking his long, silky white beard. "Susan, what are you doing? Don't bother Grandpa." I continued stroking. He had a half-smile on his face. "I'm talking to Grandpa," I explained. From Grandpa I learned that there are silences and there are *silences*; some are wordless, yet you communicate; others are like loud black voids which separate and isolate people.

I saw Mother's family less regularly. Grandma and Grandpa Miller came to visit occasionally. There had been rifts in her family. One branch converted to Catholicism, and it was rumored one of their daughters had become a nun; another had gone off to Coney Island and produced a policeman and a mayor. There was an uncle who had gone west to Texas. He got on a bus the first week there, sat in the back in the section reserved for Negroes, and refused to move forward. As he stepped off the bus in his stetson hat and cowboy boots, he was shot in the back.

Mother was close to her sister, Beatrice. They were very different but mutually protective of one another. She told me fond stories about her father but was more ambivalent toward her mother, who had been strict and authoritarian with her.

Although my parents now had achieved a measure of artistic success, financially we were on shakier ground, but even if we barely had money, my mother always kept food in the refrigerator for company, and if she could manage it, champagne. If you were hungry or out of work, she would feed you, opening her arms to a starving unknown playwright or a famous actor; the only prerequisite was talent. They came to learn from my father and stayed to eat with my mother. She made an oasis of warmth in what was almost a religious atmosphere of fervent dedication to the theater, the arts. This remained true until the day she died.

Sometime at the end of my second year, I became aware of the imminent arrival of the second Strasberg child. On the day I was born, my mother had announced, "There'll be another in three years." And three years later, short only by two days, there was Johnny, which showed, I think, a great sense of timing. When Mother had told me about the new baby, she asked, "Do you want a brother or sister?" I put my hand on her belly and replied, "What else is there?" Her stomach moved with a rebuking kick.

While Mother was in the hospital, I celebrated my third birthday. My guests refused to sing "Happy Birthday," so I stood up on the table and sang "Happy Birthday to Me." I knew that "Princess Blintzes," as a family friend had nicknamed me, was about to get a co-ruler whether I wanted one or not, and I began to worry about establishing my territorial rights. Until then, my only competition had been Honamechi, the cat, who at first had ardently avoided me until I, more ardently, wooed him into sleeping under my bed. I suspected I wouldn't be able to get a baby brother under the bed as easily.

At first Johnny was like a new doll: adorable, huge brown eyes, blond ringlets, and dimples. He couldn't walk or talk, so at least I still had the field to myself. As Johnny grew, I began to feel very protective toward him. He was little and cuddly, and I loved the way his tiny fingers would cling to my hand. There were, however, ambivalent moments. When I was taking a walk with this angelic creature, people would stop, totally ignoring me, and croon, "What an adorable little girl. Those enchanting curls." "It's not a little girl," I snapped, "*it's* a little boy!"

My mother, an extraordinary woman with an enormous amount of energy and drive, worshiped my father and was focusing now on molding his career. He dreamed his dreams, and she, the pragmatist, set out to make them realities. She clothed him, not in suits, in an aura of mystery. With great directorial flair, Mother gave parties, had meetings, began to gather people for Sunday brunches; our home resembled a European salon. She surrounded my father with the best audience she could find, the cream of the artistic world, realizing he could not be a king if he had no subjects.

Mother was then in her early thirties, a slender, curvaceous blond with huge blue eyes and a fringe of long lashes which swept her high cheekbones. Her wave of golden hair started from the widow's peak on her forehead and ended at her waist. I loved brushing it for her, feeling its silky, luxurious texture in my hands. When she went out, she would pull it back in a bun or a twist, which further accentuated the chiseled contours of her face.

Mother adored hats: frivolous ones, chic, veiled, beribboned, sequined. One was a black feather cloche whose feathers swung down over her cheek, almost touching her full mouth, which was painted a bright red. There were print dresses in silks and crepes, soft materials that showed her full bosom and slender legs. Her scent, when she bent over to kiss me good night, was of violets or gardenias. She exuded an eighteenth- or nineteenth-century quality, with her eccentricities of personality, the lace hand-kerchiefs she always carried in her purse, the smelling salts. One could imagine her having spells, fugues, and yet she was not fragile. She had a life force that flowed from her, vitalizing my life.

She was a genuinely giving woman. She had a tremendous craving to be needed, appreciated, and to be the benefactor. Perversely, she had difficulty accepting gifts or favors graciously, as if she felt undeserving. She rarely went to anyone's home without taking a present, even though it was only a token. It was anathema to her to receive a compliment. She would respond with a self-denigrating remark, a habit I assumed until I realized that I was slighting the complimentor. It took me years to learn to say thank you without apologizing. She was a woman of Rabelaisian appetites. Her laughter, coming from deep within her, bubbled up, infecting people around her.

My father's personality was in sharp contrast to my mother's. Both had passionate natures, but Mother's was mutable, softer; my father's was darker, hinting at unseen feelings and desires. He was a man who did not compromise, nor did he pander to popular fads or judgments, and my mother freed him to follow his path by shouldering the more practical considerations of money and children. Sadly, she also protected him from us, as if we would infringe upon his life rather than enrich it.

I could never imagine them having an affair, making love to one another. I think most children of my generation had this feeling about their parents. We were still in the days when you ran the water when you went to the bathroom and hummed so no one would know.

Despite any disagreements, her worship of his intellect and his talent was unwavering. It was a pure emotion, a respect that rose above any consideration of personal happiness. She was satisfied because she believed the most glorious achievement for a woman was to be a partner to an extraordinary man. I was vaguely aware that what she wanted for me was not just a nice man or one who loved me and would make me happy, but a brilliant, creative man.

My father was sensitive-looking, with strong ascetic features; he resembled a professor as much as the actor, teacher, and director he was. He was small of stature, dressed haphazardly, uncaringly, in nondescript baggy clothes, blues and grays. The intelligence and depth of his hazel eyes were extraordinary, even hidden behind his glasses, and a burning intensity lay beneath his calm manner. He possessed an ability to see through to the heart of a matter, a problem, a person, a talent; a knowledge far beyond that of more traditionally educated men. His material and spiritual needs were for knowledge, more books, more music, more poetry, as if through these he would be able to understand the core of human behavior; the very behavior Mother conversely accepted unquestioningly. She kept a sign in her kitchen: "No human emotion is alien to me."

He had unexpected flashes of humor that often came out of total silence. He could be verbal, outgoing, witty, punctuating his points with wonderful theatrical or talmudic stories and "for instances": "As to logic versus emotion, two and two don't always make four. Two apples and two pears make fruit salad." To an actor: "Just for the sake of argument, shut up."

There were moments of tenderness which disarmed both the recipient and him, like a gift when it's not an occasion. "Well, Snookie," he'd say to me, briefly caressing my hair. I'd melt.

Franchot Tone came to the house to consult my father once about something. He entered the study. "Hello, Lee," he said. My father looked up, nodded, returned to his book. The ever-present music was blaring on the stereo.

Franchot waited for Lee to turn down the sound, to look up from his book. He waited and waited and waited. After an hour and a half, Franchot gave up gracefully, said, "Good night, Lee," and left the house. At other times, Franchot would hold out his arms, Lee would open his, and they would embrace.

It was hard to imagine my father without the sound of pages turning, and the music—Bach, Beethoven, Mozart, Chaliapin, Caruso. This music colored every area of our knowledge and existence.

At a Passover dinner in our home, someone said to my brother, "Johnny, you're too young to know what the Passover is about."

"I am not," he said. "Everybody knows it was when Mozart passed over the Red Sea."

I now became aware of my father's silences in a more personal context. He would talk brilliantly and emotionally when he taught, and passionately in the all-night sessions with the theater people who gathered around our kitchen table. Harold Clurman said, "I once heard Lee Strasberg talk for one hour in the same sentence."

In his acting classes my father spent hours cajoling actors to contact their innermost feelings and express themselves without fear. "Are you a human being?" he would demand. "Then just get up and act like a human being, don't complicate things. Look at her, touch her, be aware what's happing to you, to her." But with me, he would often sit totally uncommunicative.

It was difficult to make myself heard over the thunder of

26

Beethoven, and catching my father's eye was impossible because he was constantly reading. Years before, he had begun to collect books that related in any way to the theatre—art, psychology, painting, music, great literature. Eventually this collection became the finest artistic and theater library in the country. But to me his books and music were like a fortress wall, a barrier too high to scale. Since he rarely touched me, the absence of words reinforced my feeling that I had done something terribly wrong to cause him to withdraw.

Both my parents had tempers, but my mother's, quixotic, teary, would spring up often and disappear. My father's anger would build slowly, contained in his silences, until he erupted. Mother was so intimidated by his rages she would retreat to her bedroom, her smelling salts and her tears. If my mother, who knew everything, was frightened, I reasoned there must be something to be frightened of, so I tried never to make him angry.

These were difficult years. The Group Theater had floundered, splintered apart, many of the members having been lured to Hollywood. My father, through Clifford Odets, was offered a job as a director by Twentieth Century-Fox in California, so we joined our many friends who were already there—Franchot, the Garfields, Clifford. Chaplin was still there, and Garbo. It was the last breath of the Old Hollywood. Television was an idea that would never last.

We rented an old Spanish house in Brentwood. Our next-door neighbor was a real princess—Princess Guika. The name wasn't one I would have chosen, but a princess is still a princess. We had a tennis court on which Johnny and I used to play until the bees the princess raised invaded our court and we abandoned it in favor of new entertainments.

My nurse, Jonesy, came West. She brought her possessions, including the Angora cats she bred, to fill the apartment over our garage. We would forage the neighborhood, gathering the low-hanging magnolias that reminded her of her childhood. I would fill my skirt, her apron, holding up the corners to make a basket, trying not to touch and bruise the delicate petals, intoxicated by the aroma.

Jonesy and her cats were a safe harbor over the garage; she was never too busy to hold me or protect me. Her cats had their first litter. She locked the kittens and their mother in the bathroom, as the father cat had killed and made a meal of one of his own babies. "Do you think people fathers eat their babies, too?" Johnny asked me. I didn't know for sure, but if they did, perhaps that was why my mother was always coming between my father and us, keeping us apart, saying "Don't bother him. . . . Don't tell your father about that. . . ."

One day Jonesy was gone. She had found a place of her own where she could go into professional cat breeding. She began to win medals, although she had to enter her cats in competitions through a friend who was white; blacks were unheard of in that field.

Although I could no longer run to Jonesy, I would visit her in her house in Watts, her gleaming rows of cat cages filling the backyard. In spite of seeing her, I couldn't overcome the feeling that she had deserted me—not once but twice.

Shortly afterward my mother's parents moved in over the garage. My grandfather was dying, and they hoped the balmy California days would make his last days easier.

His doctor told him, "Stop smoking those cigars and give up drinking your schnapps, they're killing you."

My grandfather replied, "Without them, I'd rather die!" which he proceeded to do.

Grandpa's funeral was sad and lonely; only four people were there, an unhappy contrast with his life, which he had lived in crowds, never learning to be alone. Mother told me about Grandpa's death and asked me to explain it to Johnny. I told him, "We're like flowers [which I loved passionately]. All flowers have to rest, and it's the same with people. Grandpa's resting."

Another "godmother," Polly Rose, came to live with us. Her brother was producer Billy Rose. She was a painter, blond, vivacious, had a lovely wide smile, and was a great tennis player.

She would take me to the ballet lessons I had just started, and we went ice skating together twice a week. I was only fair at both, but my mother decided I would be either the next Sonja Henie or the new Margot Fonteyn.

Mother, as usual, always had a house full of people. Many of our New York friends felt lost in California. They didn't know how to fill the long, empty stretches between jobs. Those who became stars suddenly had to live up to that image. In New York no one gave a damn, but in Hollywood people noticed what kind of car you drove, how expensive your shoes were. All of this was aggravated by guilt. Many New Yorkers felt they had deserted art for commerciality.

At one grand party, I remember sitting at the top of the stairs, peeping through the banister, listening to the laughter and music. I slid down a few steps, then a few more. A gentleman below caught my eye and waved me on. He began to twirl and bow.

"Do you like to dance?" he asked. I nodded yes. "Shall we? I'll give you a lesson." He took my hand, and we leaped and twirled together. My ballet teacher was Charles Chaplin.

He then proceeded to dance *Swan Lake*, playing all the parts and the entire corps. Afterward he told his wonderful stories while Oona O'Neill dozed on our couch with a faint smile on her face. Although she must have heard his stories many times over, she smiled at them even in her sleep.

Barry Fitzgerald was there and taught me to play the piano with my nose. I fell asleep that night lulled by the intense laughter, arguments, and conversation drifting up the stairs.

For his daughter's birthday party, John Garfield took over the entire Beverly Amusement Park, free rides for hundreds of children. I was impressed. This was "living" movie-star style.

I grew, and Johnny grew more adorable. At four and one-half years old, he was quite feisty and very honest, as only children can be. With his cherubic face, he was so cute my mother could rarely bring herself to punish him. When she did chastise him, he piped, "Don't tell me how to live." On another occasion he innocently asked a friend, "Why do you have such a fat belly and no hair?"

But Johnny was a great companion. We played together and

shared a room. I taught him to spell, hanging my head down under my bed while he hung his head under his. I read to him every morning, usually choosing books that were too difficult so that I had to make up my own stories.

For my seventh birthday Tallulah Bankhead bought me my first long party dress, pink tulle and satin. I loved the way it moved in the breeze. "You're a sky-blue-pink cloud," Mother called as I ran across the lawn.

I was in love for the first time. Grandma said, "Oh, yes, puppy love," but it was real for me. I could not wait for Philip to arrive at my birthday party. Philip was the one the pink dress and the special cake were for, and he had promised to come. I didn't care about any of the other children. But he did not come or even bother to call.

My friend Iris, who lived across the street, had two brothers who were always looking for a fight. One of them trapped me alone in their garden and attacked me, tearing at my clothes. As I lay on the ground bleeding, he urinated on me. My grandmother dried my tears, bathed me, and tried to console me. "People are crazy, they act like animals sometimes. Even at my age, I don't understand why." It was a side of childhood I had not seen before.

One night, a friend's daughter came to sleep over. She was a few years older than I, which was very exciting. A tall, thin girl with long, light brown braids, she had had polio and wore heavy braces on her legs. As we lay in my double bed, moonlight streaming through the window making shadows on the ceiling, jasmine scent filling the room, she suddenly screamed and began to cry. I looked; the sheets were covered with blood.

She pulled away from the stain and whispered intensely, "Do you know what that is?"

"No," I replied, wide-eyed.

"That's a curse on women from God because it's our fault, we committed the first sin, Jesus died, so every month women have to bleed to pay for their sins."

I didn't know exactly what sins she was referring to, but I could see that she was not only bleeding but crippled, so I reasoned whatever it was, it must be terrible, and she had included me in this curse too.

She held the crucifix that hung around her neck up to the shaft of moonlight. "If you kiss it and pray a lot, maybe God will forgive you."

I was totally distraught. I had always felt guilty, but no one had ever told me why before. I lay awake most of the night, praying.

In the morning, I was still hysterical, weeping and talking incoherently about the curse of God. My parents were more concerned with calming me down than deciphering what I was saying, so I never really dealt with that fear.

After several months in Los Angeles, we bought a home of our own from writer Christopher Isherwood in Santa Monica Canyon, walking distance from the ocean. You could feel and smell the damp salty winds drifting in off the Pacific.

To reach the house, it was necessary to cross a wooden bridge laid over a creek that was dry in the summer but swelled like the Mississippi in the winter. Johnny and I would tie a heavy rope around the large tree in the front yard and slide into the creek to play explorers. There were snakes there, and whenever my father saw one, he would grab a large board and bash it to death. Later, with my brother, as assistant, trailing behind me, I would dig a grave, lift the snake with my wooden spoon, and bury it, placing a small wooden cross over the hole.

One day I was invited to my old neighborhood in Brentwood to visit my girlfriend Iris. Her rambunctious brothers were there with Philip, my love, the little boy who had stood me up on my birthday. We began to play cowboys and Indians.

I wound up as the solitary Indian, and they were the cowboys. The game became a nightmare when they tied me to a tree and started to build a fire beneath my feet, threateningly waving lighted matches in the air. I was terrified as they brought the flames close to my long hair. "I don't want to play anymore," I begged, but my pleas only seemed to egg them on. They began throwing stones at me, pushing sticks up my dress, hitting me, and doing an Indian dance around the tree to which I was tied.

I was angry, frightened, and frustrated. This was my best friend attacking me. This was the little boy I adored. I remembered the ominous whisper of my crippled friend. Perhaps there was a curse on me.

Somehow I finally got loose and ran stumbling, panic-stricken, to Claude Rains's home. They took me in and called my mother, who rushed to my side. I never saw Iris again.

That year I was sent to summer school, which was in a large prisonlike building on Sunset Boulevard in the middle of nowhere. I was a dreamer, and this school was determined to make me into a doer. I loathed it and decided to run away. I went over the wall alone, headed west on Sunset, having no idea where I was going except away. In those days there were miles of Sunset Boulevard without so much as a gas station to be found.

My fair skin began to blister in the midday sun, and my feet ached. After walking what seemed like ten miles, I saw the white spire of a church. The ladies were having a tea and gave me biscuits and cookies. One of them called my home. "We have your little girl," she said. "Oh, no, my little girl is at school." "Mommy, it's me." My parents made me go back to school the next day, and I didn't find the courage to run away again for fifteen years.

Several weeks later, we were driving down Wilshire Boulevard on a clear sunny day when bells began to ring. Traffic came to a standstill, cars began to beep their horns, radios blared from open car windows. People were laughing and crying. "The war is over! The war is over!"

Things were not going well for my father at Twentieth. Although he was under contract as a director, studio management had given him nothing to direct other than tests for new actors. He had a phenomenal record in that every actor he tested was signed, which was not surprising, because with his talent, my father was able to elicit wonderful performances from even the most mediocre applicants. But this work did not offer enough challenge, and my parents decided to move back East.

Pop took the train to New York and Mother waited to follow as soon as he found an apartment, which was next to impossible immediately after the war. While waiting, Mother debated taking

Johnny and me. "I can't rid myself of the feeling I should bring the children East," she wrote my father. "Surely you must know after all these years that I don't live beyond the time I exist in. I have to live every minute . . . you, on other hand, seem to skip the present and live in the future."

It was decided that Johnny and I were to stay with my mother's sister and her husband, an ex-fighter and now a school custodian, and their two children, while Mother joined my father. They had followed us to California and owned a home of their own. We were to stay "for just a short time." As soon as my parents found an apartment, they would send for us. The "short time" got longer and longer.

"But you promised," I said on the phone.

"We can't find a home in New York. Be patient, Susan," Mother explained. She sent me ten dollars to buy Johnny and me presents.

I felt abandoned again. I would rather have slept in a cellar than in this home where I felt we didn't belong, where we were not guests and not really family. It was a cruder, less sheltered atmosphere than we were accustomed to. Johnny and I were miserable. Whatever problems we had in our own world, at least it was ours. As the weeks stretched out and became months, my parents sent money but no train tickets.

On one such predictably beautiful California day, my uncle was mowing the lawn. I remember the fresh, acridly sweet smell of the newly cut grass and the harsh buzzing of the mower.

My cousin had a friend who at eleven was three years older than I. He wanted to play doctor. I was willing, but my willingness soon palled, and I wanted to stop playing. He became harsh and abrupt. Silently we struggled as he tried to remove my blouse. I knew that if I cried out and we were discovered, he would be beaten. I also feared that he might take revenge on me in the future. His hand touched my unformed breast. I was paralyzed, freezing cold. I felt as if I was going to throw up, but there was some fascination mixed with repulsion, and for years afterward I had recurring nightmares from which I always awoke feeling unclean, responsible.

As the months dragged on, I sold comic books in the alley

behind the house, trying to raise money to buy tickets to New York for Johnny and me. The nights were interminable. I lay awake wondering what I had done to cause God to punish me this way. I kept my mother's picture under my pillow, crying myself to sleep night after night.

Finally my brother and I were on our way East, home. Danny Archer, a family friend, accompanied us on the Super Chief. Johnny was drilled to lie about his age so he could go at a reduced fare, but pride at turning six got the best of him when the conductor asked, "And how old are you, little boy?" . . . so we had to pay the difference.

We stuffed ourselves on pancakes and Southern-fried chicken, admiring our reflections in the gleaming table settings. The train rocked us to sleep at night while Danny went off to tell jokes and play poker with the servicemen who filled the train, going home after the war. Johnny, who had a lovely, high boy's voice, sang for them in the club car after dinner: "Home on the Range" and "When Johnny Comes Marching Home." He made the young men weep into their beers, applaud, and treat us to ice cream and Cokes. I wished I were able to win applause as he did.

My parents had been unable to find an apartment in New York, so we moved into a guest house on the country estate of family friend Bess Eitingon in Connecticut. The cottage was attached to a large barn that housed chickens, cows, and a goat. In front of the house a manmade lake stocked with fish ran into a stream. The banks were overhung with weeping willows, and above the lake was a gently sloping hill covered with pine trees. In the winter, the deer would come down to drink from the lake. I would spend hours alone daydreaming in the forest that covered the hill, watching for the deer.

That spring I was invited to go to the local amusement park with Tom, Bess's son, and some of his friends. Bess lent me a skirt and blouse. I was the youngest of the group, and very nervous. The hot dogs, Cokes, and ice cream I had didn't mix well with the roller-coaster ride, so my first "date" ended with disaster on the boardwalk.

34

By the following fall, my parents found a small apartment in New York on Seventy-fourth Street near the Hudson River in one of those newer buildings where you knew what everyone was having for dinner and who was having a fight. Johnny and I enrolled in P.S. 9, and we settled in. My parents had returned to their first love, the theater. I sensed from their renewed dedication that the theater was *life*.

My father began to teach at the Actors Studio, which had been founded by ex-members of the Group Theater, Elia Kazan, Robert Lewis, and Cheryl Crawford. After the first year, Bobby Lewis left and my father was asked to take his place. Among others, the membership included Marlon Brando, Julie Harris, Kim Stanley, Maureen Stapleton, Walter Matthau, Eli Wallach, and Anne Jackson. My father began teaching private acting classes and directing plays again.

Our home was a theater workshop. Guests ranged from stars to starving actors and playwrights, to painters and musicians. As always, some came to learn, some to talk, others to listen or have a good meal. Among those were a young Steve McQueen in his black leather jacket, George Peppard still with his Marine haircut, and Paul Newman with his profile from a Grecian coin. These people were supremely talented, alive, sensitive, eccentric, and some were neurotic and miserable. I thought everyone was like that. If they weren't, I assumed something must be wrong with them.

My father, without condoning or condemning neurosis, was fascinated by it. He sought to help his pupils use it by channeling it into creativity, to use it constructively for, not against, themselves. "They have the fuel, I try to give them an automobile so they can drive."

One day two young men with a gun forced themselves into our apartment. They were playwrights, brothers, whose play had been rejected, and they were going to kill themselves or my father. My mother warned me to stay in my room and made some excuse to leave the apartment. I lay on my bed, clutching my teddy bear, my ear pressed to the wall listening to them shouting.

Somehow my father managed to get hold of a knifelike letter opener, which he held behind his back. One of the young men was now naked, crouched on the windowsill, threatening to jump. The other was on his knees with gun in hand, weeping, pleading with my father to save him.

My mother burst through the door, accompanied by the New York police, guns drawn, and a team from Bellevue Hospital with straitjackets ready. At first, the police weren't sure whom to arrest— the man with the knife or the one with the gun.

At this point Johnny arrived home from school. He took it all in: police, guns, doctors, naked man, straitjackets. "Hi," he said, and turned and walked into his room.

When everyone had cleared out, my mother went to him and asked, "Johnny, didn't you notice anything unusual when you came home?"

"No," said Johnny, "wasn't it just another rehearsal?"

My parents took me to Europe that summer. My father had been asked to direct a play in Israel, and the Israeli government was assuming all expenses for our trip. Johnny was considered too young to go, and he reluctantly went off to camp.

We stopped in Paris first. With its translucent glow of age, the music of a strange tongue, it had the romance of all the novels I had read. We checked into a small hotel on the Left Bank. Marlon Brando was living in the house next door. He was courting a beautiful American girl who was living with another man in an apartment nearby. In the morning Marlon would lean out of his window, and like Stanley Kowalski calling Stella, he would moan her name in a plaintive cry. I walked down the Avenue Foch with them to a sidewalk café, rushing to keep up with her long-legged stride, feeling very grown-up and adoring them both, impartially.

By the time we were ready to leave Paris, P.S. 9 seemed not three thousand but three million miles away. We went by train to Rome, which was equally enthralling. On the way to Venice we stopped at Verona, and I stood on Juliet's balcony and daydreamed.

I would fall in love with an Italian, I would move to Europe . . . I
would . . .

We arrived in Venice late at night. Ulanova, the great Russian
ballerina, was dancing the next evening, but we were able to get
only two tickets. My mother and I argued over which of us was to
accompany my father.

She insisted, "It's once in a lifetime, a chance to see her
perform."

I was adamant. "I'm not going. I don't want you to make a
sacrifice for me."

Years later, I berated her, "You should have *made* me go."

My father left for Israel; Mother and I traveled on to roam the
streets of Salzburg, listening to Mozart in the dark. The young
Russian soldiers at the checkpoint between Salzburg and Vienna
seemed barely older than I.

A week later, we rejoined my father. Israel was like an
awakening. Everybody seemed so alive, so purposeful. The children were such a mix—dark Sephardic Jews and blue-eyed blond
Europeans, working side by side. We traveled by truck through the
tiny country with Meskin, the leading actor of the state theater. At
the Red Sea, I went swimming and heard the nearby gunfire from
the Arab borders.

Outside King David's tomb our tour guide held up a rock. "God
is everywhere," he said, "even in this." We stood at the well Mary
had drawn her water from; the stones under my feet had borne the
weight of Christ's feet, too. At the monastery on top of Mt. Carmel,
I had to remain outside because I was wearing shorts. A young
monk appeared at the door with a large red-and-white-checkered
tablecloth. "Wrap yourself in this and come see Mary's tomb." He
smiled. We stood overlooking the valleys that form the cup of
Galilee. The air had an extraordinary purity and clarity. There was
a faint sound of camel bells. My father said. "Here . . . a man
could be Christ."

The day before we left, we listened to Golda Meir speak to some
refugees. She told them how, as a child, her parents nailed boards

against the doors and windows of their homes to stop the cossacks from killing the children. "Never again," she said. "Here in this country no one will ever have to nail boards across their windows."

My father was still working on his production, so Mother and I were returning to New York without him. I didn't want to go home; life was so ordinary there. This journey had awakened new longings in me.

Mother and I spent a few days in Paris before taking the boat train to Cherbourg to board the *Queen Elizabeth*.

No sooner had we settled on the boat train than my mother leaped from her seat and let out a shriek. With her stage-trained voice, it was a very piercing cry. "The passports, the tickets, my money! I've left them in Paris in the hotel safe. Oh, my God!"

All the very proper English passengers were staring at her, so I tried to look as if I belonged to someone else.

The Cunard representative rushed over to us. "Madam, please calm yourself," said this upright symbol of the British Empire.

"I don't want to be calm," she sobbed. "What will we do? My young daughter here will be heartbroken if we can't go on the boat." I shrank in my seat.

After repeated attempts to quiet her, he said in his impeccable English, "Madam, you are the kind of woman I have nightmares about." But through her insistence and caterwauling, she got us onto that boat with no money, no passports, and no tickets.

"All right, madam," he surrendered, "you tell the U.S. Customs you left your tickets here in Cherbourg, that we saw them. That way we won't get in trouble, and we'll have the Paris hotel mail your passports to New York and they'll be on the customs boat that comes to inspect the ship."

An English doctor from the train lent her some money, the woman sharing our cabin offered us champagne. I wandered around the ship; this was a dream world to add to my others.

That night in the dining room, I saw the silks and chiffons, satins and jewels of the other first-class passengers. I felt totally out-of-place in the pink linen dress I had made myself in sewing class in P.S. 9. I was so self-conscious that I became violently seasick and was unable to leave the cabin except for the lifeboat drills we had every day (it was September, and a very rough crossing) and to go to the movies, where, unseen in the dark, I was not ill.

We sailed into New York harbor. The boat with the customs officials and our passports pulled up—only there were no passports. We waited until everyone else had cleared customs while my mother described Ellis Island, where we might be sent.

The customs official looked at us. He was very young. My mother's eyes filled with tears.

"You both look honest enough to me," he said. "Go on home."

We entered the United States with no passports, but those were the days when you didn't have to lock your front door, either.

"Don't tell your father," my mother said. "He'll kill me."

Soon after we returned to New York, we found a larger, more suitable apartment. My father's book collection was growing to gigantic proportions. We needed a lot of wall space. One afternoon, the owner of one of his favorite bookstores personally delivered an enormous package of books. My mother pointed at them and said, "There comes my life insurance and my fur coat." She was smiling, but she meant it.

We moved into an apartment house with a courtyard filled with plants and trees. There were other artists, friends, in the complex. Zero Mostel and his wife, Kate, lived upstairs, actress Betty Field lived downstairs with playwright Elmer Rice.

Zero would make up little rhymes and songs for Johnny and me. One day he came to the apartment and sang, "Roses are reddish,/ Violets are bluish,/ If it weren't for Jesus,/ We'd all be Jewish."

I had my own room at last, with large windows from which I could look down at the life of the courtyard, inventing stories about the people I saw, who they were, where they were going.

My mother was thrilled with the large house. "Come talk to me," she would say, and disappear into the bedroom. She spent hours there counseling, consoling, complaining, mothering, coaching, all from her bed. Unknown and famous, young and old, they came regularly to see her.

Ellen Burstyn said to me once, "I couldn't have survived without Paula. She gave me courage when no one else believed in me." I wondered whom Mother had turned to for comfort.

My brother and I would take our turns with her. To Johnny she would complain about life in general and her unfulfilled or aborted plans to produce, direct, and write. "I can't," she would cry, "they need me." "They" being Lee and all of her protégés. To me she would list all her grievances about Father. Eventually I dreaded going into her room because I didn't want to know those things.

If you asked her a question, she would not always answer directly; depending on who you were, she would say, "I'll have to ask my husband," "I'll have to ask Lee," "I'll have to ask your father." Other times she'd respond, "Well, Lee says . . ." "Lee thinks . . ." Often when Father was present but did not answer a question, she would fill in his silence by saying, "Well, Lee told me the other day . . ." Sometimes he would let these comments go by; at other times he would be forced into responding, "Darling, that's not it. What I said was . . ." and she would smile as he held forth.

My mother resumed her stage career in a play called *Me and Molly* starring Gertrude Berg and our old friend Philip Loeb, who had given my father his first acting job years before in *The Garrick Gaieties*. The play was a warm comedy about a family from the Bronx, and Mother played Mrs. 2C, one of the neighbors.

I went to the theater with her on weekends. After sitting backstage, watching the actors Pan-Caking their faces and checking their props, I would stand in the wings, where I could see the exchange between the audience and the actors.

At the time, we had a woman who came to clean the house once a week, Dinah O'Brien. Dinah was from Jamaica, skin black as night; she was a kosher Jew married to a Communist. She would arrive each week with a Coke and a banana because she wouldn't eat any of our nonkosher food. From the money she earned doing day work, she put her two children through medical school.

One evening Mother was ill. Although she had a high fever and a bronchial cough, she was determined to go to the theater.

Dinah said, "You're too sick to go out. You got a burning fever and no voice. Child, you got to stay home."

"You don't understand. The show *must* go on. I've got to go. I've just got to," Mother stated.

Dinah stared at her. "Mrs. S., I found there's only two things in life I've *got* to do. I've got to stay black and I've got to die."

Mother stayed home.

One day Dinah came into the kitchen horrified. "Mrs. Strasberg, what's that you've got filling your bathtub?"

"Coffee ice cream."

Mom had this passion for ice cream, and in a burst of inspiration she had hand-churned more than could be put in the freezer, so she had to find another large container. The bathtub was the largest available. In the end I invited all my friends over with spoons for an ice-cream party.

Mother used to say, "I'm going to open an ice-cream parlor à la Will Wright's. I'll employ out-of-work actors as soda jerks and waitresses." But the idea never went further than a dream and melting ice cream in the bathtub.

One weekend when I was with her at the theater, Gertrude Berg asked, "Susie, you want to go onstage tonight?"

I said, "Maybe. Yes, I guess so."

She arranged for one of the children who had a small part in the play to let me go on in her place. I had one line, "Hello."

When I walked out on the stage, I was tingling all over. The arc lights shone down, bathing the stage in a soft white aura, surrounding the actors with a halolike glow.

After this experience I began to dream about acting, although I never outwardly admitted it. If people asked, "Don't you want to be an actress, too, Susie?", I'd say, "Well, I might want to be an actress after college, but I think I'm going to study art. At least that way if I'm a flop at acting I'll have something to fall back on."

I revealed my aspirations to one of my friends, Judy, Elia and

Molly Kazan's daughter, when I spent weekends with her at their country home in Connecticut.

I became reenchanted one weekend with their house guest, Marlon Brando. He was young and beautiful, but to me he was an older man. It was a hot, humid Eastern summer. Marlon took his sheets and slept out on the roof. It was all terribly romantic until that following morning when I saw him sitting shirtless, drinking a glass of raw eggs for breakfast. It took me months to recover from that.

At school we were doing a production of *The Wizard of Oz*. Auditioning for the part of Dorothy, I got the part of her aunt. After my first line, "Watch out, here comes the tornado," I was blown offstage, never to be seen again.

Despite that disappointment, I decided I wanted to go to Music and Art, a public high school for which you auditioned by singing, playing an instrument, or presenting an art folio and taking an art test. It was the only school of its kind in the United States, and competition was fierce. When I was accepted as an art major, I felt as if my life were beginning.

I was taking dance at George Balanchine's School of American Ballet. Small for a dancer, I had strong legs, and toes so squared I could go up *en pointe* without toe shoes. This fact and, hopefully, some talent earned me a scholarship. My mother told everyone, "Susan is going to be America's next great prima ballerina." I had other plans.

Dancing began to make me violently ill, nauseous. I began to dread going to classes.

One hot Saturday morning, Parents' Day, and with my mother watching, I spun across the stage seven, eight, nine turns, to swoon and pass out on the other side. Without realizing it, I had become extremely nearsighted, 20/400 in both eyes, with an astigmatism that made me unable to "spot" properly (pick a specific spot to visually focus on at the end of each turn to stabilize my balance). I was not unhappy at the end of this career. It required grueling work and a dedication I was unwilling to give. Besides, I couldn't be a ballet dancer in horn-rimmed glasses.

We started wearing little Cuban heels on weekends, bobby socks with white buck shoes, Peter Pan collars, V-neck sweaters, and full skirts with crinolines. At less than five-feet-one, by the time I got on my petticoats and socks I resembled a walking lampshade. On weekends we would have formal dates, going uptown in taxis to dances at boys' private schools.

After I got my glasses I would hide them when I went out, particularly on blind dates—what I didn't see couldn't hurt me. Besides, I'd read Dorothy Parker: "Men seldom make passes at girls who wear glasses." I was afraid that in my horn-rims I might look like an "egghead." My dates were intimidated enough just seeing the thousands of books that lined the walls when they came to pick me up: "Boy, I didn't know you lived in the public library," or "Read any good books lately?"

Half-blinded, in the dimness of a room I would grope toward someone's lips. There were rules. You had to kiss, but you didn't have to open your mouth. It used to terrify me if the boy had pimples, because we were sure pimples were catching. The rules made decisions easier. As long as you kept to them, you were accepted, you never became a "fast" girl.

One morning during breakfast I glanced down at the New York *Times* and saw some familiar names: Clifford Odets, Elia Kazan. I began to read the article. Abruptly I stopped, shocked; included was *Paula Miller Strasberg*. The article named actors who had been accused during the McCarthy hearings of being Communists or Communist sympathizers in the 1930s and 1940s. I understood little of what I read or, in fact, of what was going on. I only felt humiliated seeing my mother's name on the front page of the New York *Times*, which was usually reserved for the bad news.

One afternoon not long after this, the doorbell rang. Two well-dressed young men asked if Mrs. Strasberg was in. They had similar short haircuts, gray suits, ties, white shirts, and looked like the actors you saw in television commercials selling after-shave lotion. I asked, "Who should I tell her wants to see her?" One of them pulled out his wallet. "We're from the FBI." In comparison to these young men, our artistic friends seemed scraggly, overly intense, scruffy.

I went to call my mother. "It's the FBI," I whispered. My God, maybe they'd come to take her to jail.

My mother seemed composed. "Hand me my lipstick." Afterward, when the young men had left, pulling me into the bathroom and closing the door, she said, "You know, Susan, we did talk about overthrowing the government, but I didn't really mean it. We talked about a lot of things. We wanted to make a better world."

All around us friends, friendships, were being affected. Philip Loeb was fired from the television version of *Me and Molly*. He came to our house and wept. John Garfield was named as a sympathizer, a term which could mean going to a party with a Communist or signing a petition in support of the Spanish Civil War. People were being damned for the company they may, or may not, have kept, and in this climate of irrationality and fear, a pall was cast over Garfield's career. He began a decline which ended in front-page headlines when he was found dead of a heart attack in a woman's bed at the age of thirty-nine.

Others committed suicide from the pressures thrust upon them, and still other artists fled to the safety and freedom of England as their ancestors had fled here to America seeking freedom from past persecutions.

It was worse for the actors than for the producers and writers; unlike a writer, who could change his name, an actor could not change his face, and many of them lost irreplaceable years from their careers.

My mother and I were quarreling more regularly now. She began going to a German psychiatrist. A lot of the mothers were seeing German psychiatrists. It was very fashionable. But suddenly all these liberal ladies who had been so permissive with their "yeses" were saying "*nein*."

As I struggled for my own identity, my mother seemed to impose her desires, her will, more and more on every area of my life; she seemed threatened by my need for autonomy. "Leave me alone!" I raged at her. "I hate you, detest you!"

My mother, who had never hit me, slapped me in the face, but her words hurt more than her hand. "You're not a nice girl. You'll never be a nice person."

Unerringly she put her finger on my Achilles' heel. I wanted desperately to do the right thing, to be a good person, to be loved at all cost; obviously it was unsafe to openly express any of my real feelings, I chose to suppress them until in the privacy of my room I would crouch on the floor of the clothes closet in the dark with the door shut. Hidden, I would tear at the old clothes or towels I had saved. Opening my mouth wide, I would scream, long strident, silent screams.

In public, tears were the only safe emotion. Tears were so much more acceptable, so much more feminine and less threatening than rage.

My mother possessed a gift of clairvoyance, which she rarely used. Years before, at a party for John Garfield, she had read for a young singer who was flying overseas the next day, and she had seen death in the cards. She begged the girl to delay her trip. The warning was ignored. The next day, the plane the girl was on crashed. This young woman had been sitting next to singer Jane Froman. Shortly before the crash she and Miss Froman exchanged places. This accident, which proved fatal to my mother's friend, resulted in the crippling of Jane Froman. For years afterward Mother did not touch the cards, feeling in some way that she was responsible; if she had not seen it, perhaps it would not have happened.

My mother read for me. She gazed at the cards she had spread on the table. "Changes . . . great, great changes." She sighed. "Travel, transformations, love. Much confusion."

"Oh, Mother," I said, "you make everything so melodramatic."

But almost everyone we knew was melodramatic. One day Father took me to a rehearsal of Toscanini's. We sat in the glass booth fascinated. The maestro was angry with one of his orchestra.

There was a long silence, the only sound the impatient tapping of his baton. "Why you look at me like that?" he shouted in his Italian accent. "You think I am crazy? No. I'm not crazy. I *hate* to conduct. I *hate* it because I *suffer*—too much!" They then proceeded to play beautifully together, Toscanini singing aloud to the music, a look of intense pleasure on his face.

Lee loved baseball like a kid. Johnny batted, I became a fan, and we had something to share. If you asked Pop a baseball question, his face lit up. When the Giants won the pennant one year in the bottom of the ninth inning, my father, Johnny, and I all began to scream with excitement—we all appreciated the great dramatic timing.

The summer I was thirteen and my brother was ten we had no plans. We were short of funds again. Nonetheless my mother was determined that we have some sort of vacation. She scraped together enough cash to rent two rooms on Fire Island.

"Mother, I don't want to go there. I don't know anyone, I won't make any friends, I look terrible in a bathing suit, and it's going to be embarrassing."

My mother paid no attention to my objections. We stayed at Birdie Irwin's Boarding House, a two-story New England-style ramshackle beach house which had withstood numerous boarders and many hurricanes. Mother and I shared one room, my brother Johnny had another down the hall.

The first girl that I met was from Music and Art, my new school, and she had a friend who had a friend, and so I became part of a group. After only a week, I was surprised and pleased to be elected lifeguards' mascot.

The head lifeguard, Richard, and I began to talk and found we had a great deal in common. One thing led to another, and I began to go out with him.

He was older, nineteen, in college—Yale. At first he was unwilling to be seen with me in public. Perhaps he didn't want to be accused of robbing the cradle. Instead we arranged to meet surreptitiously late at night.

After I went to bed I'd lie there in the dark waiting and listening until I heard him. He would sit under my window on the boardwalk next to the beach and whistle "Greensleeves." I would slip on my clothes, grab a blanket, pad down the stairs barefoot, ease silently out the front door. I knew my mother was awake, and although we never discussed it, I think she too listened for his music.

We would make our way to some private place in front of the gently sloping dunes that dotted the beach. That summer, to the rhythm of the waves, the rhythm of my life was gently, irrevocably shifting into a different gear. I was growing up.

My mother acknowledged my burgeoning maturity by asking me to explain sex to my brother. When I got to the subject of homosexuality, I said, "That's when two men like each other a lot. They sleep together, they're roommates."

"Oh," Johnny said, "I know that stuff. Like Eddie Stanky and Alvin Dark."

"That's not exactly it," I said, "but Mom told me to explain everything to you, so if she asks, tell her I did."

Summer drew to a close. Dick and I agreed that we would write and keep in touch and that fall we did correspond. "I enjoy your letters," he wrote. "It means a lot to me to see you thinking, if only occasionally." Finally he invited me up to Yale for a weekend.

"No," my mother said, "you're too young."

I knew it was the German psychiatrist she was still seeing occasionally. "Mother," I pleaded, "what are you afraid will happen that couldn't have happened on the beach at Fire Island? Trust me."

"Trust me," she retorted. Her doctor was too strong—I stayed home.

Now I made a list of careers I was interested in. Ballet was crossed off, acting was just below commercial art, but the more I hid my feelings, the more enticing acting seemed. After all, the same emotions that made me feel unacceptable in person might make me acceptable as an actress.

Almost fifteen, I decided I should become a model. As I was

extremely short for a profession that demanded height, I don't know why the idea possessed me, but I persuaded my parents that it would be a good way for me to make spending money. John Robert Powers signed me and got me my first job, posing for the cover of one of the confession magazines. I can't remember if it was *True Confessions, True Love,* or what, but I do remember being attacked and strangled for hours.

The combination of having done a few modeling jobs for which I had earned money of my own and the fact that for the first time in my life I loved school and was doing very well made the year pass incredibly quickly. Toward the end of the school year, when I was free because of final exams, I decided to visit the Actors Studio, which I had done occasionally over the years, observing my father teach or having lunch with my parents. Jo Van Fleet and I had talked about my acting aspirations on previous occasions at the Studio. This morning she approached me about playing the small role of Fifine, a young, innocent waif who is destined to become a streetwalker, in *Maya,* an off-Broadway play that Jo had signed to star in. She said she had thought of me immediately upon reading the play.

She spoke to my parents, offering to take care of me and help me with the part.

My parents said, "No. We'd prefer she wait until she's older to do any acting. You know how we feel about child actors. It's so difficult to make that transition from adolescence to adulthood. What's adorable when you are five or six or even ten and eleven can be mannered and embarrassing when you're sixteen or seventeen."

Undaunted, Jo asked, "May I talk to Susan?" They agreed.

I thought about it and said, "I'd like to do it."

My parents said, "Well, it can't hurt. We'll see what her quality is like onstage, we'll see if she's talented. Later on, after school, who knows?"

On June 10, 1953, I made my debut. Opening night I watched horrified as Martin Ritt, an experienced actor, in the course of the scene preceding mine, went up completely. Not only did he forget his lines, he choked on a glass of water and was unable to say another word. It was an actor's nightmare come true, and on opening night. They had to bring the curtain down on his scene.

With the courage and ignorance of inexperience, I went onstage as if nothing had happened. After all, no one expected anything from me. I was free. When I moved onto the stage, there was that feeling that I had experienced briefly years before during *Me and Molly*. All of my intensity, my excess sensitivity, magically became virtues, something to be shared. I felt more than incredibly alive, I felt I had come home.

The first time *Maya* had played, years before, it had been considered very risqué and the police had closed it. This time it was the critics. But what the reviewers said about me opened innumerable doors I had not even dreamed about.

Offers came into the house. My parents seemed resigned to the fact that I was on my way to a career. They asked an old friend and a fine agent, Edie Van Cleve of MCA, to represent me.

The first role I accepted was on *Omnibus*, the Sunday-afternoon anthology hosted by Alistair Cook. The script, *The Duchess and the Smugs*, was about a young English girl, Penelope, who lives in the south of France with her artist father, whom she calls by his first name. The duchess is their best friend, an eccentric grande dame, and the Smugs are a petite bourgeoisie English family summering next door, whom Penelope adores. They are ordinary, she is different; she longs to emulate them, to fit in.

After the first rehearsal, I said to my father, "Well, Lee . . ." He began to laugh. "What's so funny?" I asked.

"You called me 'Lee.' Are you living your part? Isn't that what Penelope does?"

"I like 'Lee.' Now that I'm working, I'm too old for 'Pop.'" He couldn't stop laughing.

Following that show, a rather special part was offered to me. After much deliberation my parents and I agreed that I should accept it in spite of the fact that my father felt I was too young to play Shakespeare's Juliet. At fifteen I would be the youngest American actress to play the part.

BITTERSWEET 🍂

"It's such a demanding role," he said. "On the other hand," he reasoned, "if you fail, you can always do it again when you're more experienced!"

"I knew it," my mother said. "When you stood on Juliet's balcony in Verona three years ago, I had an intuition you'd play Juliet one day."

"Did you also have an intuition there'd be Kraft cheese cooking in the potion scene?" I asked.

I was doing *Romeo and Juliet* "live" on *Kraft Television Theater*. The commercials were live, too, and as I prepared for my scene, the aroma of the Camembert cheese fondue being cooked on the adjoining set wafted under my nose.

I changed high schools because of my work schedule. The High School of Performing Arts was amenable to my missing classes if I got a job, so I enrolled as an acting major. In spite of my professional experience, they required that I do an audition for them. My major achievement there was flunking playwriting analysis. Attending the school at the same time were Suzanne Pleshette and Richard Benjamin, whose ambition then was to become a radio announcer.

A six-week NBC television series (the first in color—this was pre-peacock), *The Marriage*, with Hume Cronyn and Jessica Tandy, was my next job, followed by a number of other television appearances.

I attended my first theater party without my parents. I wore Mother's pink jersey top and her chiffon skirt pinned in to fit. Marlon Brando was there sitting cross-legged in the middle of the floor surrounded by girls and petting a cat he was holding on his lap. He wore slacks, a jacket, a beautiful silk ascot, and no shirt. I was smitten again.

In the course of the evening he asked me how old I was.

"Seventeen," I lied.

"What grade are you in?" he inquired.

"My second year of high school," I answered. He looked startled. "You see," I explained, thinking quickly, "I flunked two grades."

50

That night I dreamed of what my life would be like when I was older. The following day Marlon called the house. I didn't know what he was calling about but I heard my mother saying, "Yes, Susan's just started acting, she's only fifteen!" She's ruining my life, I thought.

That summer I went to California with my mother to visit her family. We lunched with producer John Houseman at MGM.

"Susie would be perfect for my next picture, *The Cobweb*. Let me talk to my director," he offered.

A week later I had my first movie. I was leaving my schoolgirl existence behind for Hollywood, perhaps one day Broadway. Cinderella was going to the ball, and I couldn't wait.

My mother and I were staying at the Chateau Marmont, a hotel renowned for the quality of its clientele. This rambling, faded-at-the-edges Hollywood building was caught between Sunset Strip and the Hills at a point in the Strip where it was so difficult to cross the street that Robert Benchley was reputed to have called for cabs to take him to Beverly Hills, and then, pretending to have forgotten something in his room, he would have them deposit him on the opposite side of the street. The tenants were not the nouveau riche mink-clad producers and starlets of the more famous Beverly Hills Hotel. This was the place many New York actors made their home away from home. The pièce de résistance was that Greta Garbo often occupied the penthouse. Lillian Gish, who was to appear in *The Cobweb*, was also staying at the Chateau Marmont. She, my mother, and I would share a taxi to work at Metro-Goldwyn-Mayer.

In one of the poolside bungalows, Director Nick Ray was preparing the film *Rebel Without a Cause*. James Dean and Natalie Wood were at the hotel constantly, often lying by the pool. I looked at Natalie in her low-cut bathing suit, her eye makeup, her painted nails, smoking her cigarettes, and thought: That's what I want to be like when I'm older. I didn't realize we were the same age.

Dennis Hopper, also appearing in *Rebel*, gave me a copy of Rilke's *Letters to a Young Poet* and talked to me about his aspirations as an actor, bemoaning the fact that he had consulted a psychiatrist who had told him he was not neurotic enough to need therapy. Dennis asked, "If I'm not sick, how can I be a good actor?" And I, reassuringly, said, "You *are* sick, Dennis. Believe me, you are!"

Jimmy Dean fascinated me. He epitomized an iconoclastic approach to life, opposed to the more measured, intellectual cadences I was accustomed to. I knew that Jimmy adored Pier Angeli, a lovely young Italian actress, only five years older than I. Pier was beautiful, virginal-looking, and I tried to emulate her, but in my heart of hearts I wanted to be Natalie Wood, who seemed more daring and sophisticated. When I saw Jimmy and Pier together, I could see they were madly in love. There was an invisible current between them which was very exciting, and I empathized completely with their romance, which I heard her mother was adamantly against. Eventually "Mama" was to win. Pier married Vic Damone as Jimmy gunned his motorcycle outside the church.

Years later I met Pier in Rome when she had begun her journey into the darker side of life with drugs and pills. She was still beautiful even with the heavy makeup she wore, although it couldn't cover the strain in her features. Several years later she died of an overdose. She was barely forty.

Nick Ray, Jimmy, my mother, and I used to go out for dinner, with Jimmy usually borrowing one of Nick's jackets, which made him look like a little boy dressed up in his father's clothes.

Among the actors in *The Cobweb* were Charles Boyer, Lillian Gish, Lauren Bacall, Gloria Grahame (who coincidentally was Nick Ray's ex-wife), Richard Widmark, Oscar Levant, and Paul Stewart. Also making his debut was John Kerr, who was fresh out of *Tea and Sympathy* on Broadway. William Gibson, who went on to write *Two for the Seesaw* and *The Miracle Worker*, had written the script, which took place in a private sanatorium. I played a hypersensitive, paranoid teenager with whom I easily identified.

On my first day of shooting, I had only to walk out of a movie theater with John Kerr and panic at the crowds. I had told Jimmy how nervous I was, and when it came time to shoot the scene (we were on the back lot), Jimmy roared up to the set on his motorcycle. "Hey," he said, "I came to take you for a ride."

"I don't know if I'm allowed to leave," I said, wanting to but anxious to be professional.

"It'll be okay," he assured. "Come on. It'll relax you, what the hell."

I looked for my mother, but neither she nor the welfare worker assigned to me were in evidence. I eyed the bike suspiciously—I hadn't been on one since my childhood days in California. "I'd really love to," I said wistfully.

"Then, shit, do it . . . come on." Nobody said "shit" in my family. Impressed, I jumped on.

"How do I sit . . . like this?" I tried to act blasé.

He nodded and took off the minute I straddled the wide bike. I grabbed on, hugging myself to him as we sped off. I saw people turning to look at us. The wind whipped my hair over my face, stinging it. I leaned closer to Jimmy, my face buried in his leather jacket.

"Too fast?" He laughed.

"No, you can go faster." I would have crashed sooner than admit I was afraid.

We circled the lot, arriving back at the set.

"Okay?"

"Okay, see you."

After surviving that ride, a minor detail like a camera wasn't about to scare me.

I was still sobbing after my first dialogue scene—a long emotional monologue with John Kerr—when the cast, led by Miss Gish, broke into applause. I had been baptized into films.

Charles Boyer kept largely to himself, only attracting attention as he did his vocal exercises before a scene.

"Mi, mi, mi, miiiii . . . Mi, mi, mi, miiiiii . . ." Up and down the scale.

Oscar Levant snapped at Vincente Minnelli, "Don't try to tell *me* how to play crazy! I'm crazier than you could ever *hope* to be!"

The most interesting scenes, from which I was excluded, were those that Betty Bacall held in her dressing room. I could hear Oscar's voice, the laughter, through the door. But I was "the kid"—too young. My mother and I were, however, invited to numerous Hollywood dinner parties. I could glean from the conversations at these gathering what I was missing in the dressing rooms. Risqué stories and a great deal of gossip made up most Hollywood dinner conversation. Movies were screened after dinner. The wall with the Renoir or Picasso flipped up, and a screen came down. At fifteen I was the only young person at these gatherings, and I felt that although I had glimpsed the horizons of a new world, I was still excluded from it. They treated my mother and me as if we were special; the Easterners . . . the outsiders; at once a compliment and a barrier.

I made one young friend, Steffi Sidney, the daughter of Hollywood columnist Sidney Skolsky, who was to become a lifelong one. She, too, was an actress, with a small part in *Rebel Without a Cause*—tiny, black-haired, vivacious, and bright. I could share feelings with her I couldn't with my school friends.

One day my mother and I went to visit Marlon Brando on the set of *Désirée* at Twentieth Century-Fox. Steffi, whose father was one of Marilyn Monroe's few close friends, arranged for us to see her filming *There's No Business Like Show Business*. First we visited Marlon. During his lunch break he played baseball in the wide street that bordered the sound stage. After lunch he was transformed into Napoleon, with Jean Simmons as his Désirée. I thought she was the most beautiful woman I had ever met. They had a scene on a terrace and looked incredibly romantic together, except Marlon was chewing gum and when "Action" was called, rather than taking it out, he hid it inside his mouth. Napoleon with gum in cheek. . . . I was disillusioned. I had thought of Marlon as the epitome of the "serious artist," the kind my mother and father wanted me to emulate.

We were talking after the scene when suddenly a stream of energy vitalized the stage. Heads began to turn and people stared as Marilyn Monroe undulated across the room in a dress so fitted she could barely move. I was instantly jealous of her, her *zoftig* body, her blondness, the ease with which she commanded attention.

It was strange. Years later we walked with a friend through the streets of New York. She wore a scarf and raincoat, sunglasses, no makeup, and no one paused or looked. If they did, it was only to shake their heads as if to say, "Of course, that's not her." And they were right. "Her"—M.M.—the golden pied-piper girl, was someone else, someone she became by shifting into another gear. It was deliberate. She willed it. As she walked down Broadway, unnoticed, she turned to us and said, "Do you want to see me be *her?*"

I didn't know what she meant by "her," so I nodded, wanting to be agreeable. She made some inner adjustment, and suddenly, there she was—glowing. Heads turned as they had the first time I had seen her. People began to converge on us. She smiled like a little girl.

Once, in a taxi going to classes, simply dressed, no makeup, hair pulled back, she was asked by our driver, "Where are you girls going?"

"To class," she replied.

"What do you do?"

"I'm an actress."

He inspected her through his rearview mirror. "Ya know, I betcha you could make it. You're a lot prettier than Jayne Mansfield. Stick with it, honey."

"Oh, I will," she assured him.

But when we visited her on the set of *There's No Business Like Show Business,* neither my mother nor I really knew her. They were in the midst of rehearsing for the "Heat Wave" song-and-dance number. Marilyn was perspiring heavily and kept falling out of step. Joe DiMaggio was on the set that day, so she was under additional tension, as he disapproved of the sexy roles she played. She slipped in the middle of a complicated step and fell soundly on her backside. Taking a break, she came over to us, still embarrassed from her fall. We were standing with DiMaggio and Steffi's dad.

Marilyn said to my mother, "I've heard so much about your

husband. I think he's wonderful." She seemed nervous and self-conscious. Later, when we went to her dressing room, she spoke about my father again. "I've always dreamed of studying acting with Mr. Strasberg." I stared in admiration at her image in the dressing-room mirror. This was it—the American dream.

When *The Cobweb* finished filming and we returned to New York, school was anticlimactic, boring. I was longing to work, to be accepted for myself. Only the year before at the Actors Studio benefit party, I'd hidden behind my parents, peering out to acknowledge introductions. Now I was a professional. At the next Studio benefit, Marilyn and Marlon were ushers. I chose a spot slightly apart from my parents, standing as straight as I could. "You'll never play a princess if you don't stand straight," my mother said.

I was pleased that Marilyn remembered me from Los Angeles. She had come East and was an observer at the Actors Studio. She said, "Hi, I'm Marilyn Monroe."

I noticed that she went up to people, put out her hand, and introduced herself, saying her full name, as if they might not know who she was.

In acting class it was different. Another Marilyn emerged; she was appreciated for her inner qualities as well as her more obvious physical attributes. "Hi," she breathily said to a boy she was working with on a scene. She had phoned him about the rehearsal time.

"Hi, it's me—Marilyn."

Joking, he asked, "Marilyn who?"

"You know," she said seriously. "Marilyn, from class?"

We all learned to live in a glaring spotlight. "Remember," my father cautioned, "a career grows in public, but your talent grows in private."

Johnny now demanded some attention. As I had emerged into acting, he was just entering his awkward stage; his blond hair darkened, he developed baby fat. He was almost thirteen and suddenly decided he wanted to be bar-mitzvahed. His best friend was going to be, and Johnny, feeling left out of the family, wanted to be part of his peer group.

"But, Johnny, you never even wanted to go to Hebrew school, you can't speak Hebrew, you don't know anything about the ceremony. It's too late. You've only got a month until your birthday."

He was adamant. "I want to be bar-mitzvahed. It's important to me."

My mother rose to the occasion. "If my son wants to be bar-mitzvahed, he's going to be." She began calling reformed rabbis who, she logically reasoned, might be more liberal about Johnny's lack of religious training than the more orthodox. "He hasn't studied," she said to them, "but in his heart . . ." They all turned her down, saying it was impossible for him to be prepared in such a short time, but she refused to give up.

Through a friend she went to see an orthodox rabbi, and he, too, reiterated even more strongly what the others had said: "How can this young boy learn Hebrew in one month?"

"He'll learn," she said. "In our family, you can learn Macbeth in a month; Johnny can learn this part."

"Mrs. Strasberg," he said, "it's impossible."

"All right," she said, tears spilling down her face. "If you don't want this child, I'm going to take him there." She pointed through the window toward the Catholic church across the street. "They won't turn him away. They'll welcome him."

The rabbi paled. "Perhaps we can make an exception here if he can really learn to speak Hebrew. Let me talk to him. We'll see."

One month later, in an orthodox temple, the men on one side of the synagogue, the women on the other, Johnny stood up and became a man. Then he proceeded to get high on Manischewitz and make a pass at one of my father's younger, prettier students.

"My son, the doctor," my mother would say. Johnny was beginning to talk about medical school. He rejected the idea of going into the theater, which was a turnabout, because he had been the one with the beautiful voice and ambitions. He had even auditioned at one point for a musical.

"You didn't give me the chemistry set I wanted," he shouted at my mother. They were fighting regularly now, more and more vehemently.

My father entered into the altercation. "My son wanted a chemistry set and you didn't give it to him?" he yelled.

Johnny got his set and his bar mitzvah, but not his fair share of attention. He was the only member of the family not immersed in the artistic world, the only nonpro. He would go off with his school friends on Saturdays to play football uptown in Central Park, carrying a shillelagh as a weapon because there were often gang rumbles in that part of the city. My mother forbade him to go, but he said, "They're my friends and you can't stop me." "Johnny, you have to watch what you do. Think of the family name!" she admonished. He pretended indifference, but inside he felt a desperate need to be acknowledged. My mother and I were off traveling much of the time, and Father was deep in his own dreams, so that when we were away, Johnny had to struggle along by himself. He was terribly sensitive, with a sharp, brilliant mind, a temper like my father's, and a tenaciousness that came, I think, from my mother's family. He physically was beginning to resemble my mother's father. He was going to be taller than anyone else in the family, and though he was still carrying his baby fat, you could see underneath it his sharp, classic features. Even when we were all sleeping under the same roof, a family at home, the attention was focused on my father's career and mine. Johnny's day-to-day problems were lost.

My mother would erratically try to make it up to him. "Eat," she'd say, putting some cake in front of him.

"I'm trying to diet, Mother. I'm fat and want to lose weight."

"Just a little cake," she'd say.

"You're a sadist," he yelled.

"But you love cake." She always seemed to find the wrong thing to do or say. He begged to go to Greenland for a summer construction job. He wanted to earn his own money like me, to be independent. "No," my parents said, "we worked so you wouldn't have to, you're too young." He stormed out of the room. As I became busier, I saw less and less of him.

The pressures of performing began to distort my own private life. As new feelings and sensations I could not contain streamed through me, I would become hysterical. One weekend my parents and I drove to Westport to see a friend playing at the summer theater there. During dinner I had a glass of wine that went to my head. I excused myself and went to the ladies' room, where I passed out cold on the floor. When I revived, my hands and legs were totally paralyzed. I tried to force them to move and couldn't. Horrified, I began to weep. "Why has God punished me, what have I done? Please, someone, ask my father to come in here." When he did, he proceeded to calm me down and massaged my limbs until painfully the feeling began to return. No one acted as if anything out of the ordinary had occurred, and indeed my father probably saw many hysterical actresses react this way in his classes, but I was frightened and wondered if there were something drastically wrong with me. Yet, within a few days the incident was forgotten, as so many before had been, when I became involved in a new project.

Edie Van Cleve, my agent, arranged an appointment for me to meet with Josh Logan, the director of *Picnic*. I'd seen Kim Stanley in the role of the kid sister on Broadway and fallen in love with the part. Millie was a rebel and an outsider. It was another character I could readily identify with.

I walked into Mr. Logan's office in one of my best dresses, a full-skirted dirndl, with my hair flowing down my back. He looked me up and down as we talked, and mentioned that he had known me when I was a little girl.

"Susan, you're really too pretty and feminine for Millie," he said. "She's a tomboy, and there's no way you could play that. There's no point in your even reading."

I reported what he had said to my mother, and she hit her forehead with her hand, saying "I knew it. You should have gone dressed for the part."

"But I wanted to look pretty."

"My darling," she sighed, "you can look pretty another time. This is a wonderful part."

My agent set up another appointment. Over Josh's protestations, she managed to convince him that he was in for a surprise.

My mother pronounced, "This time he won't see Susan, he's going to see *Millie.*"

That evening Ralph Roberts came over to give my mother a massage. Ralph had given up a career in the Army to become an actor, and as a sideline he gave massages to his good friends, among whom were Judy Holliday, Maureen Stapleton, Walter Matthau, and, eventually, Marilyn Monroe. He was six-foot-four, strong but sensitive-looking, a gentle giant who had entered our lives three years before. He was wearing a plaid lumberjack shirt. "That's Millie's shirt, Susan," my mother said.

"But he's over six feet."

I tried on the shirt, which came down to my ankles. "I think Johnny has a shirt like this, only a little smaller."

Two days later I walked into Mr. Logan's office in jeans, no makeup, Johnny's shirt, a baseball cap, my horn-rimmed glasses falling down my nose, and holding my brother's baseball mitt and ball, which I had borrowed for the afternoon. During the reading, I threw the ball back and forth to Josh and flipped it up and down in the air. He was impressed enough to screen-test me. I did a scene with Carroll Baker, who was testing for Madge, "the pretty one."

Within a week I got word that I had won the part. Columbia insisted on casting a young actress they had under contract for the beautiful older sister. Kim Novak was a protégée of Harry Cohn, the president of the studio. He was determined to make her a star, partially, I heard, to spite Rita Hayworth, who had rebelled against him. Bill Holden was signed to play Hal, the itinerant wanderer, Rosalind Russell and Arthur O'Connell to play the schoolteacher and her boyfriend, and Betty Field was to play my mother.

We were going to shoot the entire film on location in Hutchinson, Kansas. As a minor, I had a tutor for three hours a day and was able to act for six hours. Jean Louis was designing the costumes, and I was relieved that, in spite of my tomboy part, in the big picnic scene I was to wear a pretty flowered cotton dress; then I saw the dress that he had designed for Kim.

"Couldn't my dress be cut just a little lower in front?" I begged. "No." "What about higher heels, then?"

They sent me out to buy a bathing suit for the swimming scene. I picked a svelte one-piece tank suit. "Take it back, it's not Millie," they said. I went back and bought an ugly two-piece bathing suit that made me feel fat and short.

We arrived in Kansas. The first thing the company did was to assign "ditch partners." This was tornado season, and in the event one appeared during filming, we were to find our partners—mine was Rosalind Russell—and run together to our assigned ditch. A tornado warning was issued. We could see it ominous and black, spiraling toward us across the horizon, but at the last minute it veered off and struck a small town ten miles away, decimating it.

Bill Holden was very unhappy about his role. "Christ, Josh, I can't swing around like a monkey. I'm too old for that crap. I'm going to look like an idiot." He also complained when he had to shave his chest. No hair was allowed in 1955.

Kim was worried about her emotional scenes. This was the first part she had gotten which made real demands upon her. In one scene, she asked Josh to pinch her hard and make her cry for the camera. I watched as he directed her like a choreographer, blocking the scenes out for her by the numbers. "Turn, two, three, deeper breath, four, five, six." It worked, because she was lovely in the part.

At 5:30 in the morning I'd sit fascinated as Kim was made up. Two to two and a half hours were spent on her face and hair. Then, in the scenes where she wore a swimsuit, they would shade her body just as they had her face, thinning here, enhancing there. "Couldn't I have dark shadows on my thighs like Kim?" I begged Alberta, the body-makeup woman.

We played a scene in a locker room. I was intrigued as Josh

61

covered Kim's nipples with tufts of cotton to make sure they wouldn't show through her thin dress. Braless, she was years ahead of her time.

Nick Adams, who played Bomber, the newsboy, used to follow Kim around adoringly, carrying her chair from location to location. He ignored me.

By the time we got to the scene where I had to cry out, "Madge is the pretty one. Madge is the pretty one," I needed no coaching.

Leonard McCombe, who had photographed me a number of years before when I played Juliet, arrived on location to cover the movie for *Life* magazine. One night after shooting, Bill was particularly angry at Josh about something, and knowing that Josh had terrible acrophobia, Bill climbed out of Rosalind Russell's window and proceeded to hang off the ledge, seven floors up, holding on with only one hand, until Josh apologized. I was privy to all this, as Rosalind's room was right next to mine.

"You should have called me, even in the middle of the night," Leonard said. "God, what a picture!"

My mother was across the hall from me, and on my other side was Phyllis Newman, a New York actress, with two other roommates. At night I would put a glass to the wall and try to listen to their conversations, which varied from men and sex to sex and men.

I celebrated my seventeenth birthday with a cake and champagne. Bill, Rosalind Russell, Josh, my mother, and the producer were there. And the next day on the set, hundreds of extras sang "Happy Birthday."

All locations, with their isolation and loneliness, are difficult. As time went on, the crew became more and more rambunctious. Daily Harry Cohn was heard screaming on his direct line to Hutchinson that someone had to keep them under control. One night they threw all the mattresses into the corridor. Another evening they invited a beautiful young girl to the hotel, who, when it was discovered that she was the daughter of a local VIP, was quickly removed.

Josh was becoming more and more nervous because of the

pressure from Hollywood to finish on time despite the problems that arose on location: the weather, dealing with crowds of amateurs. The major love scene between Kim and Bill had to be completely reshot because back in Hollywood someone noticed that they had filmed it waist-high in a field of marijuana.

One day during the big picnic scene, I was called before sunset, five o'clock. The driver arrived late at the hotel, and I did not get to the set until the sun was almost gone. When Josh saw me, he began to scream hysterically, launching into a long, irrational tirade over the open microphone in front of thousands of strangers. I was humiliated and horrified. He had been such a gentleman. It was not until years later, reading his book, that I learned about his emotional problems.

When we got back to Hollywood, I was summoned to Harry Cohn's office. He wanted to see me alone, sans Mama. It seemed that he had intended Kim Novak to be put on the cover of *Life*, but instead, the magazine had decided to run a picture of me eating watermelon. After having an apoplectic fit, Mr. Cohn had decided to offer me a contract. "I'll make you a star," he said.

"Well, I'm not sure yet what I want to do with my career," I hedged. "I think I should talk to my parents before I make any decision."

"You're a very lucky little girl," he said. "People don't get onto the cover of *Life* at your age. Do you realize what that means?"

"I know that it's important, Mr. Cohn, but after all, even Lassie made it."

I sat down with my girlfriend Steffi and made a list, "What I Want to Be Like When I'm Famous: *elusive* like Garbo, *there* like Marilyn Monroe, *difficult* like Marlon Brando, *sexy* like Ava Gardner, *cool* like Grace Kelly, and *talented* like Duse and Bernhardt."

I was committed to doing a third picture, *Friendly Persuasion*, directed by William Wyler, starring Gary Cooper. I was ready to start work when my agent, Edie Van Cleve, phoned from New York.

"Paula," she said, "you and Susie are to be at the Beverly Hills

Hotel for lunch tomorrow to meet with the Hacketts and Joseph Schildkraut. They may want Susan to read again."

Frances and Albert Hackett had written the script for *The Diary of Anne Frank*. Mr. Schildkraut had been cast in the role of Anne's father, Otto Frank. "But the producer hated me when I read in New York. He never called me back. I can't understand it."

My mother smiled. "God works in mysterious ways. You probably weren't as bad as you thought you were."

Garson Kanin, who was to direct the show, was in London working on another project and had seen the old television show *The Duchess and the Smugs*. On the basis of that viewing, Garson was willing to give me the part. He was unable to be in America to interview me personally, and agreed that if they all approved, the part was mine.

"I don't want to read again," I said to my mother.

"That's absurd. Why?" she demanded.

"If I don't try and I don't get it, I won't feel like such a failure."

Even that early in my career I was trying to protect myself from rejection.

We sat in the bougainvillea-filled garden of the Beverly Hills Hotel. Joseph "Pepi" Schildkraut was holding court. My mother was unaccustomedly quiet as she listened to him.

"Suzileh, I saw you in your crib when you were a baby. You are just as beautiful today." He kissed my hand. He talked about his father, the great German actor Rudolph Schildkraut, of how he had tried to live up to his father's reputation, but that it was finally this part, this play that would fulfill his deceased father's expectations for him. As he spoke about his father and about Otto Frank, his eyes filled with tears.

The Hacketts were charming. They asked me about school, about the filming of *Picnic*. I was very nervous, as I knew they expected me to read as soon as the meal was finished, so I ate as slowly as possible, becoming almost hypnotized by the sound of Pepi's voice with its continental accent rising and falling. When I could not delay any longer, he said, "We've arranged to open the downstairs ballroom. It has a small stage, and we'll have privacy."

No I won't, I wanted to say. "Of course." I smiled.

We walked from the sunny garden into the cavelike cool of the ballroom. Someone clicked on the overhead lights and handed me a small sheaf of pages—it was the last scene in the play, a monologue when Anne talks to her friend Peter about her hopes for the future, her belief in the goodness of man. As she speaks, she looks out a small window through which the audience will see a fragment of sky.

I clutched the script—like a security blanket, to stop my hands from trembling. I almost knew this speech by heart from the previous time I'd read in New York.

The three of them sat at the tables scattered about the dance floor. My mother was not visible, but I could feel her presence. I looked out the small window over the stage. I could see a hint of green and sky. As I began to speak the lines, I started to weep, for Anne, for her courage, her belief, but also at my own cowardice. She had maintained her faith in the middle of the war; I was unable to hold on to mine on a peaceful day in Beverly Hills. When I finished, there was silence. Then I heard them whispering among themselves.

"Hello, Anne," Pepi said. We all began to laugh.

I called William Wyler to see if he would release me from *Friendly Persuasion*.

"Mr. Wyler, I wouldn't ask if it were just a part, but it's Anne Frank."

"Of course, I understand," he said graciously. "You must do it. We will work together another time."

Rehearsals didn't begin for three months, so I now had the whole summer to prepare. My mother and I flew back to New York, took the ferry to Fire Island, where she had rented a house. I had my umbrella, my hats, my sun screen, as I would have to look as if I had been shut away from the sun for two years. The months disappeared as if the tide had washed them away overnight.

I read and reread the diary itself. I stayed up late talking with my father and mother. "What do you think it was really like? . . . How could she have stood it to feel that alive and yet be caged that way?" I sensed a strange parallel with my own life. I also felt constricted, unable to release my feelings into my personal life. It was only playing a role that I felt safe enough to let my inner self show. Ecstasy, exuberance, brattiness, and even all my silent screams could be exposed and no one would think I wasn't nice. I identified with Anne so strongly that the line between her feelings and mine started to become indistinguishable.

People had heard that I was signed to play Anne Frank and began to pay attention when I walked down the beach. I was suddenly a burgeoning celebrity. We saw very little of Johnny that summer. He got his first job at a water-ski school, frequently coming home only to sleep. Marilyn came East and visited often. Turning up the radio or the record player, she would kick off her shoes and dance in the middle of the room alone, if no one was willing to dance with her. In the evenings, we would open a bottle of champagne, which she loved. In the daytime we would venture out onto the beach if it wasn't too crowded. Once people knew she was there, they gave her no peace, so instead, I lent her my sketch pad and pen and she drew and doodled with them. I saved two of her drawings. In one, with quick, round lines, depicting a feline sensual grace and movement, she had done a self-portrait. The other was of a little Negro girl in a sad-looking dress, one sock falling down about her ankles. I thought that was a self-portrait, too, of Marilyn's hidden self.

When she visited, we shared a room. Early one morning I awakened to see her standing, bathed in the morning sun, nude by the window, doing intimate things to her body, bleaching, shaving her legs. I was mesmerized. Was this what drove men wild? Was this the eternal feminine mystique? I couldn't see the sensuality of her body, but I recognized a magical quality about her flesh. It had resiliency and buoyancy, like a child's. She turned toward me as if sensing my gaze. Caught off guard, I blushed and blurted out, "Marilyn, I wish I were like you."

"Oh, no," she gasped in that sometimes whispery voice, "oh, no, Susie. I wish I were like you. I'd love to have your family.

You're going to play a great part—Anne Frank. People respect you. Oh, no." She trembled with the intensity of her feelings.

When Marilyn became restless, she would putter around in the kitchen, rolling up her men's shirt sleeves. She would fry things, eggs, chicken, anything she could find in the icebox.

We took a family photo that summer. It was a creative time, and we all looked happy. My father's contribution to the American theater was being popularly recognized. My mother was delighted with his success and the promise of mine. I was close to fulfilling her dreams, and rather than pulling away from her, as would have been normal at seventeen, I was becoming more dependent on her, professionally as well as personally. I was relying on her to make choices and decisions for me, and I was afraid that without her I would be helpless, a failure.

Together we decided I would buy a tiny gold Jewish star to wear around my neck and it would be from Anne's best girlfriend. I would be able to touch it like a talisman whenever I needed strength. My mother believed in these little secret messages to yourself. She used to say to me, "If you don't feel real, touch a chair. It's real. Touch a tree, it's alive. Touch the wall. It will put you in contact with yourself."

Rehearsals began. It was unlike anything I had ever experienced, totally absorbing, demanding, and fulfilling. All of the actors, even the old-timers like Joseph Schildkraut and Gusti Huber, who played my mother, were enthralled.

Garson Kanin, the director, was a small, slender, wiry gentleman who dressed impeccably in the finest English fashion. He was a raconteur par excellence and his conversations and directions were illustrated by stories and references to his famous friends and what they had said or done. "Justice Frankfurter said to me . . . Last year Spencer Tracy was filming and told me . . ."

We were all very impressed with his intimate knowledge of these legendary names.

There were five Broadway neophytes in our cast of ten. Eva Rubinstein, daughter of pianist Artur Rubinstein, was playing my sister, Margot. Dan Levin, a young American whom Gar had hired in London, played Peter. "Let's see what my money's bought me from London," producer Kermit Bloomgarden said upon meeting him. Lou Jacoby, Gloria Jones, and I completed the quintet of newcomers.

Actress Ruth Gordon, who was married to Gar, was present most of the time, advising and lending moral support. She was delightful, as was Gar, but he was cerebral, exacting, thorough, whereas Ruth was spontaneous, warm, outgoing, the kind of person everyone should have on his side. She had put some of her own money into the show.

"Listen, fellas," she said. "you are all so terrific, you're gonna knock 'em dead."

During rehearsals, whenever I was having difficulty interpreting a reflective passage or timing a laugh line, she'd come to my room and talk to me about her struggles when she was a young actress. She never directly or specifically told me what to do, but afterward, when I'd had time to digest what she had said, I'd realize her stories always pertained to the problem I was having.

Years later, I saw Ruth, who was then in her late seventies.

"How are you?" I asked as we hugged.

"Darlin', I've still got some ginger up my ass," she replied. She did indeed.

Gar had his own way of working. He asked us all to arrive with our lines learned, which was unusual, and as soon as we could, he blocked the play—"putting it on its feet," it is called. He had a discerning eye for timing, comic and dramatic detail, a strong sense of rhythm. He was concerned with the pacing of the performance and with restraining Pepi so he would not overact as he had a tendency to do. I was concerned about feeling rushed, unable to take time even in rehearsals to explore some of the moments. Gar would ask me to speed it up, and I was too insecure to tell him I was just trying to feel my way.

I asked my father for advice, and he told me, "Pick up your cues quickly. If you want to pause, do it in the middle of the line. Once you have the audience's attention, they'll wait."

When I had trouble with a more lyrical passage, he said, "Remember, you *have* a lyrical quality. You don't have to act lyrical, too."

Later, I wrote Steffi, "As I begin to get into the play, I've stopped being afraid of it. I haven't done anything lately but talk, eat, sleep, and primarily work! So there's not much to tell. If the show is successful, I have to stay with it until June 30; if not—well, I will just keep working. I will send reviews after we open. I can't see straight, so I will say good night."

My father came to dress rehearsal before we left for Philadelphia. The actors were more concerned with his opinions than those of the critics. When he was silent, Dan Levin said, "We must have been awful, he's not saying anything." He did not realize that my father's silence was normal, not personally directed at him.

During rehearsals in Philadelphia, Gar called the company onstage to talk to us. Actor Philip Loeb, not only a family friend but also one to many of the cast, overburdened by his blacklisting as an actor and by family problems, had committed suicide by jumping out of a tenth-floor hotel window. Gar talked about Philip, the loss he would be to the theater, and the insanity of McCarthy's political scourge. He said, "I had to talk to you. I could never have lived with myself if I hadn't."

We were to have news soon after that another fine, younger actor had been tragically killed. Jimmy Dean died at the age of twenty-four when his Porsche, "The Little Bastard," crashed outside Salinas, California. He was on his way to an auto race.

I struggled with the part, trying to find the way to make the transition from feisty teenager to blossoming young woman. Much was deleted from the original diary, and focus was shifted because certain subjects were taboo. Some of Anne's political and religious views, her sense of her own body, were tempered. She was, in the 1940s, far ahead of most of us in the mid-50s.

All of us were caught up in the spirit of *Anne Frank*. This was more than a play, it was something extraordinary. I worked harder than I ever had in my life. There was no need for my mother to say, "Susan, you must go to sleep earlier, you shouldn't go out." I had no desire to go out, to be with friends. People asked, "But don't you miss having fun?" This play was more fun than anything I had done. I was expressing all my hidden feelings and being praised for it. Through Anne, I was laughing, weeping, even rebelling against my mother as Anne had against hers. . . . "Mother is unbearable, she insists on treating me like a baby. . . ."

I was so totally immersed in being Anne that I was virtually unaware of any problems other than my own. Vaguely, I knew that Pepi was unhappy at having to mute his flamboyant style and that it was traumatic for him to shave his head in order to look like Mr. Frank. There is an old actor's saying: "Save me from children and animals." I was not really a child, but he felt I was getting too much attention. He complained that I was stealing scenes or upstaging him, that my parents were helping me do this. My father had not been within fifty blocks of the theater except for that first runthrough; my mother had kept a low profile; and I barely knew which way upstage was. He was even unhappy because it was called *The Diary of Anne Frank.*

Before we left town, the producers spoke about replacing me: I was too inexperienced and Pepi was unhappy with me. He was creating problems, and every other day he threatened to quit, accompanied by torrents of tears, which I later learned he could turn on or off at will.

Fortunately, all this was forgotten in the rush of opening-night madness. The dream began to become a reality. We opened in Philadelphia to glowing reviews. But as I wrote to Steffi, "Even though the reviews and the box office were terrific, there is no way of knowing if it will be the same in New York."

The day we opened on Broadway, October 5, 1955, I was in a dither. The previous night I had dreamed that I could not remember my lines. I was worried about being able to do my work in front of so many of my family and friends. I couldn't eat, my stomach was playing strange tricks on me.

My father said, "Your nervousness is a sign of your sensitivity. If you weren't nervous, you'd be dead. Have faith in yourself. All good actors have opening-night jitters. What's important is to use

70

it. Make it work for you. You wouldn't be normal if you didn't feel the way you do."

When I went to the theater that night, my dressing room was filled to overflowing with flowers, telegrams, gifts. One, a gold charm, was from my parents and Johnny and was engraved "The talent is yours, the love is ours." The flowers brought on an allergy attack that I got whenever tired or under stress, and my mother ordered everything removed until after the show.

"No distractions," she said. "Just concentrate on the part."

On the bulletin board was a letter from Otto Frank, Anne's father:

> . . . You will all realize that for me this play is a part of my life, and the idea that my wife and children as well as I will be presented on the stage is a painful one to me. Therefore it is impossible for me to come and see it . . . my thoughts are with every one of you all the time, and I hope . . . the play will be a success and that the message which it contains will, through you, reach as many people as possible and awaken in them a sense of responsibility to humanity. . . .

Everything went well. The audience seemed even more responsive than those in Philadelphia and Boston. When the final curtain went down, something happened which was very rare in the theater but which was to occur often during the run of the play. There was a stunned silence as the audience returned to reality. Then the applause broke over us in waves.

People crowded into my tiny dressing room. Marilyn, Franchot, Joshua Logan, my godfather, Anderson Lawler, who handed me a box. Inside I found a ring of yellow sapphires surrounded by cabochon rubies and emeralds.

"Ah been savin' this for years," he said. "It was mah mother's. Ah'd never found anyone I wanted to have it."

When my parents and I entered Sardi's for the party after the show, the diners stood up, applauding. Marilyn rushed in behind us. "Wasn't Susie wonderful?"

"Lee, isn't it wonderful?" said Josh Logan. "You must be so excited."

"No," my father replied, "relieved."

"I'm so glad Susan isn't a child actress," added my mother. "I loathe child actresses."

"Susie, if you never studied with your father, how did you learn all that?" someone asked.

"Osmosis," I replied.

Franchot raised his glass. "Little Susan, you have been launched on a long and glittering career. I drink to you."

I was ravenous, as if I had been starved over the past months, as if I had been locked in that attic hideaway. I ordered fruit salad, ice cream, a ham-and-turkey sandwich. Franchot ordered pizza. Nervously I ate my meal and his. Someone seated next to me had steak tartare. I devoured that and champagne.

The reviews finally arrived. Franchot couldn't see without his bifocals, so I read them to him. I was pleased and embarrassed at the same time, feeling that, although it was me, it was not *me* that they were talking about. The only review I can quote to this day by heart is Brooks Atkinson's in the New York *Times*. ". . . By some magic that cannot be explained, Miss Strasberg has caught the whole character of Anne in a flowing, spontaneous, radiant performance. . . ." He went on to say something to the effect that it is difficult to say what is Anne and what is Miss Strasberg, because "for the moment they were blended into one being." I was not sure any longer what was Anne and what was me.

My father turned to a reporter, saying, "When she came out on the stage, I was amazed. Truthfully, I never dreamed she had such talent." My mother said, "I always knew."

When I awoke the next morning, I read all the reviews again, plus the new ones that had come out. The phone did not stop ringing.

"Well, Susie Q, how does it feel to be a star?"

"Well, I'm not really a star."

72

"How do you feel this morning?"

"I don't feel any different. Do you think there's something wrong with me? Should I?"

I only knew that I had to go to the theater again that evening, and I was stricken by doubts. If I had been anxious before the opening, now I was petrified. I had no idea if I could repeat my performance. I struggled through that second night, and by the end of the first week I was becoming more confident, although I was bewildered by the attention I was receiving and by the change in attitude of people toward me.

My life was extremely hectic at this time, because in addition to doing the play, I appeared in a television show, *Dear Brutus*, with Helen Hayes and Franchot. Rehearsing during the day and performing at night left little or no time for me to be alone to absorb what was happening to me.

That December we gave another one of our by-now-famous New Year's Eve parties. My brother, without consulting anyone, invited his entire school football team: thirty-five fourteen- and fifteen-year-olds. My mother was furious and banished them to the back room, where Judy Holliday and Maureen Stapleton spent much of the evening with one of the best audiences they ever had. Johnny, someone told me, was throwing up in the bathtub from an excess of champagne.

One day in January, the producer Kermit Bloomgarden came to see my parents. The management wanted to place my name with Joseph Schildkraut's above the title as his costar. Both my mother and father were less than enthusiastic. "Maybe it's pushing her into too many responsibilities too soon. Her life has changed so suddenly already. As a star, she'll be responsible to the public, to her colleagues, to the playwrights, to her art. I don't know—she's so young. This will make her the youngest person ever to get star billing on Broadway."

Kermit said, "Lee, it's too late to hold her back. It's inevitable."

My father was not convinced. "If she was more experienced, if she had time from a continuous, logical rise to this point, to learn how to handle the problems of success—but unprepared, I've seen people go crazy. It's like candy. A few pieces you can enjoy. The whole box can make you sick."

Kermit was adamant. Although he was asking, he intended to do it regardless of the answer.

"At least let her continue to take curtain calls with the company, not alone," my father asked.

When my parents told me all this, they explained, "That's the way you started in the show and that's how you should continue, as a member of the cast, the ensemble."

Late that evening, after the show—at that hour when I was almost asleep on my feet—my father said, "You know, through you, I feel I touch the world." I shuddered with the burden of his admiration.

The next evening, I wandered down into the theater basement as usual to check my props, see that the microphone was adjusted. On the dusty, scuffed floor I looked at the marquee letters scattered at random. They could spell anything or nothing. I realized they could be shifted with no effort to make my name or a stranger's. Yet the night I first looked up and saw those one hundred and eighty bulbs flashing my name, I was entranced.

My parents were undergoing their own transitions. The changes in their lives seemed to have taken place overnight, or perhaps I was so immersed in my work and adolescence that I had not been observant.

My mother's was the sharper metamorphosis, because it manifested itself in a dramatic physical change. As time passed, her gay, light-colored dresses at first had been replaced by an ethnic manner of dressing. I remembered her on Fire Island the summer before I opened in *Anne Frank* in striped and flowered dirndl dresses from Salzburg. But these gave way to darker- and darker-hued clothes until eventually she was to dress almost exclusively in black. Her whimsical feminine hats of the past were now black witch's hats in straw or felt with strange peaks which protected her face from the sun or the view of people around her. I intuited that her adoption of this color had a strange logic, as if she were in mourning over the slow erosion of her robust sexuality. More

74

obviously, she was hiding the excessive weight that began to imprison her body.

Now in her mid-forties, my mother remarked to a particularly slender friend of mine, "God, you don't know how I envy you. I haven't been able to look in a full-length mirror for years. Only from here up." She made a slashing motion across her shoulders. She adopted a habit, too, of wearing long, flowing chiffon scarves that were her only touch of color. She carried huge purses, some like small suitcases. There was always some food to be found carelessly wrapped in the bottom of these, along with her perennial smelling salts (although I never saw her faint, she threatened to often); she also carried a magnifying glass, a flashlight, aspirin, assorted pills—she was a combination delicatessen, pharmacist, Jewish mother. She carried and used fans, ivory or wooden, French, Japanese, bought in every country she passed through. People began giving them to her as gifts. Sometimes she used those fans as a geisha does, but at other times they were used like a teacher's ruler, punctuating her words and explosions of anger or enthusiasm. Eventually she switched to a small hand-held, battery-operated fan.

She suffered greatly from the heat even before she began to acquire the weight, and her excessively slender feet, which seemed too slight to support the bulkiness of her body, would swell terribly. Her awareness of her own ills made her sympathetic to any slight ache or pain of mine. I remember coming back from a long night on location and having her lovingly hold my feet on her lap and massage them until I began to relax. She still loved to laugh; that full, deep laugh that came from the center of her would boom out shockingly loud in a theater or room. And at seventeen, I gave up begging her to laugh more quietly, to not embarrass me.

My father seemed outwardly much the same, but I sensed that my parents' relationship with each other was now firmly cemented by their mutual reverence for the theater rather than by any physical or conventional bond. And, of course, foremost of all my mother's passions remained that unrelenting one for my father, although now they were fighting more often. My father would slam out of the house and she would retire to her room, weep, and threaten suicide. I would stand bewildered in the hallway, saying to my brother, "What should I do? Mother's sitting on the ledge of the window and says she's going to jump." Johnny would look at me helplessly and run.

Despite this, they carried on a passionate love affair with their work and their talented disciples, protégés upon whom they lavished criticism, attention, devotion, and tolerance.

As more and more people came to the house, I became aware that the women who visited came to sit figuratively and literally at my father's feet. My mother and I watched as they leaned seductively toward him. The girls dreamed he would make them stars; the stars, that he would make them actresses. He seemed to be alternately teacher, surrogate father, and psychiatrist, and though he did not encourage this, he passively accepted these various roles. Many were beautiful women, and my mother lived under the threat, imagined or real, that she might lose him. In her fight to maintain her position, she became more possessive, and I, observing this, became more disturbed.

I came home one night shortly after *Anne Frank* opened and asked my father about an acting problem. Without a word, he turned and walked into another room. I said to a friend who was with me, "Why doesn't he talk to me? He talks to every stranger from the class who comes into the house, but he won't talk to me. I don't understand."

The world observed our family unit as the ideal one. I remember people saying to me, "Oh, God, I'd give anything to have a mother like yours. What energy, what love." An interviewer said to me, "Do you realize your father is a genius? He's one of the most remarkable men I've met, even if he is a little remote." My mother's energy was overwhelming me, and I couldn't accept the distance from my father.

Trying to deal with these two larger-than-life, extraordinary people, I fought desperately to relate to them as simply Mom and Pop. Irrationally, I wanted them to be ordinary and treat me as an ordinary child. I wanted them to adore whatever I did professionally and personally.

They still had the same approach to life that they had when I was younger. No impulse, from the most spiritual to the most destructive, was unacceptable as long as it could be transmuted into the creative experience. But I was confused by the fragmented lives I saw around me. So many wonderful actors functioned well on stage or screen but were cripples in their day-to-day lives.

I wondered if it was possible to be sensitive and yet not have a "compulsion" to create. I had an insatiable need to express myself. My nature was so emotional that if I did not transform it, channel it into some other outlet, I was afraid it would build up like a damned river and flood my personal life. I wondered if I could ever have a full life apart from the theater and acting, just as a person.

Julie Harris, who was appearing on Broadway as St. Joan in *The Lark*, presented me with a handkerchief that had belonged to Sarah Bernhardt. It had been given to Julie by Helen Hayes, whose daughter Mary had received it from a friend. It was supposed to bring good luck, and it was to be passed on, always to some new young actress. It served to make me even more aware of my professional responsibility.

A week later, Greta Garbo, who had already seen *Anne Frank* twice, through a mutual friend invited me to a small party at her home, between the matinee and evening performances. I declined, saying, "I can't go out between shows. I have to rest." Even my parents thought that was going a bit too far in one's dedication.

My first Broadway play, my first starring role, perhaps it was inevitable that I would have my first love affair. I had been saying in interviews, "I'm too old for boys, too young for men." Overnight, it was no longer true.

I began to date Richard Adler, lyricist of *Pajama Game* and *Damn Yankees*. I was flattered, as he was older, thirty-six, divorced, with two young sons. He was a tall, dark-haired man with an enormous enthusiasm for life. He was attentive but not frighteningly aggressive. He seemed sensitive to the age difference, but not intimidated by it. He let my parents see that he was concerned with the propriety of the situation and with my welfare. He couldn't have been more solicitous or proper. After the show, we might meet at my parents' home. He would cook me eggs, my father would make tea in a glass. Either my father or mother waited up for me every night after the show to make sure I was all right, to ask how the performance had gone. It took me two or three hours to unwind after a performance, and Richard and I would sit and talk, often until the first morning light began to streak across the sky. He would then tuck me into bed, we would embrace, and he would say good night.

He invited me to his rehearsals, to parties, to dinner at 21 or Sardi's. It was a long way from Fire Island and Schrafft's to El Morocco, and Richard was the perfect guide.

My mother displayed a foresight and courage rare for those days—this was 1955. Several months later, for my eighteenth birthday, she gave me, among other gifts, a visit to our family physician, to acquire a diaphragm. At the time, I didn't appreciate her gesture. I almost resented it. I didn't want her to be such an integral part of my love life. It was too confusing having her acknowledge my right to grow up in some ways while still treating me as a child in others.

Friends told me, "You'll never forget the moment you lost your virginity." They lied. I have forgotten. I have only an image, real or fantasized, of being carried across a threshold into a room, like Vivien Leigh in *Gone with the Wind*. I was pleased to have taken this step toward womanhood, and I experienced no guilt because I felt that Richard's maturity relieved me from accepting any responsibility.

Another man entered my life at almost the same time as Richard, as a friend and protector. In my mail I received some obscene letters, postcards. Strange people waited in the alley outside the theater to accost me. One night as I entered the elevator of our apartment building, someone jumped out of the dark corridor toward me. I was saved by the elevator door, which was already gliding shut. I arrived at my front door distraught and frightened.

"Oh, it was probably Zero [Mostel] or someone in the building playing a joke on you," my mother said.

We both knew that was absurd. I could hardly imagine Zero waiting up until two in the morning to leap out at me in the dark, but she didn't want to frighten me, so we both pretended.

The next day Martin Fried, a twenty-five-year-old acting student of my father's, who as a sideline owned and operated his own taxicab, was asked if he could possibly arrange to pick me up every night after the theater and see me to my door. He refused pay but accepted the assignment. Marty was an ex-boxer with a dark-haired, swarthy handsomeness. Although he had come up from the streets in an upbringing as far removed from mine as anyone I knew, I soon came to trust and confide in him. More than anyone else he seemed to understand my fear of strangers recognizing me. "I'm just a girl. People are calling me Anne Strasberg."

Marty and I worked out an act that took me a month to gather the courage to do in public. I'd sit at a party in my black dress with pearls and white gloves and he would say to me, "You know, Susan, you're a real lady." "You bet your ass I am," I'd reply.

Marty and I discussed everything, sharing opinions and experiences. Most importantly, he didn't treat me as if I were wrapped in cotton bunting. He seemed to have no preconceived ideas of how I should behave or what I should be.

I could tell him things I didn't want to reveal to anyone else; I would tell him about Pepi Schildkraut, who had become very obstreperous, more so after I had become his costar. He would pinch me onstage if I displeased him. I was not the only actor he did that to, but he restricted it to the young ones. He would pinch hard, and I would come offstage bruised and in tears. Marty suggested that next time he attacked I yell "ouch" loudly. I did, and Pepi was shocked and never did it again.

One night during the scene in which I kissed him good night, he opened his mouth. I was aghast. He would come into my dressing room without knocking.

"But I'm not dressed."

"My dear Suzileh. I saw you when you were a baby."

Pepi, I knew, had an eye for very young pretty girls, probably harmless flirtations, because he was very devoted and dependent on his blond, ethereal wife, Marie. Once, trying to pacify him, I asked, "Pepi, what would you do if I said yes?"

"Oh, my dear child, you wouldn't do that to me, would you?"

Even I was too old for this kinderspiel, but it was the onstage distractions that disturbed me most. He was a superb upstager.

Since Marty was as inexperienced as I, I went to my mother. "Ask your father. He'll tell you what to do."

"What do I do?" I asked. "He keeps hugging me just before my lines. He covers my mouth with his arm, muffling my words, kills my laugh and my lines."

"Take his hand, remove it just before your line, speak, and put it back over your mouth. He'll stop. You'll see."

And he did. Despite these shenanigans his fine performance was the backbone of the play.

Now, partially in the arrogance of my youth and partially out of a realization that I could not handle relating to him as a teacher and a parent, I decided not to study with my father.

"That way, if I'm good I'll get the credit, and if I'm bad they won't blame you," I explained.

Instead, I invented my own "method." It was called "the save-it method." Anything of consequence that occurred during the day was to be "saved," to be let out onstage. For instance, if I stubbed my toe and wanted to cry or scream, I'd say to myself, "Not now. 'Save it.' Let it out onstage." Sometimes it even worked.

There was quite a bit of controversy raging in the theater world about "The Method," the way of work that actors trained by my father were making famous. People would ask if I had been to the Studio, and "Have you ever been a lamppost or a fire hydrant?" They watched me as if they expected me to jump on a motorcycle or wear torn T-shirts and scratch a lot.

Some of the misconceptions came about because so many young actors were imitative of Marlon Brando and Jimmy Dean. Every aspiring actor who rode a motorcycle and wanted to be thought of as the next Jimmy Dean would claim to be a disciple of Lee Strasberg, and my father was unjustly accused of encouraging

80

actors to be self-indulgent or mannered. For years I can remember him yelling at his actors, "You have to speak up. Louder. I can't hear you when you mumble."

Many people found it profitable to write articles attacking the "New Realism," which was actually based on techniques from the great actors of the past. My father was constantly reiterating the point that naturalism was not realism. He felt that many actors were imitating life, speaking nicely, naturally, emoting in a way that did not seem like acting but which, on the other hand, brought nothing to the material. "If you want to see naturalism, you can stand on a street corner. When you go to the theater, you want to see realism. Art is more beautiful than life, it is the essence of life."

The way of work that he taught could be incorporated into any of the different modes of acting required for plays with styles as divergent as Clifford Odets, William Shakespeare, and Tennessee Williams. My father defined acting as "creating real thought and experience under imaginary circumstances." And for this task the actor needed all the control and knowledge of the instrument he had to use—himself. It's not easy to be *private* in *public*.

My father used to illustrate the degree of belief an actor needed with this story. A Texas oilman went to heaven. "Sorry," said Saint Peter, "there's no room."

"What do you mean?" the oilman said. "I've lived a good life just so I could come to heaven. It's not fair."

"It's not that," said Saint Peter. "Our quota for oilmen is filled. There's no room."

"Where do I go then?" inquired the oilman.

"Sorry," Saint Peter replied, "to hell."

"Listen," the oilman pleaded, "you let me into heaven for five minutes. If I can't make a place for myself, I'll go to hell."

Saint Peter was intrigued. "Okay," he agreed. "But only five minutes."

The oilman entered heaven and made a beeline toward the groups of oilmen, where he went from one to another whispering to each. There was sudden bedlam as the oilmen, en masse, began to run out the gates of heaven. Collaring the instigator, who was running as fast as the others, bringing up the rear, Saint Peter demanded, "Wait a minute! Where are they going?"

"To hell," replied the oilman hastily.

"What did you tell them?" Saint Peter inquired.

"I told them they struck oil in hell."

"Then why are you going, too?" asked a puzzled Saint Peter.

"Because," the oilman replied, *maybe it's true.*"

Outsiders or foreign actors were allowed to observe at the Studio. It was a courtesy that was offered to professionals. They would come for one time, and not understanding this was work in progress, the equivalent of seeing a pianist doing his finger exercises, would judge the work the way one would a finished project on Broadway. One day Noël Coward was brought to the Studio by Joan Copeland, a Studio actress who was appearing in one of his plays. He had asked her where she, an American actress, had learned how to work with his material.

"At the Actors Studio," she replied, and invited him to come have a look for himself.

That day, a young actor, Thomas Milian, who later became a star in the Italian cinema, was doing an improvisation from *Night of the Jaguar. Night of the Jaguar* is about a boy who has just been released from a mental institution, and in the course of his improvisation, Thomas pulled out all his emotional stops, screaming and moaning as he writhed in agony on the floor on top of broken glass. As he looked around, he spotted some candles on the stage and in his "insanity" he decided to eat them. Everyone in the studio was stunned. My father was furious. "This has nothing to do with reality. This is not what The Studio is about. If you're playing a man who's lost his fingers, you wouldn't cut off your hand to see how it feels." At this point Mr. Coward leaned over to Joan and said, "Of course not. It would simply ruin his piano playing."

Gerry Page was scheduled to do *Mourning Becomes Electra.* During the first five minutes of her scene, she seemed flustered and distracted. It was obvious something was the matter. It turned out that she was furious because the stage manager had forgotten to place the tapered candles around the coffin as she had requested.

She had no way of knowing that her candles were being digested by Thomas Milian.

I turned eighteen on May 22 and my parents gave me a party upstairs at Sardi's. I remember thinking: Now, this is when my life is truly going to begin. Marilyn gave me a lovely Chagall print and Richard Adler gave me a beautiful strand of pearls.

I was more and more confused about my relationship with Richard. I didn't know if it was love I felt or if I was in love with the idea of love as much as I was with him. He was charming and romantic and knew how to court: flowers, letters, he wrote a song for me. I cared about Richard, but it was very difficult for me to imagine myself living with a man, and I certainly was not prepared to be a stepmother to two young boys.

Many of my high-school friends were becoming engaged or marrying from a sense of "it's what one is expected to do with one's life." Most of my girlfriends still considered marriage to be the ultimate fulfilling event of a woman's life. I wanted a grand passion, too, but I was in no rush.

In June, shortly after my birthday, I was due for a vacation. Drained after playing Anne for a season, I was more than ready.

My mother was going to England for the summer to be with Marilyn Monroe during the filming of *The Prince and the Showgirl*. My father had planned to join her, and my mother insisted that I accompany my father. Richard had work to do and was unable to go. which pleased my mother, as she thought that I needed the time to myself to reexamine what I wanted out of my life.

My brother also stayed home. He said he needed money, and Richard gave him a part-time job doing errands. Johnny had two more years before he had to take his college exams. He wanted to go to Wisconsin and study premed.

When my father and I arrived in London, Mother and Delos Smith, Jr., met us at the airport. I had met Delos during *Picnic* in Kansas, where he lived. He was a genuine eccentric, loved travel and the theater, and had followed Mother and me to New York, where he promptly began to study acting with my father. Delos had come to the airport to lend moral support to my mother, who was unhappy for a variety of reasons. Marilyn, along with Milton Greene, was producing this film as well as starring in it. She had hired Laurence Olivier to direct and star. His wife, Vivien Leigh, had done the part of the showgirl in the London production of the play. She was a wonderful actress but miscast as the sexy, naive American showgirl, a part for which Marilyn was perfect. Marilyn could play this role with her eyes closed, but Olivier seemed to feel that she should play it like Miss Leigh, and he was infuriating her with his exacting and specific directions. My mother was agonizing over Marilyn's behavior, which she considered unprofessional and for which she shouldered much of the blame.

Olivier was resentful of my mother's presence on the set. He was unable, however, to establish any rapport with Marilyn as some of her other directors, like George Cukor or Josh Logan, had done. This was obvious when he asked her to "come into the room and act sexy." There was a long, heavy silence. Marilyn looked at him. "Larry, I don't have to act sexy. I am sexy."

To add to the tension, Marilyn and Arthur Miller were having problems in their marriage. Marilyn had, I heard, found his diary left open to a passage that spoke in a very denigrating, condescending way about her. She had been devastated, and her reaction lapped over into her work and, of course, placed an additional strain on Mother.

We had seen Vivien Leigh in her closing-night performance of a Noël Coward play from which Vivien was withdrawing because she was pregnant, a long and deeply desired event. Marilyn had attended with Olivier and Arthur, almost creating a riot. Unnoticed in that flurry, Olivier crossed the theater to reach the stage door, and as if he wanted to be inconspicuous, he placed his hands over his face, with the result that every eye in the house was drawn toward him.

My parents and I were invited with actress Anna Massey and a few other people to Notley Abbey, Olivier's country home outside London. Vivien Leigh was the most exquisite woman I had ever seen, despite the winter pallor of her skin and the slightly strained lines around her mouth and eyes. After luncheon she went upstairs to nap.

My mother had misplaced some jewelry upstairs, and Vivien, on hearing this, insisted upon running nervously up and down the staircase searching for it. Her husband begged her to rest, since she had had difficulty in the past carrying a child. But she was like a bird caught in a house that flutters from room to room, unable to light. The following day it was announced in the paper that she had suffered a miscarriage. My mother said, "If only I hadn't lost my jewelry."

A young Englishman, Colin Clark, invited me to visit his family's country home. Sir Kenneth, Colin's father, was curator of the British Museum, and the ancient walls of the castle were hung with Renoirs and Rembrandts.

Colin and I drove out to the White Cliffs of Dover. There was a ferocious wind blowing in off the channel, and with the daring and carelessness of youth and some champagne courage, we challenged each other to see who could lean the farthest over the cliffs. I leaned out at a perpendicular angle into the wind, which supported me, and laughing, I spread my arms like a bird's wings. Afterward, sober, I thought: God . . . what if the wind had died down? It was one of the rare devil-may-care impulsive moments I had ever allowed myself.

In London I bought a first-edition set of Andrew Lang's fairy tales. I was eighteen and still reading about princes and princesses, knowing one day I would kiss the right frog and he would metamorphose before my eyes.

We went to Paris for a weekend, the family and Delos, and in one of the stores where my father was buying books I saw an entire section of pornographic novels, which Delos dared me to buy. I picked one at random. Embarrassed, I slipped it in with the pile of books my father was getting. That evening before dinner I began to read it, and the stark contrast with my romanticized vision of life made me ill. I had gone from fairy tales to dirty books in less than two days. I didn't go to dinner that night; instead, I lay in bed restless and disturbed, trying to think of ways to dispose of the insidious pages lying on the bed in front of me. Finally, in desperation, I shoved it as far under the bed as I could reach and left it there for some unsuspecting tourist to find while searching for his shoes.

Back in London, my father and I went to the theater one night, and during the play, we both remarked on a talented young actor with a wonderful stage presence. After the performance, we walked down a deserted, dimly lit cobblestone street. We heard footsteps behind us. We moved more quickly, so did they. Then they began to run. My father and I looked at each other in panic.

"Mr. Strasberg, Mr. Strasberg." It was the young actor we had admired. "I'm Peter O'Toole. I was in the play. I wanted to meet you. I've read some of the things you've written about acting. May I buy you a drink?"

We told him how much we admired his performance but that Mother was waiting for us at the hotel.

It was arranged that Otto Frank, Anne's father, and the only survivor of the family, and I would meet. The English press got wind of this and began following me around. I didn't want reporters at this private meeting, but they proved unavoidable. In order to satisfy them we agreed to pose for some pictures. It disturbed me, but Mr. Frank handled it all graciously, with enormous dignity, even when the photographers continued to pester him.

We talked about ordinary things, what kind of cookies we liked, our respective homes, skirting the questions I longed to ask but felt I shouldn't. I told him how privileged I felt to be portraying his daughter. He gave me a souvenir of the meeting: a photo of Anne when she was fourteen, which he signed. I have it still on my desk.

Richard was an indefatigable writer; letters and poems arrived every other day. I enjoyed them, but they also made me feel guilty that I did not miss him as much as I thought I should. He, I think, was aware of the tenuousness of our bond.

I had arrived tired in England, and now I was doubly exhausted from the new people and experiences, the tension between Marilyn and Olivier, my mother and whoever, Arthur and Marilyn, the rushing about, trying not to miss anything. My mother and father agreed to let me go home early.

I was greeted at the airport by my brother, Steffi, Marty, and Richard. I knew that I would have to break off with Richard, as I was not prepared for everything that had happened to me thus far, and certainly not for any major emotional commitment.

My father, who had remained in London, now wrote me a letter which I received shortly after arriving home. "You are freer discussing these things with Mommy. I don't easily discuss these problems, but I do feel you should know how a man feels. I am concerned that you shouldn't do what I do, which is drift into a situation until it becomes inconvenient to change. It is, therefore, important that you do only what you really want to do rather than what presents itself or is done only because someone else makes it possible. Whatever you really want to do, that you *should* do."

He was accurate in his appraisal of the situation and in his perception of my reluctance to make a decision. Now, cautiously, gently, I broke off the relationship. I had an enormous feeling of relief as I realized that for that half-hour I had taken my life into my own hands.

My mother, of course, when it was finally ended, said, "Perhaps you should have stayed with him after all."

My contract was nearing its expiration, and as much as the experience of *Anne Frank* meant, I was glad to be approaching the end. I wanted, like Anne, to kick up my heels, have some fun, go to bed when other people did, get up and see the sun.

I had become so overwrought and anxiety-ridden that I was unable to sleep. I would wander around the house trying to eat myself into a stupor. Our family doctor gave me some sleeping pills, which I all too quickly became accustomed to. Even with the sedation, I would roam around the house, half-awake.

A friend of mine and Kim Novak discussed my life. "I thought," he said, "Susan would have a perfect life."

"I always knew it wouldn't be perfect for her," Kim observed. "During *Picnic*, she couldn't even enjoy a sunset."

For the last time, I spoke these final words: "I still believe, in spite of everything, that people are really good at heart." I felt both the promise of tomorrow and the insecurity of the unknown quantities it held. My life had changed; I would never be the same again.

The week after I left the play, I slipped into an evening performance, standing at the back to watch Dina Doran speaking those lines. I wanted to experience for myself what people and critics had told me about, but I was unable to be objective and I left during the first act in tears and confusion.

Anne Frank had been bought as a movie by Twentieth Century-Fox. George Stevens, the director, had come to see the original company in the play a number of times, and I heard rumors he had offered the part to Audrey Hepburn, who had turned it down, as she had the play, saying she was too old at twenty-eight to play the fourteen-year-old Anne. People kept asking me whether I was going to do the film, had I been offered it? "No," I replied, "but if it's meant to be, it's meant to be."

Shelley Winters, who was one of the first people cast in the film, as Mrs. Van Damm, and who had worked for George in *A Place in the Sun* and knew him well, said, "Susie, fly to California to see him. Tell him you want to work with him. And go alone, without your mother. I know George. He's the kind of man who would be pleased if you made that effort."

I was too involved in the "now" to worry about a film six months away. I wanted to do it, but just as I had been unable to pursue the part in the play, I found myself unable to reach out for the part in the film. Eventually the role went to a lovely young model, Millie Perkins.

A year and a half later, my friend Mary Schnee was sitting next to Mr. Stevens at a banquet. She couldn't resist asking him, "Why didn't you use my girlfriend Susan Strasberg in *Anne Frank?*"

He looked her in the eye and replied, "She never asked me." So Shelley had been right after all.

I was signed to do a film for RKO, *Stage Struck*, starring Henry Fonda, the young stage actor Christopher Plummer, Herbert

Marshall, and the deep-voiced Joan Greenwood. The film was a remake of Katharine Hepburn's *Morning Glory*, for which she had won an Oscar. I decided not to see her performance, afraid I would be completely intimidated. Instead I immersed myself in costume fittings while the producers and my parents discussed directors. Sidney Lumet was being considered. He had done television and one film, *Twelve Angry Men*. My family opted for him, and he was engaged for the film.

I flew to California, where RKO was giving a huge party to launch *Stage Struck*, the story of an aspiring young actress who comes to New York to be a star and has to choose between love and a career, as well as playwright Plummer and her producer, Fonda. On the flight I was seated next to Yul Brynner. Those were the days when it took twelve hours to get from one coast to the other and the planes were outfitted with a few bunk beds, which you had to reserve months in advance. Marlene Dietrich was on the flight in one of the bunks, and Yul and I sat up all night waiting for her to emerge from her bed, hoping that she would take off her makeup and we would see her unmasked. She was smarter than that, and when she stepped out in the morning, she was impeccably groomed and done to the teeth.

I stayed with family friends, the Schnees. Charles was an Academy Award-winning writer, and Mary, his wife, was a striking-looking ex-actress, flamboyant, tall, and dark-haired. Mary decided to mother me, a relationship I never refused. She was a very confident, charming, strong woman, or so it seemed to me, and I was shocked, years later, when she committed suicide and her husband died not long afterward.

She took me shopping for new clothes to "jazz up your image. You're not a little girl anymore. You've got to stop dressing like that." She also played matchmaker, introducing me to Arthur Loew, Jr., the scion of a famous motion-picture family. This young man had a proclivity for actresses, which all his friends said was ruining him, but we hit it off well. He was attractive and intelligent and we had many acquaintances in common. He was very much a part of young Hollywood. From my point of view, they were not especially young; at nineteen I thought anyone over twenty-five had one foot in the grave.

It was a pleasant relationship, emotionally undemanding, but he was great company and had a wonderful sense of humor. We went to parties, screenings, slipped over the border to Mexico, where I got violently sick, and visited Jean Simmons and her husband, Stewart Granger, on a cattle ranch in Arizona, where I had a devastating allergy attack. Upon our return to Hollywood, I found out Arthur was seeing his last flame, Joan Collins, on the side. He had supposedly broken up with her. I halfheartedly threw an ashtray at him, but it was not an intense enough relationship for me to work up any real indignity about.

Later, we saw each other briefly in New York, and my California mother, Mary, was quite pleased that I was acquiring the ways of the world.

I was nervous about *Stage Struck* but I was looking forward to it. The producer said he'd make me a big movie star. My mother said, "She is," and I just drifted with the current, driven by their ambitions for me. I liked the director, Sidney Lumet; he was young, theatrical, almost like an actor, which he had been as a child. Unfortunately, I was unable to communicate with him; I became overcome by shyness and fear the few times that we were alone without my mother. It was during this film that I began to recognize my total dependence on her. I wasn't even sure if I could speak for myself, let alone act. When I tried to talk to Sidney, I became so fidgety I spilled my lunch all over myself and had to leave the room. I felt I was incapable of doing anything right. At the end of the day, Sidney would leap over the door of the little fur-lined convertible driven by his wife, Gloria Vanderbilt, and shoot off into the sunset. I'd watch enviously as they drove off; I was going home with Mother.

It was a lovely company, but I was straining too hard, not able to relax enough to do what my mother or the director wanted, or even what I felt was right for the part. Actually, I disagreed with both of them. They wanted the girl to be extremely theatrical besides being intense, a quality that Katharine Hepburn had brought to the part, but which was endemic to her personality, not mine.

I resented my mother's coaching, and yet I was unable to do without it. Sometimes, mechanically, I would copy her reading, not agreeing with her but not strong enough to argue. Her demands were becoming much more exacting, whereas in the earlier things I had done, her advice had been much looser.

My mother behaved eccentrically during this film, having tantrums over trivial things such as the clothes, which she felt were not being fitted correctly, or a reading she didn't like. Although the other actors came to her for advice and she had recommended Sidney as director, she had to stay out of the way on the set. It was humiliating to her, and she vented her frustrations on me.

I had an admirer who had been hounding me since my appearance in *Anne Frank*. His communications varied from a live bird to flowers to pornographic postcards. He showed up at the studio one day, and I was forced to lock myself into my dressing room while he tried to break down the door. My Irish dresser, Kathy, a lovely lady who had been with me all through *Anne Frank*, ran for the police, saying, *"Oy vey mia."* My family felt it would be better not to press charges, and my mother sent Delos to try to bribe the police to keep it out of the papers.

My father was curious. "I wonder," he said, "what makes the man tick." Knowing my father, he was probably wondering if he could turn him into an actor.

I stood on an apple box to receive my first real screen kiss from Henry Fonda. Franz Planner, the cameraman, said to me, "This is your good side. On your other side you have a bump. You must shade it and always turn the other cheek." He had photographed Audrey Hepburn, and I listened to every word he said. I spent hours examining my face from all angles, trying to tell my good side from my bad. I remembered Hitchcock's reply to Tallulah when she said, "You're not shooting my good side." "I can't," he said, "you're sitting on it." For a number of years after that film, I did favor what I came to think of as my "all-American" side.

I was dating different men but was not enamored of anyone. I met Ali Khan at a ball. He was a beautiful dancer, and I loved to waltz. I was wearing a long black velvet dress, very low-cut, and I felt sophisticated with a merry-widow waist, which I had pulled in to nineteen inches. My hair was swept up in a chignon with a red rose in it; I had barely restrained myself from wearing it in my teeth. Elsa Maxwell, the society columnist and a friend of Ali's, introduced us. In her column the next day she said, "Little Susan Strasberg looked very grown-up last night." I was thrilled.

The next day, Ali sent roses and called. We began to go out to parties, the theater, and El Morocco to dance. He was the only man there without a tie, but after all, he was a prince, and in his black turtleneck and slacks he was more elegant than the more conventionally dressed men. He had style and was very sensitive despite his playboy reputation.

At the end of the evening we would sit in the back of his chauffeur-driven limousine in front of my apartment house and embrace and kiss passionately, but he never took the next step. I thought he had some kind of terminal disease, because after we disengaged ourselves from these passionate embraces, his legs would shake so uncontrollably they would rattle the seat. By the time I got upstairs and into bed, he would call and we would talk on the phone romantically for an hour or two. I suspected he thought I was a virgin and was respecting my condition, and I was too shy to disillusion him.

He brought his two young sons, both handsome, agile, and charming, to my nineteenth birthday party in our home. The elder was going to be the Aga Khan, and Mother peeped at us talking through the partially opened door and sighed to a friend, "Wouldn't Susan make a perfect begum?" She always wanted to cast me in the best parts.

Ali introduced me to ambassadors with exotic names, royalty, high society. I thought this must be what living was all about. The parties were gay, exhilarating, animated, with much laughter. I didn't notice that the guests' eyes were not smiling until I was much older.

As I was between jobs, I devoted myself to my current passions: collecting cashmere sweaters and eating coffee ice cream. But secretly, eagerly, I was dreaming of grander passions, impatiently waiting to be caught up by fate and hoping I would recognize it when it arrived.

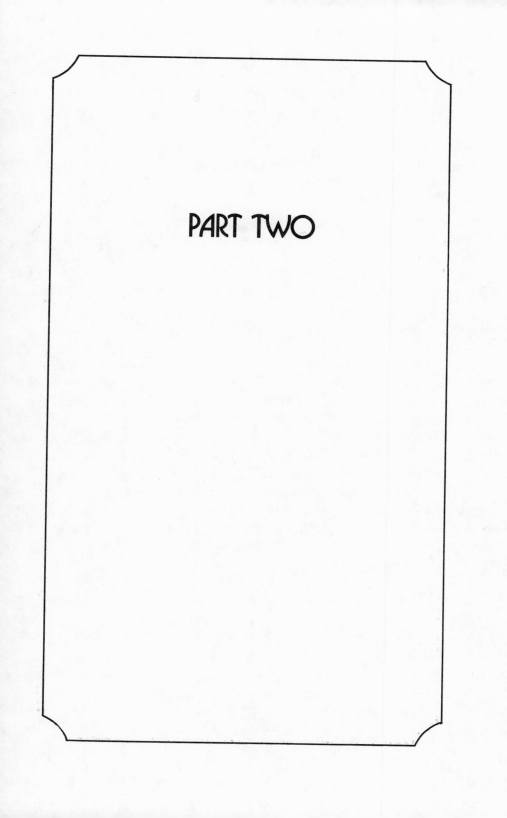

PART TWO

PART TWO

Susan's mother, Paula Miller, at the beginning of her acting career.

Opposite, top: Lee Strasberg in his Group Theater days; *lower left:* Susan with Martha Jones ("Jonesy"); *lower right:* With her paternal grandmother.

This page: As an infant.

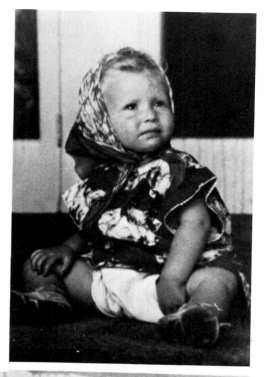

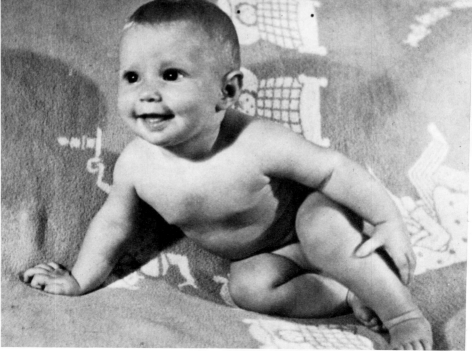

Right: With her brother, Johnny, 1942.
Below: On a chicken farm in New Jersey, 1947.

Above: With Helen Craig in *Maya*, her off-Broadway debut, 1953.

Left: Acting in *The Duchess and the Smugs*, her first TV appearance, on *Omnibus*, 1953.

On the way to a rehearsal of *Romeo and Juliet* for "Kraft Television Theater," 1954.

Above: With Lauren Bacall on the set of *Cobweb*, her first film, 1954. *Below:* Her seventeenth birthday party, on the set of *Picnic*, 1955. *Left to right*, Rosalind Russell, Susan, William Holden, Joshua Logan, Fred Kohlmar.

With William Holden, *left*, on the set of *Picnic*, 1955.

Above: As Anne Frank in a pensive mood.

Left: With Joseph Schildkraut in *The Diary of Anne Frank*, 1955.

Portrait of Susan as Anne.

With Barbara Bel Geddes and Julie Harris the night Susan's name went up in lights, *The Diary of Anne Frank*, 1955.

With Marilyn Monroe backstage on opening night of *The Diary of Anne Frank*, 1955.

Reading reviews of *Anne Frank* to Franchot Tone at Sardi's.

With Otto Frank in London, 1956.

The family at Fire Island, 1956.

With her family in their New York apartment, 1957.

Opposite: With Marilyn Monroe at The Actors Studio, 1956.

With Gertrude Berg, Eleanor Roosevelt, and Marian Anderson at a Bonds for Israel luncheon.

With Yul Brynner and Louella Parsons at a Hollywood party for *Stage Struck*, 1957.

I WAS NINETEEN years old; I had been working for five years; I was making a good deal of money and receiving a great deal of adulation, but for a girl who had everything, I felt I was long overdue to meet my prince.

I accepted an offer to do my second Broadway play, *Time Remembered*, a romantic French comedy starring Richard Burton and Helen Hayes.

I had first met Richard in England. Helen Hayes had introduced us on the set of *Anastasia* when I was visiting her and Burton was working next door. One year later, we were brought together again.

Richard had a reputation as a charmer, a ladies' man, but at that first meeting in England, I had not been impressed. He was a little too theatrical; another older man, and besides, he was married.

Our second meeting was at 10:30 in the morning in a dingy rehearsal hall in New York at the first reading of *Time Remembered*. Our stage manager, Jimmy, had warned me beforehand, "Listen, Susie, if anyone gives you any trouble, I'll be there. This Burton—I hear he's a Casanova, a heartbreaker. If he comes near you, I'm ready."

I vaguely recall that I wore a red dress, but Richard is etched in my memory. He was dressed in a blue sweater; his skin was slightly pockmarked from a childhood illness. I thought the scars were beautiful because they made him look vulnerable. His face was classically featured: straight nose, high cheekbones, full bottom lip. A lock of his fine hair fell over his forehead. His hands, which he hated, calling them peasant hands, were similar to my father's; although not physically beautiful, there was great sensitivity and feeling in them, so that when they were used, they took on the color of what was being said. He used his voice as a weapon to charm and seduce people, and the enormous energy radiating from his compact frame made people gravitate toward him.

I admired him silently, secretly, watching him covertly when he was rehearsing, but keeping my distance. He began to pay more and more attention to me. He called everyone "Luv," but I detected an extra passion in his voice when he said it to me. He would stride into rehearsals, sweep me off my feet, swing me in the air, and call me his "beautiful Hebrew princess." I was ecstatic, though trying to hide my infatuation.

People asked why I had chosen this play for my first after *Anne Frank.* "I get to wear beautiful clothes and I get a prince. What more could I want? Besides, maybe people will realize I'm grown-up. I'm old enough for a love story," I replied. In the play, the prince I fell in love with was Richard. The same thing happened offstage.

I told myself that Richard was married and that when his wife and children joined him I would be forgotten. I was afraid he was just flirting with me, and that it could never lead to anything but by the time we went on the road—Washington, Boston, New Haven—my feet were firmly planted in midair.

One night soon after we arrived in Washington, Helen, Richard, and I had an after-theater dinner at which Helen and I drank far too much champagne and even Richard, with his prodigious capacity for alcohol, was listing about a bit. We all wound up in my hotel suite. While I lay violently seasick on the bed, moaning for death to claim me quickly, they argued as to who should undress me.

Helen: "I'll do it. You go on, you're in no shape."

Richard: "Nonsense. You're obviously much worse off than I. I shall do it."

Helen: "I insist!"

She won that round. There was no way she was going to leave us alone in that room, with his reputation.

Helen Hayes was very generous to and protective of me, as she had been with other young actresses. Her own daughter had died tragically, and she tended to worry over us. She was particularly concerned by Richard's flamboyance and seductiveness.

My mother was hovering over me too, professionally and personally. I was not free of her until I saw her lights go out at night and could slip out the door to meet Richard in his hotel suite. Even then she was with me in spirit, because I knew she tacitly approved of our flirtation as long as it did not interfere with my career. Richard lived up to Mama's standards of a prince, too.

There was another, more immediate, intimate problem I faced which I could not discuss with my mother. I longed to consummate Richard's and my relationship but was unable to. I had not brought my diaphragm with me. In the fifties, no nice girl premeditated or anticipated sex. Too embarrassed to tell Richard, I pretended instead to have qualms about going further. I was concerned that he might feel rejected, but the more I held back, the more persistent he became. He deluged me with notes and letters, swearing extravagant devotion, buying me gifts—including a heart-shaped pin of diamonds and pearls that I wore everywhere—including bed. Richard became my protector, escorting me to and from the theater, making sure I was eating properly. He was a teacher, too—Shakespeare, Keats, Shelley. He showered me with words as if they were bouquets of flowers. I learned to say "I love you" in Welsh, and it became harder and harder to leave him at night. I carried an alarm clock when I went to his room, as I was afraid I would fall asleep in his arms and my mother would be confronted with my empty bed in the morning.

Professionally, the part was going well. The first weeks on the road, I was caught up with my "romance" and with learning to act with Richard and Helen, who never met in the play. Helen and I were in the first act, Richard and I in the second—even onstage my loyalties were divided.

As we got closer to New York, my deep anxieties began to surface. I had been away from the stage since *Anne Frank*. My mother began coaching me rigorously, demanding more, becoming more critical. What if the critics didn't like me? What if I disappointed people? How could I ever live up to the reviews that I had received?

I was terrified. And as my terror mounted, my voice became tight and a little too shrill. I was working with Helen Hayes and Richard Burton, each one with a most original, distinctive vocal pattern, and I was almost struck speechless. My mother was frantic. I wasn't bad, but it was obvious something had gone awry. She didn't know how to deal with it, and the more she pressed me about it, the worse the condition became.

Opening night was growing closer, as was the boat carrying Richard's wife and children to New York. I was hysterical. How could I continue to please Richard, yet still hold him at arm's length; how could I satisfy my mother by being wonderful so that she would leave me alone?

One evening when we were still out of town, I stuck my head into Helen Hayes's dressing room and called out, "Break a leg, Helen," which means good luck in theater slang. Two old ladies who were standing in the hallway overheard me. One turned to her friend and said, "And I always thought she was such a nice little girl." Another night I heard two women who had just seen the show and who obviously had seen me in *Anne Frank* discussing my performance. The more elderly said, "So what's it to you if she doesn't play a Jewish girl?" I tried to accept the fact that I couldn't please all of the people all of the time.

My father came to visit one weekend shortly before we returned to New York. He had brought an armful of books to read, among them a copy of the letters of George Bernard Shaw and actress Ellen Terry. Richard arrived from across the hall to take me to work. I was frantically finishing my dinner, and while he waited, he picked up the book, saying, "After this play is over, we'll

100

probably never see each other again. But we'll publish *our* letters to give us an annuity for our old age." I laughed halfheartedly.

We left for New York, each of us returning to the bosom of our respective families, but I was sure that our relationship was just beginning.

On opening night my father sent me a message: "For you, my darling, *Time Remembered* is the future, not the past." And my mother wrote a note saying, "Have faith."

That evening, just before curtain time, I went to the bathroom located in the hall just outside Helen's and my dressing rooms. Richard, the gentleman, had taken the upstairs dressing room, although, as second-billed star, he had the right to the one I had downstairs. All the men in the play were upstairs, and between the bar in Richard's dressing room and the general conviviality, that second floor became one of the longest-running parties on Broadway.

When I tried to open the bathroom door to leave, it held fast. I pushed harder. Sweat broke out on my face, my makeup began to run. I could hear the stage manager calling, "Five minutes to curtain." I rattled and twisted the knob, shoved the door violently. Nothing. In a calm, small voice that grew more panicky as time went on, I said, "Someone . . . I'm stuck in here. Help." I knocked louder. "Help. Someone. Anyone." No one seemed to hear, and I became frantic, tears running down my cheeks. I heard the stage manager, Jimmy, knock on my dressing-room door. I screamed out, "I'm locked in the bathroom. Get me out." He finally heard me, and after trying to calm me down through the door, ran to get help. When they unjammed the door, I fell into his arms.

It was miraculous that I got onstage at all. Steffi had flown in from California and was sitting in the fourth row. She later told me, "When they finally brought that curtain up fifteen minutes late and I saw you standing onstage shaking, white-faced, your eyes red from crying, I thought you'd never get out your first line."

I do not remember the opening performance past the fear. Onstage something took over which carried me through to the end.

101

I saw the cast smiling at me. Helen and I embraced. Richard kissed me passionately. As I floated back to my dressing room, I thanked God it was over.

There was a moment's lull, and then all hell broke loose. Friends from the audience began to flood backstage. "Wonderful!" "Beautiful." "Darling . . ." The smell of all the flowers in my dressing room was overpowering. I looked around for my parents and heard someone say, "Go in, Mr. and Mrs. Strasberg." I rushed to greet them. I hugged my father and reached out to kiss my mother.

"*Don't touch me,*" she said. "You were awful, terrible. How could you do that to me?"

I stood transfixed, ice-cold, no feelings at all. I looked at my father. He turned away and left the room.

My mother continued to berate me. "How could you? How could you do that to me? After all these years, all I've done for you, how could you be so terrible?"

I began to weep silently. My mother turned and walked out of my dressing room. The flowers in the room smelled like a funeral hall. I looked at myself in the mirror, still in the long white satin ball gown, and saw that the tears had left streak marks on my face.

Then I realized that Dennis Stock, the *Look* photographer who was doing a cover story on me, was in the corner of the room. But I couldn't control my tears.

"Susie, it doesn't matter. She was upset. She didn't mean it."

Dennis had been traveling with me for a few weeks and had seen me upset but never like this. I wanted to die. It hurt too much. I heard the rapid clicking of Dennis' camera in the background. The picture appeared in *Look* with the caption:

The accumulated emotions of weeks burst in her dressing room after the opening-night performance. She held back the tears until the last well-wisher departed, then cried alone for over an hour.

After a while, people knocked on the door. "Susan, are you ready?"

"No, you go ahead. "I'll meet you at Sardi's."

I tried to compose myself, but wave after wave of tears inundated me. Twenty minutes . . . a half-hour . . . forty-five minutes. Finally someone rapped on the door. It was my brother, with my friend Marty. They had overheard my mother's tirade.

"Susan, don't give anyone the satisfaction. The hell with them. You've got to come to Sardi's. Everyone's waiting for you."

"I can't," I wailed.

"Yes, you can," Johnny said. "You have to."

I cleaned my face and applied new makeup, combed my hair. I didn't look too bad. I put on more makeup, my new green satin dress, the diamond pin Richard had given me.

When I walked into Sardi's smiling, the first people I saw were Richard and Sybil, his lovely, prematurely gray-haired wife. My mother was not there, and I froze. I could see my father knew exactly what I was feeling.

"You're doing wonderfully," he said.

I was so grateful that he was there supporting me. Years later a friend said to me, "Susan, I think you should know what impelled your mother to turn on you. Just before they went backstage, your father turned to Paula and said accusingly, 'You let her do *that* performance?'"

His displeasure had devastated her, as hers had devastated me, a chain reaction. She must have wept alone at home that night.

The reviews finally arrived. The critics were generous. Only one or two noticed the strain in my voice.

As we settled into the run of the play, I threw myself into my affair with Richard with total abandonment and passion. When reporters asked me, "Are you in love?" I had been answering, "Yes! With life!" Richard was larger than life. He absorbed, demanded my complete attention. Up until then, my relationships had revolved around me. Now I was ready to lose myself in someone else. I did not care about the consequences. Richard didn't seem to, either. I was overwhelmed. He surpassed all my childhood fantasies when he laid his passion at my feet, publicly as well as privately. He introduced me to the legions of his friends as his "baby girl," his "angel." I was reticent at first, afraid of what people would think, but no one seemed to take it amiss. His charisma and charm set him above the ordinary man, allowed him his own rules of life, including acceptance of our affair. You could not judge someone like Richard. He was too alive to restrict. I was torn between pain and ecstasy.

His wife, Sybil, was always somewhere with the children. I had never been to their home. That whole part of his life didn't seem real to me, as he seemed so free to come and go as he pleased. The only reality was his voice swearing we would be together "forever and a day, you belong to me."

We were together six nights a week onstage and off, meeting before the show in our dressing rooms or between matinees and evening performances. After the show, we really came alive. It was 11:30 at night, but we were ready to start our day.

We dined in every restaurant, visited every nightclub. Mabel Mercer, that magical lady, was my favorite. She had her own club, where until three in the morning she would sing all the great old songs: "My love Is a Wanderer," "Miss Otis Regrets," "It's a Lazy Afternoon." I didn't drink, but to keep Richard and his friends company I'd order an Angel's Tip, crème de cacao, heavy cream, and a cherry on top. It was actually called "Tit," but we were more proper in those days.

Along with other actors from Broadway shows, we would gather at The Baque Room around midnight to listen to music. Among the regulars were Robert Preston, Peter Ustinov, Josephine Premice, and Lena Horne, who once treated us to her X-rated version of "These Foolish Things Remind Me of You." We would send out for food, everyone would drink up, slowly the excitement of the performance would dissipate, and people would wander out, some on to other drinking spots, others home to families long since asleep.

Johnny had left for college, and I had a two-room suite within our large ten-room apartment that overlooked the lake on Central Park West. Although I had relative privacy and paid half the rent, it was still my family's home, not mine, and tiptoeing in with my lover at three in the morning made me guilty and uneasy.

If I had expected my affair to be a gesture of defiant independence or a rebuff to my parents, I was totally mistaken. They knew, of course; how could they not? I was in a daze half the time, and Richard was totally verbal and extraverted about "us." He wore me like a flower in his buttonhole, especially after an evening of spirits, which was often . . . always. Instead of being angry or outraged, my mother was delighted. She had dreamed that I would have affairs with the great writers and actors of our generation, that we would inspire one another. She adored Richard. I confided to Richard, "My mother says she hoped I'd fall in love with you." In an interview she said, "Praise the child and you make love to the mother." Richard did praise me, and thus my mother lived vicariously through me.

Mother was a woman who truly believed in make-believe. She lived out her fantasies through those she loved. She couldn't just live through ordinary people, so she made us out to be giants. It was better to be extraordinary and miserable than ordinary and happy; the third possibility, happy and special, was never mentioned. We, of course, were doomed to disappoint her.

My father never really acknowledged what was happening. One night Richard and I fought after he had flirted outrageously with a starlet at a party. "I don't want to see you," I said when he called, apologizing. "I'm coming over anyway. I miss you," he said. My father was awakened by the doorbell at five in the morning. He trudged down the long hallway in his striped pajamas, half-asleep, and opened the door to find my beautiful, inebriated, married lover bellowing Shakespeare in the entranceway. The next morning Pop was silent, as if nothing had happened. Still, I began to feel there was something indecent about having my parents as co-conspirators in my love affair.

At sunrise Richard would leave to go back to his other life. After he had gone, as I cried myself to sleep, I would lecture myself: "Why couldn't I fall in love with a nice, simple young man who loves me madly and has his own apartment? This is too painful. . . . We mustn't see each other. . . . But I would die if I couldn't see him."

Just when I would resolve to end it, he would do something that would totally disarm me and I would realize I was too far gone for good intentions. Some of his relatives came from Wales, and he brought me to his dressing room to meet them. "This is my pocket princess," he introduced me, "and she speaks Welsh. Come, now, show them." I gazed into his green eyes and recited the words he had taught me. "Who do you love?" he asked. "Fi," I said. "Rwyn dy garu di." "Fiant?" he queried. "Mwy na neb arall yn y byd," I replied. (Welsh for: You. I love you. How Much? More than anybody else in the world . . .) From the way his family laughed and clapped, I was not sure that I was not saying dirty words. But the only thing I cared about was that he had wanted them to meet me. That was as good as being asked home for dinner!

I invited him to my house. He came to our family's Sunday brunches, where he sat at the kitchen table regaling us with stories about the English theater and his family back in Wales. One story, about his grandfather on a drunken spree, careening down a hill in a wheelchair into a brick wall, left us all laughing and crying at the same time.

I wondered if Sybil knew where he was and whether she knew about us. If she did, I thought she must be the most understanding wife in the world.

Richard was astonished but delighted that my father knew as much as or more than he about Shakespeare and the great English playwrights and actors. Richard's attitude toward him changed from that of a star to a student, anxious to learn and please.

"Lee, you really are the most curious, extraordinary, remarkable man," he said. "I must come to your Actors Studio."

One weekday Richard came to the house. During the run of the play he had signed to do a television show based on a Hemingway story, and as he was having problems with the part, he came to ask my father's advice. He was excited about my father's suggestions, but the day after the television show he confessed to me, "I was planning to follow Lee's advice. I just didn't have the courage, love."

When Richard and I visited his adopted father, Philip Burton,

106

he was more comfortable, less theatrical. They reminisced about Richard's life as a little boy. Rich said to me, "Little one, we actors, madmen, are capable of experiencing not just the moment but the nostalgia and anticipation of it." I didn't understand what he meant.

I wrote him a letter after that visit:

It's horrible not to be with you all the time. I wish I had known you as a child, you know. Last night for the first time in years I said my prayers and wasn't embarrassed. I don't want to hurt anyone, but I can't give you up, I love you more than life itself, I belong to you, so I prayed to God to make it all right. I'm not sure. I'm either regressing or growing up.

> All my heart, forever and a day,
> Susan

P.S. I'm going to make myself a peanut-butter-and-jelly sandwich and go to sleep and dream of you.

> Love,
> S.S.

Growing up, indeed. On peanut butter and jelly.

Richard and I decided to rent an apartment, a place that would be "ours." I asked Marty Fried, whom I trusted, to take a lease in his name for us. The first day we went there, Richard surprised me with a present: blue satin lounging pajamas with a flowing flowered skirt, in which I felt like a mistress. I hated it. I wanted an apron. We never really moved in; the apartment was a place to visit, not the home I had envisioned.

In the play, Helen Hayes says to Amanda, the character I played, when she is despondent over her prince, "The moment is now. Seize it with both hands, be greedy, for it will never come again. You are twenty years old and in love. You will never be stronger."

And seize it I did. We began to fight passionately, but we made up even more passionately. I was jealous of his wife and any woman he talked to for more than five minutes. He was possessive and furious when I went out with other people. That Christmas I was thrilled when he gave me a white mink scarf and muff, until I saw the full-length mink he had bought Sybil. After he presented me with a pair of earrings from Tiffany's, we went shopping together and I bought him a watch with "forever and a day" engraved on the back.

We were living every emotion to its fullest, playing our parts onstage and off. I believed it would never end. "I shall keep you in my pocket day and night. We will grow old together," he promised.

Stage Struck opened in New York with a midnight showing that all the Broadway actors were invited to. I sat through the movie, slumping lower and lower in my seat as I heard the strangled tone of my voice. I seemed so mannered and artificial. I saw my mother's coaching, but it seemed to lie on the surface of my performance unabsorbed, as if I had mimicked her. The close-ups were painful for me to watch. I hated myself. I was ashamed of my excesses, and I was nervous about going to the theater, afraid that Richard might be disappointed in me, but he said, "I wanted to make love to you on that screen," and I was happy.

As the play continued its run, Richard began criticizing my acting, a reading, an inflection. One night after the show he accused me of ruining his big scene, a long monologue in which he destroys the young girl whom I played. In the scene I listen to his monologue, obviously devastated, until finally I get up and say, "Frankly, you leave me cold," at which point I walk offstage. He usually got a hand at the end of his speech, but this particular night he hadn't. Often during this scene I would weep, and Rich insisted he hadn't gotten his applause because I was distracting the audience. He had heard a woman in the front row say loudly in the middle of his speech, "Look, she's crying real tears."

I ran to my father for advice. He said, "Fine, he doesn't want you to cry, don't. As a matter of fact, don't get upset at all when he talks to you. Be indifferent. Just watch him coolly. He'll find out he can't play that scene alone. Even in a monologue, the person who listens is important." The next night I tried it. Not only did Richard not get his applause, he didn't get his laughs. After the final curtain, he came up to me and muttered, "Well, just a *few* tears can't hurt."

One night I did overdo the weeping. Helen had been very sharp with me over some personal matter and had berated me in front of the crew just before I stepped onstage. Caught off-guard, I began to weep and was unable to stop for the entire first act. When Richard came onstage I was spitting out my lines between barely suppressed sobs. He thought I had gone mad. "For God's sake, what on earth is the matter with you? Get hold of yourself." One of the stagehands told him what had set me off, and Richard prepared to do battle in my defense but was luckily dissuaded.

The comic actors would make bets to see who could break Richard up. Sig Arno, a wonderful old Viennese actor would come up with outrageous business and lines. Richard would remain steadfastly serious, but I would fall apart. The things Sig would say accidentally were the ones that would catch Richard off-guard and make him laugh. He had a speech in which he says to the character I play, "Look at me! Be arrogant. Be charming. Be witty." One night this came out, "Be arrogant. Be charming. Be shitty."

Richard in turn would try to send them up. He had a wine-tasting scene which called for nothing other than a quick nod of approval to Sig, who was the anxious headwaiter. Richard was so desperate to make Sig laugh that he wound up gargling with the wine one night.

Helen would indulge in none of these antics. However, she would get terribly carried away in some of her longer speeches; she would speak very rapidly, "trippingly on the tongue"—only, like Mrs. Malaprop, she would trip over it. Then, realizing by our horrified expressions what she had done, she would inwardly begin to shake with laughter, barely managing to contain it and, bosom heaving, would make her rapid exit. I was the one left onstage, reduced to biting my tongue and pinching my hands to try to stop myself.

That whole year was one of the most intense highs and lows. I turned twenty, with the world on a string, but there were strings attached, too.

The night before my birthday, I was depressed. I wanted to wake up with Rich and be twenty, but I was going home alone. My hair was a mess and I had an appointment at an all-night beauty parlor. I took off most of my makeup, put on my old pink raincoat and pink dress, and prepared to leave the theater. I noticed that a number of the cast were all dressed up, carrying gifts off to some party or other, which made me feel more neglected.

Richard came round to my dressing room and said he'd walk me to a cab. As we passed through the alleyway, we saw that the door of the empty theater across the alley was unlocked and ajar.

"Come, my beautiful princess, let's go in," he said.

"I'm late for my hair appointment now. Well . . . just for a minute, I really do love an empty stage."

We stepped inside the darkened theater. Suddenly there was pandemonium. Henry Fonda, Tony Perkins, Julie Harris, Franchot Tone, Peter Ustinov, Laurence Olivier, Lena Horne, friends, strangers, the whole of Broadway was there onstage, newsreel camera turning, photographers snapping away, all singing "Happy Birthday." I wanted to strangle Richard. How could he not warn me? At some point amid all this hullabaloo, my mother sidled up to me and hissed, "For God's sake put on your eyebrows, you look awful."

Richard must have known I was in a state. In between smiles for the camera, I muttered, "How could you? I'll kill you." He tried to alleviate my discomfort with jokes and hugs, but everyone was watching us, and I only became more self-conscious. To this day, I loathe surprise parties.

It was a year of celebrations. The Burtons gave a grand Hawaiian luau in a hotel. They set up portable swimming pools, and Hawaiian drinks flowed literally over and under the tables. You had to enter on a slide. Naturally, someone broke a leg. Broadway was giving Hollywood a run for its money.

Laurence Olivier gave a party to top Richard and Sybil's. It was to make headlines in more ways than one. He rented a boat to sail around New York harbor. Richard and I planned to have our pictures taken with the other guests, and then, before they lifted anchor, we would separately slip off and meet. It worked. The next day, front page, there I was smiling away with Douglas Fairbanks, Jr., Peter Ustinov, and Olivier in all the papers.

A few days afterward, I picked up the *Journal American*, an afternoon New York newspaper, and went into shock. There on the front page was a picture of me in a low-cut dress, hair falling over one eye, trying to look like Rita Hayworth, the headline proclaiming "OLIVIER TO DIVORCE." I was named as the *femme fatale* who had taken him away from Vivien Leigh. The story was totally untrue; someone had confused the rumors about Burton and me with the rumors about Olivier and Joan Plowright.

Richard was insulted. He wanted everyone to know I loved *him*; I was miserable. What if Vivien Leigh believed it? What would people think? I called Cholly Knickerbocker, who had written the story.

"I swear on the Bible it's not true."

"Yes," he said, "I know. I made a mistake. What do you care? It's Laurence Olivier, not Al Capone. You should be flattered. It's the front page."

I asked Joe Hyams, a newspaper friend, "What can I do?"

"Nothing," he replied. "Just remember, today's newspaper is tomorrow's fish wrapping."

My father had a final word of advice. "If it's *true*, ignore it because it *is* true. If it's *not* true, ignore it because it's *not* true." It took me years to follow his advice.

As time passed I knew I was playing with fire, and was agonizing over the future. I wrote Richard long impassioned letters that I no longer had the courage to send. At the beginning of our relationship, we exchanged letters, love notes, poems, which I'd deliver personally. I'd write on the outside of the envelope: BY HAND. Richard would reply; his envelopes would read: BY FOOT AND MOUTH. But the unsent letters and unspoken thoughts were no longer lighthearted notes or passionate love letters. I started

111

taking a sleeping pill to numb myself after he'd gone or on nights when he didn't arrive or call as promised, which was more and more often. Groggy with the pills, I'd roam around my apartment, still unable to sleep. I tried to get drunk, which only made me ill. Alcohol worked for Richard, why didn't it for me?

Waiting for the phone to ring, I would have crying jags which left me drained and my face swollen. I was frightened by the jealousy and anger I was feeling. In the worst moments I contemplated suicide, to punish him. The contrast of the intense pain and pleasure was too much.

Richard decided to go on the wagon, or perhaps he was ordered to. In any case, I was terrified. What if he didn't love me when he was sober? It turned out that it was *himself* he didn't appreciate.

We sat on the little English swan bed in my sitting room. He was unusually subdued. He began to talk about his childhood in Wales, his dreams, his family. He was still charming and articulate, just less flamboyant. "Christ," he said, "what if I bore the piss out of everyone? Without the alcohol, when I'm stone-cold sober, I feel I belong in a university town somewhere, teaching literature or drama to grubby little boys." He felt that the artistic world brought out the worst in him.

Rich sent me the following letter written on scraps of envelopes and paper, about his vow to stop drinking.

> . . . I will stop. Shall I tell you why? Because if I don't, I shall die, and if I die, I shall not see you again, because, my sweet one, your loyalties could hardly be expected to follow me into the house of dust, the worms' pasture, the grave. So expect to be loved even more recklessly than before, even more singularly, even more intensely.
> I will be a little shaky at first and I will have difficulty with the champagne glass. . . . [He had a piece of business in the play where he picks up and examines a glass of champagne; without a pint of courage, his hands trembled as if he had palsy.] But never mind, for "Lambkins we will live."

And I will try to reestablish a nodding acquaintance with a feller called sleep. Oh, sleep, it is a gentle thing, like my Susan, it knits the raveled sleeve of care, like my beloved Susan. You may have gathered by now that I love a girl called Susan. You are not to laugh. All my heart's love, Rich.

His valiant intentions were short-lived. At twenty, my addictions were to chocolate and large doses of melodrama. I was unable to understand or commiserate with him.

The run of the play was almost over, we had made no plans, only promises in the dark. We were driving in a horse and buggy through Central Park one night, wrapped in a flea-infested blanket in the back of the carriage. The stars were out. Richard spoke. I remember hearing, ". . . I'm leaving . . . as soon as the play closes . . . home . . . Switzerland . . . as soon as . . ."

I felt anesthetized. I made it across town, home, through the lobby, up the elevator, past my mother and father, into my room, where I collapsed in despair and disappointment. He had promised "forever and a day," but he was leaving. It had to be a mistake. He would change his mind, he would send his family home and come to claim me.

The next weeks were a blur of unshed tears. It was an almost impossible strain trying not to break down in public or onstage. "I'll carry on," I said to Rich, hoping to sound rational and English but on the verge of screaming. The day before his departure I ached to cry out, "You can't go, please don't leave me, you promised." Instead, I smoked and wept, took a tranquilizer, and wept some more. He called to say he loved me, and after I hung up I sat and imagined how I would hear the doorbell ring in the middle of the night and open it to find him standing there, but the hours passed silently.

Early that morning I took four sleeping pills but could not close my eyes. Watching the late-late movie, starring Laurence Olivier, I saw only Richard's face. Toward dawn I fell into a dull, restless half-sleep, awaking every half-hour from unremembered nightmares. I forced myself to lie there in limbo until 12:30, when I knew he had really gone, that the ship had sailed and the phone would not ring. It was a relief not to have to pretend any longer. I barely left my bed, and when I did, the floor seemed to undulate like the ocean. The food lay untouched on my plate. Trying to swallow would release a flood of tears. I slept with an old T-shirt of Richard's clutched in my hand like a security blanket, comforted by the familiar scent of him. I smoked to try to stop my trembling. Trying to read made me nauseous. I was undone.

My father came into my room, and holding me in his arms, rocked me as he had when I was a baby.

"I can't bear it, I feel as if I'm dying. . . . Help me not to feel, it hurts."

He said, "Some people never live their lives. They never feel or have a great passion or love. You are fortunate. It's within you— this capacity—and no one can take it away from you. There will be other loves for you, while some people have none at all. Be grateful that you can feel so much."

My mother, as distraught as I, tried to reassure me. "Believe me, my darling, ten years from now you'll look back at this and laugh." I sobbed more loudly. "Susan, you've got to keep your sense of humor. If you lose that, you lose everything. You've got to keep life in perspective."

Marilyn was expecting my mother in California immediately to coach her in Billy Wilder's *Some Like It Hot*. Mother and Father flew to Los Angeles, where they had rented Fay Bainter's huge old house in Santa Monica Beach next door to Peter Lawford for the summer.

Now, except for my brother, Ethel, our cook, and Sweetie Pie, the cat, I was alone in the house with my misery. Perhaps I should have known Richard would leave me. I had been warned, "He'll never leave Sybil, ever," but I had never accepted it. I lay in my bed day after day, waiting for his boat to land so he could call or cable or write as he had promised. There was only silence.

My mother now asked Marty to drive out to California and bring me. He refused at first because I was so hysterical.

114

She said, "Well, Johnny has to come out, too, so he can drive with you. . . ." Reluctantly Marty agreed, and she bought him four new tires for the trip. And so on my summer vacation, I had a cross-country nervous breakdown.

It was miserably uncomfortable, shaky, cramped, and hot. But the physical discomfort was minor compared to what I felt inside.

A dreary succession of Howard Johnson's, baked beans and franks, nameless hamburger stands flowed by. I saw the countryside passing, but as I spent most of the time lying down in the backseat, I saw only the top half of it: half-letters on signs, tops of trees, and truncated skylines. Every now and then Marty or Johnny insisted, "You have to move," or, "Susan, you have to see the Grand Tetons." I would raise my head, acknowledge the mountains, and then relapse into my fetal position.

One morning Marty said, "You have to try to walk around the Grand Canyon," and to my surprise I said, "Okay." There was a two-way path around the canyon; going you walked on the inner rim; on the way back, you took the outer. I was still dizzy and queasy, as I had barely moved for over a week, and on the way back I started to panic. I came to an impasse with a little old lady who had a cane—she insisted on her right-of-way to the inside, I insisted I could absolutely not go on the outer rim. Marty and Johnny finally had to help me get around her, as I was petrified and unable to move.

The next day we almost lost Marty in the mountains, where he was totally absorbed in picture taking. We warned him not to go where the sign said "Danger." He backed up anyway, started a rock slide, and fell more than fifty feet. We got a rope and pulled him up, and I heard myself laugh out loud for the first time in weeks when he got back to the top. He looked as awful as I felt. Misery did love company.

We lost our brakes in Yellowstone Park. The boys wanted me to get out and wait while they coasted downhill for help. "No," I said. "I trust you. Anyway, if I'm meant to die . . . I wouldn't mind." I promptly fell asleep on the backseat, and when they woke me at the bottom of the hill, alive, I took it as a good-luck omen.

By Las Vegas I was mobile enough to lose one hundred dollars in quarters in the slot machines, and by California my appetite had come back. And miracle of miracles, there was a letter from Rich saying he'd been sick, unable to write before, and missed me terribly. I immediately wrote back, pouring out all the things I wanted to say, and I decided to live, just to see what was going to happen.

That summer Johnny became friendly with Peter Fonda; my parents saw a lot of Jennifer Jones and David O. Selznick. At one of the Selznick bashes, I found Marty sitting with the servants in the kitchen.

"What are you doing in here?" I asked.

"There's no one in there for me to talk to. What can I use as a conversation opener? 'Hi, I'm Marty Fried. I'm an actor. What do you do?'"

I could see his point. Among the guests in the living room were Cary Grant, Audrey Hepburn, James Stewart, Lauren Bacall, and the Fondas, with Jane.

Not long after that, Jane came to the house. She was not acting yet. Marty and I said, "You'd be terrific, Jane, give it a try," and shortly afterward she did go back East to study with my father. Lauren Bacall said, "Jane is the prettiest damn girl I've ever seen," and that summer, at twenty-one, she was—all ripe peach skin, mane of blond hair, and long legs.

We attended our first Hollywood premiere for the film *But Not for Me*. Carroll Baker was in it and had invited all of us. After the movie, I was standing next to Clark Gable when a little girl of five or six broke past the guards, and clutching her autograph book and pen, she stopped, bewildered, surrounded by anonymous legs. Finally in desperation she began to call out, "Movie stars, movie stars, anyone who's a movie star, please raise your hand." I looked at Clark Gable. He didn't, so I didn't.

The weeks passed. I rested, partied, and deluged Richard with love letters. I remembered director Harold Clurman once saying when asked what he thought of Southern California, "One thing

116

you can say about Los Angeles is no matter how hot it gets during the day, there's still nothing to do at night."

I almost learned to drive that summer. I felt it would give me a sense of freedom and independence, and Marty volunteered to teach me. My father, who did not drive, always seemed to be sitting in the backseat when I had a lesson. It was like his acting class: "Darling, be careful. Darling, you're too nervous. Relax, darling." When my father said "darling," it was not an affectionate term, it had the cutting edge of a finely honed razor. When he wanted to be affectionate, he'd say "Snookie."

I did quite well in spite of the backseat coaching, until one day my mother came along. Although she said nothing detrimental, her presence made me so nervous that I barely avoided about ten accidents. After the ride, I announced I had decided to quit.

"It's just as well," Mother said, "because you'll never have to drive, you'll always have a car and chauffeur."

We didn't see much of Johnny that summer. He and Peter Fonda had decided to drive back East together. They made the trip in three days, and Johnny bragged about it for months.

One evening, we watched the grunion run. Marilyn Monroe and Arthur Miller were there and were enchanted by the sight of these tiny phosphorescent fish that come seasonally to spawn on the shore. Marilyn was the happiest I had ever seen her.

There had been a long silence from Richard. He had not answered my letters. Marty and I lay on my bed and mapped out the strategy of a long letter, which I sent off to Richard's private post office in Geneva. "If I don't hear from you I'll call you at home. I'm worried about you" resulted in an immediate telegram with protestations of love and "letter to follow," but no explanation of the time lapse. I was sure there was a good reason that I just didn't know.

My agent called, I had an offer for a job that would take me to Europe. I was sure it was fate bringing us together. I would see Richard again.

Franchot Tone and I were to do Saroyan's *The Time of Your*

Life at the Brussels World's Fair. I was to play the sad young prostitute, Kitty; afterward we would film it for English television. I wrote Rich: "I will actually see you in two months."

It seemed too good to be true, too easy. And it was. Jean Dalrymple of the City Center, who was producing the play, was unable to get enough money, and the trip, they said, was off. But I was hell-bent on going to Europe, so Franchot and I raised the extra money ourselves. Everyone complimented us on our patriotism. But it was the love of Richard, not America, that motivated me.

Rehearsals began. I had difficulty understanding my part until my father said, "Kitty's the kind of girl who if someone steps on her toes, *she* says excuse me."

Rich's letters echoed my thoughts. "Only six silly weeks." "Now it's only four ridiculous weeks until we meet again." Four weeks, as well to say forever. I wanted it to be now.

The "now" finally came. Richard and I talked on the telephone as soon as I reached Brussels. At the end of the week I would fly to London for a day and a half and he would meet me at the airport.

Our producer had rented a large villa in Brussels, where ten of us stayed and I nurtured my secret, counting the hours.

When I got off the plane in London, my knees were shaking and there was a knot of energy that kept shifting from my throat to my solar plexus.

I couldn't see him. All the faces were unfamiliar blurs. Then I saw my name on one of those hand-printed signs drivers hold up at airports. A chauffeur stepped forward.

"Miss Strasberg? Mr. Burton sent me. He's still working, so I'm to take you to the studio." Richard was in the midst of filming *Look Back in Anger* with Mary Ure and Claire Bloom.

The trembling stopped, the knot melted perceptibly. In the back of the car, I tried not to think. I concentrated on the gray buildings, the sky, anything. We pulled into the gates of Pinewood Studios.

The driver opened the gate for me. "This way, miss."

Rich appeared at the top of the stairs and I was so excited I didn't hear what he said, or notice how he looked. We embraced and moved into his dressing room. I felt shy, awkward, as if we had just met. I waited for him to sweep me into his arms. Instead, I heard him saying something about Claire Bloom coming down to his dressing room to talk about their next scene, and would I, did I mind awfully, just for a few minutes, stepping into the bathroom?

It was so unexpected that I could not comprehend what he was asking. "But I don't have to go to the bathroom . . . oh, I see, you're afraid Claire will call Sybil if she sees me here. Claire is one of your oldest friends. Why would she care?" My pulse quickened; I wondered if they were more than friends.

There was a knock at the door and I heard Claire's cool English voice. In a daze, I moved into the bathroom. Through the door I heard them speaking and I leaned down to the keyhole to try to see them. I was horrified. It seemed so sordid, like a bad B movie. What on earth was I doing, sitting there, ashamed, in this dingy bathroom? Was this what my love had brought me to?

Without a watch, I couldn't tell if one minute or one hour passed. No, I thought, I will not cry, I refuse to cry anymore. God, why doesn't she leave? I'll run the water and flush the toilet. I'll sneeze. It's not my fault if I have to sneeze. But I sat there immobile.

By the time she left, I felt gray and cold. I wrapped my new mink coat closer about my body.

"Love, I'll take you for a drink at a pub and then to your hotel," Richard said, "but I'll have to go home tonight. We'll arrange something tomorrow."

"Something"? What was "something"? I hadn't come three thousand miles for a guided tour of London. What had happened since I last spoke with him? I was afraid to ask. We went to a pub and then drove to the hotel while he made small talk. I looked at him and realized he seemed more than withdrawn. He acted frightened. I lost control and by the time we reached the Savoy Hotel, my face and eyes were distorted and swollen from my tears.

"Please, just walk me into the hotel. I can't go through that lobby alone looking like this."

"I can't, someone might see us." For one year he had publicly flaunted his passion, and now he was suddenly afraid someone would see us. It was incomprehensible; he was behaving like a stranger.

The driver took my bag, and I asked him to register for me. Richard whispered some perfunctory words. I barely heard.

Again, I began to weep as I watched him drive away, but not with pain—with rage. Dear God, I wanted to kill him. In desperation I walked aimlessly through the evening mist, drifting with the fog until I reached Waterloo Bridge. In one of my favorite films, Vivien Leigh had thrown herself off this bridge after the loss of her great love.

I leaned over and tried to see my reflection in the murky water; a sharp, cold wind moved through my hair. Slipping over the rail would have been so easy, I could see myself lying on the ancient cobblestones of London like Ophelia, like Vivien. Yes, I thought, I'd rather die than feel this . . . this abandonment. I felt the railing pressing against me. My coat had fallen open, my costly mink coat that I had bought myself; if I drowned, it would be soaked, ruined. In a flash of intuition I realized that if I could worry about a coat at a moment like this, my life wasn't over yet. . . . I could survive.

I retraced my steps to the hotel and caught the first plane to Brussels.

While I was in England, my mother had arrived in Brussels to work with Franchot and me on our parts. She realized at once that I had suffered a traumatic experience and wanted to know all the details.

"Tell me, Susan, let me help you. You've got to talk about it."

"Leave me alone. I don't need your help, I just need to be left alone." I could see the pity in her eyes, and it made my humiliation worse.

"He's not worth it, Susan."

"It's my life, Mother, you can't live it for me, or decide what's important to me. I'm not your baby, Mother. You don't know me. You're suffocating me."

She looked hurt and pained but said no more.

When we arrived back in New York, Marty and Delos met us at the airport. Paula was the first off the plane, dressed as usual in black. They took one look at her face. "Oh, God, look at Paula. Something terrible's happened to Susie," Delos exclaimed.

"Don't ask questions," Marty said.

Driving in from the airport, we talked about the weather in Europe and the play.

I saw Richard again six months later when he returned to New York. He called and I met him at the airport in a limousine. In his hotel we drank champagne and he took me to bed. I no longer saw through the eyes of love. I saw what I had refused to see before, that he was human. On his lovely, strong peasant fingers I noticed the nicotine stains; on his firm godlike body I saw the excess; in his green eyes I saw the red veins of dissipation; on his sweet breath I smelled the alcohol; and in his poetic words I heard the lies. Someone said, "The height of indifference is forgiveness." It was true. I had made him a god. Now I forgave him for being mortal. I even forgave him for London.

I was not happy at home. I was longing for something, some coherence to my life, some control over it. I felt helpless waiting for something to happen.

Johnny returned home from Wisconsin, where he had suffered a nervous breakdown after discovering he didn't want to be a doctor after all. He had been bored and loathed college. He felt trapped and had begun to drink. Johnny asked if he could go into therapy, he felt he needed help. My parents were at a loss as to what to do and agreed to pay for a psychiatrist. A few years later, I asked him what had gone on in his therapy, did he feel the doctor had helped. "Well," he mused, "he slept and I lied."

Marilyn seemed to be aware that Johnny was suffering. That year, for his eighteenth birthday she gave him her beautiful Thunderbird. Our parents said, "Marilyn you don't have to do that, it's too much."

"You don't understand," she answered. "I really want to do it."

Johnny, overwhelmed by the gift, was unable to express his gratitude.

Now that he had the car, he would spend his days driving aimlessly around the city, winding up at the reservoir, where he would run until he was exhausted. He told anyone who asked that he was taking courses at Columbia. At night, he would go to Basin Street East, listen to jazz, and get drunk. Mother and Father had given him two credit cards. After he ran up a hundred-dollar bar bill in one night, they took them away. They seemed totally confused by his behavior. After all, I had never rebelled.

Early on Christmas morning that year, the doorbell rang. When my parents opened the door, there was no one there, but on the doormat was a wrinkled brown paper bag.

"Practical jokers," my mother uttered as she picked up the bag and moved to throw it into the trash.

"Aren't you going to open it?" my father queried.

"What for?" she said as she proceeded to peer into the bag. She drew out and opened a leather jewelry case. It contained a single strand of pearls held by a diamond clasp. "Marilyn's pearls," she gasped, "that the Emperor of Japan gave her on her honeymoon with Joe DiMaggio. She knows how I love these pearls. She gave them to me." Her eyes filled.

We were invited to Tallulah Bankhead's for dinner. My father was working, so mother and I went alone. She asked me not to leave her alone with Tallulah. After dinner, Tallulah was reluctant to let us go. Mother made some excuse about Lee waiting up for her and offered me as a sacrificial lamb, saying, "Susie will stay with you." She must have known that I would be there all night, but she had spent enough nights with Tallulah.

Tallulah seemed incapable of sleep. With the dark circles under her eyes, she looked like a bruised magnolia. We were in her bedroom, it was five in the morning. She lay in her bed in her pale blue cashmere sweater covered with cigarette burns, grasping my hand with hers, clinging to it so that I could not leave. She was too proud to beg me to stay, so she seduced me into remaining by

122

telling me about all her love affairs. I was fascinated by all of them, the well-known ones and the others I had never heard of: her English triumphs, her royalty, her politicians. "Edward R. Murrow," she said, "what a man. He was the last great love of my life."

She seemed so ill and lonely. I looked at her and wondered. This woman was a star, had traveled all over the world, done everything, but she couldn't go to sleep at night and she was incapable of calling a taxi for herself to go crosstown. As much as the child in me had once known that she was everything I wanted to be as an actress, the girl in me knew that she was everything I didn't want to be as a woman.

I began to seriously question my own life. Mother, for reasons of her own which we never discussed, reentered therapy with a very well-known psychiatrist in New York. I admired her for having the bravery at the age of forty-seven to make that commitment to change. Encouraged by her example, I decided that I needed it as much as if not more than she did. I began treatment with the same doctor, and my appointment was the hour following my mother's, at six o'clock, the last of the day.

We knew other people who had used this analyst. He was highly recommended and was well-thought-of in his field, so I will not use his real name. I will call him Dr. Mann and describe him only by saying that, except for a cutting, insistent quality to his personality, he was altogether a satisfactory father figure.

I told him my dreams in detail, hoping there wouldn't be time to talk about anything else. I was paying him to help me and perversely trying to fool him. It was usually only in a burst of energy at the end of my forty-five minutes that there was any action or interaction. After one session I confessed, "I didn't want to come here today because I have an appointment later and I didn't want to get upset, because if I cried I'd have ruined my mascara."

"You," he said, "have got to get your head and your ass together."

I was shocked that he had spoken in such a crude way. Perhaps, I thought, he's deliberately trying to shock me.

"What do you think about me as a man?"

123

"I think you're very . . . nice," I responded cautiously.

"As a man sexually," he insisted.

"I don't," I said.

"You don't think about my cock?"

I was horrified at his question, but I stood there calmly and said, "No. But could you explain what you meant about getting my head and ass together?"

"You'll understand when you feel it," he said.

"You're confusing me," I complained.

"My God, you're a complicated family," he said. "All of you." He had asked Lee and Johnny to come into the office to share a few sessions. "You're hysterical, your brother's confused, your mother is sick, and your father is brilliant but he has the best-built defense mechanism of anyone I have ever met."

When I moved to the door to escape, he followed me. The door was ajar, but in spite of this he grabbed hold of me and kissed me full on the lips, a French kiss.

"What do you think about me now?" he asked, pulling back, but still holding on to me, one hand on my breast.

"I think you're a dirty old man," I said. To myself I ruminated: It must be a test. The door is open, he couldn't really be trying to do anything to me. Maybe he wants me to get mad. Or maybe he wants me to like it. If I could only figure out why he was doing this, I knew that I could give him the required response.

Afterward he established a pattern of touching me and grabbing me as I was about to leave. Some days when there were no dreams, he would tell me about the more bizarre and eccentric behavior of some of his other patients.

"You see," he said, "you're not so terrible. Now, John Doe, he's crazy. But you're not."

Other days I was aware that while sitting in back of me, he was drinking something. Once I turned and saw him pouring himself a stiff shot. I had a friend, also in therapy with him, who said, "It's too bad you can't get an earlier appointment. Everyone knows after four o'clock is schnapps time." With the level my ego was at, it seemed only just that I should get him at his low ebb of the day.

124

I knew another girl who was going to him. She claimed that he would leap on her while she was lying on the couch.

"Well, what do you do?" I asked.

"It depends," she said.

Although she was a very beautiful girl, I felt that she was far too crazy for him to be actually drawn to her, and this proved to me that what he was doing with some of his women clients was a new, unconventional form of therapy, and so I never mentioned it to anyone, not even my mother.

Johnny's differences with my mother now exploded in a verbal battle that took place in the midst of a party. We were discussing professionalism and amateurs and Johnny said, "I want to do something I enjoy. I think that's the most important thing in life."

As if he had struck her, my mother screamed, "It isn't important to do something you enjoy. The important thing in life is to do what you're best at. You don't have to enjoy it."

They raged back and forth at one another while I ran from the room, realizing that my mother was apologizing for her own life.

I was going to the Actors Studio regularly until one morning my mother casually said to me, "You look mousy without makeup. You shouldn't go to the Studio looking like that." I stopped attending.

Shortly afterward the Actors Studio did a production of Sean O'Casey's *Shadow of a Gunman* on Broadway. I was cast to play the part of an Irish girl who's destroyed in the battle for freedom. Now that I had a job, I had a good excuse to stop therapy, and I informed Dr. Mann that I would see him when the play closed. The last week of rehearsals there was a problem with the production and my father took over the direction of the play. I was not prepared for this. My mother was backstage telling me what to do; my father was out front telling me what to do. I totally lost my voice and barely recovered it in time for opening night.

One weekend after the play closed, we drove up to Connecticut to visit Marilyn and Arthur. Marty Fried was driving. It was a four-hour drive, but we resisted stopping to eat because Marilyn had said to come for lunch. We arrived hot, tired, and starving. Arthur greeted us, but Marilyn was nowhere in sight.

"She's upstairs," he said.

There was a heavy feeling in the house. We thought perhaps they were having a fight. We sat in the living room for well over an hour. Arthur neglected to offer us anything to eat or drink. Finally Marilyn descended and went into the kitchen, and Marty followed her. She was taking food out of the freezer.

"Marilyn," he said, "if I don't eat soon, I'm going to piss on the floor. It takes hours to defrost food. Haven't you got anything prepared?"

"No," she admitted.

He returned from the kitchen, and together we drove for an hour back to a huge country-fair picnic we had passed, and bought lunch for us all. If only Marilyn had told us to bring our own food in the first place!

Not long afterward, Marilyn, while en route to the country, said, "You know, if it weren't for the work [her work with Lee], I'd jump out of the car."

Her statement startled me—I had imagined she was so happy with Arthur, just as people imagined I was so happy with my life. Marilyn, Tallulah, Vivien Leigh, so many of the women I had known were so lonely and discontented. I had an impulse to run away from it all, but I had nowhere to go.

At the Actors Studio Benefit that year, Marilyn asked Johnny to dance with her. He was paralyzed with self-consciousness and said no. I chug-a-lugged champagne to work up my own courage to dance in front of my father and the newsreel cameras.

Time passed, and I didn't return to therapy. I began to talk compulsively, eat too much, spend too much, move too quickly, laugh too loudly, weep too easily. As long as I kept moving, I didn't have to think or feel.

The play was uninteresting. I was sitting with my father. My mother was ill and I had her ticket. Two strange men approached us. One knelt in the aisle near my seat.

"Miss Strasberg? Susan Strasberg?"

"Yes?"

"I'm Hank Kaufman, this is Gene Lerner, my partner. We're agents from Italy. We have a script for you. We've been trying to reach you for days."

"I live at home and my father is in the phone book, but I guess you wouldn't know that."

"May we bring you the script tomorrow?" he inquired.

"I'd be thrilled to read it," I said.

Weeping, I walked into my father's study holding the script of *Kapo*. "It's wonderful. There's not much dialogue, but it's so *European*. It's incredibly descriptive visually. When you read it, you can almost see the movie, and the images are so haunting and powerful."

The story was about a fourteen-year-old French Jewish girl, Nicole, who is taken to a concentration camp, sees her parents murdered by the Nazis, and is saved through a camp doctor's transforming her into a criminal rather than a religious prisoner. In the brutality of her battle to survive, she becomes hardened, corrupted. Eventually, she becomes a guard, a *kapo* in the camp. She is redeemed, her humanity reawakened by her love for a male prisoner who is brought to the camp, and finally sacrifices herself in a useless attempt to save her fellow prisoners. The film ended on a cry of protest.

When I was sixteen I had said to Steffi, "If I were eighteen, had the money, and was free, I'd go to Europe and put three thousand miles between here and me." I was twenty now, I had money, I was free, but I was incapable of making the break.

"I'd like to do it," I said to my father, "but mother's going to be busy with Marilyn, so I'd be alone. I don't know what to tell them. They need an answer quickly. The director is a young Italian who's only done one other film. I just can't make up my mind, I can't decide." Like a young bird, I wanted to fly but I needed someone to push me out of the nest.

My father closed his book, an unusual gesture for him. He

would talk to you and, in between sentences, go back to his book. So this was something important.

"I think you should do it, Susan. I think you should go. I think you should get away from your mother, be on your own. Get away from . . . us."

"Lee, it's so far. And they're going to be shooting it in five or six different languages. I'll speak English, the French actress will speak French, the German actress will speak German, Yugoslavs will speak Serbo-Croatian."

My father nodded. "Sometimes it can be better that way. It will make you really listen. Besides, you need to be on your own now. It's not good for you here anymore. You can always come home."

"Pop, what would happen if I fell in love with a bad actor?" I changed the subject.

"We'll just turn him into a director," he replied.

My mother's response was, as usual, ambivalent. "Of course, you'll be all right. I know you can make it on your own. I know you don't need me. On the other hand, perhaps I should tell Marilyn that I can't work for her. If you need me—Yugoslavia, so far—who's going to take care of you?"

"Mother, I'll be all right. I don't want you to change your plans." She looked stricken. "You can come and visit me."

The relief was incredible. I felt that Europe was the escape hatch I had been seeking. There, alone, I could rise or fall on my own merits, be accepted for myself. I could learn to live my life, I wouldn't have to pretend to be something I wasn't. I'd have only myself to please.

I stepped off the plane in a fine Roman downpour. Everyone talked at once in Italian. Roses were thrust into my arms, long-stemmed, red, yellow, beauties. There were at least fifty photographers, flashbulbs blazing. A dark-haired, blue-eyed man rushed up to me.

"Susanna Strasberger. I am 'appy to welcome you."

I smiled. He turned out to be the director I had heard so much about, Gillo Pontecorvo.

He stared at me. "You no 'ave blue eyes."

"No," I said apologetically. "I never had blue eyes."

"Yes," he insisted. He produced a photograph of me. It was a reprint of a picture that had been in *Look*, except they had printed my brown eyes blue.

"I'm sorry," I said.

"Is okay. You 'ave Jewish eyes."

"I beg your pardon?"

"Jewish eyes."

"There is no such thing," I said defensively. "What do you mean by that?"

"Yes," he insisted. "Jewish eyes sad, suffer." He beamed at me with his blue eyes. "My eyes only suffer little but I'm only half Jewish. Your eyes suffer all."

I wasn't about to stand in the rain and argue.

They gave me an interpreter, but since I couldn't understand what was being said, I just relaxed and flowed with what was happening in the following weeks, letting myself be led by the elbow to photographic sessions, interviews, costume fittings, makeup and wardrobe tests. They stuck one of Jean Seberg's old wigs on my head because there was a scene in the film where I would have my head shaved. "It's too big," I said.

Pontecorvo wanted to try flaring my nostrils more to see if it would make me look tougher and coarser for the part of the film where I become a guard. They inserted plastic pieces in my nostrils.

There I was with Sophia Loren's nose and Jean Seberg's hair; I couldn't breathe, and the wig kept slipping. "I can act it," I said. "Don't you think we should keep it simple?"

Gillo came over to me and said, "It will be wonderful. I make whole film *fock*. *Fock, fock*, whole film I make as *fock*." I tried not to look shocked. "You, everybody with *fock*."

I smiled uncertainly, determined to act sophisticated. Later I learned that he meant to say "fog," that the whole film would be shot through a fog filter, which would give the film an authentic grainy look, like a documentary.

I had a penthouse suite at the Hotel de la Ville at the top of the

129

Spanish Steps. I walked out onto my terrace overlooking all of Rome. I could see flower-laden roof gardens with laundry strung on lines like a Rossellini movie. I looked into ancient terra-cotta-walled Roman apartments. I felt my escape had succeeded. I opened my arms wide.

My secretary-translator, an English girl, Jean Gribble, had the best legs I had ever seen, including Betty Grable's, and we got on fine. We had to, because I couldn't understand anyone else. We left for Yugoslavia, where the film was to be shot. The producers had recreated a concentration camp, authentic in all details, just outside Belgrade. When the natives saw the camp going up, they almost rioted. It was only fifteen years since the war. Large signs had to be posted: MOVIE SET. FILMING. MOVIE SET.

We drove from the airport in Belgrade to the hotel. I was appalled. The city had none of the luxury of Rome; the destruction of the war was still evident. They were just beginning to rebuild, and many items were still in short supply. It was the first country I had visited where they did not import Coca-Cola.

I placed a call home and asked my mother to send me a CARE package from Fortnum & Mason in London—biscuits, cookies, jam, chocolates, tins of pâté—and American cigarettes, which everyone seemed to want more than food or money. They had given me the star suite, which looked like something out of a 1920s baroque movie, all frayed around the edges.

Jean Gribble was across the hall, my lifeline to the world. If I wanted to speak, I had to call her first. For two weeks I listened silently to all the Italian, then one night at dinner Jean translated something derogatory the assistant director was saying about the Method and, by implication, my father. I lost my temper, and when I had finished a long, windy rebuttal, they all sat looking at me astounded. Unknowingly, I had blown up in Italian, grammatically weak but succinct. I realized I could understand most of what the director was telling me and that I was on my way to being a compulsive talker in two languages.

I made two friends. One was a writer, Edith Bruck, a Jewish girl who had survived two concentration camps. She had a high-cheekboned Slavic face framed by long blond hair setting off her lovely blue eyes. Her body was as muscular as a man's from the years of back-breaking hard labor in the camps. This film was dedicated to her. My other friend was Annabella, one of the Italian actresses. She was a little older than I, married, had two children somewhere in Italy, and seemed very self-sufficient. Again I had found myself someone I could lean on, a mother substitute.

Through her encouragement I started to keep company with one of the cameramen. It was not a grand passion, but most of the cast and crew were pairing off, and I was lonely and wanted someone to hold me. The work was demanding and left little time for play. The Italian cinema didn't have strong unions then, and they would work fifteen, eighteen, twenty hours a day. It was in my contract that I was to work American hours, but I didn't want to walk off in the middle of a scene, and I was pleased to be totally absorbed in the film. When I worked that intensely, I felt my existence was justified, and I didn't have to deal with my own life.

A good deal of the time we were all freezing, and I had a touch of frostbite. I was dressed in only a thin flannel prison dress and wooden clogs. I tried wearing thermal underwear beneath my dress, but it made me look too heavy.

Jean and I would accompany each other to the latrine, a hole in the ground with flimsy cardboard walls around it. We would take turns holding perfumed handkerchiefs over one another's noses.

My mother's visit coincided with my death scene. As I lay on the damp, hard ground whispering my last words, my limbs began to tingle and burn the way they had years before when I had fainted from too much emotion. I felt as if I were really dying. This time it was partially from the intensity of the scene, combined with the stress of my mother's presence. Fortunately, she could stay with me for only a week, and it was with relief that I said good-bye.

As she flew back to California, I returned to Rome for the final shots on the picture. Mother had asked, "When are you coming home, my darling?" I knew I wasn't going home, I was going to try to make Europe my home, but I didn't tell her at the time, because I wasn't sure I could fight her if she objected.

131

My new friend Annabella helped me find an apartment two blocks from the hotel where I was staying. It was a walk-up on a small, narrow, cobblestone street off the Piazza di Spagna, and it was five long flights up. "What if I forget something?" I asked Annabella. "I'm not running up and down those stairs in three-inch heels."

"We fix a basket," she said. "We lower the basket, we pull it up, we have food sent, something you forget, mail, a lipstick."

I was convinced.

Across the street was a monastery, and after a week or two one of the monks shyly approached me and asked if I would turn up the volume when I played Frank Sinatra. He said they all loved his songs.

Annabella stayed with me, showing me the ropes until her husband arrived, so that although I was on my own, I was never alone. I had a king-sized bed. The rest of the apartment was sparsely furnished. In the kitchen refrigerator I kept champagne, wine, pâté, and caviar, just as my mother had. However, unlike her, I neglected to stock the staples. It seemed romantic to me, living on only luxuries.

For a time I felt as if I were finally growing up, becoming worldly. It was midsummer and I was on a social whirlwind. At midday I would rush past the Spanish Steps, past Keats's house and the closed flower stalls, late for luncheon appointments. The Italians were smarter. They kept their slow *dolce far niente* rhythm. I would get dizzy and sit on the steps with my head in my lap. Finally I began passing out. Going up and down my own five flights of steps, I could hardly breathe. I had no appetite. I regretted the apartment. I almost regretted my decision to stay. In desperation I called the producer's doctor.

He was a tall, good-looking young man with a very suave yet fatherly manner. He listened to my heart, took my pulse, and gravely said, "*Mal di fegato.*" It sounded horrendous.

"Liver trouble," he said. "Very common for foreigners. The food is different, very rich, too much red wine. You must eat in *bianco*. White. Everything white. And I will come to your apartment each day and give you an injection of calcium."

I was pleased. Eating in *bianco* and the calcium shots sounded exotic. I knew Dr. Finger, our family doctor, would never give me calcium. He even refused to give me the vitamin-B shots I had wanted. "They're starlet shots," he said. "You're an actress, not a starlet. You don't need it."

My parents were not too pleased when I described the treatment. My mother said, "If I wasn't tied up with Marilyn, I'd be there tomorrow, but we have to go to Reno. We start filming *The Misfits* soon, and Daddy's coming with me. I won't go without him. So you come here."

My dreams of independence seemed to be crumbling. I, like most pampered princesses, was having a slight royal nervous breakdown. I was barely twenty-one years old, three thousand miles from home, and I wanted my mother.

I sat on the plane to Reno clutching my vials of calcium serum. My parents met me at the airport. I tried to act as if this was just a pleasant vacation, as if I weren't running home to Mama.

The next morning I bought a cowboy hat, some embroidered cowboy boots, and went to visit the set of *The Misfits*. Mother was dressed as usual in a black flowing dress, a black pointy hat, and carried her black umbrella against the sun. Marilyn called her "Black Bart." My father she nicknamed "The Great White Father," though she never called him that to his face. Marilyn had nicknames for all her close associates. Her publicity woman she called Sybil, for "sibling rivalry." I don't know if she had one for me.

Marilyn had only one scene, so my mother was free for the rest of the afternoon and she took me to the sulfur springs, sure that the rotting-egg smell of the sulfur was going to cure me.

That evening the hotel doctor came to my room to give me my shot.

"What the hell is this I'm giving you?"

I explained what my Italian had told me.

"Honey," he said, "that doesn't do anything but give you a rush. Take some vitamin pills, get some sun, some desert air. If you still feel dizzy, call me."

I threw the remaining shots into the wastebasket and went to the set again.

Somehow it was appropriate that this film was named *The Misfits*. Montgomery Clift stood about, thin and wan, almost transparent, obviously rushing toward his own disintegration. John Huston was late that day because he had been out gambling all night and, on a wager, was in a camel race across the desert. Marilyn was cloistered in her dressing room trying to muster the courage to come out. Arthur Miller was off trying to hurry things up because he was anxious not to lose time.

"Arthur will bring the film in on time, but he'll lose a wife," someone said.

I knew that Marilyn had been sick once already on the film. Female trouble of some unspecified kind.

Only Clark Gable held a semblance of sanity. Sitting in his wide-brimmed cowboy hat under the ferocious noon sun, he said to me, "Well, it's harder for a woman in this business." He seemed to be trying to understand Marilyn, though he was a little less compassionate toward Arthur Miller, who was always surprising him with new pages of dialogue, until finally on the last day of filming, when Gable saw the new blue pages coming, he said, "No more. That's it. This is my last day, gentlemen." He had a clause in his contract that he did not have to say one word he didn't want to. This was to avoid the profanity that was becoming prevalent in film. "I don't want to say *one word* of this stuff," he stated. "The film's over." He threw his blue pages into the air.

He sensed, I think, as I did, that Marilyn was mortally injured in some way. Like a wounded white rabbit, all pink and white and trembling.

Mr. Huston arrived soon after with a few saddle sores, and Marilyn was coaxed out of her dressing room. They managed to complete one scene.

134

For dinner we went to a restaurant in Virginia City, a restored mining town. My mother had discovered a boardinghouse run by a gourmet cook. We sat in an old wine cellar as the proprietress and her huge Mexican assistant, Ramona, waited on us and her husband served wine. Marilyn joined us for dinner alone; she and Arthur were not speaking that day.

There was a forest fire raging nearby, and Reno suffered a total blackout. They tried to hook up lights to the movie equipment, but it didn't work. The food was rotting in the hotel refrigerators, you couldn't gamble by candlelight, although they tried, and there was not a flashlight or transistor radio left in town as my mother and I learned when we tried to obtain them.

I was groping my way to my room that night when I passed the wardrobe room. Sitting in the candlelight on crates and boxes surrounded by costumes, I saw Marilyn and May Reese, her secretary, with Ralph Roberts, having a drink.

A woman passing the door stopped. "Aren't you Marilyn Monroe?"

Marilyn grabbed Estelle Winwood's old ratty wig off its stand and threw it on her head, began to tap-dance, and in a high squeaky voice said, "No. No. I'm Mitzi Gaynor. I'm Mitzi Gaynor." Marilyn felt Mitzi had made fun of her during *There's No Business Like Show Business*, and she had never forgotten it.

There was enough nervous energy on this film that without the fire they could have blown all the fuses in town. By the end of the week, Marilyn was so ill she had to be taken to Los Angeles to be hospitalized. "Wrapped in a wet sheet," I was told. Ralph drove my father and me to see her. I realized everything was relative. My "illness" in Italy was mild in comparison to Marilyn's and Monty's illnesses.

With renewed determination I prepared to return to Rome. After I left, my mother was deeply concerned for me, a concern heightened by the suffering she was watching Marilyn undergo. Unable to check up on me herself, she contacted Delos, who was en route to Reno to play a small part in *The Misfits*. My mother, with her usual determination, tracked him down in Taos, New Mexico. Like the voice in *Peer Gynt*, she intoned, "Delos, go back, go back. You have to go back."

"Go back where?" he hollered.

"To New York and get a Reuben's cheesecake."

"For God's sake, why?"

"To take to Susie."

"Where am I supposed to take this cheesecake?"

"Delos, you're going to meet Susan in Rome."

"I am? Why?" Delos asked. By then he should have known better.

"Delos, you know I have to stay here to take care of Marilyn, so you'll have to go to Europe and take care of Susie. There's a lot of publicity she has to do with her picture coming out soon and you know she can't handle all that alone. Besides, those Italians won't stop pinching her. You know what delicate skin she has, she bruises so easily. You have to protect her."

When my mother informed me that Delos was on his way, I protested, "Mother, I'm not an infant anymore, I'm not Tallulah, I don't need anyone. Anyway, sending Delos to take care of me is like sending the blind to lead the blind. He's more high-strung than I am."

"Nonsense. There's a method in his madness. He knows Europe, he'll get you organized and take care of you. I can't leave Marilyn or I'd be there myself."

"All right," I acquiesced, "but I'll be the only person in Rome with a fifty-year-old bearded *dueña* who wears strange T-shirts and has a collection of dirty words in every language."

Delos arrived ten days later dutifully carrying my Reuben's cheesecake. Annabella and her husband, Leonardo, had stayed in the apartment during my trip, which meant we were quite cramped. Now, with Delos there, she moved in with me and Delos, and her husband slept on two couches in the living room.

Delos was the eternal tourist. In the long mornings during which I slept off the effects of the night before, too much wine, too much dancing in high heels, too much romanticizing with my new

136

beau, a dashing Italian prince, Delos would take off, guidebook in hand, touring every nook and cranny of this sacred city.

Three weeks later we set off like the Four Musketeers—Annabella, Leonardo, Delos, and I—for Florence and the official opening of *Kapo*. Annabella's husband was a good-looking, volatile Italian who was prone to rich laughter and abundant tears. They argued a great deal. I took her side, Delos his. The four of us in Leonardo's little Fiat 500 screamed at one another like the quartet in *Rigoletto*.

Kapo was now going to be shown at the Venice Film Festival. Delos, Annabella, and I boarded the train for Venice while Leonardo went back to work. At four in the morning, through the thin compartment walls, we heard Delos speaking in French and a low rumble of answering French. We wondered if perhaps he had gone mad and was speaking to himself, alternating voices.

The next morning I asked, "Who were you talking to all night? Yourself?"

"Alain Delon has the room next to me." He grinned. "He couldn't sleep, so we talked all night."

"Why didn't you come and get us?" we shrieked.

Delon was the up-and-coming *homme fatal* at the time. He had just completed *Rocco and His Brothers* for Visconti and was on his way to superstardom. We had heard wild stories about his life. He was so beautiful. "God," I said to Annabella, "do you think someone like that would ever ask me out?" We giggled like two adolescents.

In my three-inch heels I wobbled over the cobblestones of Venice. Covered with pigeons, I knelt for photographers in Piazza San Marco in front of the church. *Kapo* played to a wildly enthusiastic audience who gave the picture a standing ovation. They called me "La Strasberg."

"What does it mean?" I asked.

"Ah," Gillo said, "it's a sign of highest respect. They say La Magnani, La Loren."

This acceptance meant more to me than any I had achieved in America. I had done this film on my own. I felt I was assuming responsibility for my own life, but I didn't realize that by staying in Europe I was avoiding reality.

I was prevented from any real introspection by an offer to do a film in England. The script was a well-written thriller called *Scream of Fear*, with several location shots in the south of France. I signed the contract, and Delos and I took a plane over the Alps to London for costume fittings and makeup tests. My costars were Ann Todd, Christopher Lee of horror-film fame, and Ronald Lewis as the heavy.

Delos returned to New York on business, and my mother informed me that she would be flying over for two weeks early in the shooting to keep me company and to help with the part. I had told Annabella to use my apartment in Rome until the lease ran out, that I would find another when I returned.

In the Dorchester Hotel, feeling edgy and a little lonely, I sat in my room having my meals alone. Apprehensively I waited for my mother. The only real sense of myself I had up to now came from my acting work. She had to acknowledge my need for independence at this moment. In a burst of defiance I decided to do something radical to proclaim my emancipation.

Sidney Guilleroff, the famous Metro-Goldwyn-Mayer hairdresser, whom I had known in Hollywood (he always styled Marilyn's hair), was in London to visit Ava Gardner.

I called him. "Sidney, would you cut my hair? I want a totally new look, older, sophisticated. I trust you to do whatever you want to do."

"I'll transform you," he said. "You've got to get rid of that hair. It's pulling you to the ground."

"Nothing too drastic," I said. "Not too short."

The sudden image of my mother was making me a little less courageous (she had refused to cut her strawberry-blond hair for twenty-five years). "Don't ever, ever cut that beautiful hair. You look like a madonna," she had warned for years.

"You'll love it," he said. "It's going to make you look taller, you'll have that long neck on camera, you'll look sophisticated, European. Relax. You're going to adore it."

"But will my mother?"

"If I do it, she'll love it."

"All right." I closed my eyes. "I won't look." I felt better. He had taken the responsibility. I sat there with my eyes closed, hearing the sharp snipping of his scissors, feeling like Samson being shorn.

"You can look now," he said.

I opened my eyes. "My neck does look long, almost like Audrey Hepburn's. It's beautiful, Sidney. Thank you." My hair, six inches shorter, curved gently to just below my chin.

But when I got back to my hotel, I panicked. What had I done? What would my mother say? When she arrived, although not delighted, she accepted my new coiffure but launched into a lecture on another subject.

"My God, you let Sidney see you with no makeup on? Even Marilyn would never do that. You know you look plain without makeup, you should have gotten dressed up for him. You have to learn to act like a star."

Again, I could not win.

With the advent of Mama, all my tentative self-assurance vanished. Despite this, when she returned home, as much as she had intimidated and restricted me, I missed her energy, which, although it nourished me, did so at the expense of my own will.

Back in Rome after the film, fortuitously I met Josephine Premice, the actress and singer I had known during *Time Remembered*. She was now living in Italy with her husband, Timothy Fales, Jr., and their small son, Enrico. Josephine was a tall, thin, wonderfully striking-looking woman with huge eyes, velvety chocolate skin, an agile dancer's body, a deep, throaty voice, and a small, beautifully shaped head she insisted on covering with numerous wigs. She had style, charm, and taste, and the vitality with which she embraced life was not unlike my mother's.

We had been casual acquaintances in America, but here we instantly became fast friends. And again, although I was unaware of the pattern, I had found more than just a friend, I had found the surrogate mother I seemed to need. I was still terrified of making my own decisions and was drawn to her by the decisiveness and strength of her character as well as her charm.

There was a vacant apartment upstairs from Jo and her husband in the palazzo they lived in—a palace at least five hundred years old. I was delighted. I took the apartment and they adopted me into their family. From the marble entranceway to the Renaissance angels in the bedroom, I loved it.

Up to now, my time in Europe had no continuity, I had lived from movie to movie. Suddenly I had privacy and freedom, but I didn't know what to do with it. I imitated Josephine—except she had a child and a husband: I shopped and wined and dined and vacationed. But, on a Sunday, if I awoke and no one had called to invite me to the beach or a club, I would lie in bed envisioning the empty hours ahead in panic. I had no idea how to spend a day alone with myself.

I decided to take the next six months and learn to enjoy myself. I had seen too many people exist only through and for their work and achievements; like my brother, I believed I could learn to have substance and depth and pleasure independent of my acting identity. There had to be something besides success. Artistic expression wasn't enough for me. Sometimes I wondered if I had made a mistake running away from my career in America, but as long as I was consumed by my work and what I felt to be my obligations to my family, I would never have time to know myself, to grow up.

A French actor said to me, "You Americans . . . the Italians are the children of Europe, but you Americans are the children of the world."

Before I really made any inroads in my struggle, *Kapo* was chosen to represent Italy at the Academy Awards in the Best Foreign Film category. The Italians sent me to represent the film in California. It was an ideal way to return to Hollywood.

George Cukor allowed invitations to a screening to be sent in his name to members of the Directors Guild. The Selznicks, Jennifer and David, also gave a party and showed the film at their hilltop home. I looked around and caught a glimpse of Alfred

140

Hitchcock's face, the light from the screen illuminating his cheek as one lone tear slid down it. It was the ultimate compliment. Unfortunately, the film didn't win.

In California, a friend asked me, "What do you do in Rome, Susan? I mean, when you're not making movies, what do you do with yourself?"

"I live my life," I replied, "at least I'm trying to."

"Yes, but what do you do? Don't you really think you are running away?"

"You don't understand," I responded. "I don't want a life where my only goal is superstardom. I need more than that. I'm trying to find it in Europe." But her comment stayed with me long after I'd returned to Rome.

I was back in Italy less than a month when Dr. Mann, to whom I had said good-bye over a year ago, reentered my life. He called. "Susan, I'm in Rome for a psychiatrists' convention and I want you to have dinner with me tonight, and if you have time you can show me the town."

"You don't know how happy I am that you're here," I said. "I can't believe it. It must be fate. I've really been trying to do some of the things you suggested, but for every two steps forward I take, I seem to slide backward one. I know you can help me."

That evening I took him to one of the small but famous trattorias near Piazza Navona. We ate an enormous meal at a leisurely pace, as I, finding a responsive and sympathetic listener, poured out my continuing conflicts with my mother and my fears that I could not resolve the relationship in Europe. He suggested that I try to find a therapist in Rome and offered to help. He was very supportive of my need to work out my problems alone, away from home.

After dinner, during the taxi ride back to my house, he began to feel violently ill. "Perhaps," he suggested, taking in great gulps of air, holding his stomach, "I'd better come up to your apartment for a little while. I've got to lie down."

I was concerned, because in addition to feeling ill, he had lost his coordination and was clutching his head in his hands. I realized that during dinner, as I had talked, he had consumed a prodigious amount of wine, and I remembered the rumors that I had heard about his drinking problem, which I had never believed.

Inside the apartment, he bolted for the bathroom. I sat in the living room and listened to his loud retching. Afterward he barely managed to get to my bed before he passed out. I was dismayed and disillusioned. He was a doctor, my doctor. He was supposed to set a good example. How could he behave like this? I wanted him out of my apartment, out of my life. After an hour of listening to him wheeze and moan and of watching him toss fitfully, I finally succeeded in awakening him and suggested that he leave. I called a taxi.

The following day he sent flowers and called me. "Susan, please understand, even we doctors are human. I can't tell you how sorry I am. I know how disturbing it must have been for you, but if you can forgive me it will mean a great deal to me. You know I have a special feeling for you. I still believe I can help you, and I hope this won't stand in your way if you ever return to New York and want to consult me."

"It's all right," I said, embarrassed that he should be apologizing to me and inwardly praying that I would never need to turn to him again.

Although the experience had been a disillusioning one, after talking to him I felt better. I began to think that perhaps if I had a man in my life it would resolve some of my problems. There was no one I knew that I would even consider, but one evening at a nightclub I met a young Italian actor who seemed unusually intelligent and yet had enough of a macho image that I felt I could lean on him.

He was from a poor country family and had been ostracized by the upper-class society of Rome until he became an overnight sensation in the movies. Now he was living like a prince, with not even a picture in his home to remind him of his rural childhood. But he still felt like an outsider, as did I, and it was something we could share.

We began to see one another, but after only a few weeks I

awakened in his apartment one night feeling suffocated and isolated. I looked around his richly decorated bedroom draped in a surfeit of velvet and satin. I looked at his sleeping face and realized that he drank too much, made love too quickly, and in typical Italian fashion deprecated any attempts at analysis or introspection. He had been telling me that if I just left life alone my problems would go away. I realized that I had been physically attracted to him and in order to justify that I had imbued him with the attributes I was looking for.

It was dawn. I slipped out of bed, dressed, and left his apartment to walk home alone in the pale morning light. I recalled Shelley Winters' comment about actors when she divorced Vittorio Gassman: "We had a lot in common, I loved him and he loved him."

Shortly thereafter, I bumped into Inger Stevens in a café. When I had last seen her, she had been studying with my father, her career had not been going well, and she had been in the throes of a disastrous romance. In 1970, when she had just become established as a star but was still tormented by personal problems, she would commit suicide. That day she looked radiant and was full of optimism about her future.

She was with Warren Beatty, who was vacationing in Rome after completing the filming of *The Roman Spring of Mrs. Stone* with Vivien Leigh. He was wearing a beautifully tailored Italian wool suit, a little heavy for the warm weather.

"That's a smashing outfit," I said.

"I'm glad you like it. They made it for me for *Roman Spring*. I play a gigolo."

"It's really nice, but can you sit down in those tight pants?" I said.

"Just about." He laughed. When he invited me to dinner I accepted.

We hit it off, and the next day he moved in with me for the remainder of his vacation. Warren's reputation as a lothario had preceded him. I found him charming and intelligent, with a tremendous need to please women as well as conquer them. Every

143

night for the next two weeks we wined and dined and danced with his many friends in Rome.

We spent one strange evening at director Luchino Visconti's opulent mansion. He was a salon Communist and sat in his living room surrounded by priceless antiques and a handful of beautiful young men, while advocating Communism for the masses. He seemed enchanted by Warren and ignored his young men to seductively focus on him.

Needless to say, I felt a little left out until Warren whispered to me, "I'm going to the bathroom. Follow me in a few minutes. I have to talk to you alone." He kissed me on the back of my neck and left the room.

After a suitable length of time I tried to slip out of the room as unobtrusively as possible. In the hallway, I heard Warren's voice.

"Psst, psst, Susan, in here," he said, motioning me toward the bathroom.

He pulled me inside and locked the door.

"What are we doing in here, Warren?"

"Let me show you."

I began to laugh. "Warren, isn't it a little close for that in here?"

"No, no," he breathed, "it's not. You'll see."

When we returned to the living room twenty minutes later, we were greeted by six pairs of hostile eyes. To my embarrassment, I realized my blouse was still unbuttoned. I wasn't quite sure how to act, but Warren beamed at one and all an enchanting, ingenuous smile.

Two days later, Warren became ill. I ran downstairs to Josephine. "What am I going to do with him?" I asked. "I don't even know how to make chicken soup. I want him out of my bed. I don't know how to take care of a sick person."

"Susan," she said in her deep, resonant voice, "you cannot send that poor boy to a hotel in his condition. Besides, he isn't going to be sick forever."

"Do you think my housekeeper knows how to make chicken soup?"

144

By the time Warren recovered, it was time for him to return to the States.

"Why don't you come with me?" he said. "I'm stopping in Paris on the way home."

"I'd love to but I can't."

"Why not?"

"I have to see a producer next week," I lied.

We decided I shouldn't accompany him to the airport.

Later that evening the doorbell rang. It was Warren. Sheepishly he said, "I forgot my passport."

We had a passionate reunion. The next morning he left again.

I received a call from the airport. "You're not going to believe this," he said. "I must have left my ticket at your house."

Again I welcomed him with open arms. That night we made love. Afterward, in that vulnerable time, he turned to me and said, "Have you ever thought about going into analysis?"

"That's a strange question to ask," I replied.

"But have you ever thought about it?"

"I was in therapy in New York, but I haven't been able to find anyone here in Rome. But I think you should tell me why you asked."

Intuitively, he had perceived that there was a part of myself I held back.

"That's true," I said, "but it has nothing to do with you. You're terrific. I just can't seem to overcome some of my inhibitions. I could do it in a part, but in real life it even embarrasses me to talk about it now."

"You know," he said, "it can't be easy to have parents like yours and the kind of success you've had. I think analysis could be very valuable for you."

In the time we had spent together, we had discussed our family backgrounds and I had told him a lot of the same thoughts I had told Dr. Mann.

The next morning he again left for the airport. This time he made it.

I sat in my huge living room on my Louis Quinze sofa and

wondered what was wrong with me. As soon as I began to get close to someone, I began to feel the same claustrophobia that Mama engendered in me. I didn't seem to be able to tolerate a commitment of any depth, and yet I was terribly lonely. The last two men that I had cared about and trusted, Richard and Dr. Mann, had left me feeling it was dangerous to care too much, caring meant being open to disappointment or even betrayal. As far back as I could remember, from my father's silences to my rejection by Richard, my experiences with men had been painful. And the only time I wasn't fearful was when I was working.

My agent called me with an offer to film Hemingway's *Adventures of a Young Man*. I was to play a young Italian nurse who is in love with the hero and dies tragically from a war injury. I seemed to get so many offers to die in films. The young man was Richard Beymer, who had appeared in *West Side Story*; Paul Newman, Eli Wallach, Jessica Tandy, and Ricardo Montalban were signed for other parts. The director was Martin Ritt, whom I had worked with when he was still acting, in my first play, *Maya*. I was pleased to be doing an American film again even if it was in Italy, and prepared to go to the locations in Verona where years before I had stood on Juliet's balcony, never dreaming that I would return as an actress who had played Juliet.

It was winter now, and snow was beginning to fall in northern Italy. It was good to be busy. Eli Wallach, Ricardo Montalban, and I started a running gin game to while away the days when we were not working.

There was one beautiful young girl among the extras. With her long dark hair, fair skin, and huge eyes, she resembled the young Loretta Young. "You should be an actress," I suggested. "You could study with my father." Her father was in the army and was stationed at the army base in Verona. She seemed interested but undecided. Eventually, I heard that she was headed to Hollywood via New York to be in films.

Our paths crossed again a few years later, when, newly blond and much more sophisticated, she came up to me at a party.

"You don't remember me, do you?" she said, holding out her

146

hand. "We met in Verona. You told me to be an actress. I've been studying the last couple of years and I'm just starting to get some good parts. I kind of think it was fate that I met all of you at that point. It changed my life." Her name was Sharon Tate.

Eli, Ricardo, and I all had a simultaneous week off. "What are we going to do here for a whole week?" we said. "Let's go somewhere." "Where" was the problem. The company was unwilling for us to travel too far afield in case they needed us. We decided on Venice.

It was a wonderful trip. Venice was empty. It belonged to us. I had seen it during the summer, swarming with tourists, tamed pigeons sitting on hands and heads for photographs. Now, with the canals covered with patches of ice, it was like an exquisite slumbering giant.

On the train back to Verona, Eli, Ricardo, and I became so engrossed in our gin game—I was winning—that we missed our stop.

"We have to get off, we're making a movie," I explained in Italian.

"Next stop," the unimpressed conductor said. "Si, *si*, I understand."

"All right, the next stop. What is that?" I asked.

"Ah, Milan."

I shrieked, "Milan?"

When we alighted in the Milan station, we leaped into a taxi. "Verona, please."

The driver said, "Excuse me, where?"

"Verona," I repeated. "We'll pay."

We arrived in time for the next day's shooting, but it cost us a two-hundred-dollar taxi ride.

It was Christmas, almost another new year. I would not be working during the holiday, but the company refused me permission to go to New York, as I'd planned, for my parents' New Year's Eve Party.

"What about letting me go to Rome?" I asked. "There's no danger of a plane crash, at least."

That sounded reasonable to them. After one day in Rome, I decided I was going home anyway. It would mean that I would have less than twelve hours in America, but it was worth it.

Over the years, the party had grown larger and larger, until it had reached epic proportions; more than five hundred people would come and go during the evening. A Pinkerton man had replaced the actors who had been our bouncers. George Peppard, fresh out of the Marines, had been the first.

I was greeted like the prodigal daughter. Peter O'Toole, who had become a big star in the intervening years since my father and I had first seen him on the London stage, had found a place to stand in the hallway and was proceeding to get thoroughly drunk. As the evening progressed, his lean frame slowly slipped farther down the wall he was using as a support, until he welcomed the new year passed out cold on the floor.

Lauren Bacall, in a sequined mermaid gown, and Jason Robards became acquainted in one of the back rooms. In a burst of some emotion, Jason burned her on the shoulder with his cigarette. Jane Fonda arrived with her dancer lover, who displayed bandages on his wrists, telling everyone he had tried to kill himself because Jane was leaving him. Geraldine Page and Rip Torn argued in the kitchen; he sounded like the army man he had been.

Happy New York—marriages were shattering, new affairs were beginning, in every room was at least one fireworks display of self-destruction.

I looked around at the people I cared about and respected—Franchot, Maureen Stapleton, Isaac Stern. At the party was the epitome of everything I had run away from and everything I longed for—the excitement, the intellectual stimulation juxtaposed against the neurotic life styles of many of my friends. There seemed to be no answer to my problems here, I saw too many reflections of my own struggle. I might as well have been in Europe.

I flew back to Verona with a champagne headache and a Reuben's cheesecake for Marty Ritt.

When the film was completed, I returned to Rome, where I

148

marked time, often cloistering myself in my house for weeks on end. Other periods I spent running to parties.

At one cocktail party I sat with an American friend, actor Mark Damon. We were having a wonderful time, laughing and giggling.

"Isn't it strange," I said to him, "I've never had dessert at a cocktail party." They had laid out a luscious chocolate cake cut into small squares, which I had been eating along with my wine.

Mark came over to me a few minutes later. "Susan, you know that wonderful chocolate cake?"

"Yes," I giggled, "I know."

"Well," he said, "it's loaded with hashish."

"I don't believe that, Mark," I said. "You're so suspicious."

"No," he said, laughing, "really, it is."

"I would know if there was anything funny in that cake. I'm an expert on desserts, you know. As a matter of fact, just to prove there's nothing in it, I'm going to go back and have some more." Higher and higher.

"Come into the bedroom." I pulled him to the door. "Look." On the ceiling was painted a pornographic mural. "We should leave, don't you think?"

"We don't have to," he said.

"Think what our mothers would say."

We left.

I was invited to Prince Vito's castle for the weekend. I was packed and ready.

"My God," Josephine exploded. "Timmy, come here. Guess where she's going? Prince Vito's. Susan, he's a lecher and a drug addict. He likes to deflower underage virgins."

"He's too late in my case," I said.

"They have orgies, Susan. They're infamous."

I phoned my regrets.

At other parties I attended, I would notice odd combinations of people drifting into bedrooms and locking the doors behind them. After one party I said to Josephine, "Can you believe people were taking snuff there?"

149

She said, "Oh, my Lord, Susan, that wasn't snuff, it must have been cocaine."

"But they seemed so ordinary."

"How can you be so naive?"

"You know, Josephine, it's funny, I keep getting calls from friends saying that just after I've left a party an orgy starts. No matter how late I stay, the orgy is still later. Do you think it's true? If it is, do you think I'm just lucky, or is maybe my leaving the signal to start the orgy?"

She said, "Well, let's hope we'll never know."

This period of apathy interspersed with bursts of activity was briefly interrupted when I was invited to the West Coast to do publicity for *Hemingway's Adventures of a Young Man*. I first saw the film at a private screening in Jerry and Connie Wald's house. My date for the evening was Cary Grant. I was unhappy with both my performance and my appearance. Cary didn't help when halfway through the film he leaned over and inquired, "Which one is you, dear? Are you the one with the nurse's cape?"

I had met Cary through Clifford Odets and dated him for a brief time. He was at a restless period of his life, as was I. He seemed to be searching for something. He talked about his regrets at never having children, and a few years later he married Dyan Cannon and had his first and only child, Jennifer.

Once again back in Rome, I discovered that self-imposed exile had brought me to a standstill. Nothing exciting was happening professionally or personally. In other words, I wasn't working and I wasn't in love. I followed the adventures of Richard Burton and Sybil and Elizabeth in the newspapers as if they were strangers.

Bored and restless, waiting to begin a film in Spain, I accepted an invitation to a weekend party in Spoleto, Italy, which was being given for Luchino Visconti, the director, whom I had met with Warren Beatty. The idea of a real castle appealed to me, and as it turned out, it was wonderful—very different from the English castle I had stayed in, which was crumbling and austere. This was lush, with oceans of candles, miles of tapestries, and every imaginable comfort.

The day of the big reception, the duchess who was giving the party decided I had to wear her emerald-and-diamond earrings to set off my green dress. I was very pale, as I had been out of the sun for months, and my hair was dyed almost black, my eyebrows heavily lined. I was attempting to look Italian, but I wound up looking like a short imitation of Elizabeth Taylor. As emeralds are my birthstone, I accepted. There were hundreds of people milling around, and I was talking to someone or other when a slight, young, well-dressed man came and planted himself in front of me and announced in thickly accented English, "You are my Alphonsine Du Plessis." "No," I said very clearly in case he didn't speak fluent English, "my name is Susan Strasberg." "No, no, yes, of course," he said. "I am Franco Zeffirelli and I'm doing a stage production of *La Dame aux Camélias* in New York. I've been searching for a young actress to play the part. Her real name was Alphonsine Du Plessis, and you are she. We must talk. I'm a great fan of yours."

I caught my breath. Camille was one of those magical parts, like Joan of Arc or Cleopatra, that any actress would give her eyeteeth to play. And it was being offered to me by a well-known director.

Zeffirelli had apprenticed with Visconti and had recently become famous for his beautiful stage production of Shakespeare's *Romeo and Juliet*. Later he told me it was the effect of the green dress and the earrings that had first caught his eye.

I was immensely flattered by his offer, even though I wasn't sure if he was serious or if this was party talk, so I tried not to get too excited. There's a superstition in the theater that until you sign the contract, the part's not really yours. As it turned out, he was not only seriously committed to the project, he was ready to go into preproduction except for lack of a Camille.

As in *Romeo and Juliet*, Franco's concept was to cast a very young heroine. I knew it was a wonderful part, one with the same challenge as Anne Frank. The only really artistic experience I had had in Europe was *Kapo*, and although my awards for that film had pleased my parents, I knew they had their hearts set on the stage for me.

Franco wanted me to come to his seaside home in Livorno to work on the play, and as my father was committed to conduct an acting seminar in Spoleto that summer, both he and my mother could accompany me to Zeffirelli's. I happily gave up the movie in Spain.

I flew back to New York to visit and to begin looking for an apartment to live in while I was doing the play. My parents were delighted with my decision, and in the pleasure at being back in the fold I even decided to become a member of the Actors Studio. I could have joined after the Studio's production of *Shadow of a Gunman*, but I was still trying to resist being labeled the daughter of the Method. Now my brother, Johnny, who was stage-managing the play, said to me, "Susan, remember the advice you gave me years ago? Since we have to put up with the disadvantages surrounding the Studio and Pop, we might as well take the advantages."

One incident occurred at this time which made me realize my relationship with my parents had not really changed. They were invited to the White House dinner for André Malraux, the French minister of culture. My mother was working with Marilyn and was unable to take time off, so I went with my father in her place. Many people who had been blacklisted during the McCarthy era were invited. It was a time for healing old wounds and, I hoped, an excellent opportunity to spend some time alone with my father.

We drove to Washington with Geraldine Page in a chauffeured limousine. It was a wonderful four hours. Gerry chatted away and my father was lively and open, both of us enjoying the easy rapport.

When we entered the White House there was a cocktail party in progress. After we passed through the receiving line, we noticed a couple poised in the doorway who seemed to be at a bit of a loss. They were being ignored by many of the guests and we realized it was Vice President and Mrs. Johnson, who were on a receiving line of their own, only no one seemed to know who they were. People were just streaming past them. It was terribly embarrassing.

After dinner Pablo Casals gave a beautiful concert in the East Room, and following that we danced until the small hours of the morning.

The next day we returned home. Geraldine had to fly back to New York for a performance, so my father and I set off alone in the chauffeured car.

That ride in the back of that limousine, alone with my father, turned out to be the longest four hours I'd ever spent. I had hoped it would be a chance to ask his advice about *Camille*, to make contact, but something unforeseen happened. I became tongue-tied and realized to my horror that if I didn't speak, my father wouldn't, and it would be a totally silent trip. I desperately wanted to amuse him as Gerry Page had, but the longer I was quiet, the more difficult it became to break the silence.

If I had only realized that in the same way I was obligated as his daughter to be exceptional, my father was always under pressure to be not just brilliant, but omnipotent. Perhaps he also longed to be accepted for himself, but he seemed to live comfortably in his stillness. I could not. It was a four-hour nightmare.

When we reached New York, I was in a cold sweat. How had the fear of my father built to such a degree? I had once heard my father say to a friend, "I would help Susan in the part if she were to ask me. But," he added, "she has to ask me the right questions." I was now so frightened of asking the wrong questions that I was unable to speak at all.

Two months later there was another Kennedy party, this time for the president's forty-sixth birthday. It was given at Madison Square Garden as a fund-raiser. Marilyn was flying in to sing "Happy Birthday," and I had been invited by a friend.

When the time came, Marilyn shimmied her way to the microphone, taking tiny steps in her skintight floor-length beaded dress, and throatily half-sang, half-whispered "Happy Birthday." Afterward at the private party, guests jammed into the hallway to watch Jimmy Durante perform; people were standing and sitting on the staircase. I was precariously clinging to the banister when I felt a hand on my ankle. I looked down, then turned to Alan and whispered, "The vice president's hand is on my ankle. Should I ask him to move it?" A few moments later, "It's on my calf now." Then the vice president, Southern gentleman that he was, patted the space between his legs on the stairway and said, "Come sit here, little girl."

When it was time to go back to Italy and meet Zeffirelli, my mother and father, Marty Fried, and I first drove to Spoleto together. During his seminar my father asked me to demonstrate an "affective memory" for the Italian actors. In this exercise the actor recreates strong or traumatic experience solely through sensory impressions. I was a little apprehensive that it might not work, so I was absolutely delighted when I became totally hysterical. The Italians were immensely impressed, and I knew I hadn't let my father down, but the memory of that experience was something else to tuck away in my "to deal with later" file.

As we prepared to join Zeffirelli, my mother was urgently called back to America to work with Marilyn, and Marty, Lee, and I went off without her.

I was so excited that at night I could only sleep restlessly, tossing and turning. Sometimes I was awakened by nightmares, heart still pounding, tears oozing out of the corners of my eyes. Many were typical actor nightmares, like being in front of a million people and forgetting your lines. Others were so dreadful I couldn't remember them at all.

During the day I was the central character of our drama. I felt my father's presence alone implied approval of me. He didn't have to say a word. It was the first time we had worked together since *Shadow of a Gunman*. Mixed with the pleasure of the close proximity to my father was guilt that I was relieved at my mother's absence.

Then it was time for my father and Marty to return to New York. Franco and I went to Rome. During the day, I packed my things. We had costume fittings, photo sessions. One night Franco and I flew to Milan to see Maria Callas sing *Medea* at La Scala.

"Franco, is it really true she's swallowed a tapeworm to lose weight?" I asked. "No," Franco said, "but she is having cellulite treatment by machine, very painful; you don't need it, yet."

At La Scala I observed the fickleness of the public firsthand. Callas was an extraordinary Medea, but a few of her higher notes were wobbly. The audience booed and jeered her unmercifully.

I passed the days at the beach, hiding under a huge straw hat and an umbrella to keep my skin properly white for the play. I began to dress only in black and white, an image I saw as very Camille-like. My friend Tanya Lopert remarked, "You know, I've never seen you this relaxed and happy." I was filled with hopeful anticipation.

One afternoon after a particularly happy day I arrived home to find a message that the United Press had been calling every half-hour. I was intrigued but decided I'd return their call later, as I was still punch-drunk from the sea and wine and sun. Before I even had a chance to lie down, the phone rang.

"Miss Strasberg, Marilyn Monroe is dead. She committed suicide. Do you have any comment? We'd like a quote. We've already got one from Laurence Olivier and Sophia Loren."

"No," I said, "no, I have no quote. No comment. Please." I hung up. I was stunned, it was incomprehensible. Marilyn of all people. I could understand some of our older friends who had destroyed themselves, but Marilyn was so young, so vital. She had been going back to work on her film, she had been so beautiful the last time I saw her two months before, right after her thirty-sixth birthday.

"You look better than I've ever seen you look," I said.

"You know," she said, "I am in better shape than I've ever been in." She pulled up her blouse. "My body looks better now than when I was a young girl."

And it did.

I had just gotten a note from my mother about the picture they were doing, directed by George Cukor, a fine director, famous for his handling of women. My mother had been friendly with George in the past, and she wrote in gratitude and amazement, "George *wants* me to be on the set." This was the opposite of all the other directors Marilyn had worked with, whose overbearing egos had been threatened by my mother's presence, fearing she would get credit they wanted. "He doesn't think Marilyn could go on without me." My mother was so pleased that Cukor had realized, however difficult Marilyn was accompanied by Paula, she would have been far worse without her.

I remembered Marilyn showing me her blue dishes and the straw kitchen chairs from Mexico. She had flown there personally to furnish her house. She was as excited as a child when she described what it was going to look like.

I recalled a darker time at my parents' apartment when she was sleeping in my brother's bed. He had been furious at being shunted to the living-room couch. She had taken too many sleeping pills one night after drinking champagne, and awakening groggy and dazed, needing help and unable to stand up, she had crawled on her hands and knees to my parents' doorway, scratching at it with her fingernails. I started to go to help her, but their bedroom door opened. I hid so that she wouldn't have to know that I had seen her in that way, helpless and vulnerable.

I saw her face just after she had been released from a New York mental institution to which she had committed herself upon the advice of her doctor. Either by accident or deliberately, she had been placed in a locked ward.

It took three days to get her released, and afterward there was an expression of amazement on her face as she talked about her experience. "I was always afraid I was crazy like my mother, but when I got in that psycho ward I realized *they* were really insane, *I* just had a lot of problems."

Now that she was dead, I felt ashamed and guilty that I had ever resented the attention she had attracted from my parents. Her need was greater than mine. I longed, but she demanded: Help me, feed me, love me, love me. And they had, protecting her as long as they could, except in the times when their closeness threatened her in some way and she would withdraw.

156

Perhaps for Marilyn the demands of the film world and the real world had finally become equally painful, so that there was nowhere to escape. But she had been so alive. An iron butterfly, some people had called her. Butterflies are very beautiful, give great pleasure, and have very short life spans.

I picked up the phone—I had to call home.

"Mother, do you think she killed herself?"

"Absolutely not," she said. I could hear her trying to control her tears. "She had everything to live for. She was going back to work. Your father and she were planning a TV special. She loved her new home. People are saying . . . there are rumors . . ." She began to weep openly.

"Perhaps," I said, "we'll never know."

It was strange, I couldn't imagine Marilyn old. Her childlike quality seemed to defy the demands of time.

A few days later, I read the eulogy my father delivered at the Village Church in Westwood:

> . . . We, gathered here today, knew only Marilyn, *a warm human being, impulsive and shy, sensitive and in fear of rejection yet ever avid for life and reaching out for fulfillment* . . . she was a member of our family. . . .

I wept as my father wept when he spoke those words in California. I felt a chill. My God, he could have been describing me!

The first news I received back in New York was that the production would be delayed. Cheryl Crawford, the producer, felt that "several months' more work on the adaptation were necessary." Franco absolutely refused to wait, and Cheryl withdrew from the production. The New York *Times* theater columnist called me for a comment. "I'm leaving everything to Zeffirelli, whom I trust implicitly," I stated. And I did trust him.

My furniture arrived from Rome, and I settled into the apartment I had found, which overlooked Central Park. My mother was pleased. "It takes a lot of security to live on the West Side."

157

I wasn't motivated by that kind of security. My apartment was far enough away from my parents but not so far that I couldn't get there in five minutes.

I allowed the play's publicist to convince me to pose for *Playboy* magazine to show the American public my new image; hopefully a smoldering European Camille.

In the interviews I did at this time, I gave the impression of being full of confidence, but I was saying what I thought I ought to say, I wasn't voicing any of my trepidations. Helen Lawrenson, however, in an interview for *Show* magazine, went directly to the heart of my problem. She wrote:

> At 24, Susan Strasberg is still seeking her identity as a human being and as an actress, a search that is complicated by the refusal of the public to dissociate her from her family background and from her own teenage triumph on Broadway in the title role of *The Diary of Anne Frank*. Her part as Anne, "the break of a lifetime," turned out to be, in certain respects, more bane than blessing, because her performance was so dazzling that it has overshadowed everything she has done since then. She is beset by paradox. Other aspiring actresses can leave home to study with Susan's father, Lee Strasberg, director of the Actors Studio, the most famous theatrical training school in the country. Susan has not only never studied with her father, but *she* left home and went to live in Rome by herself in an attempt to work out her own career apart from her family. "People expect too much of me as Lee Strasberg's daughter," she explains. "It wasn't fair to him or to me."

It was in this state of nervous apprehension, waiting for rehearsals to begin, waiting for a triumph that would put *Anne Frank* finally in perspective, that I first saw Christopher Jones. I had gone to dinner at Downey's. If you went to Downey's you didn't need to read the gossip columns. There you found out everything that was happening, and to whom.

The restaurant was filled with dedicated actors, writers, directors, the stars, and the starving, whom Jim Downey would feed, saying, "When you get famous, you can pay me."

I entered the room, looking for my friends. At the same time, I heard the unmistakable voice of Shelley Winters calling, "Susie, welcome home." I walked over to greet her at her table, where she was sitting with James Farentino and another handsome young actor, both of whom were appearing with her in *The Night of the Iguana*. We talked for a few minutes and she introduced me to Christopher. He had medium brown hair streaked with gold, deep brown eyes, high cheekbones, and a bowed sensual mouth. He was wearing a shirt unbuttoned to the waist, skintight faded jeans, and although it was freezing outside, only a lightweight leather jacket.

Years later, Shelley told me that when I walked into Downey's that night and waved at her, Christopher had said, "Introduce me, I want to meet her."

Shelley replied, "That's tough. I'm not going to introduce you, I don't like the way you treat your girlfriends. She's not for you. You don't even know who she is."

"That's Susan Strasberg," he had replied. "I'm going to marry her."

Shelley had burst out laughing. "You're crazy." She turned to Jimmy and said, "Is he okay?"

Christopher just repeated, "I'm going to marry her!"

I hadn't even caught his name.

A few weeks afterward, Franco finally arrived in New York. I greeted him at the airport, and from there we drove directly to his doctor's office in the East Fifties. "You wait in the car," Franco said. "I just get my vitamin shots." I could see that he was very nervous. He had a facial tic that was much more pronounced than the last time I had seen him. His doctor was nicknamed Dr. Feelgood by the socialites, stars, and politicians who frequented his office. He was rumored to treat people in the highest echelons of government.

Franco emerged from his office ten minutes later, twitch gone, face relaxed, massaging the spot where he had just been injected.

Years later it came out that the doctor had secretly laced these "vitamin shots" with amphetamines. That explained Franco's marvelous transformation.

There is a phenomenon that sometimes happens when two people are enraptured by a mutual project. It becomes like a love affair, except the lovers are linked through the play or film. Franco and I were like that. I became not just his star, but for the moment, his idealized woman. This confused me. Was it Susan the girl or Susan the actress he had placed upon this pedestal? I only knew it was a lot to live up to. He focused all his intense energy upon me, attention was paid to every detail of my life. Had I slept well? I mustn't eat that, it was bad for me. With my parents also caring for me, I was babied, spoiled, tended like a racehorse before the big race. I didn't realize that I was precariously perched atop that pedestal, that my place there was dependent on how well I performed. I felt that between Franco and my father and mother, I would be transformed, perfected, and I placed myself in their hands. I had really never faced or dealt with my loneliness or my need to be accepted while I was in Italy, so that now I would do anything they wanted as long as they opened their arms to me.

There were intimations of impending difficulties. The first was the condition of the script, which Cheryl Crawford had complained about. This was not a Shakespearean masterpiece like *Romeo and Juliet*. This was what one critic called "an errant piece of sentimental claptrap," and unfortunately, the rewrites that had been done were not sufficient. Secondly, the only theater available was the Wintergarden, which is the largest house in New York, usually reserved for musicals. Our delicate, intimate love story would be lost in this theater. I begged Franco, "Let's wait for a decent house." But his schedule was too tight, and besides, "They think I can't do it again after *Romeo and Juliet*. Even with that theater, I'll show them I can." He, like me, had people waiting to see if he would fulfill his promise. As I didn't want to argue with him, I shut up.

In his house by the sea in Italy, far from the exigencies of reality, we had been an ensemble, but here our perfect marriage was beginning to dissolve.

The play was easily and quickly cast. John Stride, the young English actor who had played Romeo, was Armand, the nobleman who falls in love with Camille. His father was played by a fine actor, Frank Silvera. There were many Actors Studio members in the cast. Coral Browne, a leading English actress, was engaged as Prudence, Camille's friend.

Franco had decided to stage part of the play behind a fine mesh curtain called a scrim. This would give a softened patina of antiquity to the production. It would also, in this barn of a theater, unfortunately serve as one more barrier between the actors and the audience, who already seemed to be ten miles away behind the huge, empty orchestra pit. In addition, the scrim deadened the sound so that we got almost no feedback from the audience and felt like fish in a bowl. This was just the beginning.

Obviously, major rewriting was going to be required, but we had very little time, as we had forgone going out of town because Franco's schedule did not permit the time. We had the first reading, and afterward Franco got up and proceeded to act out the entire play, choreographing our moves in synchronization with the lines, as if it were a ballet. Most of the actors were appalled. These were professionals used to making a major contribution to a play, not accustomed to line readings and set movement, especially before they had a chance to feel their own way.

Coral Browne, classically trained in England, was distraught. At the end of the first day she said, "Franco, I have a dreadful headache and I think I'm going to be terribly sick." She went home to bed and the next day returned to England, leaving word that she was too ill to appear in the play. None of us believed a word of it; we thought she'd seen the writing on the wall and decided to escape. It was not a good omen, even though she was quickly replaced with Jan Miner, an American actress.

Meanwhile, Zeffirelli finished casting the remaining parts. One young actor who auditioned had fascinated Franco with his looks

161

and animal magnetism. Although there was no part for him, Franco wrote a mime sequence into the beginning of the first act for this young man, who turned out to be the one I had met in Downey's with Shelley, Christopher Jones. At the time I only remarked that he was beautiful but a little too wild for my taste.

The producer wanted Edward Albee to rewrite the script, but he was unavailable. His protégé, Terrence McNally, was hired. As talented as he was, his very American avant-garde dialogue did not mix with the conventional treatment by English playwright Giles Cooper. In the midst of this turn-of-the-century, stylized, delicate love story, his rewrites called for John Stride to say to a prostitute, "You have a black tarantula between your legs." John refused to say the line, and the actress playing the prostitute, said, "I absolutely refuse to have that line spoken to me." But Franco was adamant. John finally read the line with such vehemence that it was finally cut.

I turned to my parents for help. When I described the changes Franco was making to my father, he said, "He's going off on the wrong track. I don't understand what he's doing." My mother tried to help, but she seemed distracted. She was still recovering from Marilyn's death, we had not worked together for over three years, and there was her own illness, about which I knew nothing.

My father made some general suggestions, but I wanted definite, concrete things to do, and he gave me acting exercises to try to stimulate my imagination. If I had been properly trained, had more time, or been less frightened, this might have worked. As it was, I had no idea what I was doing.

I felt that my father was angry at me for my panic and insecurity, and I began to feel that my parents were disappointed with me for failing to live up to their high standards.

New pages were being churned out every hour. The sets arrived, and they were beautiful, but so immense they had to be cut down to fit into the largest theater in New York. There were two giant turntables which spun around changing scenes laboriously, noisily, leaving the actors grabbing their hats and coats, leaping onto the next circle so as not to get whirled into the wrong scene. I felt like Eliza on the ice floes.

Franchot heard I was having difficulties and came to try to help me. He described his mother, who had died of tuberculosis, Camille's disease, detailing for me her flushes, her fevers, and high gaiety followed by her complete collapses, but it was too late, I was too frightened to absorb new information.

I was desperately unhappy about the costumes, which were overwhelming me. The skirts were like tutus for elephants. I suggested to Franco that they could be scaled down for my size, but he insisted on authenticity. I acquiesced without a fight.

I had relegated total responsibility to my parents and to Franco. I was twenty-four only chronologically; emotionally, I was a baby. The problems I had avoided in Europe returned, intensified by the extreme pressure. I had one outburst the day before we opened, when Franco directed me, "Laugh, be gay, you have to make it look like a party."

"When you write a party scene, I will act as if I'm at a party. There's no scene here," I snapped.

There was one other outburst that day. Christopher Jones had a huge fight with Franco and was fired or quit. There were rumors of physical violence. He was luckier than I.

Opening night arrived, the curtain went up. There behind the scrim I stood, bathed in soft pink lights as the audience applauded; then I had to move, and I did, lugging my hoops behind me.

One of my friends said later, "My God, I could hardly see you onstage. If you weren't behind someone, you were under something or between turntables."

It was like a *déjà vu*. My mother was the first person backstage, and as she had years before during *Time Remembered*, she began a diatribe. This time it was not directed so much at me as against the whole project.

"You should never have done it. It was a disaster tonight. You'd better be prepared."

I, of course, began to weep, but before I could say anything,

Kim Stanley, who had overheard my mother, stormed into the room, saying, "How dare you speak to an actress that way! It's monstrous of you to tell her that on an opening night." Then she forced my mother into the corridor.

I was grateful to Kim for her empathy and her caring, but I knew the play was a disaster. "Thank you," I sniffled. "You know I feel like that actress I heard scream at my father on an opening night, 'How dare you come back and tell me the truth.'"

Our Texas producer gave a huge party. "Well, the audience loved it." I was wearing long strands of black pearls he had insisted on borrowing for me so I would look "lak a reeel stah." Instead, appropriately, the black pearls and black dress were in tune with the black reviews.

Actually, not all of the reviews were terrible, but the fact that a few critics liked me, if not the play, didn't penetrate. There was room only for the fact that I had miserably failed not only my parents but also *myself*.

We ran for two weeks, every night of which was agony. Someone told me that on closing night Greta Garbo, who had made the role famous on the screen, was in the audience. I counted it as one of my few blessings that I didn't know she was there. I took a few souvenirs from among my costumes: a beautiful soft fur muff with a pink rose pinned on it, a delicate lace fan decorated with tiny crystals.

Franco took the failure very well. He had immediate plans for other work so that he didn't have time, as I did, to become trapped in self-pity and doubt.

My self-esteem, which had been minimal at best, was now nonexistent. Perhaps I had been inevitably headed toward this moment ever since *Anne Frank*.

I had no idea what I would do now. I had no goal beyond this play. If I wasn't Anne Frank or Juliet or Camille, I didn't know if I was anyone. Superficially, my demeanor was unchanged. I pretended I knew who I was, although this was given the lie by the blurred and indistinct face I would see every morning in the mirror. This was my first real professional failure, and after the exaggerated expectations I had nurtured, my feelings of humiliation and disappointment were total.

I forced myself to attend the Actors Studio, but while the actors and writers there treated me as if nothing had happened, I thought they were being nice to me as one would have compassion toward, say, a leper. In an attempt to stimulate myself, I decided to do some scenes at the Studio.

My first was with Andreas Voutsinas. I was so petrified I could barely move. My father was so nervous also that, totally out of character, he jumped up and adjusted the lights for us. The scene was acceptable, but I felt I would almost prefer to be *bad* than to be *mediocre*.

The second scene I did was *Romeo and Juliet* with Geraldine Page. I cried through most of the piece. "Is that the way you meant to play it?" my father asked afterward.

There was something about getting up at the Studio in front of an audience of one's peers, in front of Lee Strasberg . . . Daddy . . . and everything he represented that was more terrifying to me than an opening night on Broadway.

My father suggested, "I think you should do something different, simpler, choose a scene which will elicit different colors from you, another kind of character."

Estelle Parsons and I decided to do a scene from a Philip Roth book. I played a young woman who was a junkie. To work on this scene I chose to do a "private moment," recreating an activity which was so personal I had never allowed anyone to see it. During this exercise, I stripped to a bikini and did a dance in front of a mirror. It was certainly different from any part I had played.

At this time Christopher Jones was admitted to the Studio as an observer, allowed to watch, but not participate. My mother thought he had a wonderful quality. "He has that same animal magnetism that Marlon and Jimmy Dean had." He also had a reputation for being eccentric, wild. He had a disconcerting habit of sitting in the balcony of the Studio and staring down at me throughout the sessions. He made me more than uncomfortable; it unnerved me.

He was too intense, too alien. I tried to ignore him, and finally it seemed that he tired of the game and turned to other amusements.

My life went on, and yet I felt as if I were becalmed, like the sea before a storm.

I had reserved a Yorkshire puppy as a gift for my mother. The litter was born in late spring and I went downtown to pick out the tiny apricot-colored bit of fluff. I had thought for a long time before deciding on this present.

When I got home, Mother stared at the puppy in my hand. "Couldn't you give it to me later? It's so hectic right now."

God, I thought, she hates it. "No. Either you take it now or I'll give it back."

"Don't look at me," my father ordered. "I'm not taking care of that dog."

Six months later he had trained "Cherie" to play baseball, running between three pillows (bases) with a ball in her mouth.

"How did you train her?" I asked.

"I used the Method." Whatever it was, the dog adored him.

In the midst of my depression, my parents, Johnny, and I began spending every weekend in our recently acquired Fire Island home, which overlooked the beach, separated from the waves only by a large sloping dune and some rushes. My mother had called me in Rome just before I had left and asked for help with the down payment.

"It will be your house, too. That way you'll always have someplace to come back to."

I began, in spite of myself, to feel more relaxed. Nothing was resolved in my life, but I wasn't agonizing about it. I was able to enjoy the ocean, the sun, and the slow and easy life.

PART THREE

FRIENDS CAME OUT to the Island to visit, to walk on the beach, to talk long into the night: Marta and Jerry Orbach, my girlfriend Steffi from California, many of the young people from the Studio. Director Frank Corsaro had a home nearby, where he would entertain his students, including Christopher Jones. They dropped by to visit us regularly.

One weekend my mother and father were in Hollywood with Clifford Odets, who was dying. Johnny and I were alone. The Orbachs came over with their baby, along with an actor friend of Johnny's, Dick Bradford, and Frank Corsaro with Christopher and two or three other students. Christopher seemed to be a little erratic in his behavior, and I avoided him, trying not to meet his eyes. The more I withdrew, the more outlandish his behavior became.

There was a thunderstorm that night. It was terrifying, yet beautiful. Christopher tore off his shirt and ran onto the beach into the pelting rain. "I'm going swimming," he called.

"You're crazy, come back inside . . . it's not safe," we implored him.

Instead, he began to do a rhythmic, erotic dance between the flashes of lightning. It was as if in the eye of the storm he became the storm itself. And, like it, he appeared both beautiful and dangerous.

Later that night he persuaded a friend of mine and me to go swimming in the bay. It was cold and cruel weather, but we agreed. With his sure street instincts, he played on our fears until we became intimidated and did what he suggested.

"I don't like him," my friend said. "He's got that same mean streak Jimmy [Dean] had."

"Well, I like him," I said, intrigued. "He's just a little unconventional."

Not long after that weekend, back in the city, Marta Orbach suggested that Christopher, Jerry, Johnny, she, and I spend an afternoon together. I gathered it had been Christopher's idea and because Marta adored him she had readily agreed. We all took the ferry around Manhattan. Standing at the rail in a caressing wind, I shivered at the proximity of this young man who looked at me so purposefully. He brushed against me, and I felt as if I had been tattooed.

Later that afternoon the two of us walked from the Bowery uptown to my Eighty-fourth Street apartment. After twenty blocks we were holding hands, he temporarily as shy or cautious as I was. After four miles, we were arm in arm, and by Eighty-first Street my head was against his shoulder. I remembered how I had sworn after Richard Burton, "no more actors."

I looked at Christopher's clear, clean profile. The setting sun filtering through the skyscrapers chiseled his high Indian cheekbones and outlined in light the straight lines of his nose, the sensuous thrust of his lower lip. He's so beautiful, I thought. Susan, I admonished myself, you don't want to wake up in the morning with someone who's prettier than you.

Chris turned to me. "What are you thinking about?" I could hardly say to him: We're not home yet and I'm thinking about morning. Instead I replied, "You're so calm and quiet, I've never seen you like this." I wanted to tell him, but was too inhibited, that he was dazzling. Lean and tightly coiled, skin glowing with energy, he seemed strong and masculine and self-assured, unlike me, who quivered at every unexplained shadow, including my own.

"I imagine that you must have lived a very different kind of life

170

than I have," I ventured. "I've always been fairly protected and coddled. Sometimes I feel as if I've been wrapped in cotton bunting. In spite of everything I've done, I feel I haven't really lived. I suspect you're much more of a rebel than I am."

"Who told you that?" He turned on me. "Has some bastard been telling you stories about me?"

"No," I said, placating him. It wasn't true; I had heard all kinds of perverse, interesting stories about him, but instead of shocking me, they had titillated me.

"Don't believe anything you've heard. These New York intellectuals try to tear down anyone they can't control. They know I see through all their bullshit. The mothers are out to get me."

I changed the subject. "I did hear you were an orphan. Is that true?"

"Oh, shit," he said. "My mother died of T.B. in a sanatorium. They took her away from me when I was three. My daddy put my brother and me in a boys' home in Memphis after that 'cause he couldn't take care of us."

"Do you see much of your father and brother now?"

"I haven't been home in a long time," he said.

"When did you decide to become an actor?"

"When I was in jail on Governor's Island. I used to sit and look out through the bars of my cell. New York was so close I felt I could reach out and grab it. When I got out, I bummed around, met a guy who was a painter, I studied that for a while, then I made friends with a kid who was taking acting from Frank Corsaro and he suggested I come to class with him. Man, I didn't know what I was getting in to."

"Why were you in prison?"

"I enlisted in the army when I was sixteen, my father signed the permission papers. I hated it. They even told you when to take a leak. One night I got this overwhelming urge to go to New York, as if something were drawing me there. It was crazy, but I split the next day. I was on my way when the bastards picked me up and shipped me off to Governor's Island. But at least I made it to New York."

171

As he was talking, I noticed that people we were passing on the street were reacting to him almost the way they would have to a movie star. They stared at him or did double-takes. He walked with that ambling Southern gait, a little defiant, pelvis thrust forward, exuding energy.

As I examined his face, I said, "It's funny. We really have nothing in common."

"Opposites attract." He smiled, touching my hair.

We reached my apartment, and when he walked through the door, an unspoken commitment had been made. The next two weeks we became inseparable, caught in the glow of our romance, hardly leaving the apartment. Finally, when we did, we walked for miles day after day, going to movies on Forty-second Street and eventually to parties with young people who had lived on the periphery of my life and to whom I had not been exposed.

He introduced me to marijuana one night. He came over to me and kissed me on the lips, blowing the sweet-smelling smoke into my mouth. I started to cough.

"You gotta suck it in," he said.

"I can't inhale," I replied. "It makes me sick."

He handed me a small hand-rolled cigarette. "Take a drag on this. Long and slow. Just relax, baby. Now, hold it in, swallow it."

After three or four long pulls, I started to get giggly. I was having trouble talking normally, everything came out slow motion. I felt so agreeable. I had hated the party when we arrived. A lot of the people had seemed a little boring and disreputable. But now, suddenly, I felt very benevolent toward them.

Afterward, still feeling the effects of the grass, when we made love, I seemed to shatter and reform like liquid drops of a kaleidoscope splashing color and melting away. I had never felt anything like that before. Then we lay entwined in my bed, watching some terrible television show that in my euphoric state seemed like Shakespeare.

Everything was idyllic until we had our first fight. Early one evening while Christopher was taking a nap, I decided to take a bath. When he awoke from a deep sleep, he looked at me strangely.

"Who were you talking to on the phone while I was sleeping?"

"I wasn't on the phone," I replied, laughing. "I was taking a bath."

"I heard you talking on the phone," he said.

"Maybe you dreamed it," I suggested, "unless I was talking to myself in the bathtub and didn't realize it."

"I know what I heard," he said. "I heard you pick up the phone, dial a number, and talk to someone."

"Christopher, I was in the tub. Why would I lie to you?"

"I think you were talking to a guy."

He got up and walked into the bathroom. When he came back into the room, he just stared at me.

I started to laugh nervously. "What are you looking at?"

"The tub is dry," he said. "If you had water in that tub in the past hour, how come the fucking tub is dry?"

"Maybe it's a drip-dry tub," I joked feebly. "Look, Christopher, you're just going to have to trust me." I smiled, pushed the hair off my neck. "You see, I even washed behind my ears."

"You're lying," he said, "I can tell by that phony smile."

He was right about one thing. I was telling the truth, but the smile was false. I used it because he was scaring me. I could sense the anger lying under the surface of his words, waiting to explode as my father's had. My stomach was quivering with anger, and in my effort to suppress it, I was trying to be ingratiating.

"This is absurd," I said, and turned to leave the room.

He grabbed my arm, spun me around, and said, "Don't you ever walk away from me!" He drew his arm back and smacked me in the face.

"My God," I cried out, "what's the matter with you?" I covered my eye and cheek with my hand.

"Did I hurt you?" he asked. "Let me see."

"Don't touch me."

"Susie, I wouldn't hurt you. I love you, you know that. I couldn't do anything to hurt you."

I caught a glimpse of myself in the bedroom mirror. A bruise was beginning to appear under my eye.

"Jesus, you've got such supersensitive skin," Christopher said. "I hardly touched you." He was practically in tears. He ministered gently to my face, overwhelming me with his tenderness and affection, until somehow I wound up feeling sorry for him. After all, he had had such a terrible childhood and I had been so privileged. I felt as if I had failed him in some way. If I had loved him enough, he wouldn't have hit me.

We went to Sunday brunch at my parents' home. I was wearing dark glasses to hide my black eye, daring my parents to say anything. When they saw me, my mother started to say something, then stopped when I glared at her. My father looked at Chris and walked out of the room.

Christopher followed my father into his study and began to talk to him, almost a monologue.

"What did you think of Jimmy Dean?" And, without waiting for an answer, "I thought he was a great actor. He was a fucking saint. That's why he had to die so young."

My father just listened. Christopher went on about Jimmy, obviously identifying with him. Indeed, many of his friends in New York had been friends of Jimmy's and had told Christopher how much alike they were.

Christopher abruptly changed the subject and began speaking about good and evil, exhibiting a mystical tendency I had not seen before.

"They're out to destroy anyone who's too alive. But they can kiss my ass. I'll get them before they get me," he stated passionately.

Although my father neither replied nor disagreed with him, Christopher was arguing as if upset that he was unresponsive. He began to make statements that were deliberately provocative, trying to elicit a strong reaction.

He looked around at the book-covered walls. "You can't learn anything about life from a book," he challenged. "Nietzsche said, 'We can only find freedom and happiness without thought, without intellect, through pure will,'" he paraphrased. "It's all a power play. . . ."

My father never took the bait, and when I kissed my mother

good night, she clasped my hand and sighed. "That boy has such a desperate need to be accepted."

We saw very few people during the next month or so. Occasionally we visited the Orbachs, as Christopher was comfortable around them, but I avoided my other friends because I didn't want him to feel threatened. I turned down work, gave away clothes he didn't like, stripped myself of friends, family, work, cloistering myself with him in a symbiotic union like the one I had lost with my mother. We fought, apologized, made love, and every night we fell asleep like two children, curled into the curve of one another.

"Susan," my mother said, "I want to talk to you about Christopher."

"I don't want to hear it, I'm not going to talk about it . . . I love him . . . he makes me feel more than I've ever felt . . . emotionally . . . sexually . . . sometimes it's painful but I'd rather feel pain than the numbness, the emptiness I felt before I met him. Besides, it's my life, not yours!"

Now I became more infatuated, more obsessed by him. If he got stoned, I got stoned; if he was unhappy, I wept.

I wanted him to know he was the center of my universe, and so, gradually, I focused my life more and more around him. I wanted so much to be loved unreservedly, for myself, that I was willing to pay any price including subservience to secure this love, hoping that with each piece of myself I gave up he would be so pleased that he, too, would be transformed.

I moved to him as a weather vane spins to the wind, until, in an ultimate gesture of trust, I transferred to him the responsibility for my life, which I was incapable of assuming for myself. He avariciously accepted this power and, incredibly, perversely, demanded even more.

He became violently jealous, but there seemed to be no consistency to his suspicions. On one occasion he would say, "I'm sick of watching you making eyes at some guy across the room. You don't have to pay so much attention to every Tom, Dick, and Harry that comes to the table. You lead them on, and it makes me look like an idiot."

"Christopher, I only talked to your friend who came over to the table because you spent the whole evening talking to that actress you'd worked with. I wasn't just going to sit there like a piece of furniture."

"Listen, I've had to put up with stuck-up bitches all my life, and I'm sick of it. You and your father think you're better than anyone else. You better think again. You've met your match. Nobody's going to fuck with me."

The next night, the attack would be reversed.

"What's the matter with my friends?" he'd ask accusingly. "You act like they aren't good enough for you, like you're a goddamn princess. You totally ignored Larry when he came over tonight. It wouldn't kill you to be nice to him, talk to him."

I became more and more withdrawn, never sure what would set him off. It might be something as trivial as a wolf whistle on the street. One night he challenged three young men on a street corner in Greenwich Village.

"Come on, which one of you mothers whistled? I'll take on all three of you if I have to."

When I tried to pull him away, he shook me off and sprang at the young men. There was a brief scuffle as they dispersed and Christopher yelled after them, "Don't fuck with me, man!" To me he said, "You never have to worry when you're with me," and I knew he would protect me . . . against anyone but himself. I would decide to end this relationship, that I had had enough, and he, as if sensing this, would be on his knees like a little boy who knows he's been naughty, apologizing, cajoling, seducing me until my resolve disintegrated and I forgave him.

He had a Norton 650 motorcycle. I would sit on the back, clinging to his waist for dear life, until the night we skidded and flipped over in Central Park. We were thrown clear, but we were living dangerously. The next night we wrecked it going over the hood of a taxicab.

He had a friend who was also an acquaintance of mine, an actor-director from the Studio, whom we visited in his home one evening. Christopher attacked him for his good fortune, "undeserved," he said, in being born into a rich, liberal Jewish family.

176

And I knew that Christopher with his love of art was wildly jealous of the Van Goghs, the Picassos, that covered the walls.

That night, as we were falling asleep, he talked about his family. "I grew up in a shack with outdoor plumbing and a coal stove. Hell, in Tennessee that meant you were poor white trash."

"But, Christopher, wasn't the boys' home an old mansion?"

"Yeah, but so what? Nobody gave a shit about me except my brother, Bobby Joe. My father remarried and went and had three more kids. But we only went home for holidays. They didn't care."

"I care about you, Christopher. Do you know how much I love you? Forget about the past. You know you could be anything you wanted to be. You paint beautifully, and everybody says you could be a big star if you want to, but you've got to stop living in the past," I urged.

The Actors Studio was planning a production of Anton Chekhov's *Three Sisters*, starring Geraldine Page and Kim Stanley, to be directed by my father. I was offered the part of the youngest sister. I debated for days until I realized that even the thought of being directed by my father was appalling. The few days that he had worked with me on *Shadow of a Gunman* had been enough.

"I can't do it, Mother," I said. "And I don't want to." She begged me to reconsider. "Besides, there's Christopher. We can't be separated now." I knew Christopher didn't want me to do the play. My work was the only real rival he had.

Instead, we accepted an invitation from Marta and Jerry Orbach to drive to California. I gave up the apartment, put my things in storage, told my California agent that I would be available for work there soon, and we left.

The car was crowded, which left the Orbachs' bouncing baby boy not much room to bounce in. He made up for lack of movement with vocal power. We would drive all day, stopping at a motel for the night. Somewhere in mid-country, while Christopher was buying a candy bar and a Coke for his breakfast in a grocery story, he found a copy of *Playboy*.

"Jesus, you're in this. Bare-assed, too."

"I wasn't bare-assed," I said. "It just looks like it. That's the sitting I did to publicize *Camille*."

The pictures were not so much prurient in content as pitiful in the attempt I had made to look sexy. Christopher, in a fit of Southern morality, said, "Hookers pose for *Playboy*."

"So," I retorted, "do actresses. You may not acknowledge it, but there is a difference."

He was sure that strange men were watching me, leering at me, that the whole of America read *Playboy*.

"There's no point in my regretting it. I just will never do anything like that again, but it's too late to feel guilty, so let's not talk about it."

He waited until we were back at the motel before he exploded. "Why did you have to do this to me?" and began to rain blows on my body.

I locked myself in the bathroom, and he proceeded to rip and tear my clothes.

"It's just," he said as he apologized to me that night, "that you're so pure, I hate to see you cheapen yourself."

One night Christopher told me about the first time he had seen me two years before *Camille*, the year his mother died of tuberculosis in the hospital where she had been since he was three years old.

"It was a bitch. I couldn't sleep lying down the whole year after she died. My heart would start to race so fast I thought I was going to fucking die, too. I slept sitting up, fully dressed. I was watching TV. the Chekhov thing you did with Helen Hayes. What was it? *The Cherry Orchard?* In one scene they had this giant close-up of you smiling. I couldn't believe it. I had this picture of my mother when she was smiling into a camera. And, man, it was weird. Her face superimposed itself over yours, it was the same face. You looked just like her. She was small and dark like you."

We drove through snowbound counties, mile after mile of white sheets of land, unbroken except for barbed-wire fences and an occasional jackrabbit. On November 22, we were listening to country-western music on the car radio when the song was interrupted by an emotional, out-of-control voice.

"Ladies and gentlemen, the president, John F. Kennedy, has been shot. He's being taken to the hospital now, and . . ." As the voice broke down completely, another voice came on the air and recited the details.

"Oh, my God," Marta said, "he's got to live. He's got to."

Within hours, we knew the worst. "There's no justice," someone in the car said, weeping. We had all been brought up as romantics; heroes should die in battle or live to be boring old men writing their memoirs in front of the fire.

I remembered President Kennedy's face as Marilyn sang "Happy Birthday" to him in Madison Square Garden. Time goes too quickly or too slowly. You think you have a hold on it and it runs through your clenched fingers like sand.

We reached San Francisco and stayed briefly at Marta's father's old, rambling house on the outskirts of town. Christopher and I were anxious to leave for Los Angeles. I had no idea what awaited me there or I would not have rushed so.

On our arrival, we checked into the Chateau Marmont and went out to see the town, driving down Sunset Strip, rubbernecking at the pimps, prostitutes, all-night eateries, traffic jams of bored people who drove up and down looking for the action, and stoned drivers too paranoid to go faster than a crawl. I hated the loud music coming out of the rock nightclubs, the vacuous look of the young people, the frenzied movements of dancing bodies.

"I'm tired. Let's go back to the hotel," I said.

"Take one of these. It will make you relax and give you a lift so you can get it on and dance a little."

Who offered the pill? Was it a friend of Christopher's or a stranger? I accepted it, and I did dance, joining the crowd I had despised a half-hour before.

California was a generous land. Everything was available: tennis, surf, sunshine, grass, uppers, downers, cocaine. People were bored, empty. They doped themselves up so they could enjoy their boredom. Some just did not care anymore. When I asked for a Coke, they brought me a little box of white powder.

Christopher, here as in New York, didn't like my friends. "Hell, they're too square and uptight, too intellectual."

"We see your friends," I said.

"But you treat them like shit," he accused.

If at first I was watching how the other half lived, soon I *was* the other half, lost in the great rebellious, hypnotic siren song of the sixties. If you couldn't have things one hundred percent your way, you could just drop out to a better world—if you were lucky. If your life-style was too mechanized, have a snort. Man, it's out of sight. Take a trip, far-out, see the face of God, overcome your fear of death, expand your mind, ya know what I mean. Trick-or-treat flower children, flowers for the dead. Peace. Kill for the right to peace. I'm nobody, who are you?

I did one TV show, a *Dr. Kildare*, and then another with Peter Falk. At least I was maintaining a professional decorum; I went to bed on time so I could be up at five-thirty and go to work.

"Go on," I said to Christopher at night, "you go without me, I don't mind."

"There's no privacy in this hotel, Christopher," I complained. "I'm sick of stuffing towels in the door cracks so the manager won't smell the grass."

We were not alone. One young movie star was evicted for overdosing in the lobby; another set his room on fire. We decided to rent a house. We began our journey lured by a Sunset Strip Circe onto an island of discontent, but unfortunately we would prove less resolute than Odysseus, we would succumb to all temptations.

We rented a little rustic house in the Laurel Canyon hills. Tuesday Weld and Gary Lockwood had been the previous inhabitants. There was one bedroom, a living room with a fireplace, a kitchen, and a small dirt-covered patio in the front of the house, which was set against the hills.

I was learning to cook black-eyed peas with salt pork, collard greens and Southern-fried chicken, and we called Christopher's daddy to get the recipe for some very rich childhood dessert, a kind of milk pudding that vaguely resembled a floating island. His father's Southern accent was so thick I couldn't understand one word.

"Yes, it sounds terrific. I've got it. Thank you." And to Christopher I said, "I can't understand him, his accent. You ask him."

We'd go to a discotheque almost every night until the sun came up, and then we'd sleep away a good part of the day. Between the marijuana and the pills we were taking, we were exhausted the next day. The drugs gave us a false energy, which we always had to pay for.

There was always a friend or acquaintance who offered drugs. It was so available, at some Hollywood gatherings pills were served like party favors. On the nights we were alone, it gave us something to do.

"Christopher, we have to cut down, we're spending half our lives stoned," I suggested.

But if I said no when something was offered, I became the enemy, and because I still desperately wanted to be accepted, even by people I did not care about, I never refused. After a while, I didn't want to. Alone at home or while working, I never took anything or missed it. The drugs were a bond between Christopher, myself, and our peers. My addiction was emotional, not physical. I had drifted onto a merry-go-round that did not stop. And as always, the only self-discipline I had left was in relation to my work.

Christopher became intrigued by automatic writing. Two people put their hands loosely together, hold a pen or pencil, and wait until the pen moves. You ask questions, and the pen writes. At first all we got were infinity signs, over and over, covering sheet after sheet of white paper. Then slowly, letters began to appear, and finally garbled words. Christopher decided to go to the next step and ask me questins about the past. Had I dated so-and-so? What had I done in 1960? The pen our two hands held would reply.

"But that's not true," I said once when it wrote "Yes."

"Then you've got to be lying. *It* has to be telling the truth."

"What is *it*, Christopher?"

"*It's* your subconscious mind."

"Well," I said, "if it's *my* subconscious mind, why couldn't it just as easily be *your* subconscious mind controlling the pen? In which case, you're making it answer what you think but what I know is not true."

We argued endlessly. Christopher felt that I was deliberately withholding parts of my life. Only if he knew every thought and feeling I had ever had could he understand and possess me. I wanted to give completely of myself, but what he was asking seemed impossible.

"What do you want me to do? What more can I give to you? Tell me."

The drugs made the paranoia intense, the doubt more devastating, more dangerous. Jealousy became overwhelming. Like children. Yes. No. Yes. No. It became hypnotic in its repetitiveness.

The drugs also heightened my already incoherent sense of time; everything was vignettes, unconnected episodes.

One evening I cooked a pot of chili. The next time I went into the kitchen, I started to put it in a dish to refrigerate, only to find it had maggots in it.

I could get lost in a piece of music or the pattern on the wallpaper as easily as in a television show. All sense of discrimination was shattered. I watched terrible comedians and laughed; I listened to music I ordinarily loathed and became trapped in the rhythm of the drums. I was open to hypnotizing, demoralizing suggestions of roadside signs, radio, television.

After a while, Christopher decided to introduce me to mescaline and LSD. The artistic community is always the most open to and first to embrace new ideas and theories. Someone as conservative and respected as Cary Grant, I read, had gone into LSD therapy. An actress friend of the family's had written a book, privately printed, about her LSD experiences. Her father sent us a copy.

I remember a casual friend, a Ph.D. in New York, raving about

Timothy Leary when as a professor at Harvard, "He let me lick the spoon which had held the LSD he was making." She thought she was tasting the future.

I sat in my chamois-and-feather dress, a rich hippie, talking to some acquaintances.

"Well, the Indians have taken this stuff for years," one boy said. "It hasn't damaged them. They have religious experiences."

"Don't be scared, I'll be there," Chris reassured me.

"But the Indians don't have to drive on the freeway in Los Angeles or walk down Forty-second Street in New York," I offered.

"You've got to cut loose from all your tight-assed, conventional crap," Christopher insisted.

When I was a little girl I took my aspirin crushed up in a spoonful of applesauce. That was the way I took the tiny, dry, grayish-brown pieces of mescaline Christopher had bought. We lit a fire in the living room, pulled the curtains, double-locked the doors, and I sat on the low ledge that surrounded the brick fireplace while Christopher spoon-fed me.

I felt like a good little girl taking my mind medicine. This was going to unlock mysterious doors closed to my everyday self, take me into uncharted regions with answers to existential questions. Characteristically, I romanticized everything.

The mushroom was more bitter than aspirin. "This is going to blow your mind," Christopher said. He wasn't participating this time, he would be my guide.

My mouth was dry, my heart palpitating. I was sorry I had acquiesced and wanted to change my mind, but it was too late to protest.

Sitting in front of the fire, I waited for the mushroom to work its magic. The flames leaped, reaching upward, outward, as if they would envelop me. There was an antique handbag of mine hung on a peg as a decoration. As I stared at it, the light from the fire caught its silver-and-jewel clasp and danced off the hundreds of tiny colored beads. The flames made patterns within the flower pattern of the bag.

"Do you see that?" I demanded of Christopher.

"What?"

"Those pictures in the bag."

"No."

"You must. It's alive. That bag is alive."

He laughed. "You are stoned out of your mind."

Suddenly I am spellbound by the scenes beginning to be played out on the tiny screen in front of me. The first one appears like a cartoon—fast, jumpy, distorted figures. There is a man behind a desk, very large, scary, with a comic-strip face. He is screaming in a harsh, metallic voice, and the face distorts and puckers even more. He picks up a large book and throws it at the woman in front of him. There is a little girl holding the hand of a little boy, both are in spacesuits . . . no, they're snowsuits. They watch this man wide-eyed, terrified. It's Johnny and me. Now my mother is lying on the bed. She's much younger, with long hair, flowing like melting honey down and over the side of the bed, and the sunlight coming through the window warms it into liquid golden flames. I am on the ground in a basket, kicking my feet and screaming. When I close my eyes, I see red all around me, violent, violent red. A man comes and stands before the basket. Either his legs are invisible or I am looking between them. It is my father. I cannot see his face, I only see my mother's naked body lying on that bed. Then I am in my basket in the back of an old jalopy, the kind that used to have a rumble seat. I can feel the wind.

Suddenly I am in another car. The door is opening, the car is going very, very fast. I start to fall out of the car onto the pavement. Terrified, I begin to scream. I described what was taking place to Christopher.

"That's me," he said. "I feel or I was pushed out of a car when I was just a little boy."

It was not enough that I was reliving my life. I was reliving his, too.

I stood on the brick ledge that enclosed the fireplace, balancing myself on my bare feet. Christopher began to ask me about my childhood, question after question after question. As I began to answer hesitantly, stripping away years, Christopher began to strip away my clothes, until, without warning, a wave of words, an ocean of words poured out. No longer answering, I was telling everything, anything. Guilt, jealousy, meanness, erotic images, every incident, every vindictive word, every doubt, every terror, real or imagined. *Mea culpa*.

Twelve hours later, I was still standing on that narrow ledge in the same position, held there by the cadence of Christopher's voice saying, "Stay there, don't move."

When it was over, I was not tired as much as emptied. It was not an unpleasant feeling, though my body ached from being in one position for so long, and I could smell myself strong and pungent, as if I had just run a long way in great heat. I went to take a shower. As the warm water poured over my body, I understood confession, the essence of it, the cleansing of the soul. I felt . . . euphoric . . . illuminated.

When I emerged from the bathroom, Christopher saw from my face that I had undergone some transformation and wanted to be included.

"It's a feeling, not a thought. I can't describe it in words. Please, just hold me. Give me some time. I feel overwhelmed right now."

Still under the influence of the mescaline, I was wide open, so vulnerable that it was almost frightening. I felt indecently exposed.

He became fierce. "You're deliberately shutting me out again because you still don't trust me! You're projecting all your paranoid crap onto me. I've seen you, I know you. You belong to me!" He began to possessively, roughly touch me.

"Please let me rest. Let's just be still together," I entreated him.

He ignored my protests. As he took possession of my body, the expansiveness I was feeling dissolved and was replaced by a closed sensation. More closed than I had ever been. A light had gone out inside me that I feared might never be recaptured.

Another night, when I called my parents, I asked my father about some of my impressions.

185

"Yes, yes, I did throw a book at your mother. You and Johnny were just babies then. I don't see how you could remember that. Yes, we did have a car like that."

So my visions had not been hallucinations, they were memories. . . .

Years later, I asked a doctor, "What happened to me?"

"The drug removed the defenses you had acquired, some of which were necessary. It also released an enormous amount of energy. You felt helpless, and when he attacked you, you had no recourse but to totally withdraw to protect yourself," he said.

I was wary of mescaline after this experience, and determined to avoid LSD, as I saw the effect it had on people. We had a friend, a beautiful movie star, whose husband had recently left her. She remained with her two children in her Bel Air mansion with its magnificent view, tennis court, pool, wine cellar, projection room, works of art, rooms of couturier clothes, staff of three and housekeeper whom she had instructed to dole out her pills and, if necessary, hide them if she insisted on too many.

One evening when we dropped by for a visit, she told us that recently, at her doctor's suggestion, she had taken LSD. When the drug took effect, she happened to look into the mirror and saw her perfect features, her tanned velvety skin and glowing blue eyes, reflected back to her as a death's head with a million wrinkles.

Christopher was very critical of her or, in the vernacular of the sixties, "mind-fucking" her. It was well known one of her sons was taking drugs, all kinds. He seemed fine when he was not hiding under his bed from his guests. Her daughter died five years later. She shot herself in the mouth on Mother's Day. Before she used her gun, she wrote a note: "Happy Mother's Day." The autopsy showed she was inundated with narcotics.

When we got home, I sat on the trunk we used as a table in the living room. It was hard and cold under my bare legs, and for a moment I touched reality.

"The world is insane," Chris said. "It's run by assholes who've legalized it all. There's no point to anything. We'd be better off dead than living in this mess."

186

I closed my eyes. A voice murmured inside me, "Don't listen to him, Susan."

"You're nothing."

"I'm not sure of anything," I moaned.

"It's all right, I've felt like that a lot. You hold on to me. I'll pull you out of this. I'm here."

Later, he sat in bed cleaning his revolver. Cocking it and holding it to his temple, he looked at me challengingly. "There's only one bullet in it."

He pressed the trigger. Click. Silence. Another click. Silence. . . .

I reached out and walloped him as hard as I could on the cheek. "What's the matter with you? Why do you do these things? You shit, you have no right, no right. . . . You're crazy."

"Everyone's crazy." He laughed.

He seemed pleased that I had hit him, like a child whose mother paid attention. I wondered early that morning, as I was trying to fall asleep, whether there was really a bullet in the gun or if it had been empty.

My Grandmother Miller died. She had been healthy until her late seventies, when she fell and broke her hip. Then, almost overnight, feeling helpless for the first time in her life, she developed cancer and passed away. My Aunt Bea called to tell me that my mother was flying to California for the funeral.

Before she arrived, Christopher and I had another of our Pavlovian quarrels. He was violent and accusing, I was passive and defensive. By morning I was so black and blue there was no way to hide the bruises. My mother and her family could not see me in that condition.

Deciding not to answer the phone, I listened as it rang and rang, ten, fifteen, twenty times. I went into the kitchen and ran the water so I could not hear it. A telegram came; I did not read it. Finally the doorbell rang, and I went to the door, wrapping my robe close around me. It was my friend Steffi.

"Susan, let me in. Your mother sent me."

I opened the door enough for her to see me but not wide enough for her to enter. Shock registered on her face when she saw my bruised face.

"Your mother wants you to come to the funeral."

"How can I go, Steffi? You can see it's impossible. I can't let everyone see me like this. I don't want my mother to see me. Tell her you couldn't reach me. That I wasn't in. Please."

"I'll try," she said.

The next day Christopher went out, and I sat alone brooding. I realized that my mother would leave Los Angeles soon, that I might have lost my chance to see her. If anyone could, Mother would help me.

I called her and said, "I'm coming over."

When I got to the hotel, I found she was distraught, inconsolable over her mother's death. She had never really worked through her resentment of her mother. She had told me of her bitterness at being beaten by her mother, of being misunderstood by her; and yet, I knew that she needed and wanted her mother's approval. She saw my bruised face, but could not react, she was so immersed in her own grief.

"Mother, Mother, I need your help."

She sobbed. "Susan, what am I going to do? What am I going to do? My mother is dead. I can't bear it."

"Mother, can you hear me? I need your help."

"She never knew I loved her. She never knew. Now it's too late," she sobbed, lying in bed.

I tried to hold her, to comfort her. She reached for me. It was clear she wanted me to be the mother, and a feeling of desperation washed over me.

"I don't care about your mother," I screamed. "She's dead and I'm alive, goddammit. There's nothing anyone can do for her. But you can help me. Tell me what to do."

"You're so cruel," she said. "My mother is dead and you don't care."

"Please, Mother, Mommy, please look at me. Grandma is

dead, you and I are alive. It's too late for her, but not for us. I feel as if I'm going to die. I need you."

But she couldn't help me. She was a little girl weeping for her mama, as I was a little girl weeping for mine.

When I started to leave, she reached into the bedside drawer and pulled out the Gideon Bible. "Take this with you. Take it."

"That's stealing, Mother. I don't want a stolen Bible."

"No, no. They put them here for you to take. They want people to take them."

Realizing she was trying to make up with me, I accepted the Bible, hiding it under my coat as I left.

Christopher and I drove to Tijuana, Mexico. It was hot, dirty, and squalid. I didn't want to eat anything, do anything but turn around and go home. We saw El Cordobés fight a bull. A horse was gored, its insides spilled onto the ground. Afterward Christopher bought a couple of ounces of marijuana so the trip wouldn't be a total loss.

He gave it to me, saying, "Put it in your boot."

"Why my boot? You have boots on, too."

"Can't you please just do anything I ask you to without bitching?"

"Just give me the damn bag." Resentfully I pushed it down into my boot, arranging the ridges of the soft leather around it.

At the border crossing, the customs guards were checking every fourth car. I leaned out of the window trying to count to see whether we would be stopped. As we neared the United States, the lump in my boot seemed to get larger and larger, pressing against my ankle.

We were the fourth car in our line. They were ready to wave us through when the man who had been checking the trunk called out, "Hey! Hold it! Look at this!" He waved something in the air. It was a revolver. "It's loaded," he shouted.

The other tourists looked at us as if we were Bonnie and Clyde.

I had not noticed that Christopher had put his loaded revolver in our suitcase.

"That's an illegal concealed weapon, kids, and taken across a foreign border. You're lucky they didn't find it on the Mexican side."

They took us inside the station. "Do you have a record?"

"Do I look like I have one?" I asked, horrified.

"Honey, you'd be surprised what some of them look like. As if butter wouldn't melt, but they got records, all right."

In the next room a young girl was being stripped and searched. I thought about going to the bathroom to flush the incriminating package away. Christopher looked unconcerned. But I couldn't tell if he was acting or if he really wasn't worried. I decided against the bathroom. Instead, I began to drop names: Marlon Brando, Jennifer Jones, Paul Newman, Marilyn Monroe.

Finally the guard asked me, "Are you an actress?"

"Yes," I said, "yes. How did you guess?"

They became chattier. "Son, I bet you carry that gun to protect Miss Strasberg."

More likely to protect what's in Miss Strasberg's boot, I thought. *My* boot, not his.

"You kids go on home now. I'll just take these bullets out. You get a permit for this gun as soon as you can."

"Yes, sir."

I had this strong urge to strangle Christopher, but was satisfied that he paled when I told him I almost went to the bathroom.

"Oh, my God, that would have been a dead giveaway. They wait for you to do something like that."

"This is your territory, not mine. How could you expect me to know something like that?"

He laughed. "Man, I'd like to see your father's face if he knew."

It was if through me he had reached out to challenge my father and the world. I sensed how important it was that my father notice him, acknowledge him, as though that would compensate for his growing up separated from his own father.

*   *   *

190

In my next television show I played a girl who is hysterically paralyzed. It seemed appropriate. I was effectively paralyzed in my own life.

One morning, following a fight Chris and I had, during which I was unable to protect my face, I went into the studio with a large bruise on my jaw, ashamed that the makeup man would see it.

"I bumped into a door," I lied.

Matter-of-factly he looked at me and said, "Honey, don't worry. I've seen worse. Anyway, it'll never show. I'm gonna give you the Ava Gardner Special, covers anything."

On the last night of shooting, I got lost between the cables and backdrops that bordered the soundstage. Scuffling, trapped between two exits I was unable to find, trying to make my way off the set, I ran back and forth until finally I emerged pouring sweat, with tears of frustration burning my eyes.

Christopher was waiting for me outside. He drove me home, where I proceeded to take a pill to relieve my exhaustion and then another to relieve the overactive state the first pill had produced so I could sleep. This combination of drugs played Ping-Pong in my brain. Neither asleep nor awake, I sat in the warm water of my bathtub and scribbled with an eyebrow pencil on the back of a magazine, "SOS *from a Drowning Girl, She Dog-Paddled to Safety.*"

> I love him and he
> Says he loves me.
> We'll all be dead soon
> Him and I—Hymn and me.
> Help.

As if in answer, my father arrived in California to attend an Actors Studio party. I had been bombarding my parents with late-night calls, accusing, begging, questioning. They had been patient, tolerant—they did not hang up on me. I suspected my mother had insisted he see us to try to find out what was happening to me. Perhaps to convince me to come home.

We were to meet my father at the party. We arrived when it was almost over. My face was swollen from crying; Christopher and I had been quarreling, as usual. My father drew Christopher aside as if to admonish him. Chris flinched and moved away.

My father came up to the house later that evening. Christopher began to talk about his theories about Jesus. He was no match for my father, so he switched to a more personal attack, and before I realized what was happening, he and Lee were raging at one another while I sat almost ignored. It was hopeless to argue; we were living in a wasteland where reason had no credentials, but at least my father tried. I could not thank him, but I was grateful and knew that he had not forsaken me.

Christopher and I decided it was time to return East. He wanted a new car for the trip. I cashed in some more of my stocks and bought him a Corvette Stingray. The trip was uneventful until in Pennsylvania, trying to avoid a truck careening on the icy roads, we were driven off the side of the highway, where we became stranded in a snowdrift. It was hours before a truck pulled us out.

I found an apartment that overlooked the river in New York, in an old building with gargoyle carvings. I got my furniture out of storage. It was nice to see the things I cared for—the English swan daybed, the Louis Quinze desk, my Rembrandt, old friends, survivors of other eras.

We had traveled, but nothing had changed but the scenery.

Christopher and his friends had decided to take LSD. My friend Lisa and I were just going to observe. I had learned part of my lesson.

Lisa was a bright, attractive lab technician; her husband was a makeup man and very heavily into drugs. He and his brother, James, a successful painter, and his lover, Tony, with Christopher rounding out the group, were going to be the active participants.

We decided to use the house on Fire Island. It was private, deserted in the winter, and the more experienced in the group said they had found that the country helped produce a more positive trip, away from the chaotic influence and "vibes" of the city.

With Helen Hayes in *Time Remembered*, 1957.

Opening night tears after *Time Remembered*, 1957.

With Richard Burton in *Time Remembered* . . .
. . . Onstage, *left*; offstage, *below*.

Surprise twentieth birthday party, 1958. *Left to Right*, Richard Burton, Franchot Tone, Susan, Henry Fonda, Peter Ustinov. *Below:* Sunday brunch around the Strasbergs' kitchen table, 1958. *Top left to right*, playwright Louis Peterson, Susan, Richard Burton.

With Peter Ustinov, Laurence Olivier, and Douglas Fairbanks, Jr. at Olivier's party on the *Knickerbocker*, 1958. *Below:* With Vivien Leigh and Marilyn Monroe at an Actors Studio fundraising benefit, 1959.

Europe, 1959/1960. *Left:* Just before leaving; *below:* Shopping in Rome in her first Chanel suit.

Opposite: In front of a poster for *Kapo* at the Venice Film Festival.

With Clark Gable on the set of *The Misfits*, 1961.

With the family on the way to an Actors Studio benefit, 1963.

At baby shower, 1966. *Above, left to right:*
Rudolf Standish, Susan, Johnny, Paula and
Lee. *Right:* With Christopher.

STEFFI SIDNEY

In the hospital after Jennifer's birth, 1966. *Below:* With Christopher and Jennifer, 1966.

With Christopher and Jennifer on the set of *Chubasco*, 1966.

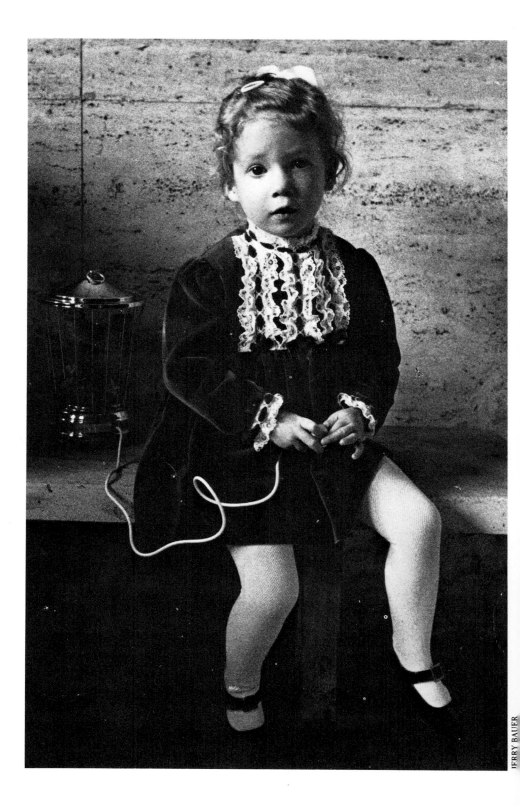

CURT GUNTHER/CAMERA 5

Opposite: Jennifer in Rome on her fourth birthday, 1970.

With Jennifer in Malibu, 1973.

In the hospital the day before Jennifer's open heart surgery, Texas, 1971. *Below:* With Jennifer in California, summer 1979.

California, summer 1979. *Front row, left to right,* David and Adam, Susan's half brothers; *back row,* Susan, Jennifer, Lee and Anna. *Below:* With Lee and Anna at an Actors Studio benefit, 1979.

Now . . .

It was freezing cold when we got to the dock. There were no ferries running, but we found a water taxi and paid him to take us out to the Island that night. He looked at us as if he knew but didn't care that we were all mad.

"You people aware there is no electricity?" he asked.

"Yeah."

"No hot water."

We nodded our heads. He shook his.

When we landed, we borrowed a red wagon someone had left at the pier to haul our groceries and overnight bags. The damp ocean air was incredibly cold; there was a wild, swirling wind. The house looked haunted, shutters closed.

The candles were lit. There was no wood to build a fire, so we went foraging, pulling the little red wagon behind us like kids.

"We better heat some water, keep it hot on the stove," someone said.

"No stove. It's electric."

"So we won't heat the water."

Everyone chose a room, staked out a territory. Lisa and I made a meal of sorts, sandwiches, milk, cookies. The little ivory box with the LSD capsules was produced; Lisa and I played happy stewardesses serving coffee, tea, and LSD.

After the acid was "dropped," the room grew quiet. We bundled into our blankets and sleeping bags, waiting expectantly— for what, we did not know. The air was charged with the energy this powerful hallucinogenic was releasing. Being in the room was enough to draw you into the vortex of the experience.

Years before on Fire Island, in my teens, my brother and I had waited for a hurricane to strike. We could sense it in the air long before we saw or felt it.

Tony, the painter's friend, began to get nervous. "It's been so long . . . I don't feel anything." He was a sensitive young man who, under the best of conditions, was prone to hysteria. For him to feel nothing promised danger. He went over to James. "I love you," he said. The painter turned away from him. Tony looked hurt and wandered into the bedroom. He emerged fifteen or twenty minutes later turning like a whirling dervish in my high heels and lipstick, incoherently talking about James's rejection of him.

We were horrified. "He's freaked out. Somebody should smack him, bring him down before he hurts himself."

"We should have known he'd go on a bad trip."

We appealed to him, shook him, tried to make contact. Finally Lisa embraced him, and her touch calmed him down. Quieter now, he informed us he was turning into a giant phallus. When that passed, he fell asleep for a while.

James withdrew into himself, meditatively watching the excited waves through the window. Christopher walked over, and standing behind him, whispered, "You really want to go into the ocean, don't you? It's beautiful. Admit it. You want to."

Christopher was very, very contained and quiet. He seemed to be taking in everything, watching, waiting. I could no longer stand the tension and walked outside, down the steps to the beach. Although it was night, the sky was not black, but a pale shimmering gray. The air was alive, dancing, moving in tiny particles in front of my eyes, as if it had form and body. I decided I must be hallucinating. The clouds began to disintegrate, and as I looked up at the sky beginning to fall on me, I realized it was snowing.

"Come quickly, quickly, it's the most beautiful thing I've ever seen," I shouted.

The water and snow were interchangeable liquid softness. It was as if I had become the snow, the sand, the ocean. I danced on the beach, embracing Christopher and my friends. We all cavorted, falling into the snow, rolling in it, laughing. This was a "good" trip for the most part.

Less than a year after this night, Tony was arrested after running up to a policeman half-naked, high on LSD, saying, "Beat me, please, help me!" He was taken to Bellevue, and after his release he spent years alternating between drugs and alcohol, finally going cold turkey one year after three successive crashes on his motorcycle, the last into a police car. He spent weekends in jail and began to put his life back together.

Four years later, Lisa's husband was found shot dead in the

streets of uptown New York. It was rumored he had been dealing in drugs, and they found needle marks on his arms.

But I was unable to see into the future, and Christopher persuaded me to join him and a friend on a trip just two months later. "It'll be like Fire Island, a good trip." So we sat in a small Italian restaurant, adding our own mushrooms to the spaghetti sauce. I refused to take LSD; peyote at least was not a chemical.

Two or three hours afterward, Christopher, Billy, a friend of his, and I were in a Brooklyn park getting ready to dive into a lake in our swimsuits. It was ten above zero and we had drawn quite a crowd. One gentleman with a cigar was skeptical. "Naw, they ain't gonna do it."

"Oh, yes, we are," I said.

He started taking bets. "What are the odds? They're never gonna do it."

"Who's going first?"

The three of us looked at one another. Everyone hesitated.

"Christ almighty, it's as cold as a witch's tit," Christopher said.

I looked at the two men. "Cowards," I called, and dived into the freezing water.

"Son of a bitch, she did it!"

I laughed, so numb I couldn't feel anything.

Afterwards, almost morning, we drove down to the Fulton Fish Market and waited for it to open to buy fresh fish, which we cooked for breakfast with noodles. An hour later I was lying on a bathroom floor regurgitating what looked like snakes moving and hissing.

Just a short week after this experience a young actor who was involved with a very sophisticated New York homosexual crowd killed himself during a trip. He was at a party on the eighth-floor terrace of someone's apartment; everyone was high on pills, peyote, and liquor. He had been standing on the terrace looking at the lights of the city, toying with some tiny dried flowers. As his friends watched stunned, he simply stepped off the terrace and fell eight stories to the street below, never crying out. When the police pried his clenched hand open, he still held those tiny flowers. He had said to me once, "We're the last of the flower children, Susan."

195

It was too dangerous; each high was followed by an enormous low. We rode the roller coaster, up and down, with no safety bars, leaving it to fate. I realized that I could not go on like this. There was nothing to hold on to, nothing stood still, nothing was real. It would have been easy to go insane if I was not already, and there was always a threat of violence under the surface. We clung to one another as drowning people, pulling each other down. I thought of ways to tell Christopher that I could not go on any longer, but was terrified of confronting him alone, not knowing how he would react.

One night we were driving down the West Side Highway going much too fast. We were both miserable.

"I don't make you happy, let's separate," I said at last. "Why should we stay together when we're both so miserable?"

I don't remember whether he or I opened the door, but the next moment I was halfway out of the door, dragging one foot on the freeway, clinging to the handle.

When we got home, Christopher took out his revolver. "I could shoot you." He pointed it.

"But you wouldn't."

He fired. I closed my eyes, tightening my whole body, hearing the bullet tearing, ripping the surface.

"You have to learn to trust me," he said.

The English Regency desk, bought with the first money I'd earned, was smashed through, leaving a jagged hole. The desk was intact, but a part of me was being smashed, too.

Christopher and I walked in the park looking for four-leaf clovers. Christopher found not one, but two.

"You've got good eyes," I said. "You found your luck today." I took a deep breath. "Christopher, we've got to separate, we can't be together right now. I can't go on, forgive me, I can't, I just can't."

He turned on me. "Here, you can have the four-leaf clovers. You can put them between glass and wear them."

"They're yours, I don't want them, Christopher."

"Run back to Mommy and Daddy, to the bourgeois world, but they ain't gonna destroy me and you'll never make it alone."

"Maybe you're right. But I've got to go anyway."

Let him have the last word; anything to avoid the explosion I knew was going to come. I would swear that the moon was made of green cheese or that I was Medusa.

In the end I was the one to explode. "Don't touch me, don't come near me. Never, ever, ever, ever touch me again. I never want to see or speak to you again." The words came from my stomach, and my ferocity caught him unaware.

He stormed out of the apartment, shouting, "I'll be back when you come to your senses."

The shattering of my desk, the feeling of my foot dragging on that freeway, all the broken pieces, I could not bear it.

In my desperation I called Dr. Mann. I could not face the prospect of exposing the horrors of my life to a stranger. Having seen him in an all-too-human light in Rome, I felt he would be less likely to pass judgment upon me. He was pleased to hear from me and shocked when I told him of the life I had been leading with Christopher.

He stroked his beard. I sat facing him in a straight-backed chair. chair.

"I'd like to meet the young man. Do you think there is any possibility you'll continue this relationship?"

"This is the last try. If this doesn't work, I've got to end it."

"Why don't you ask him to come in with you later in the week? Susan, even without the drugs you're a highly suggestible personality. It's also part of what makes you a good actress. Whether or not you're aware of it, during your drug experience, you were being brainwashed."

He seemed fascinated by the details of our relationship. He asked me about Christopher's background, his temperament.

"I've never run across a classic example like this," he mused.

"An example of what?" I inquired.

"*Folie à deux*, they call it."

"Translated literally?" I asked.

He nodded, "Yes."

"*Madness for two*. It sounds better in French, romantic . . . in English it sounds sordid."

Christopher agreed to an appointment with the doctor, which

surprised me, since he despised the psychiatric profession. He knew about the Roman episode, so in addition to that, he had contempt for the man he was going to see, which perhaps is why he agreed to see him.

The meeting was a fiasco. Christopher confused the issue immediately by demanding, "Before we talk, I want to know one thing. Do you believe in God?"

Like a rabbit into a snare, as soon as Dr. Mann tried to answer, he was caught. He didn't know that Christopher was capable of taking either side. They began arguing heatedly. By the time Christopher began on Nietzsche, whom he greatly admired— "Women was God's second mistake"—they had forgotten I was in the room.

"Who was his first? Anyway, Nietzsche died insane," I said in a small voice.

Christopher was giving Dr. Mann just enough rope to hang himself. There was no right or wrong. It was who had the most conviction, the most passion, the loudest voice. The two men, one bearded, in a suit and tie, the other in jeans, long hair, and a leather jacket, stood toe-to-toe shouting at each other.

Ignored, I sat in the chair. It was my life they argued away. Heads or tails, you get her—I sought help elsewhere.

I called my parents and then my friend Ralph Roberts, who came to stay with me. I double-locked the door.

Christopher tried to break it down later that night. Finally, his energy spent, he left. I lay in the dark wondering how long it would take for him to realize that it was over. I had reached a turning point.

Once again fate intervened. My agent called, "Can you be in London for dinner tomorrow night with Dirk Bogarde? He'd like to meet you about a part in his next film."

"Of course," I said. "Of course."

"The producers will give you a round-trip ticket and arrange for a hotel."

I was galvanized into action, thank God. I took a small bag with a change of clothes, a green suit from Italy, with a hand-knit cape with long fringe. The film was called *The High Bright Sun*. It was about an American girl of Cypriot descent who was caught in the escalating war between Cyprus and Greece.

Dinner went well, and I was offered the part, which I accepted gratefully. It was the best medicine I could have.

Back in New York I went to a doctor to have an insurance physical. He took my pulse. "Could you jump off the table, please," he asked. I did, again. "Your pulse is so low I can hardly feel it," he said.

"I have very low blood pressure," I said. "At least I'll never die of a heart attack."

He weighed me. "Are you always this thin?" I looked at the scale: 90 pounds.

"No, but actually I've been very nervous lately, doctor, and under a great deal of pressure."

He looked me up and down. "You're really in atrocious shape," he said. "You're barely certifiable. Do you think you can gain some weight and relax before you start work?"

"Yes, yes. It's very important to me to do this film. I'll do anything I have to. It's just, I have no appetite."

"Drink milk shakes with egg in them," he said. "That's a good beginning. Eat custard, rice pudding."

He was prescribing baby food.

That night Christopher came to the door of the apartment again, and when I refused to open it, screamed obscenities at me for almost an hour.

The next day when I left the house he was waiting for me. I ran to a taxi, but he followed me to the theater where my father was rehearsing *The Three Sisters* for a London production.

Christopher stormed onto the stage after the rehearsal. I was waiting for my father with Marty Fried, who was the stage manager. The two men moved between us as Christopher headed for me. My father turned color, the cords of his neck popping out. He and Chris looked as if they were going to kill one another. Marty kept them from physical violence, and somehow no one was hurt. This was the way I had longed to be protected as a little girl.

199

I left for London, leaving the past behind, hoping time would be kind and veil my memory.

After a week of preparation, the entire company left for locations in Foggia, Italy, a bleak town near Bari.

At night I lay in bed in the strange hotel room, touching myself tenuously, afraid that I would disappear. Amazingly, my body felt whole, unscathed. It responded slowly, coming alive to my touch. It had not died after all. I was surprised at my own resilience. I had thought of myself—and Christopher reinforced this conviction—as being weak. Now I felt strengthened by the experiences I had gone through. They were a terrible cleansing fire which I had come out of burned, but in one piece. I wrote to friends whom I hadn't spoken to in months: "I am still among the living and anxious to see you."

Dirk Bogarde was wonderful, as elegant a human being as he was an actor. He had brought his Rolls-Royce along with him to conquer the rutted peasant roads and to remind him, perhaps, of the civilized life we would return to. At first I thought of him as cold and indifferent, until I realized it was just the English accent. He would ring me up in the evening and say, "If you're lonely or have nothing to do, come out with us." I was grateful to him for his kindness.

I had bought books in London to read, anything on religion and history that was available, searching, I suppose, for metaphors that would correspond to my own *fall*.

Christopher wrote to me. At first I could not bear to read his letters; I couldn't even touch them, as if they were marked by his scent the way an animal leaves his trace. He justified the experiences we had gone through, oversimplified them, sometimes in his rambling capturing a glimpse of the truth.

"You must see nothing was done out of hate or indifference but out of love and the fear of love," he wrote. "I am no longer selfish, Susie. You will see this now or in three months. I will deal with my need while you are away. No matter what we have done, we will see the doing as fear. We were partners in fear."

In some of his letters he wrote long, seductive passages which repulsed and sickened me, ending with "I will come to you or you to me." I shuddered.

When we went back to London to finish the picture, I moved into the elegant Connaught Hotel, which until more recent years had had a strong aversion to actors.

Eli Wallach was staying there, and it was nice to see a familiar face. Rex Harrison had the suite next to mine, and I, coincidentally, became friendly with his son, Noel, and his wife, Sarah, who was a lovely blond ex-model, thin with piercing blue eyes, a horsewoman, sensitive and intelligent. Noel was fighting to establish his own identity as an actor, singer, and composer apart from his father. An attractive, bright couple, they had four beautiful children. I sat in their kitchen at their long monk's table for high teas or lunches, feeling I had reentered the normal world.

The car and driver from the studio would call for me at the hotel at 5:30 in the morning, and during the hour it took to reach the studio, I would sleep or study lines. One morning in a pungent English mist, my eyes still half-closed with sleep, I stepped through the front door of my hotel and a man's figure appeared before me. His face seemed enlarged, his head swollen out of proportion to his body. He had a bandage across his nose and was wearing a dark leather jacket. The mist cleared momentarily and I saw it was Christopher. We looked at one another silently.

Finally: "I sold the car you gave me to get here," he said. "I loved that car. Jesus, I've been running all over Europe trying to find you. I went to that hellhole Bari and they told me you'd gone to Napoli. I went to Napoli and they'd never heard of you. I had to see you, talk to you. You love me, you know you do."

I shivered, yet there was no chill in the air.

"Are you cold?" He leaned toward me but drew back upon seeing my involuntary retraction. He eyed me like a cameraman deciding where to put the light, how to adjust the lens. "Don't be frightened. I'm not going to hurt you anymore. I just want to be with you, near you. I've changed. You'll see."

How dare he? I wanted to scream because of his proximity. How dare he invade my world?

"I just want to talk to you," he said. "Let me ride to work with you. Did you get my letters?"

I was oppressed by his presence. And yet, because he was being charming, I seemed to have no logical reason to run. "Come on," I said.

Slowly, during the next few days, I became convinced that he had changed. Perhaps we could work things out; perhaps it was meant for us to be together. He seemed sincere and in pain, vulnerable again. I began to empathize with him.

He came to the studio with me every day. At first I sat huddled in a far corner of the car, on the defensive. But as the days passed, my concern changed from protecting myself to protecting him. At night I would drop him off at his rooming house in Soho. One evening he asked me if I wanted to see his room. Telling the driver to wait, I entered the shabby old London boardinghouse. As I looked at him in this down-at-the-heels room, I suddenly thought: This is no way for him to live, he must have silk shirts and cashmere coats. And I would give them to him.

That evening he moved into the Connaught Hotel with me. He came through the revolving door into the impeccable English lobby in his leather jacket and blue jeans, his shirt open to his navel. I was afraid they wouldn't let him in. The manager approached me, and I introduced them. From his face as he looked at Christopher, it was obvious he thought Chris was beautiful. He was much nicer to him than he had been to me.

We lunched at Dirk Bogarde's home in the country, spent Sundays at the Harrisons'. Things seemed more normal than they had ever been between us. We actually seemed to be getting on. We were less wary of each other, and there were no fights. I had a week off, and we decided to go to the south of France. Dirk gave us the name of a little hotel outside St. Tropez overlooking the sea.

We rented a little Citroën and drove down the beautiful winding coast. That trip to St. Tropez belonged to the should-have-been time or the might-have-been. We were ourselves but not ourselves. We were close but not in that parasitic, suffocating way.

We talked, and realizing we didn't agree and never could on some things, decided to just avoid those areas.

I lay on the beach and got my first tan in ten years, eating sardine sandwiches, drinking the red wine, going out to sea in a little pedal boat and drifting for hours. We felt we had conquered ourselves. We had paid our dues; now the future would belong to us.

As my film ended, Christopher received a cable from his agent in New York, and then a phone call. "Twentieth Century-Fox wants you to star in *Jesse James*, the TV series you tested for before you left. It's urgent that you arrive as soon as possible." This was the first time since we had been together that he would have a job. It's going to be different, I thought, I know it is. He will work and I won't threaten him. Let him be the wage earner, I don't care that much about acting.

We flew to California when my film finished, stopping in New York to close up my apartment.

The first day Christopher went to work at the old Twentieth Century-Fox ranch in Malibu, I watched as he leaped off his horse, ran in his cowboy boots behind the rocks, drew his gun, and pointed it at the villain. His childhood dreams had come true.

"Bang-bang," he said as he pulled the trigger.

"You don't have to say 'bang-bang,' Christopher, they put the sound in for you."

The unaccustomed discipline of his work took energy from him that previously would have been concentrated on our relationship, so I was free to play housewife, enjoying it. I loved to cook, I tried new recipes. I would arrange flowers, wax the furniture, singing, like the ads on television.

The series was not an unqualified success, but Christopher was. Within weeks after it had gone on the air, he was receiving more fan mail than any actor at Twentieth since Tyrone Power. The girls of America had affirmed my choice. He was feeling his oats, and I

203

hoped that his acceptance would give him the security that I didn't seem to be able to.

We rented a house belonging to Sir Cedric Hardwicke's widow in one of the canyons of Los Angeles. It was one of those Hansel-and-Gretel homes with a lumpy crooked roof which someone must have thought was charming fifty years before. Two stories high, it felt cozy though a little claustrophobic, set as it was close against the hill with the canyon wall rising in the back. It was fully equipped with all the conveniences, including a ghost Christopher insisted he had seen and talked to.

I refused to believe him until the owner's son came by to pick up something he had left and asked, "By the way, have you seen the lady who haunts the upstairs room?"

Vindicated, Christopher began a "love affair" with the lady in white. "She adores me, she can't stand you. She's jealous. She told me to get rid of you."

He could not move a real woman into the house, so she became my rival in this odd *ménage à trois*—me, him, and the ghost.

The precarious razor-edge balance that we had created demanded too much energy. No one could really change, shazam, overnight, and more and more jarring notes from the past crept into our relationship.

Christopher's friend Billy came to stay with us, although, like "the man who came to dinner," it was a very extended visit. I could not stand him. He was heavily involved in drugs and there was something in the nature of his personality that repulsed me. He had an aura of evil about him. I was not sure whether this destructiveness was directed at himself or others. He cared about Christopher but at the same time was violently jealous of him and of our relationship. He was a terrible influence on Chris, egging him on to irresponsible acts. They would disappear for hours, returning in the morning "wiped out."

It was during this time we visited a psychic. We were sitting in the kitchen, and I caught her staring at me. "Give me something of yours," she said.

"Like what?"

"Oh, your ring, that's fine."

She held it over my forehead. "Well, dear, there's a female soul awaiting entry over your head. You're going to have a daughter. She's waiting to come in."

"Not over my head." I laughed uneasily. "I'm not planning on getting pregnant. It's impossible. I'm very careful."

"My dear child," she said, "if it's meant to be, it's meant to be. Anyway, she's up there waiting for you."

Several months passed, and I began to feel queasy. I was sleeping more than usual and my appetite was erratic. When I missed a period, I went to Christopher's doctor in Beverly Hills.

"I think it's just nerves," I said. "I missed one period, but I've been late before. Isn't there a shot you can give to bring it?"

"Is there any possibility you could be pregnant?"

"Absolutely not," I said.

He injected me, but after three days there was still nothing. I remembered the psychic holding my ring over my forehead, intoning, "There is a female soul awaiting entry over your head." Home, I thought, I want to go home. I want to see my mother.

In New York Mother arranged for me to see a gynecologist. He came into the room to announce the results of the tests. "Congratulations on your pelvis," he said. "For a little girl, you're going to be a great childbearer."

A child. *I* am a child, I thought, but I was approximately two months pregnant. That night in my parents' home, unable to sleep, I wandered through the long corridor to the kitchen, into my father's den filled with Japanese costumes, books, records, theater medallions, and actor's masks from all over the world. I looked out at Central Park and the lake, a view that usually calmed me, but this night it appeared to me like a backdrop in a Hollywood movie, flat, two-dimensional.

I flew back to California and told Christopher. "What are we going to do?" I asked.

"Well, I guess you're going to have the baby."

"That's it?"

"That's it," he said.

A week later, Christopher came home late from work. He was arriving later and later. I would sit alone, dinner waiting cold on the table, trying not to listen for the car. That night when he walked in I was sitting on the bed reading the Bible, tears cascading down my cheeks.

"What's the matter, for Christ's sake?"

"I want to get married. I think we should get married," I managed to get out through my sobs.

"Okay," he said, "we should." His Baptist upbringing was bothering him, as was my Jewish one. "When?"

"This weekend."

"We'll do it."

Just like that.

I went to Jax and bought myself a short white jersey dress. I was determined to be married in white. I could barely close the zipper around my growing waistline but refused to buy the dress in a larger size. I was still only two and a half months pregnant. At Saks I bought myself a wedding band. At least I would not have to keep up with the Joneses anymore, I'd be the Joneses.

We discussed going to Reno but decided it would be quicker and easier to go to Las Vegas. After much deliberation, I made up my mind to wait until afterward to call my parents.

When we got to the clerk's office in Las Vegas, they asked for identification.

"God," Christopher said, "you're not going to believe this. I left my I.D. in Los Angeles."

"How could you? You did it deliberately."

"I swear I didn't, Susie. I forgot. Really."

"If you forgot, it was Freudian. You meant to forget."

"We'll have to come back next week."

That Friday after Christopher finished work, we tried again, accompanied by my Aunt Bea and Christopher's best friend, Billy. This time I had his papers in my purse. We checked into a small hotel on the Vegas Strip, changed clothes, and were off to find the justice of the peace. I had on a blue garter, a new dress, an old pair of shoes, something borrowed from my aunt, and was carrying a white Bible she had given me.

So on September 25, 1965, William Frank Jones and Susan Elizabeth Strasberg were married. "I'm going to marry that girl," he had prophesied to Shelley Winters two and one half years before. He had kept his word.

When the justice of the peace said, "Till death do you part," I felt a trembling in my legs that spread upward, erupting from my mouth as giggles. Christopher caught my eye and began to laugh too. "Till death do you part." We laughed until I cried.

We went back to the Stardust Motel, changed our clothes, and went gambling. I was uninterested, having taken enough of a gamble for one night. But my child would have a legitimate name.

Much later that evening—it was already morning in New York—I called my parents on Fire Island to tell them.

My mother answered the phone. "My darling girl, why haven't you called? I've been so worried about you. I've been thinking about it, Daddy and I would like you to come home—"

"Mother," I cut her off, "everything's going to be all right. Christopher and I got married. We're in Las Vegas."

She didn't say anything. Then: "Call your father. He's working in New York today."

"Mom, would you please do it for me? Christopher's waiting for me. I have to go now. Talk to you tomorrow. I just wanted you to know."

When my mother put down the phone, she let out a cry.

"What's the matter?" asked the friend who was with her.

"I hurt. I have such pain. My Susan married that boy, and no one told me. Why didn't they tell me?" She collapsed in tears and cried on and off for three days. Then she sat down and wrote Christopher a letter welcoming him to the family.

We had gone through a ceremony; I had changed my last name; there was a ring on my finger; yet everything was the same. I had expected that this contract would add a new dimension to our relationship. Now, I was just as unhappy, only I was unhappy and a Mrs.

One month after our wedding, during an argument, Christopher hit me, knocking me to the floor.

"Wait a minute," I said, "there's another life to think of now. You can't behave like this any longer."

He looked at me uncomprehendingly. "Is the baby all you can think about?" He seemed almost jealous.

Realizing the wedding had been an enormous mistake, I considered an annulment. I talked with a lawyer friend about it, and he thought it was possible.

"Will you broach it to Christopher?" I asked. "He should agree. He was never that anxious to get married in the first place."

Christopher was furious. "Never!" he declared. "Till death do us part," he said.

"We're not living in the Dark Ages. You were the one who didn't want to be married. Why can't you just admit it was a mistake?"

But he remained adamant. "That's *my* child you're carrying."

I decided to go home, to think, to rest, home again to Mama. That there was a baby growing inside me had never seemed real until now.

The first night in New York, I picked a book at random from the shelves lining the walls of the back bedroom. Books now spilled over onto the floors, into the bathroom, the bedside table. I chose Jung's *Man and His Symbols*. After reading and rereading it until the sky began to pale, outlining the skyscrapers of New York, I fell asleep and dreamed.

I carried my small dog, Camille, in my arms. Christopher and I were racing through a jungle, being chased by savages who would destroy us if they could. We came to a large, seemingly impassable bramble bush, and I turned to Christopher.

"On the other side of this barrier is the water, and at the water we can drink, we'll be safe."

"But there are beasts at the water's edge," he protested.

"Yes, but there's enough water for everyone, and they won't harm us there. You've got to press this button, and it will trigger the fuses I've set throughout this jungle to blow it up, destroy the natives, and we will be safe."

"I can't do it," he answered.

"Then I will."

I took the fuse box and detonated it. As the explosion took place, I threw my dog over the bramble bush into the water and then leaped over myself and fell into those clear waters, holding my dog in my arms.

I awoke knowing somehow it was right for me to have this baby and that, if within one year our relationship had not radically improved, I would leave him. For now, it was only a dream. I was still incapable of carrying it out.

The next five months passed quickly. I made no conscious effort to be or do anything. For the first time in my life I felt totally justified for what I was, not for what I did.

Once back in California, I could not bear to take even an aspirin, and the smell of marijuana made me violently ill; I grew round and soft and more sensual, happy and magnanimous in my sense of well-being. Feeling like this, I would surely envelop not just my baby but also Christopher in my infectious joy. I would wait and give him time.

The days passed quickly at first, but as I grew heavier, more lethargic, the time too seemed to weigh upon me, and I was anxious to have my baby.

Jesse James was coming to the end of its first season. Twentieth Century-Fox decided to send Christopher and Alan Case, his costar, on a publicity tour of the country to build the ratings in the event the show was picked up for the next season.

"Why don't I meet you in New York?" I suggested.

The tour through Texas, the Midwest, and the Southeast by train was not really a trip I looked forward to making.

"I won't go if you don't come with me," he said.

So, though preferring to stay home, I agreed to go. I cannot remember the names of the towns we went to or any of the faces of the people along the way. I only recall curling up and clinging to

209

the rungs of the berths of the trains we slept on at night, trying to make myself smaller to fit into the tiny, narrow beds. One night Christopher and I had to share a single berth. We slept head-to-toe, with my belly protruding over the side like a mountain through the curtains of our bed.

In one of these unremembered towns, Christopher disappeared. The publicist, Alan Case, and I waited for him to reappear. They talked about canceling the tour if he wasn't back by morning. When he finally turned up with no explanation, we continued on as if nothing had happened.

When we arrived in New York, my mother announced that she was giving me a baby shower. In our living room, she gathered over one hundred people who supported me with their love and friendship, as well as more tangible proofs of their affection. Champagne flowed. My mother moved about barefoot in a loose dress, laughing, from group to group. She was so alive that day, she glittered and crackled.

Renewed, carrying some gifts in my arms (the others were being sent), I boarded the plane eight and a half months pregnant.

Home in Los Angeles, I went to bed for three weeks. The trip by train, Christopher's disappearance, the huge shower my mother had given me, had drained me, and I had picked up a bug of some sort. So now in my ninth month of pregnancy, I ate and slept and read and slept, waiting in a state of suspended animation. Spider, our cat, lay on my pillow, wrapping herself in my long hair, sucking her tail like a baby.

On March 14 at 2:30 A.M. I woke out of a deep sleep. I had been dreaming of swimming in the ocean but found myself lying on the bed, my legs bathed in liquid. I didn't know if I was really awake or still asleep until I realized that my water had broken. Christopher panicked when I awakened him.

"It's all right," I reassured him. "My contractions are far apart. We've got time. If you get hysterical, I'll get hysterical. Where's my comb?" I shouted at him. "I need my comb."

"Let me get it for you. Lie down. Don't move."

210

"I'm not moving, I'm having a baby and I want to comb my hair."

"Oh, Jesus Christ," he said.

When we checked into the hospital an hour later, it seemed as if the whole world had decided to have a baby at the same time. It was bedlam. Because there were so many people, the nurses did not prep me totally, but I didn't know the difference.

The woman next to me was breathing deeply and evenly, clinging to her husband's hand. I regretted not having trained for natural childbirth. Even if Christopher had not come with me, I should have done it on my own. Perhaps I still could. I looked at her and tried to synchronize my breaths with hers.

They moved me to a private room, where Christopher came to see me. He stood well back from the bed, as if he were afraid I would burst and inundate him.

"I have to go to work," he said.

"It's four in the morning. You don't have to go to work until seven-thirty."

"It's the last day, I should be early."

"There's not even anyone there at four in the morning," I said, reaching a hand out toward him. "Christopher, don't go to work. Please don't leave me alone. Stay with me."

"You know I can't."

"Then at least go in a little later."

"They don't give a damn about this baby," he said, "they just want to finish filming. I'd stay if I could, you know that, but I don't have a choice."

When he left, I realized vaguely that it was all somehow too much for him, but I really didn't want to be alone. Time passed. I couldn't tell if it was minutes or hours. I heard moaning, an occasional scream filtering through the thin walls.

A nurse who came in to check me explained, "She's just screaming because she's frightened. It doesn't hurt that much."

Bitch, I thought to myself. It does hurt. I'm hurting. But she had made me ashamed to call out. They gave me a mild tranquilizer, which made me groggy but didn't stop the pains from becoming sharper and more insistent, worse than I thought they would be. Afraid I was going to scream, I rang for the nurse. "I need more medication now. He, my doctor, said I could have medication when I need it."

Another nurse came into the room. "Now, dear, you're going to have to push a lot harder."

"What about my medication?" I asked.

"You push harder and we'll see."

I breathed as deeply as I could, and as the breath seeped out of me, I released the pain together with the air and drifted into another part of my room. My consciousness seemed to hover over my own head. I knew there was pain in my body, but I was not in that body until the sharp cramp searing across my abdomen again, pulled me back to reality. This painless state was as real to me as the presence of the pain.

"Oh, my God," the nurse said, "did they forget? You just wait, I'm going to get a bedpan."

"I'm not waiting for the damn bedpan," I said. "I'm trying to have my baby. Why is this taking so long? It's taking too long. Why hasn't my doctor sent me medication?"

"Your doctor's not here yet, dear."

"I'm not dear, I'm in pain and you're lying. He's standing right outside my door. I can feel him standing there. You promised," I shouted toward the door. I was angry and didn't give a damn who knew it.

Later, when he came into the room, he said to me sheepishly, "How did you know I was standing outside the door earlier?"

I didn't reply.

"Susan, we have a slight problem here. I can't give you any more medication. We need you to be wide-awake and alert. You're going to have to push harder. The baby's head isn't in quite the right position, and if you push very hard, there's a chance it will correct itself naturally. By the way, your mother called. She said to tell you she loves you and that if she weren't very sick, she'd be here."

212

How can she be sick when I need her? I screamed silently. She's shared almost everything else in my life, I'm finally willing to let her share this—my pain. I had no way of knowing she was bearing her own pain as I was bearing my child.

"Please, what time is it? Where's Christopher? It's been so long, why isn't he here?"

"He's still at work," someone answered. "Your aunt and your friend Mr. Roberts are outside."

My Aunt Bea and Ralph cornered the pay phone in the lobby and set up a relay system. One held the booth while the other went to find out what the latest progress report was, and then that information was relayed long distance to my parents.

"I should be there," my mother kept saying to them. "If you don't think I wouldn't rather be there than anyplace else on earth. She needs me, I know she needs me."

More than twelve hours passed. I had pushed until I was lost in the steady syncopation of pain, breath, push. Suddenly, I started to laugh.

"What is it, dear?" the nurse asked.

I shook my head as the next pain hit. It had just crossed my mind that this was what was meant by "when push comes to shove."

Finally they wheeled me into the delivery room. Now that I no longer cared, when my pain and I had become friends, they gave me an injection which numbed me from the waist down. I was wide-awake but unable to see what was going on between my legs. It seemed absurd that I should not be allowed to observe what was happening.

Before I saw her, I heard a cry. A high, sweet, piercing sound. My baby was crying, and then they told me, "It's a girl." I smiled. She had this little cap of strawberry-blond hair covering her head, and she was all milky white. I looked up at the clock on the wall: exactly 4:43 P.M.

"She's so beautiful," I said. "Isn't she beautiful?" As I looked at her I felt a wave of tenderness pass through me. Her skin was glowing almost phosphorescently under the burning overhead

213

lights. Her tiny hands were knotted together like a boxer's. The psychic had been right. There had been a female soul awaiting entry over my head.

They took me to a flower-filled hospital room. "I'd like to hold my baby now." The nurse left without saying anything.

When the doctor came into the room, he was blandly reassuring. "Susan, now it's nothing to get upset about, we just want to examine her a little more thoroughly. She has a slight problem. She has a partial cleft palate. That's the soft part of the throat where the uvula hangs down."

He spelled it out for me, simply, as if I were a child who didn't quite speak the language, which was true in a way. "Don't be upset, slight problem." I did not understand.

"What does that mean?" I demanded.

"Eventually, she'll be operated on. For the moment she's probably going to have difficulty feeding. It's pointless to try to nurse her. With that piece missing, she'll never be able to get enough suction to draw milk from your breast."

I wanted to hold my baby now, immediately. I knew that the touch of her would assuage my fears.

"She's in a special-care ward, Susan," he said. "She's going to need constant watching. She has to be on her stomach for the next few days. If she were to roll on her back, she might choke on her own saliva. But she really is the prettiest baby in the nursery."

The baby and I had been so self-contained, invulnerable against the world. Now, suddenly separated, we were exposed, prey to life.

Christopher came in a few hours later. When he kissed me, I could smell the alcohol on his breath.

"I had to stay and have a drink with the crew. You look terrific."

We both knew he was lying. I could feel the swelling in my eyelids, the tears puffing up my face. The phone rang.

"Mother . . . yes . . . yes, everything's fine . . . no, I'm fine . . . I don't know . . . Katherine or Elizabeth, maybe Jennifer. Then she'd be the *real* Jennifer Jones."

"I'm sending your brother out on the next plane," Mother said. "What do you want from New York?"

"I want a whole chocolate roll from the Ginger Man. It's my favorite dessert in the world."

"You'll have it tomorrow morning," she said. "What else do you need?"

What I needed she couldn't give me. I needed for Christopher and I to love each other. I needed for my baby to be in my arms, healthy and whole.

Then they brought in Jenny and I saw that she was truly beautiful. Her huge eyes looked at me briefly before she closed them and fell asleep in my arms.

"I'd like to try to nurse her," I said, pulling open my gown.

"But the doctor said it was impossible."

"I want to at least try."

I held my baby close to my breast, trying to place the nipple in her tiny rosebud of a mouth. The nurse sharply flicked her fingers against the baby's bare feet.

"What are you doing?" I asked. "You're hurting her."

"Well, she can't nurse if she's asleep, can she?"

For a few moments I tried to pump the milk into her now half-open mouth.

"Really," the nurse said, "you'll feel much better if you'll just let me give you some pills to dry up your breasts."

I saw Jennifer Robin, as we decided to name her—Robin was after Christopher's mother—five times a day, right on hospital schedule. She was always slightly drowsy, and just as we began to make contact, it seemed it was time for her to be taken back to her crib.

On the third day, Christopher barreled into my room and starting flinging my clothes into a suitcase. "We're getting out of this fucking place."

"Why? What's happened? What's the matter?"

"They almost killed my kid," he said. "They almost killed her."

A half-hour before, Christopher and his makeup man, Bob, from the show, whose wife was having a baby in the same hospital, went to see Jenny. Christopher left him gazing at the babies to come to see me. As Bob watched, Jenny had rolled over on her back and begun to cry and cough. This was exactly what this

215

intensive-care ward was to guard against, but apparently the nurse had stepped out for a moment, and that was all it took. Unattended, the baby began to turn red, then blue. Bob ran to get the head nurse, who called for emergency equipment. They had to put a pump down her throat to remove the fluid she was choking on.

I got out of bed to go to see Jennifer, who was sleeping now with her hands in an elegant position, little finger and forefinger raised into the air, two middle fingers secure in her mouth. I looked at the glaring overhead lights, the rows of sleeping babies. It looked like a huge mechanical hatchery. I felt responsible for what had happened. I had briefly thought of finding a hospital where they would allow me to room-in after I had the baby, but the doctor made me feel it was so unreasonable and unnecessary that I had dropped the idea.

My brother, who had arrived from New York, was waiting for us at the house with Katie, the baby nurse who was going to help me take care of Jenny during the next weeks. Katie was a minor miracle. Tall, almost six feet, and kind, with sparkling eyes behind her thick glasses. When I told her I felt a disaster as a mother, she assured me she'd seen a lot worse.

Jennifer had eating problems. She could not get enough suction to take more than an ounce of milk an hour. At the end of two hours and two ounces we were all tired and frustrated. In a few days she began to lose weight, and we rushed to the doctor, who told us there was a special nipple with a rubberized attachment that would block the passageway to the part of the throat that was missing. We bought one, but it did not work, and over the next few days we watched her melting away from a sizable seven pounds, six ounces to seven pounds, to six pounds, six ounces. She was listless and crying now, but so exhausted from the effort she had to expend to eat that she would quickly fall asleep.

Finally Christopher said, "What the hell, those doctors don't know anything. It's my kid."

He went into the kitchen, got a pair of scissors, and proceeded to cut a large hole in all the nipples on her bottles. At the next feeding, we tried one, and it worked, though we had to be careful to

216

hold her up enough so the milk didn't pour down her throat too quickly, because then she spit it up through her nose. She was drinking three ounces in one hour now, and we were jubilant.

"To Dr. Kildare," we toasted.

Jenny steadily began to gain weight, and Katie left to go to another baby, as our girl was too grown-up for her at three weeks old.

She slept at the foot of our bed in a Tibetan cradle, enameled in burnished orange and gilt, and hung with good-luck pieces that dangled above her head. My friend Valerie, who presented it to us, described it as a cradle of princes that would bring blessings on the child who sleeps in it.

Soon after I got home, I called Franca Moore, an astrologer Jess Stearn had recommended, to have Jennifer's chart drawn up. She knew nothing of her throat condition, she had only the time and date of her birth, but when the chart was ready, she announced, "This child was born under a square, it is a learning pattern for mother and child. There is some affliction in the throat and chest areas, which will affect the extremities, causing deficiencies, shortage of oxygen, breathing problems. This condition will lift completely when the child is six years old."

She was correct about the throat area, but the doctors had not indicated problems as serious as she had described, and Jenny's throat would be repaired, hopefully, when she was between two and four years old. Six years was a way off. No one was right one hundred percent of the time, so I thanked Franca and put it out of my mind.

A call came in midmorning from my father and mother's business manager in New York, David Cogen. "You and Johnny had better get back here immediately . . . today. Your mother hasn't much time. Why the hell aren't you here?"

My mother was dying. In my roles, I had played at life and death, but I was totally unprepared for the reality.

"But I spoke to Pop last week and he said there was no need to come home. He didn't indicate that she was that sick. I had no idea it was this serious."

Although I had no conscious recognition of the severity of my mother's illness, I had smelled my mother's cancer over the past ten years. Whenever she embraced me, I had to stop myself from pulling away from that odor. I couldn't know that it was death, her body eating itself. She smelled it, also, and took to bathing and perfume several times a day.

I made reservations on the evening flight for Jenny, Johnny, and myself. I wanted my mother to see her only grandchild, to take pleasure in her. Perhaps it would give her new life.

That afternoon, Jenny and I went to her appointment with a new pediatrician recommended by Jennifer Jones. Jenny was just six weeks old. He was very down-to-earth and fatherly. He examined her silently, then looked at me, fondling the stethoscope in his hand.

"I know you plan to fly with this child, but it's really not advisable."

"But she's gained weight, she's eating now, sleeping well."

He looked at me measuringly. There was a silence, as if he was giving me time. "Didn't her doctor say anything about her condition when she was born?"

"Of course," I replied. "They told me about her cleft palate."

Another silence. Then he said to himself. "Well, perhaps they thought she'd outgrow it, some babies do."

I knew I was supposed to ask him what they thought she'd outgrow, but I could not.

"It's her heart. She has quite a severe murmur. Perhaps it was slighter when she was born, but at the rate she's registering now, unless she were tested first so that we knew exactly what's wrong with her, it could be dangerous to fly with her. Airplane cabins are pressurized to altitudes as high as five thousand feet. Her heart may not be able to bear that much stress."

I could hardly absorb what he was saying to me. I had so looked forward to seeing my mother holding my child in her arms.

As if to make things easier, he said, "A house with death is no place for a child this ill."

So I took Polaroid snapshots of my beautiful red-haired, milky-skinned daughter with such a fine translucent complexion that all her veins showed through. I had thought it was so lovely, not knowing it came from a shortage of oxygen created by her heart condition. Cyanosis is the medical term for it. There would be no way of knowing the details of her condition until I returned and had extensive tests done. There was no time now, I was afraid my mother would not wait for me.

I left Jennifer with her father and the young Scandinavian baby nurse who was living with us.

Johnny and I took the night flight to New York, the red-eye express. We arrived at Kennedy at six A.M. and by seven o'clock we were home. Although I had not lived there for over eight years, it was still home to me.

It was a cruel April day, the city was veiled with a thin cloak of luminous fog like a woman in mourning.

When my brother and I walked into my mother's bedroom, she sat up in bed, radiant like a candle that flares up before it goes out. Her honey-blond hair, shot through with gray, fell in a cascade down her back; she had on a white batiste nightgown. She looked like a child, flushed, gay. We had come back to her. Her babies had come home. It seemed impossible to me that she could look like this and really be dying. Perhaps they had made a mistake.

But within three hours, she was half-delirious, seeming not to know us. She brushed aside the photos of Jenny as if she had no time for them, plucking at the sheets of her bed, pulling at her gown as if she would rip it off. Although it was chilly, she seemed to want them off her body, as if they were placing an intolerable weight on her fragile bones.

"The window. I want the window open."

It was as if she would send her soul out the open window into the mist of the morning, as once she had threatened me, "I'm going to jump out this window. You'll all be sorry." There was no need to jump anymore.

Her lips were parched and cracking, and she continuously ran her tongue over them. She looked as if she had come across a desert. She was totally dehydrated and unable to draw any liquid

219

through the straw we held for her. She reminded me of Jenny's desperation when she was unable to draw milk from her bottle.

Her sister, my Aunt Bea, was there, too. She had received a call days before from my mother. "I'm in such pain, I'm desperately ill, and no one will believe me."

Why, I wondered, didn't she call me? It was true, each of her loved ones, for our own reasons, might not have believed her. She was the woman who had complained over so many years that when she was truly in pain, we had learned to no longer listen to her. My father, who had sat keeping vigil outside her room for months, nursing her himself, did not want to believe her. My brother and I, still swaddled by our need of her, were not ready to release her by believing her.

The ambulance came within the hour. I watched as they strapped her into the narrow cot. She seemed more helpless than my baby now, but where my child was fighting for her life, my mother was fighting to let go of hers. Aunt Bea and I sat in the back of the ambulance, trying not to hear the screaming siren. Hunched over, I tried to hold my mother's hand. There was no returning pressure, and I wondered if she knew it was me, that I was there. Every bump, every pothole made her moan and toss her head in protest at the pain, and now her hand gripped mine, clutching in a reflex action.

"Can't you give her something for the pain?"

"At the hospital. We're not authorized, lady."

It was rush hour, and we were caught in the stream of cars heading downtown over the bridge. The siren blared but, like a Fellini movie, the ambulance was immobilized by the traffic. Inside we sat, feeling the ambulance creep forward a few inches at a time, seeing the curious faces of the commuters glancing at the window, then quickly looking away. People don't like to linger on the face of death. My mother's pain rose and her cries became more insistent. The pain was worse than the dying.

Finally we arrived at the hospital. My aunt went straight to the head nurse on the floor. "My sister is screaming in agony. You've got to give her something immediately."

The nurse looked at the chart. "Her doctor's left no instructions about medication. As soon as he gets here, we'll take care of it."

I could hear my mother's voice at the other end of the corridor screaming at the nurses. "Get your goddamn hands off me, you bitch. Leave me in peace. For God's sake, you're hurting me. Please, don't touch me, don't move me. I'm in pain, please let me die." And then, "No, I won't have them, I don't want those tubes." I had never heard my mother curse before.

I moved to the doorway of her room, afraid to go in, and saw that they were trying to insert intravenous tubing and that as quickly as they slipped it in, my mother ripped it out.

"If you don't give my sister something, morphine, whatever she's been taking, if you don't ease her pain now before her doctor gets here," my aunt said to the nurse, "I will stand in the middle of the corridor and scream bloody murder and you will have to carry me out of here."

My aunt was tiny, but the force and rage contained in this statement made her seem enormous, powerful.

"All right," said the nurse, relenting, "I'll get one of the other doctors."

They gave my mother something, and the hallway grew still and quiet. My father and Johnny arrived with Marty Fried.

"Visiting hours are over," the nurse said.

How insane to have visiting hours for someone who was dying. Marty refused to go. "I'll just sit here outside her room a little longer," he said.

After we left, he conned his way into her room, saying he was a relative who had to go out of town that night. He was afraid it would be too late tomorrow. He took her hand, and she slowly opened her eyes.

"Marty," she said lucidly, "I have so much to do. I have to finish my book, and tomorrow I have . . ." Her voice trailed off and she fell back to sleep.

In the night, she died. Not of the cancer; her heart went into fibrillation caused by severe dehydration, and she suffered heart failure.

Mercifully, I was so numbed I could neither think nor feel. I could not bear this. My mother's heart, my child's heart.

People came to the house to help make decisions. Where will she be buried? When? In what? David Cogen got on the phone and bought four plots in Arlendale Cemetery on Long Island, one for each member of our family.

"Don't buy one for me. I'm going to be cremated," I stated. "And I want my ashes scattered over the ocean." They ignored me.

Should the coffin be open or closed? "Closed," my brother insisted.

"But people will want to see her."

"If they don't remember what she looked like when she was alive, that's their problem," he said.

I had brought a black dress with me knowing, I suppose, that she was truly going to die, and found my mother's black lace mantilla. We each bought one on a trip to Venice years before, fine delicate lace made by hand by the nuns. I put on my dark glasses but for the moment did not weep. I had no tears for my mother, I would not grieve for her. She could not leave me so suddenly. I was not ready.

At the funeral, when my father and I got out of the limousine, we found photographers and reporters surrounding the entrance to Riverside Memorial Chapel. Inside the chapel, I realized there was a "full house" for my mother, standing room only, from the young neophyte actors to the famous stars. It was like the guest list for one of her parties.

The service began; Shelley Winters spoke:

It's incredible to me she was so vital and now that woman is gone. What she gave to me and other Hollywood girls, the dignity she gave to us as artists and women. . . . Yesterday when they told me, my first thought was very selfish. I thought, there's no reason to live in New York anymore. Where do you go on New Year's Eve?

People laughed through their tears. In his eulogy, playwright Sidney Kingsley said:

Paula was the quintessence of Mama, she was Mother Hen, Mother Hubbard, Mother Goddamn, but most of all was Mother Courage . . . dragging her cart through the unending wars and tending her many children, not only Suzy Q and Johnny, her legitimates, but all us hordes upon hordes of adopted children she picked up off the battlefields on her long, hard march. And along this road she saw many of her golden children fall and die: John Garfield, Clifford Odets, and the beauteous drummer-girl, Marilyn Monroe. And she mourned them as her own, but she kept right on pulling the cart to the wars.

Among her friends, protégés, and co-workers who had come to pay respects, to say good-bye, were Anne Bancroft, Kim Stanley, Estelle Parsons, Harold Clurman, William Gibson, Arthur Penn, Senator and Mrs. Javits, Ellen Burstyn.

There were more than seven hundred people there that Sunday, May 1, 1966. Seven hundred people and yet she had been a lonely woman.

At the cemetery my brother scattered her favorite gardenia petals into the grave. I was still dry-eyed, but the heavens wept for me, a fine, cleansing rain which ran in rivulets down my cheeks.

The rabbi said, "We'd better leave." My brother stayed behind as we moved off, my father and I leaning on one another. When the rabbi saw my brother lingering at the graveside, he turned around as if he had made a mistake and started back, calling, "People, we're not leaving yet."

Did he know my brother wanted to bury her himself or was he afraid that Johnny would throw himself into the soft, damp earth that contained her coffin? We waited until Johnny turned to go. No one spoke as we left.

Afterward, there must have been two hundred people from the funeral floating around the apartment. I wandered into the long hallway. There was a picture of my mother in some early play wearing a wedding dress. She looked so young.

Elia Kazan came up behind me. "The first time I saw Paula, she came striding up over a hill, sunlight was falling on her blond hair, she was one of the prettiest girls I'd ever seen. She came over that hill like the sunrise."

I moved into the living room. Her doctor was talking to a few of our close friends. "It's for the best. If she hadn't had the heart attack we could have kept her alive another six months, maybe even a year, on machines, of course. But even with drugs, she would have been in unrelenting pain. The cancer had spread to every part of her body. It was in her bone marrow and had reached her brain. Perhaps it was a blessing she went this quickly."

I heard him talking about her medical history. She had had a breast removed, and numerous operations for tumors. She had insisted she was in the hospital for miscarriages. He had finally said, "Someone has got to make her accept the fact that her breast has been removed, that she has tumors."

"But she'll be so miserable," a friend replied.

"I'd rather have her miserable than insane," the doctor said.

I had been vaguely aware of some of this, but she never spoke to me about it; occasionally she would tell me she was pregnant, and I would just nod. She had covered her once lithe body with layers of fat and denied it further pleasure, but in the end, with her illness, she reendowed it with all the attributes of fertility of the earth mother she represented. She had made a bridge of herself, and when we had all crossed over the bridge and it had borne our collective weight, the bridge had collapsed.

I saw my father in the kitchen drinking his tea in a glass. He seemed so much smaller and grayer; I had not really looked at him at the burial. He was such a private man, and I did not want him to know I had seen him momentarily lose control. Now I saw that his back was no longer bent, as it had been at the cemetery, but seemed as if there was a steel spine supporting him, and I wondered if his rigidity would allow him to breathe and go on with his life or paralyze him. He was sixty-four and he and my mother had been married for over thirty years. It was hard to imagine him without her by his side. His eyes were dulled with his pain, and I felt as if they mirrored the sadness in mine. We did not touch or speak.

I walked into the back room, the one my mother had been in in

224

these past months, and wandered around, letting my fingers flutter over her dusty books, touching her jewelry sitting in a dish by her bed. I did not know what I was looking for—a note, the last words she might have scribbled on a pad. The pictures of Jenny I had brought her were still lying discarded on the bedside table. I traced Jennifer's face with one finger and remembered Clifford Odets saying, "If you live life only at the tip of your fingers, you will never hold anything in the palm of your hand." Perhaps I was looking for signs of life.

Sitting down on her bed, I stared at the stark whiteness of my knees protruding from beneath my black dress. I lay down on my side. The sheets had not been changed and were cold from the wind that whistled through the cracks in the windows. The smell of the perfume she had worn, mingled with the aroma of her sickened body, clung to the bedding. My legs began to move slowly upward, curling inward toward my chest until I lay in my mother's bed curved in the fetal position. I pulled the pillow over my eyes and mouth and there in the darkness I finally began to weep.

I wept in rage at the pain of this cancer that was her final protest and outcry against her life and with sadness for the loss of the past and the aborting of the future. I wept for the words we exchanged and those we left unspoken: "I love you, Mother. Forgive me." I lay there in the same bed she had been lying in for six months, where she awakened at night still crying at fifty-four, "Mama, Mama, please help me."

I didn't realize that there was no way to end a love relationship, that it remained a part of what you are forever, and through me, through my child, the seemingly fragile bonds of our tempestuous but caring relationship would prove unbreakable.

Aunt Bea and I decided we had to give away mother's things. My father could not, and we knew she wanted her friends to have a memento of her. She had begun this willing shortly before she died. She had called Marta Orbach and said, "I want you to have my *Gourmet* cookbooks. I won't be needing them."

"Oh, Paula," Marta replied, "of course, you will. Don't say things like that."

Mother had told a friend, "I don't care if Lee remarries. He can bring someone into my bed, but I don't want anyone to use my kitchen things. Tell Susie to take them."

And so I did, leaving behind what I could not carry. I took the collection of antique watches she had worn constantly around her neck. She had left a small hand-carved tortoiseshell butterfly pendant in a box marked "for my granddaughter." Some of the pieces I remembered were missing, and we never discovered who, if anyone, had taken them or if my mother had sold them or locked them away in the secret bank vault she claimed to have.

There was a diary or notebook with notes of her unfinished book, which she had been working on intermittently for years. "I hope everyone realizes I'm going to tell everything, the truth. I'm calling it *Are You Decent?*" (a phrase used before entering a dressing room meaning "Are you dressed?") One day I saw these notes, the next they were missing, as if she had dematerialized them and taken them with her to complete at her leisure.

I called up old friends I had lost touch with to tell them, to talk. I sat and looked at my address book. At twenty-eight, I was too young to know so many dead people, so many names with pen lines slashed through them. Sometimes I would forget what the line was for and ask, "Has so-and-so moved or died?"

It was time to go home and begin taking care of Jenny. Home had always been Mother, but now I would have to make my own. I could no longer run to her for strength, and I was afraid that some part of me had died and been buried with her.

Back in California, I held Jenny in my arms and thought: My mother is here, her blood is flowing through these veins. I could surely feel her presence. I talked to her now when I was alone, more than I had talked to her in these last years, belatedly trying to reaffirm our love.

Johnny decided to move to Los Angeles and came to live with us until he found a place of his own. He was out most of the time and I saw very little of him, but when were together, we never spoke about Mother.

226

On the evening of June 1, barely a month after my mother's funeral, at three A.M., the insistent ringing of the telephone awakened Christopher and me. I was half-asleep as I answered. The call was from an anonymous friend. Johnny was at County General Hospital dying, could I come immediately? I called my friend Ralph to drive us downtown; I needed someone close to me.

When we arrived, my brother was on the way to surgery. He had lost seven pints of blood and was, the doctor intimated, still hallucinating. "Perhaps," he gently prodded, "it might be LSD?" The police asked, too. I knew that it probably was. John had taken it before, always good trips, but this one had boomeranged.

He had gone out of a window above Sunset Strip; his life was saved by a balcony. Instead of falling forward to the ground, he had bounced backward from this railing, fallen on the broken glass from the window, which had then punctured his lung and almost severed one of his arms. He was an actor, and even in the torment of this act had covered his face as he went through the glass. His body was deeply scarred, but his face was untouched. Actors, actors, I thought.

The hotel had called the sheriff's office when they heard Johnny screaming in the second-floor room. The sheriff's deputies had arrived to find him naked and bleeding profusely, lying in the midst of the plate-glass window he had shattered. I could hear my brother screaming now farther down the corridor as they wheeled him toward the operating room.

"Get your goddamn hands off me!" He echoed my mother's words to her nurses at the hospital. As his stretcher moved closer, I saw that he was holding the bottles with tubes in his own hands, and as he passed Christopher and me, I called out, "Johnny, we're here." He turned his head slightly and smiled. I grabbed at his free hand, losing touch with him as they rushed him into the elevator.

I found a pay phone and called my father. It was two in the morning in New York, and he was awakened out of a deep sleep. "Lee, Johnny is in the hospital. He went out of a window. Two hospitals turned him down because he was a John Doe. We need you."

227

"I can't come," he said. "I have to teach at the Actors Studio today." I heard the fear and panic in his voice echoing mine. It was as if his half-asleep mind, unable to bear more sorrow, had refused the information.

"Pop, he's your only son. I don't know what to do. He may die. The doctors say it's critical. Please hurry." I had a child sleeping at home who had four holes in her heart; I could hardly bear to speak about dying.

I remembered years before my mother saying to me, "I'm not worried about you. You have strength, like your father. You'll survive. Johnny, he's too much like me. I'm afraid he'll go out of a window someday."

He was in the operating room for four hours. Finally the doctor came and told us, "You understand, he's on the critical list. A lot depends on him now, his will to live."

My father arrived that morning. A friend drove to the airport to pick him up. I stayed at the hospital, calling home to check with the nurse about Jenny, sitting in the gray hallway on a hard wooden bench, making trips to the candy machine, waiting. My father and I embraced, clinging to one another.

A nurse came. "He's better, so we're moving him out of Intensive Care. You can go in and see him now." We stood around his bed silently, Christopher, my father, and I. Johnny was pale. His face looked like a piece of litmus paper, and he was so weak. There was a urethra tube and a tube in his chest. He did not have the strength to speak, and my father and I stood awkwardly, not knowing what to say. We wanted to ask: Why?

The large ward was fairly quiet; the beds only partially filled. Directly across the way was a woman on a life-sustaining machine. The bubbles were spewing up, making a gurgling noise like a long, constant death rattle.

Johnny parted his lips. Christopher, being closest, bent over, then straightened up.

"What did he say?" I whispered.

He shrugged. "We'll be back next visiting hour, Johnny."

In the car going home, Christopher sat leaning his head against the headrest in exhaustion. He sighed. My father, who was sitting in the back with me, reached over and touched Christopher's head. He cradled it for a moment in his hands. No one spoke.

As he walked into the house, I realized my father was unshaven. I could not recall ever seeing him that way. He had one small battered suitcase in his hand as he walked up the stairs to the guest room, he looked bowed down with defeat and sorrow.

When Johnny regained his strength, he told us what had led to that leap into the darkness. "I was with friends and we decided to take some LSD. I'd been in despair since Mother's death and I thought the drug would help me release my grief. I felt so damned inhibited, stuck, I wanted to move. We sat around the apartment screwing with a deck of tarot cards. My number, whatever it was, kept coming up. I was restless. I went into the bathroom to wash while they went out to get some fried chicken. Sally had this ocelot in a cage in the bathroom. There was this acrid smell, and that wild, caged cat reminded me of my own imprisoned feelings. I was so damned lonely, and the drug intensified all my feelings." He shook his head as if shaking off the memories. "I never wanted to kill myself. I wanted to break through, break out . . . the longing was too much . . ."

He had hurled his body through the glass window. It was strange, but the scars he bore looked as if a wild animal had slashed at his body.

My brother's desperate leap toward freedom reminded me forcibly that I would have to make a move in my own life. Unless I could help myself, I would not be able to help Jennifer, and I wanted to do that more than anything in the world. I wanted her to live, to be well.

My father returned to New York to pick up the pieces of his life. Christopher and I lived in a state of semitruce over the body of our daughter.

My friends from England, Noel and Sarah Harrison, arrived in Los Angeles. He was doing a television series. They took a house nearby, and their home became an oasis for me. I could relax sitting by their pool with Jennifer, listening to their children playing. I thought: This is the kind of life I want.

In August, Christopher was offered a film, *Chubasco*, at Warner Brothers. It was a combination sea-adventure/love-story. Once he had signed for it, they started testing actresses to play the eighteen-year-old girl who defies her father in order to marry the wild young sailor played by Christopher. I received an urgent phone call from the director.

"Susan, Christopher is acting a little rambunctious with the girls we've been testing. He bit the last one when he kissed her. He is balking at doing the love scenes. What we were thinking was . . . how would you like to play the part?"

"First of all, I'm too old. I don't want to be the oldest ingenue in Hollywood. I'm not eighteen."

"You could look it."

"Well, I'm almost thirty pounds overweight. I haven't lost the weight from the baby yet."

"Don't worry," he cajoled, "your face is still thin. You can go on a diet. We'll hide your body with clothing. It's a nice part, you get to go to San Diego and Catalina."

"Why don't you do it?" Christopher asked.

"I don't know, I just feel strange about it. It's your first film."

"Well," he said, "that'll make it even better. Anyway, you should lose some weight, and besides, we can use the money."

Looking at myself in the mirror, I said, "Christopher, those don't look like eighteen-year-old circles under my eyes . . . on the other hand, maybe she's suffering from love. Maybe she's an old soul . . . I'll do it."

I had lunch with Chris and the old-time cameraman, Charlie Stromer, who went back to the days of silent films. He talked about working with Valentino. "I remember when he was shot in the stomach, right in the stomach." Christopher, fascinated, asked for details. I left the table.

Our nurse wanted to be an actress. She brought Jenny on the set every day, and the director gave her a small, two-line part. The next thing I knew, she was off to become a full-time actress, so I had to look for someone else.

Jenny was having all of her heart tests at UCLA. Her doctor, Forest Adams, was the head of Pediatric Cardiology there. The testing went on all day—terrifying for a little baby who was too young to know what all these strange contraptions and wires were. Dr. Adams asked if he could have samples of Christopher's and my blood. He explained that they, like other hospitals, were doing research to try to determine what caused these birth defects.

I asked, "And will it be possible to determine from the blood sample if something I took affected her?"

He shook his head. "We just don't know," he replied. "Drugs during pregnancy definitely have an effect, alcohol can make a baby alcoholic. I've seen babies born addicted. Smoking can affect a fetus, genetic irregularities . . ."

"I didn't take any drugs while I was pregnant, but could it have been the drugs taken before she was conceived?"

"We can't say for sure," he said.

"When will you have the results?" I asked.

"Within a week. I'll call you as soon as I get them," he said. "Will your husband come in for a blood test?"

"I don't think he can, he's filming right now," I lied.

Christopher had refused. "I had an aunt who had a cleft palate. I'm sure it comes from my side of the family. You know I hate needles, Susie, they're not sticking a needle in my arm."

"Wouldn't it be better to know or to help someone else than to just imagine?" I asked. "If it's genetic, it's not your fault, for God's sake."

"No one of those mothers is going to suck my blood," he said.

The doctor explained that the defects had occurred in the eighth week of pregnancy, when both the throat and the heart form. I tried to reconstruct what had been happening to me then. I remembered that Christopher and I had been agitated, but I knew that women had carried normal babies in the midst of wars and earthquakes.

Dr. Adams called. My tests revealed nothing abnormal that

231

could have affected Jennifer, for which I thanked God, but still in the corner of my mind there was that one shadow of doubt. Finally I realized I could do nothing about the past but I could help in Jenny's future. I would do the very best that I could for her. I could give her as much love as I had in me, day by day, one step at a time.

When the filming of *Chubasco* ended, Christopher seemed content to return to our old pattern of life as though nothing had changed.

I was insistent. "Christopher, we can't go backward, nobody can. And nothing can stay the same. If we don't change, we'll rot."

We fought acrimoniously. I kept a mental count as if when we reached some undetermined number of battles, I would say, "That's it. Enough." I wanted just to have some peace in the house, an end to the verbal and physical violence. But I was cowardly, too, knowing that the severing of this relationship might be as perilous as the union had been. At least during the filming, the work had preempted these problems. Now they were renewed with a vengeance, as if Christopher sensed I was imperceptibly moving away from him into a more private space.

We needed someone to replace the nurse we had lost. Jenny was almost seven months old, so I decided to get a companion instead. I placed an ad: "Nurse/companion. Warm, intelligent, mature woman to help with six-month-old girl. Free to travel."

A woman walked into our home for an interview. She was mature, gray-haired, blue-eyed, with a clear, steady, twinkling gaze and, unusual for California, she was wearing gloves. She had a pink-and-white complexion which hinted at her Irish-English extraction. Mrs. Journey—Florence. I felt an instant empathy with her. She was totally different from most of the people I had grown up with as well as the ones that Christopher and I saw. There was a sanity about her, a down-to-earth quality laced with humor and wisdom which in no way detracted from her sensitivity. She was from the Midwest and had been living in Eugene, Oregon. Her husband had passed away, her children were in different states, and lately she had been caring for a sick friend. She was a woman of independent means and had been thinking of going home to Oregon, but my ad had caught her eye. One of her children was a daughter, she loved little girls, and the ad said "travel." She had decided to look into it.

She moved into our house, and a breath of fresh, wholesome air came with her. Christopher responded well to her and was on his best behavior when she was around, so that things were much quieter.

I had noticed that Sarah and Noel Harrison and their children seemed to be blossoming, becoming even more relaxed and open than before.

"I wish California would do that for me," I said.

"It's not California," Noel said. "We've been seeing a doctor. A psychiatrist."

"The whole family?" I asked.

"The whole family except for the cat and dog," Sarah said. "We're in Reichean therapy."

"What in the world is that?"

She explained the theories of Dr. Wilhelm Reich, suggested I read some books on the subject, and gave me their doctor's number.

Before I called him, I decided I would get the books Sarah recommended, as I was still wary of psychiatry after my experiences with Dr. Mann. The clearest explanation was in Orson Bean's *Me and the Orgone*.

The gist of it was that Reich had broken with classical psychoanalysis because it dealt only with words, and he believed most of the damage that causes neurosis is done to children before they can talk. He developed a bioenergetic principle of functioning—not energy in a mystical sense, but physical energy—the life forces which, unimpeded, allow us to feel fully, to function as holistic beings. Unfortunately, man, over the centuries, had interfered with the natural flow of this energy, producing what Reich called armoring. For example, a child cries or gets angry or is very unhappy; he is told to stop that, behave, be good. In order to obey and be rewarded, the child clamps down on the muscles involved in his emotions until this conditioning becomes chronic and the feelings are trapped in the armor of the body and he is out of touch with his own emotions. Reich worked directly, physically, on the armor to break it down. By kneading, prodding, jabbing the muscles, he released long-pent-up feelings that in Freudian therapy might have taken years to even become aware of.

I had known dozens of people in other therapies who had observed, "I know exactly what's wrong with me, I just can't seem to change it." Reich offered hope of a concrete transformation, emotional and physical, and he stated what I had dimly perceived: you could not separate the instinct and the intellect, the body and the soul.

I called the doctor for an appointment. I didn't say anything to Christopher, knowing he would be violently opposed.

In my first session, I was skeptical and more than a little embarrassed as I lay undressed on the couch and the doctor began to press and prod my muscles. Involuntarily I let out a yell when he hit a sore spot. He continued, and again, unable to stop myself, I began to kick my legs violently against the couch as if I were desperately running away, and I began to scream harshly, throwing my head from side to side. "No, no, no, nooooooo"—the "no" I had kept silently locked inside me for years. I wept, but the tears were different. Deep, racking, wrenching sobs tore out of me. "How could I," I said, "how could I let all this happen? How could I have done this to myself—how could Christopher?" Finally I lay there spent and aware that I would do anything I had to, no matter how painful, to extricate myself from the trap I was in, even if it meant facing myself. I felt as if I had awakened from a long trance, and for the first time that I could remember, I felt at peace.

The next session was Jennifer's, and when, as the doctor worked on her, I saw her bluish skin turn pink and felt the warmth of her increased circulation and saw the relief in her eyes, I became more determined that nothing must stand in the way of this.

Christopher was incensed. "We can work out our problems alone," he said. "Doctors are the sickest people around. They live up in their heads, they don't know anything about real life."

"This is different, Christopher. Why don't you come with me and talk to the doctor? If we went together, it would be better."

"They'd just try to destroy me. We wouldn't have any problems if you'd accept the fact that you're only a woman and let me be the man in the house. I'm the strong one."

I pretended to be conciliatory and counted the days to my next session.

When the lease on our residence was up, I found a lovely large home at the top of Benedict Canyon, set back from the road. It had two stories plus a basement rumpus room, and from its back, wide glass doors looked out on what was still wilderness. The deer came down from the hills at night to drink out of our pool, raccoons and coyotes foraged in our garbage. I took Jennifer for picnics, making our way down the hill to lie amidst the wild daisies and geraniums that grew there.

One night I sat rocking Jenny in my arms, humming, when her eyes opened wide and looked into mine with an expression of such intelligence and comprehension that I stopped rocking and heard myself saying, "Don't worry, I'll take care of you. You're going to be all right." I spoke to myself as well as her.

Johnny was amazingly recovered from his surgery. In the months that had passed, he had refused to take even an aspirin. He had sworn off drugs forever, but he and Christopher began going out in the evenings, and I had time to breathe. Chris painted some portraits of me in softer, more lustrous colors. There seemed to be love in those paintings, if not in our confrontations. When Johnny rented an apartment, Christopher painted it for him, covering the walls with Christ-like figures in purple robes.

I was sleeping more and more. Withdrawing to bed after dinner I slept on my stomach, holding my hands clasped over my solar plexus. It was as if the rest combined with my therapy sessions was rebuilding my depleted body and allowing my mind to clear itself. Christopher would often wake me when he came home at all hours of the morning to accuse me of strange betrayals and acts. If I protested at being awakened, he became more intense.

235

I realized all of this must be affecting Jennifer, that she must be aware of the violence of our feelings as well as the undercurrents of fear and distrust. I did not know what to do. Although therapy was making me feel stronger, I had just begun, and the therapist was not willing to take responsibility for the decisions I had to make.

Christopher and Johnny would box in the playroom every night, emerging genial and sweaty to have a beer or go out on the town. They were becoming fast friends, spending more and more time together as I began to seclude myself.

On this night, Johnny appeared at the top of the playroom steps, covering his nose, his face drawn with pain.

"Chris broke my nose."

"Man, you didn't move fast enough," Christopher said, appearing behind him, laughing. "I'm a fast mother, Johnny. I didn't mean it, but you just didn't get out of the way of that right cross. Anyway, I think you look better like this. Don't you, Susie, he looks more manly. Jesus, his nose looks as good as Marlon Brando's. He should pay me."

"I think he should go to a doctor," I said, "and get it set."

"Oh, God, you women are always complaining. Johnny's not upset."

"No," Johnny said, "I'm just sorry. Chris, it was my fault. I didn't move fast enough."

Johnny's statement horrified me. He was beginning to act and sound like me.

The cumulative effect of the LSD he had taken had left him confused, fragmented. He turned to Christopher for help in putting the pieces together again, and Christopher encouraged him, as he had me, to confront my father, to ask him to answer for his actions. Johnny began calling him late at night to demand, "Do you love me? . . . Why didn't you and Mother help me when I was younger? . . . If you love me, why didn't you tell me?" My father listened and tried to respond as best he could, until one night he heard Christopher coaching Johnny in the background, "Tell him he didn't love you."

"Johnny," my father said, "that's enough. When you want to

ask me a question of your own, I'll talk to you. I'm not going through this anymore."

The next time the four of us were together, my father, Johnny, Christopher, and I, the boys began to pick an argument with him. They encouraged me to join in, but, unable to stomach the senselessness of it, I turned and left the room.

One morning Christopher came home alone after a night out with Johnny. He awakened me from a deep sleep and excitedly accused me of seeing other men while he was out. I was too tired to respond, and when I pulled the covers over my head to shut out his voice, he became violent. I wound up cringing in the bathroom, my hands in front of my face.

"No more! I hate you! You bastard, you have no right to hurt me like this. What's wrong with you? For God's sake, stop it!"

Afterward he cried and apologized. I listened, making sure my face showed no change or emotion. I was realizing the depth of the quicksand I had sunk into these past three years. Soon there would be no breath left in me, and I knew I had to extricate myself from this before I suffocated. I was like the man in the joke, drowning in a cesspool up to his mouth, shouting at his rescuers, "Don't make waves." How was I going to get out without making waves? I had chosen the role of victim but I could not let our child be victimized by our excesses, nor would I tolerate it any longer.

The next morning I drove down the hill to the Harrisons'. They tended to my bruises, put ice on my eyes.

"I have to think," I said. "I can't go home. What am I going to do? He says he doesn't want help, he doesn't need it. . . . That's his privilege. I have to leave, but what will he do alone? His mother left him, his father, now me. I'm frightened."

Sarah said, "Susan, he's a survivor. He won't be alone. Stop making excuses, face reality. You must think of yourself and Jennifer. Does it make it easier if I tell you he was here last night with a girl?"

I stopped. "He was here with someone else and came home and attacked me for being unfaithful and betraying him. . . . Oh, God. . . ." I almost laughed. "Thank you, thank you," I said.

I had never been jealous; I always sensed my real competition was his love for his own pain. So now I felt free to go.

I called Jennifer Jones Selznick. "May I use your guest cottage? I'm leaving Christopher and I need someplace to go where he won't think to look for me until I get myself a little straightened out."

She said generously, "Come as soon as you want."

I got into my car and drove around, trying to work up my courage to go home. When I finally did, Christopher was asleep on his side of the bed.

The next morning, I got up and drove around again. I parked at Robinson's, a department store on the outskirts of Beverly Hills, and wandered inside, not knowing what I was looking for. On the first floor I saw a black leather chair from Italy with bronze feet in the shape of lion's paws. That chair looked like Christopher. I paid them the four hundred dollars and had it put in the back of my car. A four-hundred-dollar chair, and I did not know where the money was going to come from to live. I had sold the last of my stocks so Chris and I could live in style.

At home I sat in the driveway, put my head down on the steering wheel, and wept. The American Dream: I had bought him a gift because I had no more love to give . . . money equals love.

I spoke to Florence. "We're going to leave now, immediately. I'm not taking anything, just some baby things. If you want, you can get a suitcase. I just want Jenny, and I'm taking my dog. I'm leaving Christopher the dog the Harrisons gave him."

Christopher was still asleep upstairs when we walked to the car in the blazing California sun. The trees cast strange shadows over the house and the man who lay sleeping upstairs.

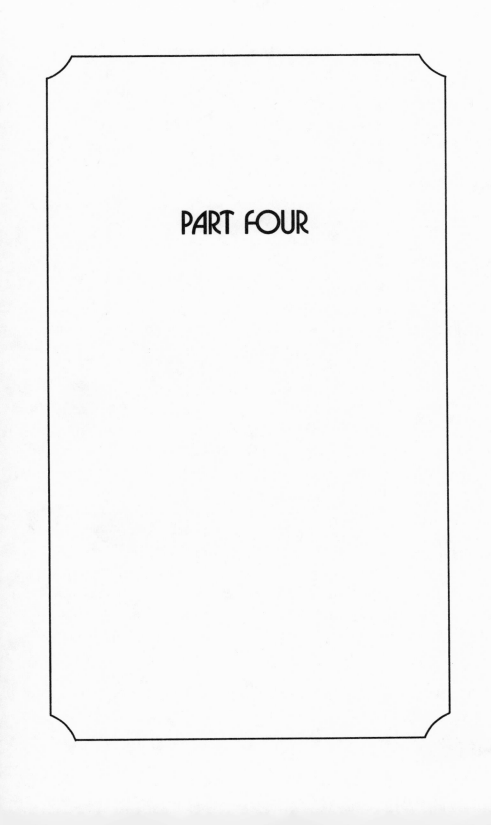

PART FOUR

*A*FTER AVOIDING decisions for so long, I now had to make them: where would we go from here, what should I do?

I slept, read, ate, knowing I could not prolong this interlude indefinitely, that I must make a move. Reprieve from an immediate decision came when Jennifer offered me her Malibu apartment.

"You can use it until you find someplace for yourself. Rex Harrison is in it now, but he'll be leaving."

It was perfect. The beach had exactly what I needed, the sense of freedom that I would get looking at that unbounded skyline. Perhaps that's why so many divorcees move to the shore.

In the meantime, I had written Christopher a letter that I would get in touch—I wanted a divorce. I asked a friend to call him and get his reaction.

"What did he say?" I asked. "How did he sound?"

"You know Christopher. He doesn't mean what he says . . . he said he was going to kill you."

"When I walked out that front door, I accepted responsibility for Jennifer and myself. There aren't going to be any more pointless confrontations."

A few days later, I hired a private detective to go up to the house with me to get some necessities, clothes. The books, paintings, the few jewels I had, I would leave. Things, I didn't care about them.

The private detective opened the front door with my key. "He didn't change the lock. Just get what's on your list."

I gasped as I walked into the living room. The house was in complete chaos. All the pictures that Christopher had painted, the portraits of me, the sunsets, lay slashed, frames smashed to pieces on the floor. I felt inexorably sad.

Upstairs, I packed a suitcase, some of Jenny's clothes, Florence's things. The detective came into the nursery.

"Jesus, he's got a loaded revolver under his pillow. I'm getting rid of it. Do you think he'd use it on you?"

"No," I said. "Anyway, if he wants to shoot me, he can always get another gun."

"Let's get out of here," he said.

"There are some things in the garage," I said. "We can stop there on the way out."

I walked into the garage and stopped, stunned. Clothes were ripped, torn, strewn all over the floor, dirt and filth all over them. And the dog, the little dog the Harrisons had given him, was sitting in their midst chewing on an old hairbrush of mine, looking unkempt.

"I'm going to take him back to the Harrisons," I said. I went up to one of my favorite evening dresses. "Maybe I'll just take this one." As I lifted it, I felt a weight in the center and as I opened it, a dead rat fell out onto the floor. "That's a clear message," I said, feeling ill. Christopher had had the last word, but for what? It wasn't a game; no one was going to win or lose.

The ocean was like a soporific. There was no pressure, no need to think or feel. After a few weeks I found a small apartment upstairs from the one Jennifer let us use and we moved in.

I heard from various friends that Christopher was looking for us. I sent a message to him: "When you calm down, we'll talk."

The detective was costing a fortune, so I decided to let him go. Johnny came down and stayed with me for a few days, sleeping on the couch. And then my friend Ralph. Their support gave me courage.

242

I went to a lawyer and told him to sue for divorce, that I would waive alimony and wanted only minimal child support.

Christopher was told where we were and given temporary visiting rights with Jennifer. But after he used his first visit to attack me, I took out a restraining order against him. I no longer would continue the battle.

"If he wants to see her," I said, "he can, but not in my presence, with a third party."

"Johnny, would you be willing to come down when Christopher comes to visit?" I asked.

He seemed very ambivalent, and confessed, "I feel sorry for Christopher. I identify with him as a man, cut off, rejected, separated from his child."

"Johnny, that's bullshit."

"Susan, I think you'd better get someone else," he said.

I did not pressure him further, sensing he was still not himself; he had recovered physically but not emotionally from the accident.

Christopher came banging at the front door. "Susie, I'll kick it in," and began to, screaming at me.

"I'm calling the police," I said. "Please go away." I sent Jenny and Florence to the back of the apartment, telling Florence to "play some music, loud."

The sheriff's men arrived. I explained briefly, feeling it was none of their business. They were polite and businesslike and quite paternal toward Christopher, who had adopted his wistful hangdog look when they arrived. I thought I detected a flash of antagonism in their eyes: What's she doing to this nice young man? But I didn't care.

During all of this, Florence had been a bastion of strength and humor. Now, unexpectedly, she had to leave for home; her son had been killed in a tragic accident. I had not realized until then how much I depended on her.

Christopher held on like a dog with a bone. He decided he wanted custody of the baby, I was an unfit mother. For the first time in my life, I knew that I would be capable of killing. I was glad I had thrown away the small pearl-handled revolver Christopher had bought me, because I could have shot him when he threatened, "I'm going to get you. I'm going to get the baby."

I was terrified, watching him yelling and cursing through the plate-glass window. I called the police again but didn't press charges because I was afraid it would incite him to further threats.

When I answered the phone, I never knew what to expect. He would say, "Get out. You're not needed. Get out from the middle. I'm going to get the baby." The baby. Not "Jenny" or "my baby," but "the baby."

The Malibu sheriff's office called. They said, "Your husband's here. He just wants to see Jenny." How sweet it would have sounded if I had not known better.

I spoke with my father. "I don't know what to do."

"You'll do whatever you have to do," he said. "I'll help, you have friends. If you need money, let me know. You're doing the right thing."

Finally, I sat in court shaking, my palms wet, looking as calm as I could. Christopher was in pants and a shirt, his feet up on the seat in front of him. He wandered in and out of the room, the doors slamming noisily behind him. "Will the young man in back stay in or out," the judge ordered. He stayed in, glaring at me, making obscene gestures behind his cupped hand.

Against my lawyer's advice, I held firm to waiving alimony. "I have been earning my own living since I was fourteen years old. I can take care of myself. I don't want money from him. Just my freedom."

The divorce was granted on the grounds of irreconcilable differences—our partnership in fear had been dissolved. In one year the decree became final. As I left the courtroom, someone said to me, "How do you feel? You must be awfully sad."

"Yes," I said, and I was saddened, because Christopher had really left me long before, he had shut me out of his life bit by bit, day by day. His eyes, which at first had questioned me, had ceased to believe me; his hands had lost all their tenderness. He had, in reality, divorced me long before I had left him.

244

I knew it would be a while before any seeds I planted grew. But I had felt my baby's life inside me flourish, and I felt I could renew my own life, make it grow. Mingled with my sadness and regrets was relief—incredible relief—that it was over.

When I received a film offer, I accepted, not caring what it was. I was thrilled to be working, thinking about something other than myself. I played Peter Fonda's wife in *The Trip*, a film written by Jack Nicholson about an LSD experience. It was highly romanticized, containing none of the destruction that I had seen.

In the love scene I was to appear in the nude with Peter. In fact, I was wearing a G-string and cotton patches over my nipples so if the camera saw the front of my body, it would pick up the white cotton and they would have to cut the scene.

Someone came over to me. "Susan, Peter wants to talk to you. He's thought about it and decided he can't play the scene truthfully if he's not naked."

"I understand," I said, "he can be naked, but I'm going to *act* naked."

I went over to the double bed we were using. Peter pulled the covers up around his chin.

"Susan," he exclaimed, "I want—"

"I know, they told me. It's all right."

"No, no. There's something else. I just want you to know, if I get an erection, it's nothing personal."

After I finished *The Trip*, another script arrived that required filming in Arizona. I was pleased. Christopher was still behaving erratically, and I felt the month or two away would be a relief.

The Name of the Game Is Kill was an inexpensive mystery. My mother was played by T. C. Jones, the female impersonator, so you can imagine, *Mother* turned out to be *Father*.

Each day I traveled up to the old mountain mining town we were shooting in. One morning I heard my name echoing across the hill, followed by a string of obscenities. When I looked across the horizon and saw Christopher gesturing obscenely at me, I wanted to run and hide. The company manager called the sheriff's deputy, who was on the set, and he called his boss. When the sheriff arrived, he stated, to Chris, now in custody, "Young man, you can get out of my state or you can go to jail."

"I'm going, I'm going," Christopher said loudly, and under his breath, ". . . old bastard."

I accepted another low-budget film, *Psych-Out*, with Jack Nicholson and Bruce Dern, which dealt with the flower-child culture. I played a seventeen-year-old deaf runaway searching for her brother, a spaced-out religious fanatic, in Haight-Ashbury. Jack was the love interest; the denouement was me freaking out on STP in the middle of the Golden Gate Bridge.

When I climbed into bed for the obligatory lovemaking scene, this time in a bikini, I felt something funny.

"Jack," I said, "I don't mind your blue jeans, but could you please take off your boots? This is not a death scene."

Haight-Ashbury was incredibly depressing. I watched the young people on the streets seeking more drugs, a new thrill, the old high, or the way out. Some careened toward suicide, some drifted into communes, some rejoined "society," and some disappeared God knows where. People kept telling me, "But, you should have seen it in the beginning." I wondered if that beginning had been in their fantasies.

This could have been me, I thought. This was a world that I might have fallen into if I had been ten years younger, if I had been from a different background. Many of these young people had just been less fortunate than I.

What I felt about this film and the others that soon followed was succinctly stated by actress Vera Miles when she appeared with Katharine Ross and John Wayne in *Hellfighters*. Katharine, who was forced under her Universal contract to do the film, was furious, and when she was asked what she thought of the movie, she told the press, "It's the worst piece of crap I've ever done." Miss Miles was asked to comment on Miss Ross's statement; she thought for a moment and said, "Well, it's not the worst piece of crap *I've* ever done." Still, I was working with good people, making a living, and it was a beginning.

When the films were over, I had to deal again with my constant, unrelenting concern about Jennifer. I would awaken four, five, six times a night and tiptoe into her room to make sure she was still alive.

Finally one night, standing in terror over her bed, listening to her breathing, which was more shallow than usual, I had a talk with myself.

"All right, Susan, what's the worst thing that can happen? Say it! She could die. But you aren't God, you don't control her destiny, you're doing the best you can. You've got to treat each day like a gift, stop wasting it in guilt and anxiety. You have to stop agonizing 'what if,' 'if only,' stop worrying about yesterday and tomorrow. You know, Strasberg, they're just dates on a calendar. The most important thing you can do is love her, and the heart has no calendar."

In facing the worst of my fears, I took the first step in letting go of them. It was a turning point. In facing her possible death, I resolved to live more, not less.

Johnny called and said he wanted to come out and visit. It was not the pleasant afternoon I had anticipated. He had run into Christopher and after some initial hostilities, they had declared a truce, and during the course of the evening, Johnny had become convinced I was in fact trying to destroy Christopher. Johnny identified with Christopher and was determined to make me see the error of my ways.

"If I didn't love you," he said, "I wouldn't even bother arguing. But you need help."

"That's why I'm going to a doctor," I said. "I don't think at this point, Johnny, that you and I are strong enough to help one another. If you really love me, you'll leave me alone. I don't want to talk about all of this anymore."

I was furious, but my rage was tempered by the knowledge of how persuasive and ingratiating Christopher could be when he wanted to, and I knew Johnny was still recovering from the shattering experience he had gone through.

"He's using you, Johnny, to get to me."

247

"He said you'd say that."

I gave up trying to reason with him. "Johnny, you and I have to work out our own problems, and I think it's better if we don't see each other for a while," I said regretfully.

More confident, I agreed to go to New York to make *The Brotherhood* with Kirk Douglas for director Martin Ritt, with whom I had worked years before on *Hemingway's Adventures of a Young Man.*

Jenny, Florence, and I settled into a hotel, and I called my father. He had unexpected, startling good news. He was to be married to Anna Mizrachi, a beautiful, bright young woman he had met in California several months ago. I had been with them on their first date. Franchot had given a dinner party at Don the Beachcomber's for about fifteen people, and my father was to have his car pick me up. When he arrived, he was accompanied by Anna. At the restaurant, everyone inquired, "Who is she?" "She's awfully young, isn't she?" "She's gorgeous, where did he find her?"

"I just met her," I said. "All I know is, she's from Venezuela. She's a nice Jewish girl who was schooled in a convent, and worked in the UN. It's a small world—we just missed being introduced there twelve years ago when I made a personal appearance with Mrs. Roosevelt. She met Pop at the Actors Studio. If you want to know more, ask her."

It was an emotional evening. I watched my father with this lovely young woman and thought how happy he looked, how alive. Impulsively I reached out and hugged him. "I love you, Pop."

"I love you, my darling."

We clung to each other for a moment. How long had it been since we said those words to each other? Too long. He wept, I wept, and Anna wept. I knew that my mother would not begrudge my father his life. She had always taken pleasure in other people's joys, and my father was the kind of man who needed a woman.

The wedding was scheduled a week after I returned to New York. They planned to be married by a justice of the peace, but Anna's mother said, "Until I hear a rabbi say those words, to me you won't be married." The day of the wedding I was as nervous as they. Anna's mother and I were the only witnesses. There was one awkward moment when the rabbi said, "Lee, do you take this woman as your mate and chattel?" Anna's back stiffened and she whispered, "Chattel? I never agreed to chattel." Her mother nudged her with her elbow, and the ceremony continued.

When we cut the cake, I knew I was leaving a part of my life behind.

Christopher arrived in New York on his way to England to do a film, *The Looking Glass War*. He had completed two films, *Three in the Attic* and *Wild in the Streets*, and was becoming a big star. He had the kind of flesh, like Marilyn Monroe's, that the camera loves, and his charged-up hostility and his sensitivity and charisma were captured on film. My leaving him seemed to have been the best thing to happen to him. As he had when I left for England before we married, he had mobilized himself and begun working.

He asked to come up to my father's house to see Jennifer. I agreed, saying I would be absent. During the visit, he asked Jenny to kiss him, and she started crying.

"Why is she crying?" he asked, upset. "Doesn't she like me?" To Anna he said, "They've turned my kid against me. I want her." He held on to Jenny tightly, and her crying intensified.

"Let me take her, Christopher. She's just tired, and you're talking so loudly, it scared her," Anna said.

"Don't say that," he yelled. "She's not frightened of me."

My father came in, and Anna took Jenny out of Christopher's arms.

"Take it easy," my father said. "The baby should nap now. You can come back tomorrow."

Christopher exploded. "I want my kid! I've got rights! You'll be sorry!"

"Christopher," my father said angrily, "you don't frighten me. I want you to leave now."

"I have the power to destroy everything you love!"

My father looked at him. It had been true; it no longer was. "Get out," he ordered.

Slamming the door, Christopher left.

Chris was not the only one guilty of precipitating an argument with my father. One evening Lee and I were watching television and I made some comment about an item on the evening news which he took exception to, and before I knew what had happened, we were in a heated argument. In the old days, I would have fled from this kind of confrontation, but now I refused to back down. We were fighting not as father and daughter but as two adults. The battle climaxed when my father, irritated to a point of exasperation, at a rare loss for words, said, "I've been around a lot longer than you have. You don't know what the hell you're talking about! You . . . you . . . shitface . . . you!"

Allowing him the last word, I rushed to tell Anna, "Pop just called me a shitface! Isn't it wonderful? He really cares."

It had taken years, but we were opening the lines of communication.

I accepted an Italian-American co-production to be shot in Rome. After a month there, it was obvious that the film was never going to be made. I had been paid expenses but had neglected to get my salary up front, and it wasn't likely I would ever see it.

My last night in Rome, I ran into Nick Adams on the Via Veneto. I had not seen him since *Picnic*. He, too, had not been paid for a film that had fallen through.

"I was counting on the money," he said despondently. "It was the first movie I've had in a long time. What a rotten business."

I was shocked to hear months later that he had taken an overdose and died. I was more fortunate than Nick. I sued the American production company for my salary, and two and a half years later I received a settlement. I was learning to stand up for myself.

Back in New York, Jenny celebrated her third birthday at her grandfather's house. I helped her blow out the candles, as she did not have enough breath.

When I returned to Los Angeles I found a home in Malibu Colony, a private group of about seventy-five houses lining the beachfront and the adjacent street which had a tennis court, a backyard for Jenny to play in, and access to the beach. There was no through traffic on the street, and it was safe to play on. Everyone knew everyone else, and, everyone else's business.

No sooner had we settled into this paradise than I was offered not one but two films in Europe, one to be shot in Italy, the other in France. It was very good money, up front, which I needed, and interesting scripts and parts, so I began packing.

Two old friends, Peggy and Bill Trayler, had decided to come to California with their daughters, Susan and Stephanie. They needed a place to stay, and I sublet my home to them.

We traveled again via New York so that Jenny could rest and we could visit my family. We celebrated Anna's pregnancy, and I said, "Jenny, you're going to have another aunt or uncle, but a lot younger. You can change their diapers."

We arrived in Rome during one of the coldest winters they had ever suffered. An old acquaintance found me a one-story home in the residential area near the zoo.

The film, *The Sisters*, was about two siblings, very melodramatic and Italian, but I enjoyed the work in spite of the plot.

One day I received a call from Christopher in London. He was arriving in Italy to do another film with Pia Degermark, the lovely actress who had filmed *The Looking Glass War* with him. He wanted to see Jenny. I tried not to anticipate any problems.

When he finally arrived, he looked well, his work seemed to have agreed with him, and he was on his best behavior. He even handed me $5,000 in cash, "in case you or Jenny need anything." I was touched, and when he asked me to dinner, I thought, why not, we were being civilized, after all. That evening, lulled by wine and longing for contact, I let down my defenses and we made love.

On his next visit, he revived our old arguments. I was furious with myself. Christopher had almost eased his way back into my confidence. I had reexperienced the attraction I had once felt for him, but I realized it was not my desire he awakened as much as the memory of that desire.

He and Pia took Jenny out for a ride in his new Ferrari, a gift from the producers. When they returned, Jenny was crying. Christopher had had a near-miss with a large transport truck.

I was furious. "Your child was in that car, Christopher. If you want to kill yourself, go ahead, but not her."

"Oh, you're turning into an old lady, Susan. Loosen up."

The next night he showed up unannounced, although we had agreed that he would give me a day or two warning. It was late, the baby and Florence were asleep, but he had not come to see them, he wanted to talk to me.

"Seeing anyone?"

"That's none of your business."

"How's your sex life?"

"Also none of your—"

"Hey, I just wondered if you were getting any."

He could still make me cringe when he felt like it. I was exhausted, and I had to go to work at 5:30 the next morning, which meant that I wanted to look relatively good. I told him to go; then I asked him to. The more I asked, the more mulish he became, refusing to budge.

I threatened, "I'll call the police."

"You'll have all the paparazzi in town here if you do," he said.

"Then I'll call your managers to come get you."

He remained intractable. Finally I did something that was probably long overdue. I swiftly drew back my arm, made a fist, and aimed a perfect right cross at his solar plexus. In the instant that the move took, I felt guilt at the pain I was going to cause, and pulled my punch, just enough to deflect it. It landed not in flesh but on bone. I heard a pop, felt an incredible pain tear through my arm, and realized I'd broken something.

In agony I begged, "Now will you go?" He thought it was all a great joke, and in an ironic way, it was, too little, too late.

After he left, I woke Florence and she packed my hand, now swollen into a pulpy mass, in ice. After a stiff drink I fell into a feverish sleep.

The next day the X ray showed I had a broken wrist. As I had to continue working, they put it in a removable cast.

252

That night I awoke, my heart palpitating from a dream. I was a young French girl, Marie, in the eighteenth century. I lived in the country with my father. I fell in love with a young, charming soldier. I clearly saw his blond hair, blue eyes, his soldier's cape worn dashingly across one shoulder. He took me from my father's to Paris, and there I began a life of debauchery that led to my death when I was less than twenty-one. I knew and repeated the soldier's name in my dream so I would remember it. As I looked at his handsome face, it began to waver and disintegrate before me, changing into other features. "Oh, my God," I said, "it's Christopher." Then, still in the dream, I said to myself, "You see, Susan, you still haven't learned, you must love the *soul* and not the *flesh.*"

All my values were shifting. Life moved on. My arm healed along with some of my emotional scars. I left for France to do the next film, *The Bait,* with Stuart Whitman and Sterling Hayden.

Christopher had signed to do *Ryan's Daughter* in Ireland for David Lean. "I'm going to be stuck there for nine months," he said. "I'd like to see the baby again."

"Perhaps," I said. "Let's see how things go."

If Rome had been cold, the north of France was Siberia; bitter winds roaring in off the coast and the Dover Channel.

The film was so obscure, no one in the cast understood it; I don't think the director did either. He insisted on shooting in such dark light that in one scene, with my dark hair and dark fur coat, I totally blended into the doorway I was standing in front of, only a little piece of my nose showing in profile.

"Is that somebody there?" the producer said in the movie theater when we saw the rushes. "Who is that?"

"It's me," I said, "in my darkest hour."

On Sundays I would assuage my dissatisfactions. Florence, Jenny, and I would drive to restaurants around the countryside. I would order the same meal each time, fish in white sauce, wine, French bread, and an entire chocolate soufflé, which I shared with Florence. I got the big half. I would throw up every Sunday, too.

After the film ended, we went to Paris for a week of sightseeing. But Jenny had tooth trouble and awoke screaming in the middle of

253

the night with an abscess. When that was taken care of, she caught what the doctor diagnosed as German measles, so we went into quarantine.

Christopher had been calling, and I agreed to go to Ireland. After one or two days there I realized it was impossible for me to stay. Christopher was unhappy and behaving strangely. Of course, so were his costars. One got drunk and almost drowned in an ocean scene. Another blew marijuana in the director's face and pulled down his pants to shock someone who asked for his autograph. David Lean would get his actors keyed up, ready to film, and then wait for five days for the sky to have the proper-shaped cloud he wanted in the scene. Months in Ireland, with three more to go, had them all stir crazy.

I discussed it with Florence, and we decided she would stay on a little longer with Jenny and then we would meet in London and head for home.

I was being offered other films now at tempting sums with top European directors and actors, but I felt Jenny should see the doctors in America. She was going to need extensive dental surgery in a hospital, as her teeth were debilitated by the lack of oxygen. I thought she would get better care in America and I would have friends to help me. Besides, I was lonely, and seeing Christopher made me anxious to get back into therapy.

It was lovely to settle again into the ocean rhythm of Malibu. The Traylers, who had watched over my home for me, moved down the road with their daughters, and Susan, the younger, soon became Jenny's first and best friend.

Jennifer was limited in her activities. She could not run and play with the other children, she could not keep up. When she walked, it was slowly, stopping to rest every few feet. I was used to going too fast, too impulsively, but now I was forced to restrain myself, to be patient.

The other children played with Jennifer until they tired of her sedentary activities or pace and ran off. All but Susan Trayler.

"C'mon, Su-su," they would cry.

"I'll wait for Jen, you go on," she said in her deep, gravelly voice, so incongruous in a little tow-headed four-year-old. It's a lie that children are cruel.

In addition to this problem, Jenny had a speech impediment, which would be partially corrected by surgery. In the meantime, her voice was very nasal and there were sounds that she was unable to make or that were barely distinguishable. I comprehended her most of the time, Florence and Susan part of the time, but with strangers she had to struggle to be understood.

Jennifer was scheduled to go into Children's Hospital for her dental surgery.

"Is it dangerous?" I asked.

"The anesthetic is the risky part. Anytime someone is unconscious for an operation, there is a certain risk factor, but otherwise it's minor surgery," the doctor explained.

I was numb through the entire experience. I just wanted to have it over and done with.

As soon as the anesthetic wore off, Jenny asked, "When can I go home? I'm hungry."

"What do you want?"

"Spaghetti," she said.

Her doctor overheard. "If that child wants spaghetti, you can take her home and give it to her. Usually these kids don't want to eat for days."

"Spaghetti," I said.

"*With* meatballs," Jenny said.

She was underweight, but growing, putting a little more flesh on her bones, and she was getting to be quite a load for me. She had become used to being carried everywhere. She didn't want the stroller any longer; it was "too babyish."

"Jenny, you'll just have to rest, and then we'll go on. I can't carry you anymore. It's hot, my feet are killing me, I've parked the car in Timbuktu, and I'll never make it carrying you."

She looked at me. "Well," she said, "you're lucky you didn't park in Timbuk-three."

Her heart doctor said to me, "There are advantages and

disadvantages to waiting longer for her heart surgery. When she's five or six, she could be stronger, more able to tolerate it. But there's a danger in waiting too long, because she might become psychologically crippled. I've seen that happen to children who, after they are operated on, still think of themselves as being handicapped. We could do a helping-out bypass operation, but for now, as long as she's not passing out or falling on her hands and knees, we can wait. Those are the danger signs for a child with her condition."

These next years passed too quickly and too slowly. With Jenny's illness, a different sense of time colored my days. I had a heightened awareness; how quickly *now* became the past. There was less time for "what ifs" and "might have beens," and I was grateful to wake up in the morning, hear Jenny breathing, see her crawl into bed with me in the morning.

I partially lost sight of my own life as a woman and an actress during those years as I centered on Jennifer, but I was rewarded by the pleasure of watching her blossom despite her physical handicaps, seeing her courage. I never felt that in turning the focus of my life toward her I was sacrificing anything; everything I did was for myself as well as for Jenny. I was growing with her, through her.

"Mommy, I don't want to be a grown-up. Grown-ups don't seem very happy. They're so nervous. Why are you like that?"

"Well," I replied, "I think I'm like that because I *didn't* grow up and I'm afraid someone will find out."

Now Jennifer started nursery school. On her first day, she had to go into the school on her own. The other children ran down the stairs, passing her by. I saw her shoulders shrink and then I watched her straighten her back and move purposefully, one step at a time, down the stairs, clinging to the railing.

Whether I liked it or not, I was going to have to let her go. She had to stand on her own two feet.

She was scheduled for her first major surgery, the partial correction of her soft palate at St. John's Hospital in Santa Monica. This hospital was different from the others we had been in.

"Mommy, it's nice here," Jenny said. "It's almost not like the hospital."

The doctor told her that when she woke up her throat would be very sore and she would have to eat soft food for a few months but that she could have all the ice cream she wanted.

I walked by the side of her bed as they wheeled her down the corridor into the elevator.

"That's as far as you can go," the attendant said.

Jenny looked at me, tears in her eyes. "Mommy, I don't want to go. I'm scared."

"The sooner you go, my sweet girl, the sooner you'll come back. I'll be waiting for you, and you'll have a lovely new throat."

"I know, but I'm still scared."

"We have to move along now," the attendant said.

My God, I thought, I can't let her go. As they wheeled her away, she looked so tiny, her body lost on the large cot.

Anna had flown in from New York to lend moral support, but it was a four-hour operation and the waiting was interminable. By the time the doctor came to tell me that it was successfully completed, I was demolished.

"How," I said to Anna, "am I going to make it through her open-heart surgery?"

"Cross that bridge when you get to it," she said.

When they brought Jen to the room, she was still asleep. They handed me a strange-looking contraption, bands of material, straps attached to two boardlike sticks.

"What's that for?" I asked.

"Her arms have to be tied into these splints to make sure she doesn't suck her fingers or put anything into her mouth. We do it with all the little ones. They can't remember not to touch the scars, and the stitches can be ripped open and then she'd have to have the operation over again. You can't trust a child, you've got to put it on her now."

"But she's asleep," I said. "If she wakes up and finds her arms paralyzed, it will be terrifying. I will put them on," I promised, "but not until I can explain to her what they're for."

"What if you fall asleep and she puts her hand in her mouth?"

"I won't fall asleep. I can't. Not until she wakes up."

Anna and I took turns sitting up in her room. When she finally opened her eyes, I explained to her what we had to do. She cried at first but then said, "Okay, if I have to. I don't want to ruin my operation. I don't want to go through this again."

The doctors had told me she would have to wear this contraption day and night. I talked to Jenny about it.

"Mommy, I won't suck my fingers. I promise. But I can't stand *that*. I'll wear it at night, but please don't make me wear it in the day, too."

I thought about it, worried that it would be too much responsibility to place on her, and decided, "Let's try it and see how it goes."

I kept an eye on her all that day and the next and the next, and I saw that every time she started to move her fingers to her mouth, she stopped herself, examined them, and moved her hand away. She showed a discipline and strength that many of my adult friends have yet to acquire.

We had a celebration when the doctor said that her throat was healed. We broke the splints into pieces and threw them into the fire, and Jenny and I went out for spaghetti and meatballs, her first solid food in months.

School was difficult. She was extremely susceptible and caught everything that anyone had. She was absent as much as she attended. The longer periods of concentration that school demanded were difficult for her because of the shortage of oxygen. She fell behind in her work, but the teachers were very understanding and the years passed.

A crisis arose. "She's got to have the catheterization now. It's disgraceful that it hasn't been done. And she's going to need a helping-out operation. You know that," a new doctor said, on examining her, to her heart doctor and me.

It was a fairly standard procedure for children with this type of

258

defect. There would be a temporary bypass to help them until they were older and strong enough to have the major corrective heart surgery. It was usually considered imperative, but her doctor had felt that it could wait, as she was *not* having the classic danger symptoms.

I went to still another doctor and then another for confirmation. Should I wait? Should we proceed? Two experts said, "You must go ahead or you're risking her life." Two other experts said, "As long as she's not having those symptoms, she can wait."

I realized I was going to be the deciding vote. "We'll wait," I said. "We can always change our minds if we have to."

An actress and her daughter moved in across the street, and shortly after, the divorced father moved in five houses down. I was pleased because the little girl was just Jenny's age.

"Hi," she said when she came in to introduce herself. She was a pretty, vivacious, extroverted little girl. "I'm Jennifer Grant. My mother's a movie star, Dyan Cannon; my father's a movie star, too, Cary Grant, but he doesn't work anymore, he just sells perfume [Cary was associated with Fabergé]. What do you do?" she asked.

I looked at her and cleared my throat. "Well, *I* act, too."

Cary was lovely with Jennifer. She was not seeing much of her own father and was longing for male company and attention. I went to pick her up at his home one evening when his daughter was spending the night. They were all three lying on his king-size bed watching television, Cary in the middle, in his pajamas, his arms around the two girls.

He kissed and hugged my child, tossing her in the air as if she were his own. "You're a lovely girl, Jennifer," he said. She blushed with pleasure. She had never seen him in a film, but he rated star billing in her book.

Seeing them together, I realized how lonely I was, how nice it would be to have a man around the house . . . but the right one was hard to find, and I was not prepared to devote the time and energy necessary to maintaining a relationship. Jennifer came first now. I worried that it was unhealthy, but the priorities had set themselves. Some men resented this, others ran scared at the mention of problems, still others wanted to be the baby, and as I changed in therapy, what I was looking for in a man changed, also. Men I had previously found dull or too nice started to look better. I didn't want to live in the fast lane anymore. Danger no longer excited me.

Shelley Winters and I talked about our different therapies. "It sounds terrific, Susan, but aren't you afraid that if you got well and weren't neurotic, you wouldn't be as good an actress?"

"That's rubbish," I said. "I hate that implication, because we're sick or neurotic, we're talented. The talent is there first, and then maybe because we're supersensitive, so open to life, it affects us more strongly. But we function *despite* the craziness, *not because* of it. Its always seemed so strange to me that, on the one hand, people condescend to and denigrate actors—'You know actors, they're all crazy'—while on the other hand they make us the keepers of their dreams. How can they give all that responsibility to people they think are crazy."

For a while, frightened of being forever alone, I became frantic searching for "Mr. Right." I said to my friend writer Rona Jaffe, "You wrote that Mr. Right is dead, but I'm not giving up yet."

However, indiscriminate dating left an empty feeling in the pit of my stomach, so I stopped. Lee Grant asked, "How can you be alone for so long?"

"I'd rather," I said, "be alone by myself than feel alone with someone else." And inwardly I perceived that it was important for me to assert my independence now because I had been so totally dependent before.

"I don't," I said, "want to lean on anyone ever again. I also don't want to use men like disposable Kleenex, so I'll just hold out a little longer."

"Men aren't easy," a fervent women's libber actress friend said. "My first husband was a Communist, my second was a fascist, and neither one would take out the garbage."

Fortunate as an actress, I was financially independent, I traveled, had friends, met a lot of people, was constantly engaged in new projects, and there was no stigma attached to being single in my milieu—it was, rather, a plus. My nonprofessional women friends would tell me of being excluded because they were an odd number. That never happened to me, and I knew how lucky I was to be able to lead a full life on my own. Obviously, it wasn't ideal. I wanted someone to share things with, to love, to complete my life, but my life did not *depend* on it.

My therapy was inching forward. In retrospect I saw that I had had choices but had been incapable of making them. "I see," I said, "that it wasn't Mama or Papa or Chris, but *me* who's responsible for what I've done with my life. I think I sensed that Christopher would bring out the dark side of me. When I met him I felt that he'd break through my 'armoring,' but not that it would be like being picked up and dropped off the Empire State Building."

As I got deeper into therapy and it got rougher, there were days I wanted to say to my doctor, "Forget it, it's too painful." Then I'd remind myself of how I had felt before. As layers of protective coating came away, I was alternately angry, lonely, longing, desperate, and sad. When, I thought, do I get to the good part, to the relief I'd felt at first, the sense of being grounded, in touch with myself? And, I wondered, if I were ever going to reach the end of this, to let go of the ghosts of the past.

My father had once gone to the theater with another director. After the first act, he had asked his friend, "Do you like it?"

"It's wonderful, it's so . . . *confused!*"

After the second act, Father asked again, "What do you think of it now?"

"It's not so good . . . it's *clearing up!*"

I was in the clearing-up stage of my life. "It's so damn painful to grow up," I said to my doctor, "no wonder most people refuse to!"

"If you'd done it back then when you were supposed to, it wouldn't hurt so much now," he said.

Florence was leaving. I was losing a friend. She had become Jennifer's adopted grandma. She had first come to us when Jennifer was just seven months old. She was going home to Oregon, but we knew that she would always be a part of our lives, our family.

While I was living in Malibu I began to see the illusionary quality of the life I was leading, the instability of breathing rarefied air. My girlfriend Nancy, who lived in Beverly Hills, came down to the beach, bringing a new acquaintance. He was a short, almost squat, powerfully built man in his middle to late thirties. He was looking for a house to buy in the Colony. In private, swearing me to secrecy, she whispered, "He's Howard Hughes's adopted son, but he's asked me not to tell anyone. Hughes found him as a young man and is training him to take over his business."

On the hills, just beyond the Colony, loomed the Hughes research plan. "That must be why he wants a house here, to be near his work. He's keeping a very low profile," she said, "so please don't tell anyone else."

He drove us in his brand-new Mercedes up to the Hughes facilities. It was Sunday, the plant was locked, and he promised, "I'll bring you ladies back on a weekday for a full tour." We listened as he detailed his life. He had run away from his foster parents and been discovered by Mr. Hughes sleeping on his doorstep when he was eleven years old.

There was a home available directly across the street from me, and in less than a week he had made a bid that was accepted. I heard that he paid $350,000 cash for the house. He moved in, and by then his identity had spread through the Colony and he became very popular. All the broke producers in the Colony wanted to meet him, and the businessmen who were putting together financial deals were anxious to talk. Soon he was making deals involving millions of dollars with people highly placed in the financial world. He was also talking to a friend of mine about financing films. I was duly impressed, although I observed that, despite his intelligence, he seemed very, very neurotic.

One day he was very critical of my behavior with Jennifer and her baby-sitter. I turned to him and said, "I don't care who you are, it's none of your business. I don't want advice from you and I don't want you in my house. I think you're a very sick man and that you need help." After that we hardly spoke and only nodded at one another if we passed on the street.

Not long after this, he was out jogging when he had a heart attack. He rushed into a neighbor's house. Refusing a doctor, he rested for a half-hour until he felt he was well enough to leave. As he left this house, a group of men who had been standing around on the street began to converge on him with drawn guns, and he was whisked out of the Colony.

"Did you," I asked the gateman, "see what happened to Mr. Fleet?"

"I sure did," he said. "I saw him going out of here with the FBI and the police."

Herbert Ames Fleet was, it seems, a professional con man who had done time in the Big House. He was within reach of collecting millions of dollars on all of his deals, and what had tripped him up was a fourteen-dollar bad check he had given to the attendant at the gas station across the street. Everything, from his background to his heart attack, had been fake.

Usually I was the first to be taken in by a persuasive personality. This was one of the rare first occasions I had trusted my instincts and extricated myself from an unpleasant situation. I felt that at last I was getting my feet on the ground, which meant I could afford to leave my head in the clouds.

My girlfriend Patty, an intense, good-natured redhead, was a psychic. We had met when I was pregnant; she had been reading cards for me for four years. Approximately eighty percent of her predictions had come true. One day she spread her tarot cards out on the red Spanish shawl I was using as a bedspread.

"Cut the deck three ways with your right hand, toward you," she said, "and make your wish." She pulled out three cards and reversed them. "Keep your wish focused in your mind, concentrate on it." Her normally high-pitched voice became deeper.

263

I sneezed. "I wonder," I said, "why I always get a cold when you read for me. Nerves. Maybe what I don't know won't hurt me."

"Well," Patty said, ignoring my comment, "first of all, you get your wish, whatever it is, and I'd say by early next year."

"That's nice," I said. "Next year is only seven months away."

"You've also got the fulfillment card here, and the cards show that you're very, very anxious."

"I'm always anxious these days." I laughed.

"Your worries are passing within six months."

"It's June now. That means December or January."

"Susan, you're going to be taking another trip by plane. Someone else is paying, so you're probably going for work somewhere in this country. The South . . . Southern part of the country. But I also see New York . . . East. Yes, I'm sure it's for work. I see you reading a script, and you're traveling alone."

"It's not very likely I'd leave Jenny to go and do a film," I said.

"This is a short trip. Not months, maybe a week."

Patty moved the cards around. They made a pretty pattern against the florid peacocks and roses of the spread.

"You're going to meet someone on this trip. A man."

"Well," I said, "is that good or bad?"

"This man is going to be very, very important to you. I'd say he's a Scorpio, young, thirties, maybe forty. Lightish hair, blue eyes I'm picking up, and a very successful businessman, head of his own business, he has children, too. Maybe . . . I think he's divorced. He's going to be very important to your wish card. He'll lead you to your wish, whatever it is. Oh, Susan," she said, "this is . . . Gee, I'm getting goose bumps."

"What is it? What do you see?" I leaned forward. The pictures meant nothing to me.

"Jenny is dancing on the beach. She's twirling around, dancing. It's sometime next year, early in the year, and, Susan, she's one hundred percent better."

"Well, if she is, it will be a miracle," I said. "Because she's not going to have her open-heart surgery for at least a year. I've just

264

discussed it with her heart doctor. We're going to do some preliminary tests in six months, but that's not going to make her a hundred percent better." Wistfully I stated, "I believe in miracles."

"Well," Patty said, "whatever. You're going to be very happy. I see blessings all around you."

"God willing," I said, and knocked on wood.

Five months passed. Jenny was scheduled to go into UCLA Hospital for a catheterization to see exactly where the blood was impeded, what was missing. It required an anesthetic, and as a preparation for her open-heart surgery, it was necessary.

Just before her tests in October, I was committed to appearing in a film a friend of mine, Barney Rosenzweig, was producing. It was a cameo part, little money involved, not a great role, but I said I would do it. It required only a week's shooting, but it meant being in Little Rock, Arkansas, and I asked the producer to make the ticket to New York and back to Los Angeles so I could visit friends for a day or two. When they sent tourist tickets instead of the first-class ones my union required, I said, "Look, it's not worth it. Let's forget it."

"Insist on first class," Patty said when I called her.

But by then I had decided I really didn't want to do the film. It required too much energy and time.

That night I dreamed that Faye Dunaway was pulling my hair. She seemed to be asking for something, but I couldn't decipher what. When I woke up the next morning, I thought it was strange but put it out of my mind until my friend Steffi called.

"What's happening?"

"Don't ask," I said. "I've got to call Barney and tell him I can't do his film. Do you think he's really going to be upset?"

"Don't worry," she replied. "I talked to him yesterday, and the actor who's playing opposite you in your scene is living with Faye Dunaway, and she told Barney if you didn't, she'd like to do the part."

"Well," I said, "if it's good enough for Faye Dunaway, it's good enough for me."

The day I left for Little Rock, a friend, Barry Parnell, drove me to the airport. At the airport he handed me a huge hardcover book, *The Seth Material*, by Jane Roberts, saying, "This is for your trip."

"But it's enormous. There won't be time to read it, and it's too heavy. I only carry paperbacks when I travel. Listen, with my makeup kit and my camera and tape recorder, if I take this book, I'll need a donkey."

"Take it. I feel it's important to you."

On the plane there was no one seated next to me, so I settled down to study my lines and read a bit of the book. After a while I got up to go to the bathroom, placing the book, cover up, on the seat next to me.

When I came back, the man seated across the aisle came over to me. He was young, somewhere just under forty, and had beautiful, intelligent blue eyes.

"Mah name is Louis Dorfman an' ah hope ya'll 'scuse me," he said in a thick Texas drawl, "but ah happened to see the title of the book you're reading and ah had a strange experience ah'd like to tell you about."

Oh, no, I thought. I had hoped to have time to myself on this trip, but impulsively I said, "Please sit down."

He was on his way home to Dallas, Texas, after some business in Los Angeles. The plane was stopping there on the way to Little Rock. We ordered drinks, and he proceeded to tell me about an astral-projection experience he had had.

I was fascinated, and we continued to chat. He was a lawyer and businessman, divorced, and had two sons. Suddenly, in the midst of this casual conversation, I had an overwhelming urge to tell him about Jenny and her heart operation.

"My daughter," I said, "I'd like to tell you about her." And I plunged into it all. Her birth defects, her throat operation, her impending tests to be followed eventually by open-heart surgery. When I finished, he looked at me, and again I noticed what lovely blue eyes he had.

"It's funny," he said, "one of my good friends in Houston is Denton Cooley. As a matter of fact, I'm going to a party at his

266

house this week. Do you know who Dr. Cooley is?"

"Yes, I know."

Dr. Denton Cooley was the man I always wanted to do Jennifer's surgery. I had read about him in an article some years back, which described his phenomenal success doing open-heart surgery on children. Although Jenny's doctor in Los Angeles was a fine one, I had thought often about Dr. Cooley.

"May I tell Denton about your little girl?" my new friend asked.

"I would be thrilled. Here, let me write the name of her condition down for you. And this is my phone number. I'll be in Arkansas and New York until the end of the week. After that, I'm home."

"I'll let you know what Dr. Cooley says."

The work on the picture went painlessly, and I flew into New York, where I was staying with my friend Ara. Just before bedtime, I suddenly turned to him and said, "I met this man on the plane. No, no, not that way. Just a man. But it's so strange, because I have this urge to call him. I started thinking about him an hour ago. But I can't just pick up the phone after midnight and call a stranger."

"Why not?" Ara said.

"What will he think? What if he thinks I'm trying to pick him up?"

"Go ahead and call," he urged. "You've got nothing to lose. Trust your instinct. You can always hang up."

"I'd better do it quickly before I chicken out. Okay, here's the card he gave me."

A woman's voice answered the phone. "Just one moment, Mr. Dorfman is at dinner."

I realized it was earlier in Texas and relaxed a little until I heard his soft voice.

"Louis, it's Susan Strasberg. We met on the plane last week."

There was a long silence. I've made a total idiot of myself, I thought.

"You must have ESP," he said. "I've been trying to reach you all day. Your phone in California doesn't answer. I looked up your father's number in the New York directory, but all I got was a Spanish maid who'd never heard of you."

"Since I'm only here for twenty-four hours, my parents don't even know I'm in town."

"I've spoken to Denton Cooley about your daughter," Louis said, "and he'd like to take a look at her, do those tests you mentioned, two weeks from yesterday. I told Denton I didn't know if you could be there, but he said that he was sure you would."

"Of course I'll be there. Of course."

"My boys and I will take you and Jenny to dinner the night before you check into the hospital."

I put down the phone in a daze. What if I hadn't followed my hunch, what if I hadn't dreamed about Faye Dunaway, what if I hadn't taken that book on the plane, what if. . . ?

As soon as I got home I canceled Jennifer's appointment at UCLA and two weeks later Steffi, Jenny, and I, she in her new red-and-yellow print dress, checked into the Shamrock Hilton. Louis took us for a glorious meal with his sons, and the next morning, before we checked in at the hospital, Jenny ate a breakfast fit for four marines. She remembered the hospital food she had had before.

Most of the day was spent running from one floor to another, doing various tests, EKGs, blood tests; the important one was the next day. First thing the next morning, they sedated her. By the time she left the room, she was lying half-asleep on the hospital cart.

"Mommy, come with me." Her voice was thick with the medication and her speech defect.

"It's all right," the nurse said. "You can go with her in the elevator and all the way to the O.R."

Dr. Cooley came to our room later that day. "We've evaluated the tests. The way it looks to us, you couldn't have come at a better time. I'd like to operate on her."

"When?" I asked.

"The day after tomorrow."

"But I hadn't planned on doing it this soon. Not for at least eight more months. After she's six." My heart was pounding. "It's just so sudden."

"Susan"—he looked at me—"my hands will do the best they can. After that, she's in God's hands."

"May I let you know in the morning?" I asked.

He nodded. "But you have to decide so we can make preparations."

I went into the room. Jenny was still sleeping off her sedation.

"Steffi, he wants to operate on her the day after tomorrow." We talked about the pros and cons. "We could come back in six months."

Jennifer sat bolt upright in her bed. "Mommy," she said firmly, "I want to get it over with now. I don't want to have to come back here." Out of the mouths of babes. I decided to go ahead.

The morning of the operation, they began sedating her at about 5:45. Cooley usually operated on the youngest patients first unless there was an emergency. He was reputed to do between eight and twelve operations a day, moving from operating room to operating room. The patients were lined up, already cut open, ready for him.

I rode down in the elevator with Jenny, holding her hand, her drugged eyes looked frightened. As they began to wheel her away from me, I clung to her, saying, "Remember, angel puss, I promise you under the Christmas tree this year is going to be a little puppy just for you."

She released my hand and smiled. There was nothing more I could do, so I went to the waiting room to sit with Steffi.

At nine, there was a phone call from my stepmother, Anna. "Your father is flying in tomorrow. He wasn't able to make it today. I'll let you know when he's arriving."

"Thank you" was all I could say, pleased that my father had made this gesture. I knew he was not a man who took easily to hospitals and doctors.

Soon afterward there was another phone call. It was Christopher screaming, "Why didn't you tell me? She's my child, too."

I tried to calm him down. "Christopher, it happened so quickly there was no time. I didn't want you to be concerned."

I couldn't tell him that Jenny and I had discussed it the day before the operation and together had decided not to tell him.

"You should have asked me," Christopher said.

"I didn't ask you about her throat surgery or her dental surgery. You were never there to ask, Christopher." Then I realized he was frightened. "Don't worry. She's going to be all right. I know she is. I promise you."

Shortly after 11:30, Dr. Cooley's assistant came into the waiting room in his green hospital gown. He said to me, "They're just sewing your daughter up. It was a beautiful job. You're lucky. Cooley would never tell you this, but I don't think any other surgeon could have done what he did. There was more damage inside her than had been indicated on the tests."

"Thank you," I said. "Thank you for coming to tell me." Tears of joy streamed down my face.

When they finally let me in to see Jenny, I was prepared for the tubes coming out of her mouth, the needle in her arm, the tubes in her nose, the wide bandage across the center of her chest. What caught me off guard were her fingernails and toenails. For the first time since her birth, they were glowing pink like beautiful rosy seashells.

"How long do you think it will be before she comes back to her room?" I asked the nurse.

"If her fever goes down and her lungs are fairly clear, she could be back late tonight, but more likely by morning."

They wheeled her in early with the sun the next morning.

"We'll get her up out of bed the day after tomorrow," the doctor said. He had come in to put an extra piece of tape on her scar. "Because she's so pretty and delicate, I don't want her scar to stand up too much. Sometimes the extra tape makes it smoother."

"Isn't the day after tomorrow awfully soon to be getting out of bed?"

"It's amazing," he said, "the younger they are, the more

270

quickly they recover. They haven't learned they can't do it. They believe they can, and they do."

The first thing Jenny wanted when she was fully awake was spaghetti. The doctor was afraid it would be too harsh on her throat, but she was adamant. So they brought her a huge bowl of spaghetti covered with something that did not faintly resemble an Italian sauce. She was furious, but her anger pleased me. The fear was gone.

When my father arrived, he came directly from the airport to the hospital. We embraced and I took him by the hand and led him into Jenny's room.

"How do you feel, Snookie?" he said.

She held out her arms to him. "Hi, Grandpa. Don't hug me too hard because of my stitches."

"Look at her nails," I said, holding up her hand.

"They're not blue anymore," he said in amazement. Tears sprang to his eyes, and he began to fuss over her like a mother hen.

That evening, he took Steffi and me and Bill Trayler to dinner. Bill had been filming a commercial nearby and had flown in to give Jennifer a kiss. My father had never been more charming or gregarious, telling jokes and being a gracious host. I wondered if he had always been this way and I had not noticed, or was he, too, changing?

The day we left for home, they handed me a slip of paper that stated:

OPERATIVE PROCEDURE: 11/10/71. Total correction. Dacron patch to VSE. Resection of infundibulum. Excision of pulmonary valve; pericardial patch to pulmonary outflow tract. Direct closure of asd.

I comprehended little of that, but then it read:

CONDITION ON DISCHARGE: Not treated.
Diagnose only.
Improved.

> Not improved.
> Recovered.
> Died.

"Recovered" was circled in blue ink. It was such an ordinary word.

On New Year's Eve, I invited some close friends to usher in 1972. I dug a pit on the beach and filled it with logs for a bonfire. At midnight, under a beautiful, almost full moon with a ring around it, we drank champagne to toast the new year and Jenny's new heart. Jenny insisted on staying up "all night."

After midnight in the new year, we gathered around the fire and sang folk songs. As we sat in the flickering light of the fire, Jenny got to her feet and began to dance alone on the beach. Her face was radiant.

I turned to Patty. "Do you realize that everything you told me came true? The trip I took alone to the South for work and to New York, the blue-eyed Scorpio divorced businessman who would help me in the fulfillment of my fondest wish—that Jenny be well—you said, 'She'll be one hundred percent better by next year. . . .' You saw her dancing on the beach one hundred percent recovered." covered."

"Did I say all that?" she murmured.

"Yes, it's on tape. Patty, do you think life is all preordained, or is it probabilities you see, which means we still have choices, free will?"

"I don't know the ultimate answer myself," Patty said. "It could be fate or destiny. Skeptics would say it's coincidence."

"Or," I asked, "do you suppose all those 'coincidences' were really small miracles?"

Six months later, Patty read for me again. "I see you," she said, looking at her cards, "going across water. A long trip. Not Europe. Australia, I think. I see you on an island in the Orient. There's an Aries man you'll meet on this trip. He's very impetuous, outgoing. He's going to sweep you off your feet. Oh, Susan, I can see you, you're actually in his arms, swept off your feet."

"I've never been near Australia, much less the Orient, Patty."

"That's what I see," she said.

Less than six weeks later, I received a communication from my agent about a TV film to be shot in Australia.

"But there was no island in the Orient," I said to Patty. "Too bad. I would have bought you a Buddha if I'd gotten there."

A week before I was to leave, the production company called to make sure I had my cholera shot.

"You don't need a cholera shot for Australia," I said.

"Didn't your agent inform you that we've changed our plans? We're doing part of the picture in Australia and the rest will be shot in Singapore."

"Is Singapore an island in the Orient?" I asked.

I called Patty. "You've got your Buddha."

On the plane I met an attractive man who, coincidentally, was staying at the same hotel as I. He wined and dined me, escorted me to my door. He'd had a little too much to drink. Australian men consume larger amounts of whiskey and beer than I have seen put away anywhere else in the world.

"Good night," I trilled.

I attempted to handle him diplomatically, but he was past listening. As I tried to shut the door, he pushed it open, picked me up, and carried me to the living-room couch. He had . . . swept me off my feet!

"What sign are you?" I asked.

"Aries," he growled.

It figured.

After I convinced him to leave, I called Patty in California. "Well, the Aries turned up, Patty, and swept me off my feet. But it wasn't what I had in mind."

This was the first time I had left Jenny for more than a week, but she was so well now, I didn't have to worry.

It was announced that *Toma*, a television film I had done, was being made into a series. Tony Musante, the star, requested me for the role of his wife, Patty Toma, and I signed on for the run of the show. The character I played appeared only in every other episode, which allowed me a great deal of free time during the shooting.

On one of my weeks off, I flew to Israel. I was invited as one of the celebrity contingent going in honor of Israel's twenty-fifth-anniversary celebration. I joined a group in New York to fly to Tel Aviv: Barbara Walters, Alan King, Earl Wilson and his wife, and Hugh O'Brien. Others were meeting us in Israel, arriving on William Levitt's yacht, *La Belle Simone*. Josephine Baker came from Paris. Nureyev was going to dance and Isaac Stern and Pablo Casals were already there.

Barbara, Hugh, and I slept in improvised sleeping bags on the floor at the back of the plane. Only on El Al, I thought. On arrival, there was a shortage of limousines, so Hugh O'Brien and I wound up sharing a taxi into Jerusalem.

It had been over twenty years since I was last there, and along the roadside I saw flowers blooming where before there had been only barren desert.

Hugh and the driver chatted about the country, one thing led to another, and soon they were in a discussion about religion and one of the Irish lord mayors of Dublin, Mr. Cohan.

"If you're a Cohan," the driver said, "you can always give the blessings in the Jewish religion."

"What about George M. Cohan? He wasn't Jewish."

"If he's a real Cohan," the driver said, "he can give it. Maybe it's one of the lost tribes."

As we passed the Jerusalem gates, he turned to Hugh. "We Jews believe that when our messiah comes, these gates will spring open before him." He saw Hugh's face in the mirror. "Mind you, Mr. O'Brien," he said, "I'm not saying that when the messiah comes it won't be Jesus Christ."

Although Casals, at ninety-seven years old, had to be helped onto the stage, he played exquisitely the Catalan melodies and nursery tunes of his childhood. It was his last public performance.

There was a full moon over Jerusalem, and when the sounds of the prayers and the distant ring of camel bells began at dawn, the past and the present became one.

274

Four days later, back in the modern world at Universal Studios, I crawled into bed with my TV husband, Tony Musante.

I was invited to lunch at the Beverly Hills Hotel by a girl I had met in my Mind Dynamics class. The other guests were Jess Stearn, Glenn Ford, and Ann Miller; all of us had a common interest in the occult. The host was a young man from San Francisco. He was starting a new business—an offshoot of Mind Dynamics amalgamated with hypnosis, metaphysics, existentialism, and reprogramming, plus his own personal theories—and wanted stars to draw attention to it. He called his organization EST. His name was Werner Erhardt.

Glenn allowed him to use his home for an introductory lecture, which I attended with Jess and Warren Barrigan, my singing teacher. We asked questions.

"It sounds terrific, but what exactly is it?"

"I can't tell you what it is, but what it isn't. It is what it is."

"Sounds like something Gertrude Stein would say."

Werner was a great salesman, vacuums or evolution, but I wasn't shopping. I had learned the instant nirvana and self-realization offered by the numerous organizations born out of the sixties didn't work, at least not for me.

I received a telephone call at home one day. A clipped Englishwoman's voice announced, "This is Mr. Orson Welles's secretary. He'd like to send you a script and would appreciate your reply by tomorrow."

"I'd love it, but I'm working," I replied.

"Oh, Mr. Welles only shoots on weekends," she said.

I called my agent and told him about the offer.

"I have another client who did a film with him six years ago and loved it," my agent said.

"Really? What film was that?"

"*The Other Side of the Wind.*"

"That's the same film," I exclaimed. "It must be a very long one. . . . I'm going to do it."

The script was a complex, fascinating dissection of Hollywood, past and present. The cast included Jack Nicholson, Lili Palmer, Mercedes McCambridge, Edmund O'Brien, Jean Moreau, Orson's companion, Oya, a beautiful Yugoslavian actress, and assorted midgets.

Actress Lee Grant gave me some advice. "Whatever he asks you, don't take off your lip gloss or mascara."

Not knowing what to expect, I arrived on location in Carefree, Arizona. The first morning I had just consumed a huge brunch when a call came, "Mr. Welles would like you to join him for lunch in one hour." I'll eat again, I decided.

As I approached the desert house we were shooting in, Orson appeared on the balcony in a flowing white caftan. In the midst of the surrounding sea of sand, he resembled a beached great white whale. We spoke about the part, a vicious film critic, and I mentioned how much I was looking forward to working with him.

John Huston, who was playing the film's central character, an aging macho film director, said, "I'm no actor, dear," when I complimented him on a scene. "I don't know what I'm doing." His smile was charming, he called everyone "dear," and his eyes were intelligent, critical, and cruel. His disdain seemed to include himself as well as others. But for Orson, he had only admiration. "By God, he's extraordinary. I'd like a movie of him making this movie."

Orson's wit and brilliance seemed unflagging except when he was stymied or unable to stimulate his imagination. He would sit waiting for the muses to favor him.

"Where do you want us to set up the camera, Orson? What do you want in this scene?"

"Idiot, can't you see I haven't the foggiest notion of what I want?" he stormed. "I wouldn't be sitting here if I did."

In one scene I had to recite a long string of impossible names, which I barely had time to memorize. Mr. Huston observed my struggles and said, "Don't worry, it'll be fine, dear." But I knew I was awful.

276

"Susan, Susan, where's Susan?" Orson asked after the first take.

"Orson, I'm right in front of you."

"You can't possibly be Susan. She would *never* do a scene that badly."

Chastised, I tried again.

Orson had told me when I began this film, "Don't bother with costumes, just wear jeans. And no makeup. Nobody's wearing any." Remembering Lee Grant's admonishment, I subtly applied full makeup every morning.

One afternoon, Oya was shooting a scene with me. Until now, on the set she had been dressed in baggy clothes, no makeup, almost unkempt. She now made a stunning entrance from the bedroom, dressed in a form-fitting black dress, low-cut but elegant, her hair impeccably groomed and her makeup looking as though it had been professionally applied. At least, thanks to Lee, I had on my mascara and lip gloss.

Orson and Huston reminisced about the actors from the old days of Hollywood. They had found memories of Errol Flynn despite his fistfight with one of them, his unusual and prolific sexual activities, and his slow, painful demise brought about by drugs, alcohol, and boredom.

"By God, there was a man. He lived on the edge."

How could these two remarkable men admire Flynn, whose ultimate achievement, as far as I could determine, was his destruction of himself? Perhaps they were fascinated by danger, as I once had been.

We finished filming in the desert and continued the following weekend at Peter Bogdanovitch's home in Hollywood. We were shooting a party sequence during which my character reveals what she believes to be the secret *raison d'être* of the great director whom she has hounded during the film.

"'I know why he does these insane things—casting midgets, discarding actors, his outbursts. . . .'"

"'Why?'" the crowd of extras asks.

Orson had instructed me to look directly into the camera with no expression on my face and dead-pan the answer: "'Perversity.'"

I wondered if it was an autobiographical statement of Orson's.

In the intervening years, while I had gone to Europe, Australia, and Texas, Johnny had gone East, where he met a young actress whom he married. They moved to Canada, where he was offered a job working for the French-Canadian Film Board and teaching acting. I had seen him only twice during that time, once when he came to California and briefly taught acting at Columbia Pictures. I had gone to observe one of his classes, and it happened that on that day Johnny was doing the "To be or not to be" monologue from *Hamlet*. He was wonderful. All the experiences he had had were distilled and refined into his acting.

"I'm teaching and directing, but my heart is still set on acting," he confided.

The second time I saw him was in New York. He and his wife and I had dinner.

"Have you," I asked, "seen Christopher?"

Johnny had never been one to mince words. "No, and I'm not going to. When Christopher and I drifted apart, I realized how destructive our friendship had been, if you could call it a friendship."

"You know, Johnny, he made almost a million dollars the first years after I left him, but he hasn't worked since *Ryan's Daughter*. That was four years ago. Psychiatrists are saying that the stress of success is as great as the stress of failure. I think Christopher, like so many of us, thought that when he became a star everything would change overnight, his problems would be resolved, he'd be 'happy.' Before he was successful, he had something to look forward to. When he tasted the reality of it and it didn't live up to expectations, he had nowhere to go. What was that thing that Pop said: 'The moment of the actors' greatest success is the moment he has to be careful or he starts to fall.'"

"What does he do if he doesn't work?" Johnny asked.

"He paints, drives around in his Porsche, he can afford to do nothing. The Sharton Tate murders hit him very hard. He had become friendly with Sharon while he was working in England, she had just become pregnant. The house she was murdered in is the one he moved into when we separated. It belongs to his manager. I don't see how he could move back in there—I couldn't live in it." I looked at Johnny across the table. "You realize," I said, ". . . it could have been us."

We clasped hands.

After that last meeting, we began to correspond regularly. He wrote saying he was probably going to be divorced and would be moving back to New York to teach at my father's school and rededicate himself to his career as an actor. He already had an offer to do a play off-Broadway. I still thought of Johnny as my kid brother. The little towheaded kid in his snowsuit getting divorced? Where had the time gone?

Jennifer had only one more operation left, the final correction of her soft palate. It was at least two years away, and I knew that I had to begin to put my own life in order. Professionally I felt like a horse running in the wrong race. In my thirties, I was one of the oldest *ingenues* in Hollywood, partially due to my height and bone structure, which made me appear younger. I was racing against newcomers, long-legged blonds who burned out by their thirtieth birthdays. I couldn't compete with sprinters like that, but after twenty-four years of acting, I knew I had staying power.

"I think of us as Chanel suits," I said once to Lee Grant. "They can hang us in the closet but we're always in style and good shape when they take us out."

Lee said, "They told me I couldn't do comedy if I didn't go blond. I compromised: I'm a redhead."

"I was turned down for a part the other day," I said. "They thought I was 'too short.' What happened to the dreams that brought me into acting, from Cleopatra to this? And the actor who rejected me has a wife who's smaller than I am. I met him at the studio yesterday. He asked me how I was. I told him, 'Too short.'"

Lee asked me to do August Strindberg's *The Stronger* on film as part of the American Film Institute's Program for Women Direc-

279

tors. Ellen Burstyn and Anne Bancroft were also taking part in the program. *The Stronger* is a half-hour monologue for two women: one speaks, the other listens. At last my compulsive talking was not a total loss. Like everything else in my life, every experience and feeling, it was money in my actor's bank, to be drawn upon when needed. Working on classical material again with Lee, who cared, and who demanded more from me than anyone had in years, reaffirmed my love of acting, which I often doubted in the years when I worked less discriminately, and this gave me the courage to return to the stage after an absence of fourteen years. My last stage role had been Camille. If I waited one more year I would never have gone back. The production of Shaw's *Heartbreak House* was not a success, but I did not die of fear. I threw up every night before curtaintime, and prayed a lot, but I lived through it. How sharply my perspective and values had changed! Nothing would ever be life-and-death again, except life and death. I began to suspect the most important work of art I might ever have to create was my own life. There certainly was a diversity of roles I was playing. "Star" was redefined as "actress." "Princess" disappeared from my repertoire; I stopped looking for frogs to kiss. The child who had never made her bed or washed the dishes metamorphosed into the paper-towel queen of Southern California. The half-empty bottle became half-full.

Jerry was a successful businessman twelve years older than I—ultraconservative, somewhere to the right of Barry Goldwater. He wore silk undershorts with his initials hand-stitched on the flies—in case, God forbid, he or anyone else should forget who he was. He was intelligent, high-powered, and not just a father figure. The first night we met, he promised, or threatened, "I'm going to marry you." I was impressed with his self-confidence. Six months later, he prophesied, "You'll never find anyone to take care of you like me." It was true: he was attentive to the most minor details of my life, but he was also *buying* my life. Whenever he was unable to give emotionally, I would receive a piece of expensive jewelry. I could have acquired quite a collection. He sent me off to the beauty parlor so I could look like "the little doll I was."

After one afternoon of searching in my muddy garden on my hands and knees for a broken false fingernail, I admitted defeat. "Yes," I reassured him when we separated, "it's my problem. Maybe I am crazy, but I don't want to be taken care of like this."

Browning had his last duchess. I fell in love with my last married man, although he was separated when we met. William was a musician and a gentleman farmer, and I was wild about him. I felt an inner glow, a fullness of feeling I had not experienced for a long time. Finally he couldn't decide whom he wanted or loved— his absent wife or me. I was like a hungry child who's offered a lollipop, only to have it repeatedly snatched away. We separated by mutual consent, but I was grateful for the experience because I realized that I had been able to let go, to love with an open hand.

In the past, my life had vacillated between Technicolor ecstasies and black-and-white despairs. As I began to feel stronger my life took on new dimensions. I saw the chiaroscuro that I had been oblivious to. Everything began to feel so much better. I had periods of a kind of happiness, which had always seemed outside my reach, and I had no regrets. The past had brought me here, and here was the best place I had been so far. Ironically, it had been the pain that had awakened me, not the prince.

The last vestiges of my identity crisis began to fade. Years before, I had cringed when the well-meaning lady called out, "There's the little girl who made her father famous." I had been depressed when the delivery boy asked, "Lee Strasberg—isn't *she* the one with the famous father?" Now I was able to laugh at an encounter with an enthusiastic fan who said, "Oh, I know you . . . What's your name? No, no, don't tell me . . . really, you're one of my favorites . . . I'll get it, your name is right on the tip of my tongue. . . . Damn! Of course!" She lit up. "You're what's-her-name, what's-his-name's daughter! Can I have your autograph?" I couldn't handle relating to my father as a teacher *and* a father, and

I decided it was more important for me to have him as "Pop." He had given me so much of his knowledge anyway, through osmosis.

It was lovely, seeing Adam and David, my half-brothers, growing with Jennifer. And watching my father blossom into a movie star. Johnny remarried and was acting, directing, and producing, finally—doing what he enjoyed *and* what he did best. Christopher had taken a long hiatus from acting, in which he produced a beautiful baby boy and many paintings. He began to talk about returning to acting, and it seemed as if he was coming into his own again.

When I saw myself reacting to Jennifer, I realized what my mother must have felt. I empathized with her. Even after years of therapy it is still difficult for me to stop wishing for my child what I wanted for myself, confusing my needs with hers. Somewhere, I am sure my mother knows all this.

I used to think I'd reach some plateau in my life where everything was wonderful and I'd just freeze-frame there. But life is movement. One takes the bitter with the sweet.

As I've learned a little bit about myself, I seem to know less about the answers. I asked the ninety-five-year-old grandma of a friend of mine from Texas, "Belle, what's life about?" "Honey," she said, "all I know is it's not about who your family was, what religion or color you are, it's not even about what you've done. . . . I guess life isn't about where you've been, it's about where you're going."

Twenty years ago on Fire Island my father, who loved the ocean, would walk down to the shoreline every day and wade in, but never any farther than his ankles. "Lee," Anne Bancroft said, "you're so crazy about the water—how come you never go in past your ankles?" He gazed out at the horizon, seeing his own dreams and visions. "Darling," he said, "I just don't want to get involved." Yet he did, totally, as an actor, a writer, a director, and a great teacher.

That same year he and I missed the ferry to Fire Island one Friday, which meant we had a two-hour wait in the cold for the next one. "You're so calm," I said. "Why aren't you upset? It's freezing, we're missing dinner, doesn't it bother you?" "A little," he said, "but after all, the important thing is, we're traveling."

Every now and then, with a flash of clarity, I see my life with the inner eye of love, and things fall into perspective. I remember Laurence Olivier, when he came backstage after *Anne Frank.* "Susan," he said, "you were absolutely wonderful." "No, really, Larry," I responded, "tell me the truth, what did you think?" "Well, dear child," said Sir Laurence, "actually, half the effort would have had twice the effect." It was true of my whole life thus far. So many of the things I agonized over then were now unimportant.

Time passed more quickly. I turned around, and Jenny was eight. She was ready for her last operation. She was at St. John's Hospital near the beach in Santa Monica for surgery to complete construction of her soft palate.

"Mommy, if I go to sleep soon and sleep fast, will it be *now* quicker?" she asked. "I want it to be over. I want it to be done now."

"Jen-Jen, you have to learn there are a lot of things we can't have 'now.' You have to learn to be patient, to wait. You can't push a wave onto the shore any faster than the ocean brings it in."

Did she suspect how many nights I used to, still do, lie awake dreaming about all the things I want now?—if I can't have it now, I don't want it.

When this operation was over, we would have cause to celebrate. Jenny asked me for some crayons and a new coloring book, and I went out to buy them for her.

I picked up a paper and stopped for a cup of coffee. As I sat there reading, a headline caught my eye: "BURTON WILL REMAIN HOSPITALIZED A WEEK." The article stated:

Richard Burton will remain in St. John's Hospital another week recuperating from a lung infection, bronchial influenza . . . an injured left hand hurt during a fight scene in his latest film, *The Klansman*, costarring Lee Marvin . . .

the Burtons announced they will get a Swiss divorce after
ten years of marriage. Miss Taylor remained in seclusion at
the Beverly Hills Hotel and has not visited her estranged
husband. . . .

Two weeks before, one of the gossip columns had run a long
article with more explicit revelations:

Burton was so drunk he couldn't make it onto the set . . .
he was in the hospital at Oroville . . . Burton is wonderful
in the picture but everybody was drinking. . . . He was
loaded . . . he's decided on the "cure." . . . It's Elizabeth
or the alcohol.

On my way back into the hospital, I saw Richard standing on
the steps. He was on his way out for a walk, with a bodyguard on
either side. He was leaning heavily on both of them. I folded the
newspaper so he would not see that I had been reading the article
about him.

"Richard," I called.

He turned. "Yes?" He looked at me blankly. I was stunned and
then embarrassed for us both. He didn't recognize me.

Trying not to stare, I saw that his hands were shaking. His face
was pale, with dark circles under the eyes, and his hair was shot
through with gray. The papers had not exaggerated.

"Rich, it's me, Susan. Susan Strasberg."

He shook his head bearlike as if to clear his vision. "Little
Susan," he said, "give us a kiss, then."

He gave me an awkward hug, a European kiss on both cheeks,
then pulled away and looked at me. He reached out his hand and
gently brushed his trembling fingers against a vein I have in the
middle of my forehead which always stands out when I am upset.

He smiled. "You still have that beautiful vein. What are you
doing here, Luv?"

"My daughter's here for surgery," I answered. "I have a
daughter, just the one."

"My God," he sighed, "where have the years gone?"

"How are your girls?" I asked. "They must be grown up practically."

"Fine, growing, and beautiful," he replied. "Why don't you come visit me later in my room?"

"Why don't you come down to our room? I'd love you to meet Jennifer. She looks like my mother."

He didn't answer.

"I don't like to leave Jenny alone for too long, otherwise I'd come by to visit."

The years had reduced us to small talk. We looked at each other through an awkward silence.

"It was lovely seeing you," I said inanely.

I turned away and climbed the steps to the hospital. I thought of the twenty-four years I had been acting, of Europe, and of Christopher. I realized how many of my friends and colleagues had succumbed to the pressures of a public existence—too many. I had survived. I felt blessed.

Time catches up with us all. For years mutual friends had brought me messages: "Richard said to give love to his little girl." As I opened the door, I hesitated, but I did not look back. . . . All these years he had sent love to his little girl, but he had not recognized the woman.